AMONG SHADOWS

ALINE P. MORA

Copyright © 2021 by Aline P Mora

All Rights Reserved.

This book is a work of fiction. Any resemblance to actual persons, living or dead, business establishments, events or locales, is entirely coincidental. This work, or any portion thereof, may not be reproduced in any form or by any electronic or mechanical means, including information storage and retrieval systems, or used in any manner whatsoever, without the express written permission of the author, except for the use of brief quotations in a book review.

Cover Design by Moonpress | www.moonpress.co.uk
Map design by Cartographybird Maps

To Andre Mora,

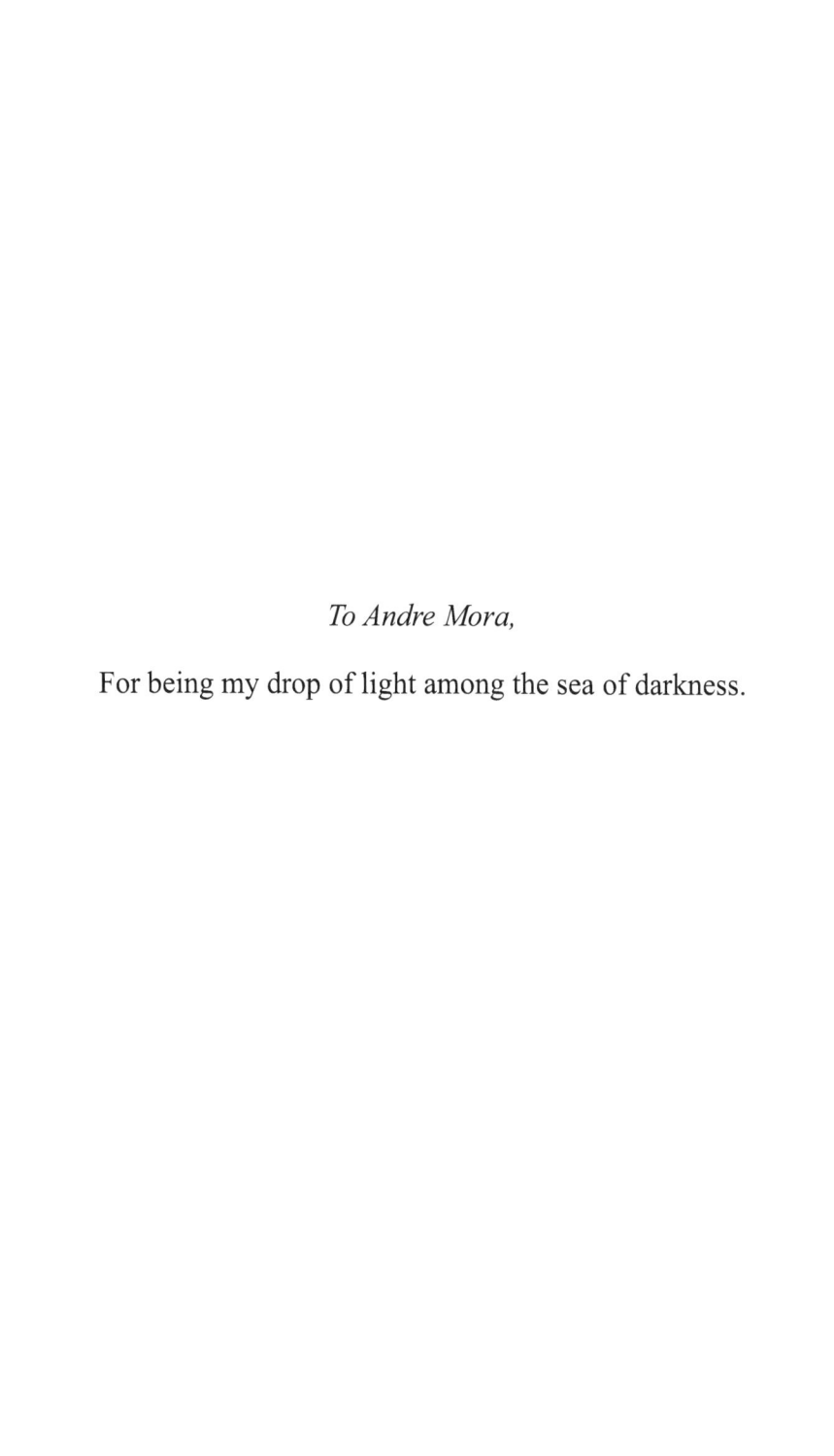

For being my drop of light among the sea of darkness.

THE ALIZIAN PLATEAU
MIREH
ALIZEH
SHANTI
THE ISRA MOUNTAINS
URIAN
GODDESS FIRST TEMPLE
TOCI
TLALOC
THE GOLDEN SE
TEFNUT
KAIT
NIRAM
NAHR
LEGEND
CAPITAL CITIES
TOWNS
VILLAGES
KINGDOM BORDERS

THE ELEMENTAL KINGDOMS OF
THE KNOWN WORLD

SUMMER CASTLE RUINS

KALINDI

SITAARE

NURI

THE ENDLESS SEA

Chapter 1

The man beside me breathed quietly and deeply as I slipped out of bed. I covered my naked body with a black, sheer robe and moved through the dark room, glancing at the open window. Nothing but moonlight illuminating my steps and highlighting the swift movement of the open fabric around me.

With a gentle, salty breeze coming from the ocean beyond, I crossed the big doors to the lit antechamber and sent a stream of darkness behind me, covering the closed door with a misty, dark veil to avoid waking up Aiden. *Not yet*, I thought. For now, I needed the silence and solitude that only the night could offer.

My quarters at the palace were big and imperial, like everything else in Nuri, the proud capital of Niram - the Kingdom of Fire. A land of scorching summers spent on sandy beaches, of high, colorful cliffs and never-ending wetlands. A place of passionate urges, of fierce people devoted to easy pleasure, as much as to untamed viciousness. A Kingdom forged by the magic fire of its royal family.

The room was filled with light wood, and white linen

furniture, lending a rich rustic look to the open chamber that gave way to a small balcony overseeing the palace garden and entry gate. Light curtains and pastel painting collections were carefully selected to highlight the luxury and value of every single item. A silent testament to the power behind the ambitious King and to the influence his magical abilities – one of the greatest in the world – could gather.

I glanced around under the warm light of dozens of fire lamps, my eyes falling on a vase of bright red roses I'd placed by the entrance earlier. I admired the contrast of the vivid color against the pale patterns of the room and smiled at the thought of that little rebellion to the veiled order around me.

Finally, I sighed and sat on the corner sofa by the balcony door and reached for the folded letter I'd left on the small desk when Aiden arrived. I'd been unwilling to let the two sides of my life collide, even if I couldn't do anything to stop it.

I felt the smooth texture of the paper in my fingers, its black seal still unbroken, unwavering. Sometimes I felt like the fox-stamped seal could speak to me, see me.

It had been a few weeks since I last heard from Ivo and, if history served as any indication, his disappearance could only mean he was scheming, and he would need me soon – sooner than I would like.

I surveyed the room once more: simple luxury and power, such a difference from the scarce and hungry years of my early childhood, from the shade of a life I had before Ivo found me. I took a steadying breath and reminded myself I was safe and cared for. That I could trust him. Only then I broke the seal.

"Breakfast at ten. Don't be late."

A summons and a message. The spy master had use of me again.

I let my gaze wander from the balcony, to the night sky, admiring the bright stars and the full moon as I called the shadows to me, relishing in the cold, silky feeling of its magic against my soul. Despite the danger and the secrecy, I'd learned to love the darkness, to cherish it, to worship the little place it occupied in my soul. It was a part of me, and I felt less alone for it.

I closed my eyes and commanded a soft, dark tendril towards the letter now resting on my lap. I watched as it crushed the paper, disintegrating it into nothing more than powder in the cup of my hand and let the breeze scatter it before making my way back to my room.

I did not bother being quiet now. In no more than a few hours, I would need to be ready to lie and scheme, I would step back into the skin of the best spy in Niram, and, in that life, there was no time for naïve hopes and pleasurable company. I couldn't bear for Aiden to be near that version of me.

The darkness lessened as I drew the veil back to the corners of the room and ignited the lamp on the small bedside table.

I poured a glass of wine and leaned against the wall, waiting as the young, fiery-haired man started to move under the drawn-canopy netting. The well-defined lines of his bare chest seemed to glow in the warm light of the lamp, his sharp jaw and beautiful face turning from sleepy into lusty as he saw me half naked, peering at him from the corner.

"Getting ready for more?" he smirked glancing at my

glass.

"Who would have thought you needed me drunk for that?" I said with a smile.

Confidence poured out of him as he stretched out on my bed and locked his sight on me. Thin lips curled in a roguish smile; kind, brown eyes glimmering. He leaned against the bed frame, strong arms casually behind his head and the defined lines of his stomach peeking from the white sheet. Sensual and commanding. Aiden Brunt was, indeed, a sight to admire.

"I think it is past your bedtime, my Lord."

"You know I hate when you call me that. Come back to bed, I prefer when you are half out of your mind." He winked.

That pretentious and sometimes insufferable sense of humor was one of the first things that attracted me to him. His station eventually became a bonus, but it was his mind that kept me tethered to him, his unfailing personality.

I sat down by his side, hand trailing round lines on his chest, sensing the warm skin respond to my touch. I let my eyes rise, sharp and determined.

"Although I appreciate your propensity to warm my bed, I do think your father would be rather disappointed to find you mingling with ... well, me."

He winced at the mention of the king. It would have been imperceptible to most people, but not to me. Not after so many nights together. Not after we became friends.

"You are usually more creative when you kick me out, and not nearly as eager." Some of the brightness had dulled from his tone.

"Just preserving my reputation, Sir," I feigned a look of innocence, trying to lighten the mood and avoid sending him down a spiral of bitter memories.

Humor flashed back in his eyes as he got up and put his clothes on ever so slowly. He took my hair from my face and reclined to kiss me on the cheek as his spicy cologne washed over me. He said on a gasp of air near my earlobe,

"Happy to oblige to all your needs. Especially the ones involving your bed."

As he walked to the door, he raised an arm in silent goodbye, moving idly through my antechambers and finally into the palace corridor. I listened to his steps getting farther away and willed my darkness to the lamp, suffocating every ember. With a satisfied motion, I savored the comforting emptiness of my bed for a few moments before letting the warmth of the night evade me.

No matter how many quiet nights we spent together, when the sun rose again, he would still be the Kingdom's Heir and I, a ruthless spy. Hoping for a different life, even in the comfort and solitude of my chambers, would do me no good.

I held to that familiar thought as I let the darkness rock me to sleep.

◆

I woke at dawn to a pleasant early-summer breeze coming through the window. I changed into my exercise clothes and sneaked through the servant's passageways into the empty grove behind the palace, avoiding the large training area the guards used.

I had found the grove in my first few months at the palace, when I spent most of my time exploring the ins and outs of its grounds. That was also when I found the small, mostly unnoticed corridors favored by the servants.

As a court lady, I couldn't roam the palace grounds freely, but this early in the morning, the silence was heavy and the few servants easy to evade. This early, I didn't have to worry about the propriety of a woman sweating in tight pants, I could simply run.

I did it as much for fitness as for mental control. When I was on the leafy trail, I let my thoughts fly in a perpetual chaos of random images. I adjusted my breathing and let the images wash over me, there and gone, until every one of them faded behind the thunderous rhythm of my beating heart.

It was my ritual, my release. One of the things that allowed me to remain myself. On that day, I needed it more than most. I needed it to help me forget I was about to go on another mission. I needed my mind to quiet so I could, once again, be the spy I'd been raised to be.

It was only when my thoughts were blank, and I couldn't take another step that I made my way back to my chambers to change into a simple dress and fashion my hair in an unadorned up-do. It wasn't even eight am when I left my room for my daily dance class in the city.

The inconspicuous dance studio was set in a quiet street near the commercial center. The shrieking of the common children which permeated most of Nuri was inaudible in this area.

A comfortable reception room could be seen through the large store-front windows. Inside, there was a small coffee table, two light-green sofas on one corner and a large desk on the opposite side of the room. The only visible person, a middle-aged hostess writing a few notes behind the massive desk.

She peeked up the moment I opened the door, letting

a swirl of hot air inside with me, and smiled pleasantly. "She is waiting for you in studio six."

I nodded, going straight across to the small backdoor that led to the corridor inside, a bland smile curling my lips. I was greeted by a series of small rooms with big mirrors on most of the walls – what passed as a traditional dance studio befitting a Lady. Half of those were occupied by groups of young girls learning ballroom dance styles.

At the end of the corridor, a staircase led to the second floor, and to the hiring rooms for advanced classes. Without so much as a thought, I made my way up.

Studio six was a large room, taking roughly half of the building. It was designed differently to the other rooms: fewer mirrors, some hidden wardrobes, and no windows beside the skylight, which gave way to a cloudless, cerulean sky. In the corner there were two big racks with most of the conventional weapons, sandbags and dummies.

The fighting room was designed for combat training and sword fighting, a gem hidden only a few blocks away from the palace. A clever charade that kept the world thinking I was doing nothing more than what was expected from a young Lady in search of marriage: taking advanced dancing class.

One of the many perks of Ivo's power and influence.

"Heya," I said cheerfully while dropping my small bag in a corner and changing into training clothes behind a set of wicker panels.

"Morning," said Dara with a bored expression.

Dara was a middle-aged woman with short, blond hair and an unwavering, serious expression reminiscent of her years as captain of the King's Guard. She'd been under Ivo's employment since my early childhood and, even though I didn't know what the agreement between them was, or why she'd left the Guard to come and train me twenty years before, I knew he trusted her enough to tell her who I was. Even if that trust didn't go as far as to tell her about my power.

She'd lived with me at the Villa and led my combat training since I first picked up a sword. And we may never have gotten close through the years, but we had forged a sense of mutual respect over bruises and sweat. So, when Ivo brought me to Nuri, it felt natural that she would come back to the capital and continue to oversee my training.

For the past two years, she'd trained me every morning at eight a.m., but I still sneaked in the studio every other night for the chance of practicing with my shadows where no one could see me.

As if responding to my erratic thoughts, my power pushed against my skin. A silky, familiar feel spreading through my limbs, begging to be wielded, unleashed. And for a glorious moment, I let myself feel it, I let myself revel on its presence just beneath the surface, until I remembered the danger that came with it and, reluctantly, convinced myself to smother it, shove it back to that deep place in my soul.

I finished stretching and went to the weapons rack. I was versed in most close combat weapons, but I always favored the smaller ones, easier to conceal and to underestimate.

I touched my preferred pair of sai. The hilts were exquisite, adorned in the faintest red hue, while the blades and guards carried the most profound black, with glittering gold patterns throughout. These were the first weapons I ever mastered, and I traced the blades with a fondness that only those who'd drawn blood too many times could understand.

I tested their grip and took them to the center of the

room.

"No niceties, I suppose," Dara said with a side glance at me.

"No time, nor disposition," I said swirling around, feeling the weight of the sais in my hands.

"Very well," she said while picking up her spear.

Without saying another word she moved at me, and we danced, as we had done so many times before.

I was barely ten years old when she decided I was strong enough to spar with her, and we had done it many times since. At first, I wouldn't last more than two minutes without ending up with my back in the dirt but now, we could go on for a whole hour without a clear winner.

I had mastered the skill she taught me, but not my arrogance. "Never let the thrill of winning get to your head. The more you believe you are winning, the worse you will lose," she kept saying.

And I kept forgetting.

That day, she anticipated all my moves, completely blocking me before I could get close to her. It was mere minutes before she swiped the shaft of her spear under my foot, leaving me slammed back at the floor, cursing.

"You are unfocused! Give yourself to your weapon or go away, but do not insult me and your blade with your distraction." Harsh words as she helped me get up.

I knew she was right. Entering a fight without focus was foolish and stupid. The fastest way to get killed.

I took a deep breath and gave her one certain nod. I closed my eyes and let my mind descend into that cold place inside of myself where there was no space for mercy or doubt. Then, I let it consume me until I found some focus.

"Give me all you got," I said when I opened my eyes

again.

She did.

She came at me with a strength she rarely used. Her speed was phenomenal for her age and every time I saw her in action, I was reminded why Ivo had trusted her with my training.

This time, my head was clear, all my distraction secured away and my sole attention on her movements, on her skill with the spear. She came for my right shoulder, forcing me to feint to the left and giving her an opening to maneuver the shaft in my stomach. I used her momentary retreat to swirl around the spearhead and get a step closer to her, and once I did, the dynamics of our fight changed.

From a closer distance, her spear was nothing more than a shaft - the pointy head rendered useless against my sai, leading us to an intimate flow of feints, blocks and close body attacks.

That had always been my advantage: what I lacked in sheer force, I compensated in agility. And, as such, I managed to deflect enough of her blows to create an opening on her left. I swirled around her weapon and blocked her body with my own, my right sai point immediately under her chin.

Her only response was a side smile. And I knew she was satisfied. Which was as close to being proud as I ever got from her.

"Again." She switched to a small sword.

We sparred again and again, until my muscles were limp with the effort and my dread was silenced. She bested me more often than I bested her, and when I sheathed my weapons, I felt finally ready to hear whatever mission Ivo had for me.

◆

By the time I made it back from Dara's training, the maids were already preparing my bath in the small en-suite in my chambers, and I quickly relieved them of their duties. I'd always preferred to dress myself, never quite growing accustomed to the intimacy of someone changing my clothes.

I chose a yellow sleeveless dress, light and veiled, adorned with little white flowers at the hem. It fit my curvy figure and embraced my round breasts without requiring any of the tight bodices that were usual in court. Black wavy hair knotted into a single elaborate braid behind me. I left most of my round, feminine face nearly untouched: a hint of glow on my lips, a touch of rouge on my high cheeks and a strong kohl line along with a tiny emerald stone on my right nostril, to bring out the depth of my big green eyes.

Finally, I adjusted the silver satin choker back in its usual place and studied the image reflected in the mirror. A vision of harmless beauty and sharp mind, inviting and distant. Alluring and tempestuous. The exact persona that Ivo had groomed me into for the past several years.

The look was as much disguise as it was protection, for only a fool would wear their heart to a meeting with Ivo.

With practiced ease, I squared my shoulders and lifted my chin, letting the weight of my inescapable role wash away the final echoes of lingering laughter in the room.

Cunning, treacherous, spy.

Minutes after I left my wing of the palace, I was in front of Ivo's chambers, the sun behind me and Billy blocking my way. The scarred face of this short, strong man was serious and attentive, with no warmth towards me, he was a soldier through and through. More than a bodyguard, he was

Ivo's closest friend and advisor, the only person who seemed to have known him before he came to Niram. I knew he had never understood why Ivo went to the trouble of passing an orphan off as his niece, but I supposed it was one thing to trust a brute like this with your life and a completely different matter to let him in on your deepest secrets. And so, Billy remained as oblivious as the rest of the world to Ivo's secrets, including my magical abilities.

I kept a cold and arrogant glance. "What do you want? He is waiting for me." No need for pleasantries or good behavior.

He scowled and led the way through the massive and opulent doors of Ivo's private quarters—as if I hadn't been here a thousand times before. As I walked through the corridor, I couldn't avoid appreciating the beauty stored in each corner of the massive room again.

A lot could be said about Ivo Timal, but no one could deny his impressive taste. His personality was stamped on every choice of furniture and art, on the pattern carefully designed to seduce and involve.

The breaking of the waves on the cliff below the palace was the only sound, when I found him waiting by the window, facing the clear sky and turquoise sea. Even though he seemed lost in the scenery I knew, deep in my bones, that every inch of his posture was calculated, a portrait of what he wanted me to see. The light-grey tunic, with an impecable fit on his broad shoulders, the pants outlining his legs in an elegant way, the black hair perfectly combed back as if not a single strand would dare disobey his wishes.

It was years before I learned to read that posture, years before I stopped hurting at his aloofness and fearing his cool detachment. And, even as I learned to recognize it for the act it was, I couldn't silence an unstoppable need to be worthy of a warmer embrace, of a loving stare. And, as that old need flooded through me, I couldn't deny I still craved it as much as I loathed it.

In a subtle and delicate movement, I claimed the space by his side, linking my elbow through his own.

"Uh-oh. Such a worried man on such a bright morning," I said with a pout.

He took his time, a show of bringing his thoughts back to the present moment as he slowly looked towards me, observing every detail of my appearance with bright and perilous black eyes.

His features as harsh and cold as ever. Unyielding and unforgiving as the ocean beneath us.

"I like the goatee. It suits you," I said, interrupting his stare.

"You are too generous to me, Aila dear."

A small and absent smile was plastered on his lips as he took me towards the breakfast spread on the table behind us. "It has been too long since we had time to enjoy a meal together. Tell me about you." He said, patting my hand in a display of affection.

We had played this game too many times in the past few years for me not to read every little intention behind his words, the treacherous remarks, the sharp humor, the condescending advice. Still, a silly part of me continued to believe it more than empty pretense. He'd saved me from certain death once, and I knew he cared, even if it was only in his own way.

I was too young to remember much more than the cold, hunger and empty violence of my years before Ivo. All I remembered was the loneliness of the streets, I'd been an orphan long before he found me and the kindness and caring moments of whatever family I had were blurred, weakened with the weight of time

I'd spent twenty years with him, twenty years of growing into what he needed me to be, of him becoming my family. And somewhere along the way I stopped wondering if he was good enough for me and started worrying if I was good enough for him.

I learned to follow his orders without question, to yearn for his approval. But more than anything, I learned to love him and to trust his vision of the future, until I no longer knew the difference between my own dreams and his command.

He was the closest thing to a father I had ever known, the only one to have offered me a hand, as tarnished as it may have been. For that alone, I would have remained his spy for the rest of my life. I would have stayed by his side even as I loathed the secrecy and vileness it entailed, even as I hated myself a little bit more every day for the thin line between treachery and loyalty that I walked.

At this point, I didn't know what I'd been born for, but I did know I'd been *made* for this life.

So, I smiled and said, "Watched some plays, read some books, danced with some bachelors. You know, the perfect lady in search of marriage."

"You make your uncle very proud."

"I assumed so." And my heart did swell at the words.

"Any new connections I should know about?"

I knew he was aware of Aiden, I knew that was what he was really asking about, but I'd been more protective of him lately, less willing to spy on the only friend I had.

"A few people back in town, but no one of notice."

"There are a lot more whispers in loud parties than in silent libraries. Maybe you should spend less time ... *alone*, dear."

Or with Princes you don't intend to use, the unspoken advice rang loud on my ears. The disapproval crunched my heart.

I remained silent as he leaned back in his chair, eyes on the wine glass resting in his hand. After so many years, I could sense the shift in him: the smile colder and sharper, the courtesan charm slowly replaced by pure cunning. He was done playing the kind uncle.

I placed my napkin on the table and, with a sweep of my arm, willed the few pockets of darkness around us to grow thicker and denser. I moved the shadows through the room and filled every little crack in doors and windows with a misty veil until all sound was sealed inside. No more than a couple of seconds later, my shield was fully in place, and I leaned back in my own chair to wait. My lips slowly curling into a lazy and provocative smile.

By the time I faced him again, his eyes were dark wells focused solely on me, a gaze able to undress bodies and read souls.

"Despite your private predilections, I hear your connections with Prince Aiden are growing strong."

I remained silent and relaxed, knowing he was evaluating me, judging my reactions.

"And I wonder if you'll learn to use that to your advantage, before he's scared away. He can be a powerful ally," he continued.

I strangled the pointed reproach that burst in me, not letting my mind dwell on all the reasons why Aiden would inevitably *move on*. All the reasons that only Ivo had ever ignored. I was, after all, a spy with a darkness-tainted soul and too many buried bodies in my past.

Instead, I shrugged and waited as his eyes assessed my every breath. I knew I was his only chance of getting a spy so close to the crown and he was furious that my relationship with Aiden never seemed to grow beyond casual.

But what existed between Aiden and me was my own business, and with no short amount of surprise, I realized I didn't want Ivo involved in it.

After a long and silent minute, he seemed to decide to let it be. Following his cue, I pushed down my lingering thoughts and let the instincts of a lifetime of serving Ivo take over my mind and body.

"Valran is throwing a ball in five days. You are to accompany me."

Apart from the king, the Premier, and Aiden, no one knew Ivo's real occupation. To the world, he was a rich lord with close ties to the court. And, even among those who knew him as the master of the wider spies' network in the Kingdom, I was no more than a niece he'd embraced a few years before, after his estranged brother passed away, an oblivious girl with no idea of what her uncle's role at court truly was.

So, there was no one else – or none better – that he could disguise in a court event. The real question was what he wanted me to do.

"As your niece or spy?"

"Can't it be both?"

Between marriage prospects and personal friends, I had access to a wealth of information a simple spy could never have. For the past two years, he'd had me eavesdrop, steal reports, poison enemies ... but I didn't need to go to a ball to do any of that. Not unless he wanted me to spy on his commanding officer, the Premier himself – Lord Valran.

I nodded, the everlasting smile on my mouth, and waited.

"It seems the King has given Valran a mission I'm not privy to. I need to know what it is. He is, of course, too aware of my usual methods, but he won't expect you."

No one would.

I took my glass to my mouth slowly. Lord Valran was a young man. Too young to be Premier, and second to the King himself.

He was known to be a kind and intelligent man, married to one of the most ambitious women in Niram. Lady Lidya – his wife – had guided him through an array of favors and positions until he was able to secure the most powerful position in the whole Kingdom. A fact Ivo was yet to accept.

"What whispers have you heard?"

His face was intent, considering. "Well, it seems his choice of Urian for his states is not as innocent as it seemed."

I furrowed my brows. Urian was a small city near Alizeh, in an area almost destroyed in the Great War, peppered with nothing more than a few half-forgotten cities. He continued, as if he could hear my unspoken questions.

"There is an increased number of soldiers transiting through the area. Too many soldiers if you ask me. And so much communication between Lidya and their home state …" Irony laced his every word. "Most troubling."

"Do you think the King plans to move against Alizeh?"

He shrugged. The King wasn't known for being reckless, and an open war would be madness.

"That is for you to find out, isn't it?"

He was a careful portrait of boredom and relaxation.

A master in his own right. My master, compelling me to provide the help only I could give.

But after so many years, I knew his tells: the strong hold on his glass, the visible vein on his neck and the simple fact he was willing to deploy me in an open function told me enough. Whatever he expected me to find – and he did expect something – was big enough for him to have hopes of taking Valran down and claiming the position he had been working his entire life for: Premier to the Kingdom.

I knew Ivo well enough to know he would go to any length for that role. As much as I knew he wasn't telling me everything.

I measured him as the tension between us increased.

"Ivo, what else do you know?" I finally asked.

"What makes you think I know more?"

"Well, for starters, you are no fool. And I know what being Premier means to you. So, I don't think you would risk having my cover blown without being absolutely sure there is something to be found. Something big."

"Are you questioning me, Aila dear?" His tone was low and dangerous even though his face remained as pleasant as always.

"No. But I need all the information I can get, to avoid being exposed. To avoid exposing you! And if you need me to find anything of meaning in there, you have to tell me what I'm searching for."

I could see the rage behind the surface. Ivo was never as dangerous as when he believed himself crossed.

"Let me remind you of something, niece." Disdain and cold rage laced his words. "I don't *have* to do anything. If it wasn't for me, you would be rotting in the bloody gutter where I found you. You would have been tortured and killed for the dark magic you possess, you would be no-one and nothing."

He dropped his voice to a low, cold rasp that made my stomach hollow and heavy. "So, you would do well to remember how much you need *me*. I gave you love and safety despite the darkness swelling through you and now you will do whatever I tell you to do."

Anger poured from him, and I watched as he took a deep breath to control himself, as his features softened at the sight of my large, shocked eyes, his hands relaxing around the wine glass. He reached to me, holding my cold hands in his own:

"I do all of this for us, Aila. For our safety. You have to trust me."

And I did. I trusted him with more than my secret, I trusted him with my life. I hated what he made me do, but I knew he wouldn't ask any of it from me unless he had to.

So, I swallowed my dark thoughts with another sip of wine and said, "Of course. I didn't mean to disturb you. I'm sorry, Ivo."

But no matter how much wine or sweet words I took in, the bitter taste of his rage never truly left me.

Chapter 2

I walked out of Ivo's room half an hour later with all the details he had on the reception ball plans. The guest list and house layout would be waiting for me in my chambers later in the evening. Being Ivo's niece guaranteed me an invitation, so breaking in wouldn't be an issue, but now I had two days to figure out the security scheme and design a plan of action.

I had to prepare, and shopping seemed as good a start as any. So, I headed to the gardens and the city beyond it.

The palace main building had been built on the edge of a cliff – the highest in town – with a patio and a garden nested behind it. A refreshing green oasis at the heart of the palace grounds connected all the smaller buildings. The air was always filled with a salty breeze, a familiar smell that reminded me of long nights and private conversations.

The place was a striking combination of vivid flowers and leafy trees around a large water mirror. A wooden pathway curled around it and through the trees beyond, leading to the farther training arena and a virgin grove.

Comfortable chairs and macrame cushioned swings were spread among the trees forming small alcoves for a languid read or a quiet conversation.

My balcony faced this exact spot, which was either a convenient stroke of luck, or Ivo's own design. One way or another, it gave me an easy, hidden access to the streets of Nuri.

Now, under the late morning sun, the patio was far from empty and peaceful, and I had no need to hide. Flocks of ladies walked around the pathways, guards patrolled the edges of the whole garden, and a few gardeners busied themselves reviving patches of bromelias and sunflowers, none of which would survive so close to the sea without their Earth power keeping them healthy and blooming.

I started hearing the heavy steps behind me when I crossed the water area. A small and furtive smile appeared on my lips, but I didn't slow my pace, despite my better judgment. It was not until I was halfway through the path leading to the palace main gate that he approached me.

The closer to the gates, the quieter the pathway became. This far from the water mirror, only a handful of people strolled by, all far enough away for our conversation to remain private.

"Lady Aila, you seem hurried. I trust everything is well this morning?" Aiden purred as his left arm casually brushed against mine.

I stopped and turned to him in time to see his eyes hovering furtively over my body. I faked an expression of pure modesty.

"My Prince." I curtsied with a docile smile before looking him in the eyes.

A mocking scowl crossed over his face at the sight of

my curtsy, despite the faint amusement in his features.

"I'm fine, thank you. Just on my way to do some shopping. I heard a new ship arrived yesterday," I said, before glancing at the sky, "and it is such a lovely day."

"Indeed. The weather is getting warmer. I hope you've been able to sleep through the tepid night." An intimate and daring smile flickered in his lips.

"Well, I suppose I can't complain."

He laughed openly, and a part of me rejoiced in the carefree and honest sound. He was good and caring, the only friend I'd had in a long time … maybe ever. He knew so much of who I was and yet, he knew nothing, that fundamental piece of my identity forever forbidden to him. I had always been and would always be a long-lost niece to his father's spy master, a lady in search of marriage. Nothing more.

"We could have lunch in the city. Before you buy every new dress the merchants brought in?" he said with an inviting smile, echoes of laughter still in his voice.

I made a show of peering around the garden and pointedly jerked my chin towards the group of intent girls wandering closer and closer to our path. "I couldn't dream of keeping you away from such pleasant company."

He winced at the sight of them.

"And besides, I just had breakfast with my uncle," I continued before he could say anything else.

He grabbed my hand and pulled me from the main pathway, towards the shade of a jacaranda tree. His touch on my hand was a tender caress, and my heart ached for him and for all I could never tell him. He was too good and trusting to be anywhere near the games Ivo played, the less openly associated to me, the safer he was. And yet, I couldn't help myself. I couldn't walk away.

For the briefest moment I let myself think what it would be like to say yes to him, to lunch. How it would feel to give myself a chance to decide if I wanted the casual sex to become more.

"You can't leave me to their mercy. I can't hear about dances and silly gossip again! I'll die of boredom." His eyes were intense, pleading. "Come on, Aila! You know I'll behave."

But as quickly as those thoughts swirled through my mind, his burning need brought me back to reality: saying no to him was the kindest thing to do for both of us.

"You are in no luck, Aiden. You'll find no reprieve from the balls and gossips with me this afternoon."

He seemed intent on insisting, but his shoulder dropped an inch, instead. He knew me well enough not to push.

"Tonight, then?" he whispered, glancing to the group of girls now only a few meters away.

"Sorry." I shook my head gently. "I'll be extremely busy with all the dresses I am about to buy. But I'm sure one of those lovely ladies can keep you entertained." I chuckled, curtsying quickly, and continued to walk before he had a chance to see the flash of doubt crossing my face.

His low laugh followed me through the path as I wondered how long it would take for him to let someone else get close, and how that would make me feel.

◆

In the merchant district the midday sun was scorching hot, the constant sea breeze the only reprieve. The sandy streets near the palace slowly gave way to stone pathways and white storefronts with big windows. These filled with rich ladies and their husbands who browsed through the new merchandise brought in from other Kingdoms: dresses with the most soft and beautiful fabrics from Alizeh, the Kingdom of Air; exotic spices and candied fruits from Tlaloc, the Kingdom of Earth, and fine glass sculpture and china from Tefnut, the Kingdom of Water.

The magic running through those Kingdoms were no longer as pure and separated as they once were. Power had been blended and diluted over the centuries, the elements weakening as it crossed borders.

The richest of Niram were in a frenzy, buying and gorging on food while spilling out thoughts and judgements about the ordinary events of the day-to-day in court. A sea of mundane gossip for them, and a well of information for me.

I spent most of the afternoon hopping from store-to-store, collecting all the latest gossip on Lady Lidya, knowing Ivo's men would never even consider her as a threat or look at 'women's gossip' as a source of worthy information. They often forgot how much of a man's life was decided in bed.

When the afternoon passed, I had a full report of who was confirmed to attend the ball, what staff had been hired, and which kind of entertainment would be provided. But the most interesting piece of information reached my ears as I tried on a red, lacy dress in one of the most expensive boutiques in the capital.

The corner shop only saw clients by appointment, unless you had endeared yourself to the helpful manager. For months, Izobel had guaranteed me a visit whenever I needed but, more importantly, she'd made sure I was informed about all scheduled visits of some of the most influential ladies of the court.

When I arrived at the store the small 'Appointments Only' sign, was firmly in place on the front door and the curtains drawn across all the windows, which told me an appointment was still underway.

Izzie turned at the delicate tinkle of the golden bell attached to the door, and a warm smile spread across her face as she saw me. "Let me guess … Premier's ball?"

"Tell me you have something wickedly sexy for me, Izzie."

"Of course, I do."

"You are my own miracle worker."

"Get yourself inside. I'll take it to you in a minute."

I crossed the small foyer in a smooth stride, not bothering to examine the few dresses displayed on white, iron, mannequin-frames. Izzie had impeccable taste and I wasn't here for the fashion as much as I was for the chatter. In the internal chamber, three chairs and a small table were arranged for tea, at it sat two matrons. Lady Ophelia and Lady Bethany had weekly appointments and were two of the most notorious gossipers in court.

I greeted them with some pleasant passing words before entering the closest dressing room, knowing that, by the time Izzie brought me my usual pile of dresses, they would be back in relaxed conversation.

I heard them talking about their daughters and husbands, about the next theater season and their summer plans, until finally, they started talking about the ball and something piqued my interest.

"I heard the young captain will be back for the ball," Lady Ophelia said.

"Really? Do you think Valran called him back?" Lady Bethany questioned.

"Or maybe Lidya," Ophelia added in a pointed voice. "One way or the other, he is coming back."

"How long has it been? Three years? I wonder what he's been doing all this time. Things were more fun around here before he left."

"You say that because there was more gossip." Ophelia laughed a low rumble.

"I heard he went away because the Prince demanded it," Bethany confided in a lower voice.

"You'd think two boys that grew up together would get along, but they were always water and wine those two. Always water and wine."

"Pity. My Rachel was devastated when he left." Bethany's voice was laced with a touch of something sounding like regret.

"I heard he was stationed up north …" Ophelia continued unphased. "I wonder if he was hunting those savage rebels. They are getting close to – "

But before she could finish, Izzie's voice rang clear. "Can I bring you anything else?"

"No, dear," Bethany replied. "We are all settled."

"Perfect! I'll get your dresses delivered by end of day."

The two ladies left shortly after and soon I was wrapping up my own acquisitions. Although I knew the Premier had a personal guard, I always assumed its captain – as its guards – would be of no consequence.

But people of no importance are always *under* the radar of rich, powerful matrons and their daughters.

If they were right, he'd left court before I ever set foot in the castle. Still, it was surprising I'd never heard of him. And the trained part of me had a habit of paying attention to surprising things.

I wrapped up my purchase and asked Izzie to deliver all of it – a pair of red sandals, three new dresses, a tiara, and perfume – directly to the palace. But as I prepared to leave the store, a simple box by the counter took my mind away from court gossip and mysterious captains. A wooden box of dark mahogany with two candied apples placed within a bed of white silk paper. A delicacy constantly present in the villa where Ivo raised me.

For a brief moment, I was filled with memories of my childhood, of the little bits in between training that made me believe I had a small piece of normalcy. Fireworks at the beach for the New Year's celebration, the fire pit where Ivo taught me history and politics, useless and never-ending religion lessons and, of course, the candied apple he would always give me for my birthday. 'A tradition from my own childhood,' he would say.

Without thinking twice about it, I asked Izzie to deliver the fine box to him with a note. "To wistful memories," I wrote. After all, he was the only family I knew.

◆

Dinners at the palace were events on their own: long meals, unending evenings and very uncomfortable dresses. The court savored them, adored them. But I often found myself otherwise occupied, usually taking advantage of the fewer eyes roaming the palace grounds.

That night I had a light dinner in my chambers, waited until anyone who could recognize me was deep in conversation and wine, then snuck through the patio to the city beyond.

Half an hour later I was no more than a hooded figure in normal clothes – simple black pants and loose shirt – discretely positioned on the roof of one of the commercial buildings on the base of the cliff that held Lord Valran's estate.

Without a hint of makeup and with my hair arranged in a simple braided bun, no one would recognize the furtive girl as one of the court ladies. There, in the thick of the night, I was free from the rare magic and the constant lies. Happily pretending I was nothing but an ordinary girl with a simple life.

I sat with my own thoughts while observing movements through the lens of a small spyglass. Cataloguing the ins and outs, the number and frequency of the rounds and the general interaction of the house guards, turning the blueprints in my hand into a mental image of the building's interior.

The big, white house sat at the edge of one of the lower terracotta cliffs that surrounded most of the beaches in Nuri, its white walls seeming to spike from the ground itself. The elegant, large construction in the richer area of town was as impressive as the palace. A heavy iron gate at the base of the cliff gave way to a carved staircase to the house portico and a few flowery corridors.

The double green doors in the center of the portico were the only visible way in and were monitored by a regular round of guards (always in pairs) supported by a small, relaxed contingent stationed on random points through the perimeter. Eight big windows were distributed across the two stories, seemingly unguarded from the inside. There was almost no movement visible beyond the first floor, where the reception would be held. On the second floor, only one room could be the office: no drawn curtains, no servants walking by.

I marked it down on the blueprints.

The more I observed the guards, the less challenge they presented. Since Ivo had found me half dead in the middle of a massacre, I'd thrown myself into training: sword fighting, war strategy, politics, venom and, of course, using every stolen hour I could, learning to control my magical power. I'd been lucky when Ivo found me but wouldn't rely on good fortune anymore.

Instead, I became skilled, lethal.

Now, the notion of the lazy and out of formation guards stepping in my way was laughable. I could take them all down in a few minutes, get the information I needed from Valran by force, and be done with it, but Ivo wanted me to do this the hard way. Or rather, the secret way—the way that would allow me to be invisible enough that no-one would suspect anything out of the ordinary was happening.

The one thing I was not capable of doing was going against Ivo's command. The one thing I wouldn't risk was stepping out of his shadow and protection, especially when there was nothing for me outside of it: no luxury, no friends, no refuge.

There were only two things I knew how to be. As a lady, I had no power, no hope of building a life for myself without the blessing of a husband, And as a spy ... well, if killing and lying was what I was going to do for a living, then I'd continue to do it under the splendor of the palace roof and the shelter of Ivo's influence.

So, I continued to observe.

Hours later, alertness shot through the air. The guard's postures straightened, their small laughs died, and they stumbled into formation as a man climbed the wide stairs, silent command rippling through the night.

He moved nimbly, each step overflowing with swagger and prowess. Two sheathed swords rested on his back over dusty, travel garments and his short, black hair danced in the wind as he stopped at the top of the stairs barking orders. My own body was tense, immediately alert, as the instinct I'd honed most of my life took control and responded to the warrior across the street.

I knew everyone on Valran's and the palace guard. Someone like this would never escape my radar, not unless he'd been away my whole time at court.

Where have you been all this time? And why are you back now? I couldn't help but remember Ophelia and Bethany's earlier conversation.

As he strolled by, the guards were left in perfect positioning with renewed alertness, and I found myself understanding the matron's remark. Looking at the man across the street, it wasn't hard to believe things were about to get more interesting. Even from a distance, I could feel a silent pull towards the mysterious figure.

A moment later, he squared his shoulders and crossed the heavy main doors, meanwhile, I was left intrigued by the unexpected player making an entrance in the deadly game that was my life.

Chapter 3

It was almost midnight when I returned to my room. My mind was still racing as I secured the blueprints and notes under a false bottom in the drawer of my writing desk.

Not even the fresh, inviting bath and glass of red wine were enough to calm the adrenaline pumping through my veins, and soon I found myself walking to the deserted library instead of relaxing in my bed.

I loved the intense smell of old books, the quiet sense of peace and belonging. I had always found solace in the written word, a soul-warming refuge that could placate the loneliness of my real life. In the open pages of a book, I had found fierce friends, a loving family and unbiased wisdom. For many years, it had given me a reason to survive.

But the Royal Library was more than that. Since I had moved to the palace, it had become the one place I didn't need to hide, the only place where I could simply be. Under the veil of night, I could read for pleasure and not for the image it cast over myself. I could be smart, daring, passionate. I could think and exist beyond the role of a docile, educated woman.

The corridors were all empty and heavy with silence as I moved. The airy, entry room clean and organized without people walking around. No books left in the few study desks, no mumbled words, no librarians walking among the gigantic shelves. Nothing but the crash of distant waves finding me.

I stopped at the center of the room and breathed its stillness before taking the first of the four corridors that opened into smaller sections with tiny studies and hidden alcoves. A maze of tomes and comfortable chairs flanked by beautiful large windows.

I retrieved the book I'd been reading for the past few nights—a thesis discussing the ethics of the trials using non-wielders to transfer magical powers - and made my way to my preferred spot in a hidden armchair by the window. Moonlight touched my skin as I climbed into it.

I was a few pages in when I felt a voice against my ear.

"I thought you were busy tonight," Aiden whispered.

"I am," I said, pointing my head to the book in front of me.

The corner of his lips tugged up and amusement covered his features as he claimed the armchair across from me. The set of chairs formed an intimate and protective retreat where we'd been meeting for the past two years. The same spot where we first met.

It was here we became friends. And, even if I couldn't admit it then, the chance of finding him was the very reason I continued to choose that same chair every other night.

He offered me a brown paper bag; I opened it to find a Dream Cake and a grin spread over my face instantly.

"Careful with the sugar now. It took me months to get the head librarian to allow me back here after the mess you made last time."

I would have argued it was his fault if I wasn't so busy stuffing my face with the sweet delicacy. Dream cakes were the ultimate guilty pleasure; soft, ball-shaped, fried cakes covered in sugar, evenly cut in the middle, and filled with so much creamy vanilla custard that one bite was enough to get chunks threatening to fall. This one was deliciously warm, and I had to concentrate to stop my moan.

"How can you come up with these at this hour?" The palace chef was responsible for the best dream cakes I'd tasted in my life, and Aiden had made it his mission not to let me miss those sweet bastards.

"Well, it helps when the chef has known you since you were born. Although I'm sure he is wondering how I developed such a taste for Dream cakes in the past two years."

I distracted myself licking the sugar from my fingers and didn't notice Aiden observing me until he spoke again.

"It has been a while since I last saw you here."

"Too long," I agreed, stroking the book in my lap. "Too many dinners and parties. Ivo is set on finding an appropriate suitor this year." I evaded the question before he had a chance to ask it.

He ignored my words, he always did. Over the past few months, my supposed search for a suitor had stopped being an inconsequential joke. Somewhere along the way, we had started avoiding it, repressing it, if for different reasons.

"Is it true you got the Premier captain dispatched from court?" I tried to change the subject.

"What?" If I didn't know Aiden as well as I did, I might have missed the subtle tightening of his lips and wrinkling of his nose as scorn marred his features.

"Wow. You are really not a fan of the guy."

"How do you know about him?"

"Well, nothing goes better together than shopping and gossip, Aiden."

"Why on earth are people talking about him again?"

"Well, *he*," I gave him a pointed look, "is coming back to Nuri."

Aiden eyes were suddenly wary. Brows furrowed and tense shoulders. Displeasure leaked from him as he faced the ceiling.

"Perfect. That is all I needed. Maybe Ivo will set you two up; I'm sure you'd make a perfect match," he mumbled ironically.

"Bad history?" I asked ignoring the pained look of his eyes and the dryness of his words.

I hated using Aiden for information, no matter how small, but there was no one else I could ask about Valran's man without raising questions. Besides, it was clear Aiden had a much more intimate knowledge than I'd find anywhere else.

"He is a prick. That is all! Just do me a favor and stay away from him, will you?" He faced me fully now, a touch of a bitterness in his usually warm eyes.

"May I ask why?"

He shook his head and I understood that he was done talking about it.

Which meant I was done asking.

I let a silence form between us. Easy, familiar. I turned my gaze to the sky beyond the double window by our side and let my mind wander, relishing in his comforting presence.

I'm not sure how long we stayed there before I felt him taking the book from my hand, brushing against my finger.

"Is this what is keeping you busy, then?"

I nodded. "Tonight, at least."

"Heavy reading," he muttered, more to himself than to me after flipping through a few pages.

"You know there is more to me than dresses and dream cakes." I winked.

His face softened under damp red hair, leaving behind the intimidating command of the prince. His square jawline suddenly more delicate, as a tender smile curled his lips and his eyes locked onto mine. The tension from before vanished.

"So much more." His lips parted and his gaze slipped over my body, longing and desire shining in his face and igniting the air around us despite the comfortable set of pajamas I wore.

He shuddered almost imperceptibly and handed me the book. "Care to explain the choice?"

"Well, a girl needs to be able to make conversation." I threw him a sly, sugary smile.

He ignored my banter, his amusement disappearing as a grave look overtook his face and he dropped his voice.

"I'm serious, Aila. Some would consider this dangerous reading with the rebels getting more active."

"It is just a book, Aiden."

"It is never 'just something' with you, though, is it?" He closed his eyes, as if deciding whether to continue speaking or not and, as I remained silent, he followed with, "I love perky and snooty, the Goddess knows how much fun we have! But sometimes I swear it's like we never met beyond my father's dining room. It's like you are so afraid of anyone seeing anything real, that you just keep everyone away ..." He took a breath. "At some point, you are going to need to let someone in, Aila." When I didn't reply, his voice dropped to no more than a whisper. "Somehow, I got this glimpse into what is beneath the polite surface, and I want more."

His sole focus was on me and I could see him searching for a way in, so intent and open that I looked away. It was unnerving how much he paid attention, how much he noticed, and yet how much he did not.

But I knew, even then, that much of what he saw was tainted by his own needs and hopes. That the only realness he expected to find in me was that of a sweet lady, in need of protection and love.

I wondered if it had been a mistake to allow him to get so close, to cross the line from powerful resource to … whatever he was now. Somehow, he had slipped through the cracks, and I no longer knew if I wanted to push him out again.

"I'm not joining the rebellion, if that's what you are asking," I said.

"It is not."

And I knew it. Of course, I knew it.

I took a deep breath and gave one last look at the stars before dropping all the masks I could and sharing the little truth I dared. "Sometimes I think about the world, and I wonder if we can ever be content with what we have, with what we are. We have used people; for years we have experimented on those too poor or too weak to defend themselves and we still want more, always more! It is part of human nature to desire power as much as it is to wish for change, no matter how wrong it may be. So, I understand the Alliance, I do."

I ignored his worried glance because every single word of it was true. The Rebels had been fighting for the last sixty years to stop the experiments that magic wielders performed on non-wielders. The same experiments that caused the Great War in the first place; a short but vicious war that pinned wielders against non-wielders and culminated in the Alliance becoming no more than a desperate group of rebels.

"In many ways, I'm no different to them, Aiden. I don't have any big secrets. I'm just a regular girl who wishes for more than she should."

"Are you saying you wish for the Alliance to spread and destroy the Elemental lines?" The sarcasm in his tone was unmistakable.

And how could it not be?

For the Alliance to succeed in stopping the Elementalists' quest for more power, his own right as an heir had to be overruled. The elemental lines destroyed, eviscerated. Because nothing else would give power and safety to non-wielders; nothing else would stop the experiments.

"No, dumbass!" I threw a pillow at his face, a smile tugging at my lips.

"Then what?" Laughter sounding on his voice.

"What I'm saying is I understand what it is like to wish, to hope. Even if I know the risks." I sighed. "These books? They give me the opportunity to think and dream, to muse about what it would be like to have a choice over the future. When I'm here my life is full of endless possibilities and meaningful opportunities, and yet the stakes are low. I'm safe!" I whispered then, the humor completely vanished from my voice, "for the few hours I'm reading these books, I can believe whatever I *want,* and I can pretend I'm brave enough to make a difference. I can wish!" *Little lies woven in deep truths.*

I let the silence ground me, wash away the vulnerability of the partial truth I'd shared. Then, I continued before I could think better of it. "I don't make a secret of these books, I just don't advertise my silly pastimes around your court." *Because dreams and hopes are not for orphans and spies.*

His eyes were glowing when I looked back at him, that deep and hopeful glow I came to admire.

"There is nothing silly about it. We can make a better world, Aila." He gestured across the library. "We can learn from all the thinkers and heroes of our time, of all times. We can stop the divide between the Alliance and the Elementalists." He leaned on his knees and stared at me. "I'll be a better King than my father one day. We can make a difference together."

I could not avoid smiling at his passion, at the strength of his dreams. At the thought that maybe, one day, the magic in one's veins – or the lack of it – would not be cause for persecution.

It was a beautiful dream, and if anyone could succeed it was him, not us. He needed to remember who we were. Who *I* was.

"I'm sure you will, my Lord. And I'll be proud to bend my knee to you when you do." I knew I'd chosen my words well when I saw the flash of pain crossing his face at the subtle reminder of our roles.

"Despite the enjoyable thought of having you at your knees, I'd rather have you by my side." A dashing and provocative smile back at his lips almost immediately.

"Your father would surely be happy with the addition of a non-arcane nobody to the family." I laughed sarcastically.

"Aiden, you know this will never happen, right? You know I'm here to find a nice suitor that satisfies Ivo and you … well, you are you. Well above my station."

He didn't let more than a shadow of disappointment show as he dismissed his words as a harmless joke. "Naturally! Still, it doesn't mean I can't help you do more than dream about a better world. Change is already happening, Aila."

"The Alliance?" I asked warily.

He nodded.

"They are violent savages, but change is still needed. My father is receiving reports from all Kingdoms. There is more movement at the borders lately … they have wielder sympathizers now."

I wondered if this had something to do with whatever the Premier was involved in.

Aiden continued.

"Change will come whether we want it or not. We should take this chance and make it worthwhile. End the division, find a way without violence, make the experiments lawful …"

It was a hopeful thought as much as it was a naïve one. Wielders had been hiding behind the idea of lawful experiments fueled by paid volunteers since the war, but whether you kidnaped someone in their sleep or controlled them through excessive pay, it didn't matter! Trying to use a non-wielder's life as an amplifier of magic was risky, barbaric, and oppressive. It also meant only one end of that fight had the ability to win it: the side holding the power and the money.

"As long as the Elementalists insist on continuing with the experiments, the rebels won't be overthrown, Aiden.

Non-wielders are dying because Elementalists want to find a way to increase their own arcane power, and until *that* changes there will only be bloodshed." I knew it too well; I'd been in the middle of it.

He leaned forward, his body tensed on the edge of his chair.

"Then we stop the experiments and find a way to co-exist! We have done it before!"

"That was over a thousand years ago, Aiden! When magic first found its way into the world, and no one knew it would get diluted after generations!" I took a deep breath before continuing. "Your own father is the head of the Elementalists council. Do you think he would let go of his dominance, would let go of an inch of power? That the other Elementalists would put the dominance of their own houses at risk?"

He shook his head and dropped his shoulder. Aiden knew as well as I did that the council was not about ensuring magic balance anymore. It was about power. Undiluted power.

"They are just a group of old men with a fancy name."

"I would say a council formed by the head of each Elemental family is a bit more than that," I laughed. "They govern our whole world, Aiden. And they've proven they aren't easily swayed."

He sighed, some of the fight leaking out of him. "Maybe you are right, or maybe we just have to try harder ... I don't know. What I do know is change is coming, and I won't wait for the world to define my role in it. Maybe I'll start by making my father see it."

I could have reminded Aiden of how much his father

loved power, of how much of the violence used by the Alliance was instilled by him and the Elementalists. I could have reminded him of how this was one of the main reasons his own relationship with his father was strained. But I didn't.

Instead, I let the silence fill the space between us, the stars as witnesses to the intimate quietness.

"I hope you make a difference." I smiled at him, having never wished for anything more. "Be careful, though. Some would call your speech treacherous."

"Some would say you are worried about me," he said in a gentle voice as he moved closer to me, kneeling in front of my chair and taking my hands in his. I remained silent as he caressed my fingers, a small part of me welcoming the softness of his warm fingers. "You should never feel silly for dreaming and wishing. I see the light in you, and I know you can do much more than just find a husband that will make your uncle happy. You can make a difference in many lives, if you dare."

He gave me a tender kiss on the cheek before leaving me to wonder if he would still believe that if he knew the whole truth.

Chapter 4

The city slums were not a pleasant place, but could be a useful one.

This far from the white sandy beaches of the palace area, it was easy to forget we were still in the rich capital. The farther I moved towards the hills on the edge of the city, the cheaper and smaller the houses got. The more irregular the streets turned. Until the whole area was nothing more than rustic, flimsy sheds huddled in a chaotic pattern and only interrupted by a few small makeshift stores and empty taverns. Most of the uneven wooden constructions were smaller than my quarters at the palace and still harbored entire families. The whole district was a contradiction to the big white houses and large streets that covered the rest of Nuri.

This was the type of place from where people disappeared to fuel the Elementalists' experiments. Anonymous faces followed me as I walked by, face hidden behind the long hood of my thin, blue cloak.

Dirty children played in the street, women sold

trinkets in improvised tents and drunken men made their way home. Penniless souls and forged criminals alike owned these streets.

For me, the slums were nothing but a place that blurred the lines and exposed hard choices. A place that never failed to remind me that when you are left with no choices in life, you can rarely afford to have values.

In many ways, I fit right in.

After strolling a few minutes, I spotted a blond boy sitting on the corner of a street lazily watching two younger children playing with a ragged, leather ball. He was a portrait of boredom, but his stares at me were too frequent to be casual.

I leaned with one foot on the wall behind him, facing the match.

"I need to see the Scorpion," I said barely above a whisper.

"Does *he* need to see you?" he replied flatly.

"I would assume he needs my coin purse. Or at least will enjoy it."

"And you are?"

"Not someone you want to know, boy."

He turned to me for the first time. Maybe he caught a glimpse of the daggers on my waist, maybe he simply didn't care. But one way or the other, he rose slowly to his feet.

"I'm not taking anyone I don't know there, so what name do you want me to give him?"

"Just tell him what you saw here. He will know who I am."

Then I waited.

A few minutes later, the boy came back and, without a word, led me through a series of alleys to a rusty, red door.

Inside, I found a poorly illuminated room with hundreds of jars stacked in old wooden shelves. The monthly change of premises was an annoying habit to avoid detection, but it always amazed me how every place looked the same inside.

Scorpion was waiting behind a worn-out counter. The frail, old man had small round glasses and a slight hunchback and his freckled arms rested on the counter while his gaze focused solely on me. If I did not know him, I would never believe the white-haired man was the best poison-maker in the Kingdom.

"Long time," he said with a sly smile.

I nodded. I never liked small talk, but Scorpion would not do business with people he didn't know, or didn't like, so I played along.

"Yeah, well, my supplies are mostly in good shape," I said, threading a thin line between nicety and evasion.

"At least you aren't working too much, then." He gave me a poisonous, black-toothed smile, his face alighting in anticipation. "What can I help you with today, my dear?"

I wondered how many had suffered for underestimating the old man, and a flash of delighted admiration may have flickered across my face.

"Let's say I need to render someone unconscious, very quickly. What would you suggest?"

"Well, there are many possibilities. By what method?"

"Inhalation." After a moment of consideration, I added, "Or injection, if it must be."

"I could prepare you a tonic."

I thought about hiding the large bottle on my gown before replying. "I can't carry a large bottle, no more than a vial."

He considered for a few minutes, consulted some of the jars and drawers behind him. "Nightshade." He turned back to me. "I could make it into a concentrated oil, add a few other things to make it more stable, faster."

"Would nightshade work like that?" I asked, doubtful. The natural poison was effective, but usually by ingestion.

"A challenge, indeed," his eyes gleamed with excitement, "but with the right carrier, and the right dosage, it would."

"How would I administer it?"

"You'd need to pierce the skin. A knife? A blowgun?"

"A knife is too messy, and I don't want to risk leaving anything behind."

"A syringe of sorts?"

He put a pair of hair sticks in front of me. Each one was a striking gold stick with a massive onyx stone on its top. He motioned for me to look closely and with a touch of his finger on the side of the rock, a needle shot from the tip. He then proceeded to remove the onyx and reveal the concealed chamber inside the body of the stick. An exquisite and mortal accessory, apparently.

As I took it into my hands, he continued. "It is effective and will remain hidden for as long as you wish. Dosing won't be precise, though. The chamber will fit about two doses, but nightshade requires an exact bodyweight ratio, if your target is smaller than anticipated and you administer the full dose," he shrugged. "You may end up with a corpse rather than a sleeping chump."

"Collateral damage, I suppose," I said more to myself than to him. "I have no way of anticipating their size."

The gold would offer a nice contrast with my hair and the stone would fit the dress I'd selected. The mechanism was imperceptible and easy to activate, a dangerous and undetectable weapon.

I smiled viciously. "Make sure they are both full; I need them in three days."

♦

I spent most of the following nights hidden on the rooftops near Valran's house with a spyglass in hand. And, although the guards seemed more alert and disciplined, I hadn't seen the captain again. Which gave me both a surge of relief and a pang of disappointment.

By the time I left my position on the last night before the ball, I was satisfied. I had a clear view of the guard's rotation and house layout, a full list of guests and a clear distraction – courtesy of the theater director hired by Lidya being in my pocket for months.

Their number during the ball would be the perfect distraction for me to break into Valran's office. Everyone else would be enthralled in their number. Simple but effective.

When all was ready, it was with no little amount of satisfaction that I soaked in an early, warm bath for the first night since Ivo had summoned me.

I was already in my nightgown when I heard the two light, familiar knocks on my door. I debated not opening it, but I knew I couldn't evade the Prince much longer without raising questions I didn't want to answer. Besides, I could use the distraction.

Aiden entered the room swiftly, wine bottle in hand.
"Care to join me?" he asked with a dashing smile.
"How could I refuse?" I grinned.
I leaned against the table on the corner of the

antechamber as he filled two glasses out of my personal set. He didn't offer me one of the cups until he was mere inches from me, his chest almost touching my own. I could feel the warmth of his breath on my face, his spicy cologne surging up my nose. My body awoke in response.

I raised my glass and we toasted, his intense gaze flickering between my eyes and my mouth.

"I came last night," he said in a whisper, "and the night before."

"You know better than to come here so often."

"No one saw me."

"That you know of."

He was generally careful, but he also didn't care.

"I thought you were tired of me," he said, ignoring my comment, hands tracing circles around my arm as he inched closer. "Or were with other company." A flicker of jealousy on his voice.

I wouldn't offer him unnecessary lies, so I remained silent, losing myself a little in his touch.

"Maybe I was wrong?" His whisper was a caress an inch away.

He leaned forward to kiss me, warm and sweet. But, as our bodies touched, the kiss deepened, growing hungrier and stronger. He lifted me into the air, my legs around his waist and arms clawing his broad shoulders. Savage need rippled through me as he took me to the bed.

I could feel the hunger in him as he kissed every corner of my body, his hands lazily caressing my thighs and breasts. Demanding.

A groan escaped me, and he took me. Deep and slow, letting me indulge in the power and pleasure of feeling him inside me, my nails clinging to his chest and back muscles.

I moaned into his mouth and the sound seemed to send him into a spiral of primal need. His movements became more eager, his body succumbing to ravenous desire. I shifted on top of him, in complete control, retracing every muscle of his chest with my mouth before guiding him inside me once again. My fingers touched the small bud between my legs, while his hands held my breasts, leaving me moaning and relenting to the small waves of melting heat in my core. His voice was a soft groan, repeating my name half in adoration, half in madness, until we yielded to one another and our bodies exploded in a welcoming pleasure that still echoed between us as we collapsed on the bed, legs intertwined and hands resting on each other.

It was a long time before we stepped back into real life.

Aiden picked up the wine glasses we had left in the other room and placed them on the bedside table as I observed the beauty of the body walking through my chambers.

"So, were you? With company?" he asked a little too casually as he reclined on my bed once again.

"Do I really need to answer?"

A sweet smile found its way to his lips.

"Then where have you been?"

"Nowhere, really." I dismissed his question as best I could. "What did you want so intently, though? I'm sure you didn't come all this way just for the amazing company," I said, giving him a side glance.

He threw one of the pillows at my face, making me fall behind in surprise, a playful look on his face. He continued to cover me with every pillow and bed sheet he could reach, while saying: "Don't. Be. So. Smug."

In spite of myself, I laughed. He had that effect on me

sometimes, mostly when we were alone, with nothing to remind me of all the lies that floated between us. In those rare moments, I forgot about the darkness in me – magical and otherwise – and I wondered if I was worthy of these little glimpses of happiness.

We threw pillows at each other until we were both catching our breath, recovering from our silliness. When the echoes of laughter were over, I asked, "So, tell me. Did you need to talk?"

He sighed. "Bad council meeting, a pile of unsavory reports … I guess I wanted to distract myself."

"Something happened?" I asked.

"Just more Alliance disturbances. I don't know if I'm more pissed about the reports or the messenger," he sighed.

He and his father would often confront each other in those meetings. Aiden was a dreamer who believed in a world he could forge to be better, and he never hid his hopes and desires from his father. Never stopped using the little influence he held to try and persuade him to embrace the same dream.

But the King was ruthless. He'd clung to power his whole life and wasn't interested in letting an ounce of it get out of his control, especially not for his naïve youngest son. Heir, or not.

More often than not, their different views resulted in an open confrontation that Aiden could only lose.

I waited in silence, caressing his hair.

"The Alliance is growing stronger," he took a deep breath. "They have entire towns under their control, and now that my father knows which ones, he wants to attack. I know we must free the people from these rebels but I'm tired of the empty violence," he finished, sight lost in the ceiling.

"*Free* the people? You do realize this is a non-wielders movement, right? They represent most of the people in any of the Kingdoms."

After centuries of mixed marriages, most common citizens had little arcane power, if any.

"You know what I mean."

"No. I don't think I do."

"We were made to rule, Aila. We have to protect those who can't, and sometimes this means making hard decisions."

Of course, he'd think that. All royal families were of the purest arcane lines; all their heirs the most powerful among each line. Aiden himself had been elected heir for having more arcane power than his older brother, who ended up leading Niram Naval Forces far away from court.

"I'm a non-wielder myself, lest you forget, Aiden." Or so he thought.

"I know you are! And I don't mean it in a bad way, you know that. I just mean that all this power," his eyes were hollowed as he faced me, "it has to mean something! If I can't use it to stop the violence, to save innocent lives, then what good is it?"

"You know that is not why your father wants to stop the rebels. He doesn't care about innocent lives, Aiden. None of the Elementalists do."

I took his silence as a sign to continue.

"He has all the power now, and those rebels are a threat to it, so he will say he is protecting you, protecting his Kingdom. Then, he'll do whatever he can to squash the Alliance, no matter what or who is lost because of it. Why wouldn't he?"

"He can't pass that off as protecting us, and we can't expect to thrive if we keep endangering innocents." His voice was tired, strained.

"I'm just saying that he holds all the cards, and I don't know if anyone in his position would act differently."

"I would! I will. If I ever rule."

I looked at the pain in his face, wondering if his need to be a hero would save or doom him. I placed my hand carefully on his cheek. "If you find the strength to keep believing, I know you will."

He seemed satisfied with that, relieved someone could hear him, see him. Even if only for a few stolen hours.

◆

We spoke through half the night, until the moon started to settle, and our voices grew tired. We were both arranged comfortably on my bed, clothes back on, reclined on one another when I felt the acute and immediate need for sleep. I gave Aiden a small kiss and forced myself to sit up, despite his protests. "You have to go."

"Why? It will be hours before the servants come here."

"But not before they start to roam the corridors. Besides, I need to sleep."

Without thought and with the flicker of a finger he snuffed out all the flames in the room while holding his arms to me in a silent invite.

I couldn't stop the bitter longing flickering in my heart at his casual use of magic, at how second nature it was to him, at how it would never be that simple for me. I knew it wasn't his fault, but he had power in more ways than he realized.

In our world, survival required magic or money. If

you were lucky enough to have both, you could rule the world; if you had none … nothing but hunger and violence awaited. And if, like me, the magic power running through your veins was cursed, there was only hoping no one would ever find it out.

I pushed the unwanted thought away.

"You know I prefer to sleep on my own."

"Just because you are too stubborn to let me stay. Maybe you are afraid you won't be able to sleep without me again," he said with a teasing grin.

"You can believe that if you want. As long as you are back in your room before anyone can suspect you were here." I found my way to the bathroom. "Don't forget to light my damn candles before you leave, smart ass," I added playfully.

He could believe what he wanted, but the truth was I never allowed myself to sleep with anyone by my side, not unless I had a dagger under my pillow and made myself stay half alert, in a shallow, inconstant sleep. Not the kind of rest I needed that night.

Yet, I couldn't avoid wondering what it would be like to tell him about my overbearing fear of being vulnerable. What would he say if he had truly seen any part of the real me?

If we had the courage to look at the hard truths, maybe our story could end up differently.

Chapter 5

The dressing table in front of me was a mess of cosmetics and vials. The servants had taken the better part of an hour preparing me for the ball, but my final touches were not something to be shared or witnessed.

I used the quiet moments to replay every step of the night in my mind while I carefully placed a dagger in the hidden strip on my thigh and adjusted the golden hair sticks behind the elaborate bun and intricate crystal drape holding my hair. A deadly weapon, beautifully designed. Not so different from myself.

"Remarkable." Ivo's brittle voice rang out behind me.

It wasn't often that someone walked in on me, especially in my own chambers, but the surprise that flared in my mind as I saw him through the mirror had little to do with it. There was a rough emotion on his face, a rare silver line in his eyes.

I turned to him just as he bent down in front of me, lips curling in a smile.

"I never thanked you for the apples."

"It was nothing but silly nostalgia."

"It was thoughtful." He paused before adding in a small voice, "Made me remember happier times."

I felt my face, and my heart, soften at the memory of those times.

"Do you remember the first time I gave you one of those?" His eyes glinting.

I recognized so much of the man I grew up with in his face, that a part of me forgot the heated words we'd exchanged mere days before. In that moment, it was as if they never happened.

"Yes. It was the first gift anyone ever gave me." The first time anyone cared enough to give me anything.

His gaze was distant, as if momentarily lost in thoughts. "You were so small back then, so quiet. I don't think you said a word to anyone for the first few weeks, actually."

"I was afraid, I guess."

"But you had a fire in you. Even then. Restless, unwavering." His attention was back at me, unfaltering "A bright, scorching light that could burn the world if you let it."

My heart warmed to him.

"I think those apples, simple as they were, made me trust you."

"Not the tutors and the roof over your head?" he asked with feigned skepticism.

"No." I laughed and shrugged. "I figured if you were going to hurt me, you wouldn't bother giving me expensive sweets first."

A genuine grin bloomed in his face as he took my hand. "We've come a long way, haven't we? I'm proud of you, Aila."

My heart burst, as it did each time he spoke this way. There was always a part of me that sparked brightly at the idea of making him proud.

"I'm sorry for the other day ... all I do is for us. To give you a place in this world where you can be undeniably safe. And I hate that sometimes I must be so hard on you." He took a deep breath before continuing, a thin line forming between his brows. "I'll be better. Can you trust me?"

In the end, I knew it always came down to that; to the inescapable battle between love and fear; to the inevitable choice between uncharted freedom and dangerous trust.

"That is not ... I'm sorry." I said without thinking. "I guess I was just afraid I wouldn't find what you need, that I would disappoint you." It was the truth.

"You couldn't possibly, my darling!" He touched my chin affectionately before offering me a silk-lined, black case.

A delicate emerald necklace sat inside, the stones interwoven with the most graceful web of golden threads.

"When you were growing up, I wondered if I would ever have a chance to indulge in a true father-daughter moment with you," he mused as I touched it reverently.

"This was my mother's. One of the few things I have of hers. I know she'd be honored to know it rests in your hands." Ivo never told me what happened between him and his mother, but I knew he loved and missed her. "It matches your eyes," he whispered as he stood and turned me around.

"Ivo," I said with a breathy voice. "It is beautiful. I don't know what to say."

"Just say you'll use it." He clasped it on my neck "Just say you'll forgive me."

The rage and coldness in my heart melted. For there, in front of me, was the man who'd raised me. He was not quick to love, but he did love me.

So, I hugged him and whispered in his neck, "I'll cherish it."

And, despite myself, I forgave him.

◆

The streets were busier than ever with the endless movement of carriages. The sky, a blend of orange and pink with the sun behind Valran's house, disappearing over the sea. A whimsical backdrop for the lords and ladies making their way down the long staircase.

Tall bordering torches followed the stone steps as I climbed each slowly, arms interlinked with Ivo, intent on drawing as much attention as I could to our little family portrait.

The guards were in perfect formation, in the exact positions I'd expected. Satisfied, I let pure joy radiate from me, schooling my features to show all the signs of delight and amazement that a twenty-five-year-old girl would be expected to show at her first big ball: amazed face and parted lips.

I wore a sleeveless, mermaid dress with a long slit from the middle of my right thigh, the fabric forming a dramatic gradient from black to white and glittering with thousands of tiny, embroidered crystals. The emerald necklace sat proudly on my neck.

As we approached the door, Ivo squeezed my fingers on his arms and said low enough for only I to hear, "Anything I should know?"

"Be visible when the entertainment starts but avoid the center of the room," I said squaring my shoulders.

He cracked a charming smile as we crossed the

doorway. "Then let's begin."

The first floor of the house was as I imagined from the schemes I had collected: a relatively big antechamber giving way to a large reception room, surrounded by ample windows. The room was as big as some of the palace chambers and as elegantly decorated.

The central area was empty, forming a spacious dance floor. On each corner, tables with an array of different drinks were combined with various comfortable chairs and sofas forming relaxing and intimate areas. Astounding white flower arrangements were placed on every surface.

When night descended, thousands – maybe millions – of fairy lights littered the ceiling, mimicking the evening sky with surprising and delightful accuracy.

Knowing the theatre would not start for another two hours, I spent some time mingling with guests and making myself noticeable. I jumped from conversation to conversation gracefully, engaging different people and laughing at different jokes, all while being careful to never stay too long in the same place, to work the room so no one would know where to find me or think too long about where I might be.

Only when alcohol passed freely and no one took notice anymore, did I start to venture to the edges of the room, farther and farther away from the main body of guests, as if admiring the exquisite view from the windows and the lavish works of art on the walls in between.

With every careful step, I marked my distance to the few guards posted inside, I identified the deeper pockets of shadow and traced the path that would, in time, take me to the correct corridor. A few minutes before the start of the presentation, I cast my power wide in the room, discretely locking some of the shadow pockets in place to ensure that no unexpected light would reveal my later path. Then I made my way back to the crowd.

As I turned, I bumped into someone. A man. He gently, yet firmly, held my arms to keep me steady.

"I've got you." A husky voice rang out with a charming, yet arrogant smile. If I hadn't seen him arriving in the dead of night a few days before, I could have mistaken him for a lord.

From across the street and under the veil of night, he'd appeared intriguing. Inches away, he was the most strikingly beautiful man I had ever seen. Soft yet strong facial lines, sensual mouth, a slender, defined body and bottomless amber eyes, the color of molten gold and mesmerizing fire. Utterly captivating and deeply mysterious.

It took me some measure of self-control not to gasp at the sight of him, to remind myself I had a mission ahead, and no time for distractions.

"Thank you, I guess the lights got me a little distracted. I feel like we are under a starry sky." I gave him my most charming yet innocent smile. Nothing more than an overly excited lady.

He measured me for a few seconds, lingering on my toned arms and shoulders—too toned for a rich girl. When his eyes locked with mine again, something other than amusement shone there.

"Alluring," he briefly trailed my mouth, his charming smile never fading, "and dangerous, I suppose."

"What do you mean? It is so lovely." I arched my brows slightly, a sign of surprised innocence.

"That it is." he said, relaxing his stance, "but who says beauty can't also be dangerous?"

I had the good sense to lower my head a few inches and appear alarmed. He continued before I could talk again.

"It is better if I escort you back. Safer!"

"Is it?" The words left my mouth before I could stop it, not much of the innocent girl showing in my voice anymore.

"Safer or better?" his gaze snapped back to mine. Interest seeming to shine in his features.

"Both."

He shrugged in response.

"It is certainly more appropriate. Don't you think?" he said, seconds later.

"I've been known for not caring much about what is appropriate," I said, despite knowing I should have taken the opportunity to leave.

He laughed, a sonorous and arrogant laugh that crept under my skin. "Maybe you should care, love."

"And why is that?"

He casually slipped his hands in his pockets. A tantalizing appeal in the clearly practiced movement.

"You are a lady, are you not?" For the briefest second, he glanced at my shoulders and arms again. "What is there for you if not enjoying balls and gowns and spending a lifetime being appropriate?"

Everything about him was smug: posture, tone, look. Entitlement poured out of him. It had been years since someone had been so arrogant towards me and I didn't know if it was the way he measured me or the audacity in his voice that annoyed me more. And yet – or maybe because of it – he intrigued me.

The presumptuousness of his remark made my blood boil and my heart race in rage. Before I could reply, I felt a gentle touch on my bare, lower back, a possessive touch.

"Lady Aila! I've been looking for you." Aiden was rarely reckless enough for such obvious demonstrations of our intimacy, but he seemed not to care this time.

I thought I saw a flash of surprised understanding in the stranger's face, but it was gone before I could be certain. I turned to Aiden slowly, curtsying. "My Prince."

Aiden's gaze remained fixed on the man, no warmth left in his features.

After a few silent seconds, he spoke.

"I'll leave you to it." A shallow bow to Aiden and a weary smile to me.

Aiden pointedly turned to me, ignoring his presence and words. "You look stunning."

I thanked him, and when the man was far enough from us, I dropped my voice enough so no one could hear us.

"What was that all about?" I said, stepping away from him.

He looked at where his hand had touched me, and I knew my evasion had not gone unnoticed.

"Was he bothering you?"

"No."

"I don't trust him."

"Don't trust or don't like him?" Aiden looked at me with pursed lips and sharp jaw. Cold rage simmered in his face. "Who is he anyway?" I continued, maybe too eagerly, before he had a chance to reply.

"Flynn Wheelan," he said, taking a deep breath and leashing his temper. "Annoying captain of Valran's personal guard. Looks like he really is back."

"Flynn," I repeated under my breath as I watched him walk with the same prowess and confidence I had seen a few nights before.

◆

Aiden lingered, so I had to drive him towards a group eager for his attention before I slipped away, his gaze following me briefly through the crowd.

I did not have long to find my position before the show started. A part of my mind kept searching for Flynn, an invisible pull tugging at my core. I was painfully aware he was oblivious and unprepared, but he was nowhere to be seen, and there was no time to adapt my plans so I carried on, despite the memory of his suspicious stare still burning on my skin.

I found my place at the edge of the main crowd and waited for the lights to dim before I moved.

Just a few more moments.

The clock stroke nine, and a near darkness swept through the room as the millions of fairy lights adjusted and a delicate music started. A strong beam of light drew attention to three people standing at the center of the room: a man dressed in red and gold finery and, at each side, a woman in an exquisite white and gold gown. They were frozen in space as the music grew louder and the crowd closer.

Beckoned by some invisible power, we all moved in sync. The dancers to start their performance, and me to find shelter in the darkest shadow pocket.

I had three songs.

I summoned my power to veil me in darkness, enough that the crystals on my dress wouldn't flicker at every glimpse of light. And, soon enough, with all eyes focused on the play, I was nearly invisible.

When I reached the long corridor leading to the second floor, I had no worries about being silent, knowing the music would stifle the noise just as the shadows would hide my figure. The corridor was empty, even the servants too drawn by the spectacle to roam around.

On the second floor, I moved swiftly to the two windows on the right side of the building where I knew Valran's office to be.

Almost at the same time, a bored guard emerged from the end of the corridor. Events like this would either make an officer jumpy or lazy, comfortable knowing any threat would be stopped before reaching them. This guard, in the calm second floor, fell among the latter.

I hid in a small recess in the wall, docked between a pillar and a small table, and slightly loosened my grip on the darkness around me, letting it dissipate enough to shield any attention before it was time.

I unfastened one of the daggers from the garter belt at my thigh, reached for one of the sticks on my hair, and waited until he was close enough for me to reach him. As soon as he was, I relinquished my cover and, in a single movement, took my dagger to his throat and my left hand to the crook of his neck, not sparing a second before piercing the exposed skin with the hidden hair needle. The nightshade took root before he could react and by the time he tried, his body was already limp from the poison.

"Sweet dreams," I whispered pleased with the venom as he slumped to the floor. It would be long enough before someone found him without a trail of blood.

I tried to drag him to the closest room, grunting and straining under his weight, but after a few moments, I had to relent and form a shadow tendril to shove him through the door of the luxurious guest room. I had no time to struggle with his heaviness.

Seconds later, I was back at the corridor, breathlessly making my way to the room I'd identified days before.

My lips tugged upward in a humorless smile when I tried to open the locked door; all the confirmation I needed before I sent a small tendril of darkness into the lock, rendering the mechanism useless.

As I crossed the threshold downstairs, the first song finished.

◆

Valran's office was elegantly decorated: a grand cedar desk, lavish rugs, and translucent white curtains, complemented with shelves full of old tomes.

There were no cabinets or drawers other than the ones on the desk itself.

I quickly examined the books displayed and the walls in between for any sign of a secret door or vault, but it was slow work, and it wasn't long before I heard the second song approaching its climax. I would not have time to examine the whole place, so I moved to the desk instead.

I sat on the tall chair behind it. A pile of meaningless correspondence and service orders for tonight's ball lay on top of it. The two cabinets and drawers were also useless.

I reclined and peered around, cooling my rushed blood, the music downstairs escalating my sense of urgency. *I'll need to come back for a full sweep.* I tapped my fingers on the chair's arm, irritation taking root in my core. Then I remembered the fake drawer at my own desk back at the palace, the extra precaution I took even where I felt safe, *especially* where I felt safe.

I traced my fingers underneath the desk, touching every inch of wood, looking for any signs of mechanisms or hollow sounds. When my finger brushed the edge of the drawer, I noticed the bottom seemed rather shallow in comparison to the robustness of the wood. I opened it again.

There was no visible alteration, yet the texture of the material was a notch different. I emptied and turned it around, finding a small lever hidden on the back. With a simple touch, the bottom of the drawer opened up to me, revealing a series of piled up papers and books only a few seconds before the second song finished.

I hurried through the documents, with little time to examine them properly. There were lists of names and locations, encoded letters along with a cypher and maps, many maps. The round symbol used by the Rebel Alliance etched in most of them.

As always, the symbol seemed to prick at an old and faded memory I couldn't quite place. I'd spent hours, uselessly trying to identify a memory that was likely too old to bear any real meaning.

I flipped through the documents in haste. There were maps of every Kingdom, with small notes and marks on the page edges. Downstairs, the final song was gaining in intensity, approaching its middle point, there was no time to figure out what any of it meant now.

I tucked as many documents as I could inside my dress bodice and put the rest back in place. I left the office as swiftly as I came in. I assumed it would be at least a couple hours before anyone found the sleeping guard or noticed the breach, and a few more before they had a full account of what was taken.

I made my way through the stairs as quickly as I dared, knowing the spectacle was reaching its climax and I would have little space to hide with the lights back to their brightest intensity.

I reached the edge of the corridor and waited for the end of the song and the loud explosion I knew would follow.

Chapter 6

For a few seconds, the ball room was bright and chaotic. A mess of movement and screams: guests fleeing, guards rushing and a dense cloud of smoke where dancers had stood before.

I had a brief moment to slip away from my hiding place and into the crowd. Effortlessly copying the desperate, screaming ladies with a scared look on my face.

Guards and servants directed people towards the smokeless garden, as I found a place with some of those I'd spent time with earlier in the evening. Unsurprisingly, it wasn't long before we were in hushed conversation about how terrible it was to see such a beautiful dance end in unexpected flames and smoke.

The theater director had assured me the explosion would be small, controlled. And I knew Aiden would be nearby to smother any lingering flames. What I'd really needed was the distraction, and the smoke, to leave the impressionable young ladies flustered enough that my movements would go unnoticed.

Although the outdoor area was not as grandly decorated as the interior, the scenery more than compensated for it. The back garden was a beautiful space with small rose bushes and a pleasant sitting area near the main building. At its end, a sharp cliff that, under sunlight, would give way to a privileged view of a sandy beach and the ocean beyond it. The only other structure visible from here was the cliff where the palace sat: the southern tip of Niram territory.

By the time Lord Valran and Lady Lidya came out of the house, apologizing for what had been a *"terrible miscalculation of the special effects in the theatre number,"* half of the crowd had already dispersed through the garden.

The couple was extremely young; although Valran had a delicate and gentle build to him, Lidya had the type of ruthless face I had seen few times in my life. As they walked around, however, apologizing for the incident and inviting the guests back inside, I was surprised to note their caring touches and sweet smiles. I wondered if there was more than ambition and power behind their union.

I made my way back inside before the hosts took too much notice of me, taking a deep breath to quiet my thrumming heart and checking my facial expression.

Most of the guests were back in easy conversation as I walked around the edge of the room. I kept my gaze wandering in a careful show of uncertain curiosity as I trailed the area where the dancers had performed.

After the description the theatre director gave me, it wasn't hard to imagine the events from minutes before. The presentation had finished with the three dancers moving around a chemically induced blaze, a careful combination of ingredients that would slowly rise in a pattern of high and mesmerizing flames before dying out in a thread of smoke that would be manipulated through air wielders into a series of swirling tendrils around and in between the dancers. Luckily for me, careful combinations of ingredients could be miscalculated, easily changed to generate a hefty and unexpected explosion. As I looked at the marks of the fire on the floor, I wondered if he'd given his dancers any type of warning regarding what would happen during their final number. One way or another though, he'd provided the distraction I needed.

Soldiers were positioned around the room, more alert than before. I could see Flynn giving orders to three men on the edge of the corridor where I had been hidden only minutes before, gesturing towards the exits and windows of the room. He did not seem as relaxed as before and, as his eyes found mine, I knew the fallen man I had left on the second floor had something to do with it.

I joined one of the less ostentatious groups and put all my effort into blending in, despite the predatory look that burned through my skin and kept me incredibly aware of the documents hidden beneath my dress.

Too soon, he started walking in my direction, with certain steps and a taut jaw. I glanced around the room, searching for a way to delay whatever conversation he had in mind, and found Aiden a few paces in front of me.

Before I could think better of it, I touched his arm, ignoring the few courtiers he was chatting with. Flynn halted as I looked at Aiden, letting him study my face. Without a second thought, he took me to an empty corner of the room, dismissing everyone that tried to approach us.

"Are you ok?" he said extending me a glass of water. "I searched for you, I thought you had left."

"I'm ok. I was not at the front, but there was so much smoke …" I let my voice break at the end.

Flynn was still observing us. Me.

I shook my head and continued. "Have you seen my uncle? I can't find him."

"He is fine. I smothered the flames, no one got hurt." It had probably taken him seconds to extinguish the fire.

I made myself release a deep shuddering breath as he continued. "Come, let's go back to the palace!"

"We shouldn't!" I couldn't hide the cold bite in my words completely, but it was the truth. We both knew it.

He ignored my words and offered me a hand. "It will be my pleasure to escort you back. I'll make sure Ivo is told you are safe." The certainty on his face faltered before he added, "Unless you want to enjoy the rest of the ball?"

I glanced one last time towards Flynn and knew that, as vexing as it was, I had no more tricks. I would either leave with Aiden or face whatever questions were brewing behind the sly face.

I silently took his hand and let him guide me through the room, ignoring the few looks cast towards us. I would worry about the very public statement we were making later.

But whatever relief washed over me as Flynn allowed Aiden to take me through the door, was short-lived. For Ivo stood on the outside portico, an intent expression on his face, heartless smile on his lips and a glass raised in my direction.

◆

The ride to the palace should have been short and pleasant. The coachman followed a beautiful path by the sea, intent on giving his Prince and myself the pleasure of privacy.

Seated by the window, I observed the distant lights of the few boats anchored near the coastline. The streets were mostly empty, no witnesses for the royal carriage passing through the quiet streets.

I half-registered Aiden's attempts to talk but couldn't bring myself to respond. I couldn't stop thinking of Ivo's smile, of the greedy gleam I'd seen in there.

I always knew getting close to Aiden was reckless, but not until that moment did I truly understand it was also dangerous.

Anger and frustration crept under my skin, slowly settling in my core. An overwhelming rage at his careless display of intimacy and at my foolishness to believe I could keep the real depth of our relationship hidden from his court, and from Ivo. Tonight, more than every other night, I had been selfish and naïve, two things usually payable with pain and death.

The prince's hand touched mine as we approached the palace gate, a painfully soft and caring grasp. I didn't know when we'd gone from a fun distraction to this messy and heart-breaking affair, but I knew I cared for Aiden as much as I knew he wanted more. And sometimes I wanted nothing more than to find out if I could give him more than sex and friendship.

Yet, I was no lady in need of protection, I was all twisted darkness and carved strength. And even if we were not heir and spy, I couldn't erase that part of me. Not for him, not for anyone.

Tonight, I'd used him to escape. I'd shown Ivo exactly how big my influence on Aiden was. I'd crossed a threshold we would never be able to come back from. I knew in my core there would be consequences. For months, I'd evaded Ivo's questions, hidden my real influence over Niram's heir, but there would be no more denying him. He'd suspected our involvement for far too long and I'd finally given him all the confirmation he needed.

No matter how much Ivo loved me, how much he protected me, the small, quiet part of me couldn't stop fearing what he would do now. Because I knew what that gleam on his eyes meant, I'd seen him blinded by greed before.

And the kind of power my connection with Aiden could give him, was not something he would ever walk away from. So, whether Ivo would make me lie, betray, and use him; or whether he'd use Aiden's own life to control me, no good would come from this night.

As I looked at my friend's face under the moonlight, I just hoped I wouldn't have to break his heart to keep him safe.

He held my hand as I descended from the carriage and led me through the palace doors, dismissing every servant on our way.

Aiden had stopped making conversation a long time before I removed my hand from his. We walked in familiar silence until the main hall and, when he finally faced me, I didn't have to fake the concern and anger in my face. I knew there were too much of my real feelings lacing my manners.

His gaze was intent as he raised his hand in a tender caress of my cheek.

"I know it was scary," he whispered, "but you don't have to worry. I'll always keep you safe! I promise."

After all the time we spent together, he still misread me, he still saw me as a helpless lady in need of protection. At that point, I was not sure if that was a testament to my skills or to his naivety. Either way it did nothing to calm the storm brewing inside of me.

I took a step out of his reach and faced him, clenching my fists and using all my self-control to keep the simmering anger out of my voice.

"I don't need to be protected, Aiden! And I'm not yours to keep safe."

A flash of pain passed through his squinted eyes, but I continued before I could think better of it.

"You should remember the position you hold. You can't afford to have jealous tantrums over every girl that goes into your bed."

The cold sharpness that took over his face told me he knew exactly what I was talking about.

"You are not every girl, Aila. I think you know that by now." His tone softened slightly as he continued. "I want you by my side, not in my bed."

"Can't you see how naïve this is, Aiden?" The arrogance I tried to convey didn't come true. I sounded tired and pained. "You don't get to choose who you'll have by your side. You marry an ally, you rule and, if lucky, you choose who you bed. You want to make a difference in the world, don't you? That is the price you pay."

"I can do both," he insisted.

I laughed a bitter laugh.

"Even if you could, I was made for something else entirely. My uncle has a purpose for me, and I assure you it has nothing to do with changing the world."

"A purpose? What? Marriage to mid-level nobility?" he sneered.

He ran his hands through his hair and shook his head, disbelief marking his features, in a thick voice, "I know a life with me would not be easy, but I never thought you would prefer to be a pawn for your uncle instead."

I inhaled sharply, briefly facing the ceiling before pushing the words through gritted teeth. "I'm just warming your bed. My *future* is not your concern, my prince."

He flinched. But before I had a chance to regret it, I turned away and left him standing in the hall.

◆

A bath was all I needed. The lush foam and scented oils coated my skin as the perfume slowly calmed my senses. The hot water relaxed my muscles, unravelling the tension from my shoulders and neck. With every second, I regained an ounce of control over myself.

I'd always been able to reason with Ivo, I just had to give him what he needed first. So, I dressed myself comfortably and spread all the documents I'd stolen across the bed. The maps showed scattered, red crosses near small cities in devastated areas. Some of which I recognized as cities the King claimed to have liberated from the Alliance.

Urian appeared near the border – one of the biggest red marks by its side. Under the city name, a count of fifty soldiers and a date of a few days before, the same date Aiden claimed to have received a new report on the Alliance.

On a side pile, three letters and a cypher awaited. None signed beyond the Alliance insignia: a circular shape formed out of two intertwined arrows. The cypher would need to be decoded before it could offer me any insight.

Before I made any real progress, I heard a low tap on my door. Only two people would visit my chamber in the middle of the night, and I knew for a fact Aiden wouldn't be coming here so soon.

Ivo was leaning against the side of my door when I opened it.

"I hope I'm not interrupting." A poisonous, wry smile danced on his lips.

I opened the door freely to allow him in and ignored the prod in his question.

"I wasn't expecting you."

"I had to check on my niece after such an eventful night."

I served us both a glass of brandy and he continued.

"What did you find?"

Absently, I raised a shield around the room as I moved the documents from my bed to the table at the foyer. "He hides things well but has a mostly amateur guard."

An image of Valran's very intriguing, and apparently skilled, captain popped into my mind before I shoved it back.

"He had maps of all the Kingdoms. I believe the red marks are rebel camps, but whether they are accurate or not, I don't know. I couldn't bring all of it, but I thought you would be more interested in Niram, anyway. It had considerably more marks than any other Kingdom."

I moved my focus to the letters: "I'm assuming he intercepted these. I'll know when I crack the code. Give me a day or two," I turned my gaze back to the cypher.

"What else?" Ivo prompted me out of my silence.

I shook my head and faced him again. "Nothing. His office seemed clean enough. He may have another hiding place, but … I doubt it. He put too much effort to hide this, I don't think it was just a decoy," I finished with half of my attention still on the cypher.

"So, nothing concrete?" he tilted his head.

"Well, he is investigating the Alliance, that much is

clear. What exactly he wants out of them, though …" I shrugged. "I'd guess he is trying to find their leaders, crush their advances, but it is too soon to tell. Maybe when I crack the code."

Ivo took the letters in his hands and calmly examined them as he spoke without ever facing me:

"I need you to find out what the King asked of him. Not to guess it, I need you to *know* it beyond doubt."

I laughed. "How do you expect me to do this? Shall I torture it out of the Premier or the king?" Most of the dealings between them were off-book, and Ivo wouldn't need *me* for the ones that were recorded. Any of his spies could get to those, probably already had.

He watched me with a stare as cold as ever. Not a trace of the man who gave me his only family heirloom only hours before.

"I'm sure you have more pleasant ways to figure it out." A dangerous smile twisted his lips.

Aiden. A frigid shiver ran through my spine in expectation of the one choice I didn't want to be forced to make.

"You seemed very cozy with our Prince tonight. I'm actually surprised he is not here right now." He continued eyeing the bed chamber behind me. "It was very caring of him to escort you back to the palace."

"He doesn't trust me enough to share his father's secrets." The lie flew smoothly from my lips.

"Oh, but I think he does. I think he does." He placed the letters and cyphers in his pocket and leaned closer to me. "You better find out soon," he continued in a murmur while placing a kiss on my cheek, "before he tires of you."

"I don't want to use him, Ivo."

He stopped his move to the door mid-turn and tilted his head with a penetrating gaze following my every breath in cold assessment. "Why? You certainly don't seem inclined to take advantage of your power over him."

Because I can't let go of this little haven I built with him. Because I can't force myself to repay his friendship with betrayal. Because I'm too tired to lie and to use and to destroy...

"I can find another way," I said instead.

"You think you can be together?" His voice was flat judgement as he ran a gentle hand through my hair. Such a cold motion travestied as a fatherly gesture. "We've been here before, my dear. It is not only the secret of your magic that sets you apart. You are a spy, an assassin. No one can really accept the truth that lies beneath your pretty surface, they all run when they see the dark poison in your heart. All, except me."

And I knew it. By the Goddess I knew it. How many times had my heart shattered over the promise of love and friendship? How many times had I paid the price for the tiniest crack in my docile lady disguise?

I could keep my magic secret, but there was no hiding my true nature, not for long.

Every one of those times must have showed in my face, my body as I felt my shoulders drop. Ivo's voice was softer when he continued: "So, either claim the influence he is so clearly offering you or use him for the information he is worth."

Maybe he was right, maybe there was nothing other than heartbreak waiting for me. But then this was never about Aiden's love or devotion. It was about mine. About how I could choose to spread poison, or wish for compassion.

This time, I was willing to wish.

I held my hands together in a bid to hide my trembling fingers.

"And ... if I don't?" a pained, frail whisper.

Ivo sighed, his temper threatening to flare, his voice once again laced with nothing but icy detachment.

"Don't test my limits, Aila! You won't like what you'll find."

"You won't hurt me, and you won't hurt the heir."

His face turned wolfish. There was sharp cruelty in his pursed lips and strained jaw as rough fingers held my chin. I'd seen this look before, but never towards me.

"Are you sure about that?"

His words were a painful jolt as I realized I was fully and undeniably replaceable. Whatever illusion I had of being anything more than a powerless piece on his infinite strategy game, any hopes I may have harbored of an emotional bond and a sense of belonging, were just that: carefully designed illusions. Empty wishes.

I flinched. Sorrow and fear clouded my thoughts as he began to turn away.

"I need the letter to break the code, I didn't make any copies." *Maybe if I do break it, if I can be certain of all that Valran knows ...*

"Leave that to me and focus on the task at hand, dear," he said without looking back.

I was desperate enough to be reckless.

"You are sending me on a fool's errand, Ivo! I can't help you if I don't investigate every lead."

"Let's hope you can, dear! For yours, and your prince's sake."

My world shattered as he left my room, for I finally

understood I could be his most well-guarded secret and his best agent. But I was also a tool for the direst of situations.

I was the one agent of whom the King had no knowledge, the one person Ivo could not be held responsible for. I was his last resource. But that didn't make me special, it made me a controllable liability. And he had just gained another weapon against me.

◆

My legs gave up the second the door closed. Knees too wobbly to keep me standing. Arms trembling and thoughts in a vortex. Shadows raged around me, as I struggled to recover the grip I should have on myself.

For a long time, the room seemed to get smaller and smaller, the floor less stable and the world meaningless. I kneeled, trying to command myself to breathe slowly and my power to quiet. Unmoving as the familiar touch of terror started to take root inside of me, threatening to engulf my senses. It had been years since I'd felt the hopelessness that comes with terror. The despair of having no options.

Refusing to give in to fear, I allowed myself one more minute of self-commiseration; one more minute of uncontrollable crying for the hurt I would inevitably cause Aiden.

When I stopped, I forced myself to get up and remember that I was alive, despite all odds.

I took a deep shuddering breath. *I am not a child anymore, I'm no longer helpless*, I reminded myself.

Another deep breath.

"I will not be helpless," I repeated, this time out loud. "I will not let anyone make me helpless again. Not even Ivo."

One more calming breath, as I observed the now static shadows in the room and savored the inch of control I had found.

I poured myself another dose of brandy and drank it at once, only then did I sit and replay Ivo's words, painfully striping my sentimentality away.

A part of me still doubted he would really threaten the king's heir, but I knew him too well to discard the idea. He might have given me a home, but whatever the complicated relationship we had forged over the years, he was not, and would never be, good.

Even if I wanted to believe he loved me, he loved power more.

I couldn't deny all the ugly truths I knew about him, not when he was willing to threaten me. He was dangerous, ambitious and he knew every one of my secrets and hopes. There was no safety outside of his shelter, as much as there was no true freedom under his service.

He'd never before given me a reason to doubt his will to protect me, but I couldn't count on this to protect anyone else.

I would need to make my relationship with Aiden useless! Gain time for our supposed affair to live its course, for me to end things rather dramatically. I'd suffer Ivo's rage for being foolish, but it would keep Aiden safe. Heart-broken, but safe.

But for that, I needed time. I needed to placate him, to give him information he wanted. I needed to keep him happy.

The Alliance came to mind, and I wondered why Ivo didn't want me to investigate that particular lead.

For the second time that night I remembered the reports Aiden had received on their movements. It was clear that he was aware of the latest developments with the Alliance, but that didn't mean he knew about any agreement between the King and the premier.

Somehow, after hours of guilty deliberation and desperate planning, I'd convinced myself that looking into reports I wasn't supposed to know existed was less of a betrayal than using my bed to interrogate the prince.

So, instead of thinking about Aiden, I focused on the one route that would give me a lead: the reports, and whatever stories they could tell.

Hours passed by and I watched the night clear into a rosy sunrise as the cool breeze brought the sound of the early birds flying through the sky.

As I prepared to defy my master's direct order and betray my best friend's trust, I knew all too well the life I knew would never be the same.

Chapter 7

There was no word from Ivo, nor Aiden, in the following days, and I didn't know if I should be grateful or worried.

Even so, with time, my immediate panic eased. As many times before, I convinced myself Ivo was only stressed, that his threats were not real. That, once I gave him some concrete information, it would be easier to take his attention from Aiden long enough for me to distance myself from the Prince again.

I just needed the right lead. I needed the reports Aiden mentioned.

Those pages were my only chance at finding anything on the Alliance, yet I hesitated. A part of me not wanting to use any information from him, not wanting to commit even this small act of treason.

But despite my mind's turmoil, I knew those days were crucial. I had to maintain my routine: go to my classes, walk by the beach, read at the library.

Everything should remain ordinary, even though it wasn't.

My walks were no longer silent, no longer peaceful. Wherever I went in the palace, a constant flow of whispers and stares followed.

The little contact I had with the Prince did nothing to reduce the gossip, or the interest building around me.

That morning, like every morning since the ball, I had a quiet breakfast in my room, plastered a pleasant smile on my face and went for a mid-morning stroll through the garden, in which I proceeded to ignore the envious glances and excuse myself from the ladies and courtiers suddenly seeking my company. The only difference this time was that, consciously or not, I drifted to the training grounds where I knew Aiden would be training the new guards. As heir, he was head of the army until he assumed his position as King and, often, that involved training and selecting the palace guards, the Elite of Niram soldiers.

I was only a few meters from the big salon where he usually sparred with the guards, when Flynn approached me. His hair was dark brown and perfectly messy, the swagger in his steps as prominent as the arrogant smile on his lips. As insufferably dashing with common clothes as he'd been with the fanciest attire.

"Lady Aila, isn't it? Ivo's niece?" he said as way of greeting.

I nodded once, as he caught up to me.

"Flynn. We were never properly introduced," he dipped his chin graciously, a daring and inquisitive look blooming on his face. There was nothing casual about this encounter.

"I don't see why we should have." Aloofness lacing

my words.

"You are beautiful," he offered with a shrug as if it was an explanation.

"And what does that have to do with anything?"

"Well, I like to know pretty things." Smugness seeping through his voice as he offered me an arm. "May I accompany you?"

"Do I have a choice?"

He tilted his head with surprising eagerness, as if he wanted to coax deep, uninvited thoughts out of me: "Would you say no if you did, love?"

The warm golden in his eyes was magnetic, intriguing. I signaled the way, silently.

"Pity I couldn't catch you before you left the ball."

If I was an innocent lady, I would have believed the sorrowful tone of his voice. But I wasn't and he didn't trust me any more than I trusted him. That much was clear.

"What did you think of the night?" he continued when I didn't reply.

"Lovely ball, terrible entertainment."

"Curious how even the best can make basic mistakes, isn't it?" he asked softly before continuing. "I heard you are quite a fan of their work?"

"I'm familiar with it, yes," I admitted.

"Don't you think it was an odd performance, then? What do you think happened?"

"How would I know?"

"Well, we've already established you are familiar with their work."

He had a predatorial grace, a relentless focus. It was like being watched and tested by ... well, me. And I was growing tired of it.

"What is it you want?" I said, stopping and facing him.

Something bright and fierce flashed through his face.

"Many impossible things." For the briefest moment his gaze became almost unbearably intense, searching. "But for now, I'll settle for the answer to a puzzle; who are you really?"

"You seem to know plenty about me, Wheelan!"

"Ah! So, you do know who I am." His features easing in an arrogant smile.

"I've heard things, yes." I lowered my voice in mocking confession, "The Prince is not a huge fan."

"Oh, well ... he was a sore loser as a child. I suppose not a lot has changed." He slipped his hands into his pockets before prompting me to continue walking.

"I'm sure it had nothing to do with your delightful personality."

"We can't all be as charming as you now, can we, love?" A side smile tugging his lips up.

"I do have a name, you know?"

"That you do." After a heartbeat, "So, any thoughts, about the other night?"

Maybe it was the half whispers and glances following us, or maybe he just had a way of making my temper flare. One way or another, I could feel the hot spike of irritation in my temple. If there was no avoiding this conversation, it was time I played along.

"Did anything happen, Captain?" The hint of a smile reached his eyes at the mention of his title. "Should I avoid the theatre? You're making me worry," I added in a sugary voice.

"I'm just curious. Being a dancer yourself, I assumed – "

I interrupted him before he could finish.

"Careful, Wheelan! You seem to be asking an awful lot of questions about me. One might say you are interested." I took a small step closer to him. Provoking.

He sneered and dropped his voice to a low rumble that crept through my skin. "I'm sure some would be very displeased at that." He indicated the path behind me.

Emerging from the training room was Aiden. At the sight of us, his icy gaze pierced me. Then, without a word, he turned and found another path to the palace. Faint smoke in his wake.

"Maybe you should fix that. He never liked having me around his belongings," Flynn said in a hot whisper against my ear.

"Jerk," I replied.

He bowled, smirking.

"You can give me an answer next time, love. I'll find you."

◆

The image of Aiden's cold glare followed me as I put distance between myself and Flynn, I longed to call for him, to find him and ease his worries. But whether I liked it or not, Flynn had inadvertently given me a way to keep him at bay, a way to use whatever bad history existed between them to break the relationship I had with Aiden, to create the hurt that would finally lead the Prince away from me.

No one can really accept the truth that lies beneath your pretty surface. Ivo's painful words ignited in my mind. Except this time, my truth would be a boon rather than a curse. This time, I would be hurting him for a good reason.

I steeled myself and turned around, conscious that I was letting Aiden walk away. But before I could leave the garden behind, Ivo found his way to me.

"Niece! What a pleasure. I thought you'd be otherwise occupied." He approached me quickly.

His pointed comment was not lost on me. Yet, I schooled myself into my most charming, and oblivious, self.

"Uncle." I gave him a kiss on the cheek. "I found a few minutes to enjoy the scenery."

I made a show of adjusting his tunic in a loving, caring gesture.

"New friend?"

I didn't have to follow his gaze to know he was talking about Flynn.

I shook my head. "He was just asking about the ball."

"He seemed quite interested."

"Nothing but speculation and curiosity," I dismissed his worries.

Ivo watched me. "Careful, dear. He is a smart one and you know you can't afford to let people look at you too closely."

I simply nodded, anticipating where this conversation would lead us.

"It seems you just missed the prince." The hint of a question behind the remark.

"It appears so," I replied coldly.

With a quick look around and a deep sigh, he pulled me under the shade of a big tree, away from too many ears and eyes.

His voice was softer, gentler. A swift reminder of why I'd always believed him. "I'm sorry about the other night, my dear. It breaks my heart to see you so devoted to people who will inevitably leave. I don't want to pick up your pieces again. I ... I just want you to remember our priorities."

The promise of a loving embrace lay on every word, the pull, the craving for someone to love me despite knowing the real me. Yet, now that I faced him, there was no convincing myself of his good intentions.

The quiet voice inside of me refused to be leashed again and there was nothing I could do to unhear the threats he'd made, the coldness with which he'd looked at me.

He was dangerous, and for the first time I wasn't sure I was any safer than anyone else.

He affectionately caressed my chin. "I'll be away for a week, use this time. We can discuss your findings when I'm back."

"I understand."

Something on my face must have given my intention away, because his expression turned wary, a small vein pulsing at his neck.

"You know your job, Aila," he said in quiet warning.

He was struggling for control, but I didn't let it stop me.

"I do! And how I accomplish it is up to me, is it not?"

"There is no other way to accomplish it."

"You want to know their deal, I'll find out their deal! But I won't use Aiden until I'm sure there is no other way," I insisted.

He took a deep breath, still struggling to leash his temper.

"I don't know what has come over you, but don't test me, Aila!" his voice a low hiss.

I held his stare, unafraid.

"I've never failed, Ivo. And I will find what you need,

but I will do it on my own terms. Even if I have to find the fucking Alliance myself." My voice was no louder than a whisper, but I knew he could sense the sharpness of it.

Something I couldn't place flared beneath the cold anger distorting his face. "Let me be clear. I'm not asking you to go on a fishing expedition; I'm not asking you to eavesdrop; I'm not even asking you to think. I'm telling you to ask the damn prince! Your only choice in the matter is if you'll do it before or after he fucks you! Are we clear?"

I flinched at his ruthless command, anger and hurt mixing in my gut. But then I realized Ivo never cared about how I finished a job if I secured what he needed. Except this time.

This time he was very particular about what leads I should and shouldn't follow, and, somehow, I knew his hostility had very little to do with his control over me.

He didn't have a choice but to use me to uncover the Premier deal, but even as desperate as he was for that information, there was something in this whole story he didn't want me to know. I couldn't stop wondering why.

So I held my temper, suffocated my anger, and said in a low voice, "Yes, uncle."

◆

I didn't wait another night. If I only had a week, I needed to get my hands on those reports, whether I liked the idea of using information Aiden trusted me with, or not.

A small treason is better than a big one, I told myself as I changed into black, tight pants and shirt, after a very long and visible dinner with the other courtiers. I secured my hair in a loose bun with a metal stick and hid a small dagger inside my boot. I wasn't expecting a fight, but one couldn't be too careful when breaking into the Royal Archives.

Every report and official document had a copy in the archives. In this case, most likely in the military section.

Ivo usually deployed other spies for this type of job, but I had studied the layout of the place and was familiar with the guard's rotation. In theory, if I made quick work of the main lock and kept to the servants' corridors, I would be fine.

There is no better way to test questionable theories than through impetuous decisions, thought my most reckless, stupid self.

Before I could consider my own impulsive plan, I waited for the guards doing rounds to clear my room's corridor and made my way to the servants' passages – a maze of old, connecting pathways I had spent many sleepless nights exploring – and headed to the back of the palace.

The small one between the palace and the cliffs was quiet and poorly illuminated, offering constant cover under the many balconies encrusted on the side of the building. It was mostly used by servants to avoid the main areas of the buildings, and more importantly, was mainly empty at night. Except for the occasional patrol.

I timed the guards' patrol before throwing myself at the familiar passage. I should have about fifteen minutes to reach the path that would lead me to the archive window. *More than enough time.*

But as I approached it, a silent figure crossed my path coming from one of the building accesses.

"What an unexpected meeting," Flynn's voice was a cool caress.

He was the last person I expected to find in the palace at this hour, let alone in a back passageway, and I knew this encounter would do nothing to quench his suspicions.

I sighed and did my best to look bored. "A girl needs to be creative to find some ... *privacy* around here."

He leered over my whole body, slowly.

"Some would say this type of exercise is not an appropriate activity for a lady."

I took a minute to assess him, trying to muster all the disdain I could as I scanned *his* body. *His beautifully sculptured body.*

"Some would," I said finally.

"But you don't care about what is appropriate," he teased.

"I guess you already know the answer to that."

"And what do you care about then? Quiet midnight strolls? I'd be happy to offer you inappropriate company for those."

"Aren't you a smart-ass?"

True laughter burst through him. So fresh and sincere it surprised me. A wary smile bloomed before I could stop it.

"What are you doing here, Wheelan? Shouldn't you be strolling around the Premier house?" Some of the tension in my voice somehow gone.

"Well, I've enjoyed the *privacy* of these corridors since I was ten, so I should be the one asking what you are doing here."

"Well, a lot has changed in the past two years; pity you didn't catch up."

I wasn't sure when he'd moved, but he was closer now. Inches away. Patrols would reach us soon, yet, I felt rooted to the floor, pulled into him.

"This passage will become even less private soon," his whisper echoed my thoughts.

I didn't have to ask to know he didn't want to be seen any more than I did, but before I could ask why, the sound of heavy boots reached my ears.

I glanced around, searching for a nook in which to hide, keenly aware that I couldn't use my magic with Flynn standing by my side. But before I found a spot, he reacted.

In no more than a breath he had me pressed against the wall, a hand swiftly loosening the stick holding my hair in place. The smell of green grass and fresh rain washed over me in an intoxicating gust. His smell.

Every hard muscle of his body pressed against mine. His warmth wrapped all my senses as his bright golden eyes held mine.

Beneath all of that, something tugged at my core. Something in him fascinated me, spoke to my very soul. And to my own surprise, I wanted to know what it was.

He flexed one elbow at the side of my head, the other hand firmly on my waist. By the time the two guards turned the corner I knew that, between my loosened hair and his own body, I was unrecognizable.

"Some privacy, boys?" he said in a slurred, drunken voice as he looked at them briefly before turning back to me.

The guard's hurried steps and muffled apologies quickly faded, leaving us alone and unmoving for a moment more than necessary.

Even if I doubted it'd been for my benefit alone, he'd just saved me from a very unpleasant situation.

"Why?" I asked in a low, husky voice before I could stop myself.

"That is the question, isn't it?"

He moved a strand of hair from my face, slowly. *Too slowly.* Before I had a chance to blurt another hasty question,

I loosened his grip on my waist and turned away. But, just as I did it, he caught my arm and he breathed against my ear, chin deep in my hair.

"I wouldn't mind seeing this outfit again, love. Not one bit."

He was gone before I could think of a reply.

Chapter 8

I tossed and turned for the whole night, the strangeness of Ivo's demands and the encounter with Flynn playing over and over in my head.

I didn't know why Flynn let me walk away. But there would be no breaking into the Royal Archives now. Not less than a week after he'd seen me lurking in the grounds.

By the time the sun was up and the memory of the captain's body against mine had popped into my head for the millionth time, I'd had enough. So I sent a note to Dara dismissing her from my lesson and went to the one place where I knew I could find a friend.

Even though I never visited Aiden's quarters before, I knew he had his own wing not far from my bedroom, and I couldn't help but be surprised at the sheer size of it. The double doors were beautifully decorated with gold paint, not unlike the others in the palace, but somehow they were grander and more sophisticated.

Behind the doors there were a few chairs where

courtiers waited for an audience, and a small office in front of the long corridor to his chambers where Karl, his valet, and a few servants waited to tend to his every need.

It was easy to forget who he really was when we spent most of our time at the library – or in my bed. But here, in front of his doors, it was impossible to think of him as anything other than Niram's Heir: the most powerful fire wielder of his generation, the future King and leader of the Elementalists. He was pure power, and I was only an orphan-turned-spy.

"May I help you?" Karl said with a polite wave of his hand from the office door.

Lowering my chin and willing my face into the shyest expression I could muster, I spoke in a tremulous voice:

"Hi! Oh, I'm sorry. I wanted to surprise Prince Aiden, but it was silly of me to come here." Hopefully even if he didn't know about Aiden's visits to my room, he would have heard about us as much as anyone else by now.

He seemed uncertain for a moment.

I made a movement towards the door, "Please, don't worry. Sorry to have bothered you, sir."

"Wait, dear," he said before I touched the door.

He looked around and only spoke again after being sure we were alone.

"The Prince just came from sword practice. You go ahead, it is the third door to your right."

I beamed at him,

"He is a nice boy, my dear. Deserves a friend." A knowing smile at the edge of his lips, before going back to the small office.

"I told you I'm not in the mood – " Aiden stopped dead when he found me standing on the threshold.

"Not even a tiny bit?" I said playfully.

He moved away from the door giving me space to enter. He was fresh out of a shower: wet hair, loose white shirt and simple beige pants.

"Karl let you in?"

I nodded, taking in the interior of the room. It was enormous and richly decorated with ancient pieces of Crown Treasure. But it was still possible to see him among it all: in the choice of books, the comfortable furniture, the bright curtains. I smiled, despite myself.

This must be his inner chamber. A few comfortable reading areas, a study desk and his bed were visible through the open door across the room.

Most of the northern wall was formed by three sets of double doors, leading to a large balcony that ended right at the edge of the cliff.

"What do you want, Aila?" He sounded tired.

"You didn't say hello." He stared blankly at me, "Yesterday? You didn't say hello."

"I didn't want to interrupt your pleasant walk," he said contemptuously.

"I missed you," I blurted before I could stop myself.

"You seemed well enough."

"I'm sorry. I was upset after the ball. I shouldn't have talked to you like that. I truly am sorry." It was true, more than it should have been probably.

He scoffed and sat at the nearest sofa. "The ball," he said pensively. "What is it about him? How does he get everything he wants? I know you will need a husband someday, but I thought you wanted … better." Scorn bled from him like I'd never seen before.

"Are you talking about Flynn?" I asked.

He waited, silently. I knew it was the chance I needed to deepen our rift. But I didn't.

"I don't know what you think you saw, Aiden, but I don't think you could be more wrong." I sat by his side, exhaling slowly. "You know, I now spend half of my day ignoring hateful looks from every eligible man and woman in this palace. And the other half smiling and listening to people who want your favor. Nice spot you've put me in, by the way."

A small smile tugged at his lips, but he remained silent, leaning on his knees and facing the floor. There was a vulnerability in him that made my heart ache, a loneliness that made me wish to never walk away.

"I don't know what it is between you two, but I honestly don't even like the guy," I offered quietly.

"You'd be the first," he mumbled before taking a deep breath and reclining, face turning to the ceiling. "He came to the palace when we were children, and we were friends for a while. Turns out he is an arrogant bastard who gets to have everything I'll never be able to."

"Oh, so he has always been delightful then?"

He grimaced, facing me fully for the first time.

"Well, you are the heir, that should count for something."

"Seriously, Aila, what do you want? What do you want from me?"

I sighed. This was the moment of truth; I knew he would listen to me this time, no banter, no playing around. He would respect my ask. So, I prepared to say goodbye, to end things before he could get hurt. Ivo be damned.

But when I faced him, I remembered the endless, sleepless nights, his shiny laughter, his caring touch. I remembered it was easy and comfortable to be around him.

I tried to tell him that he would be better off without me in his life, but the words never left my mouth.

I wasn't built for dreams and unfaltering love, wasn't worthy of it, but maybe I could hold onto this comfortable friendship a little longer.

"I care for you, and I want you safe, Aiden. That is all."

He held my hand before saying "Me? You should be worried about you! You are right, you know? My father would not be happy if he knew what you mean to me. I know you don't need a hero, but …" He took a deep, shuddering breath before continuing. "I know I shouldn't have exposed you—*us*—like that, but I couldn't bear being away, I couldn't bear seeing him … I'll find a way to keep you safe from my father. I won't let him touch you."

"I'm not worried about that."

"You should be."

"I'm disposable, Aiden. I'm just an orphan. I'm bound to be forgotten." He started to protest, but I stopped him. "But you? You are the heir, you are important. And us? I don't know what we are, but I know we have no future together, not beyond what we have now."

Even if I didn't know if I would ever want more, I knew I didn't want to let the little we had go. I didn't want to let *him* go any more than I wanted to use him.

He pulled me to his chest, resting his head on mine and breathed in my hair. "I know."

He held me as if I was his last breath of air, with such need and devotion that it startled me. I searched for his eyes and found the same painful resignation I'd found in his voice.

For a moment, I thought about telling him everything,

about not hiding, about revealing every dirty secret I had, every shameful thing I'd ever done. But Ivo was right about one thing: I only ever brought pain and hurt to those near me, and I couldn't bear to deepen the pain I saw in him, I couldn't bear to turn his care into scorn.

Most of all, I couldn't bring myself to trust him not to hate me when all was said and done.

"Promise me you will be careful. Promise me you will always be alert," I said instead.

Even as he did, I knew he had no way of knowing just how much danger he was in, how easily he could be replaced as heir by his weaker brother. Ivo would never stop threatening him, unless I found a way to *make* him stop.

He said under his breath, "Promise you won't hurt me like everybody else. I don't know what I would do if you did."

There were no words for the vulnerability in his rough voice, nor for the knot in my stomach that came with the knowledge I would, inevitably, break his heart one day. So, I held him tight and said nothing, unable to lie about this most fundamental thing.

"Hey," he said after a few minutes, interrupting my dark thoughts, "this is the first time you've come to my room. Hell, it is the first time you've even sought me out during the day. I'm feeling less used now. Definitely less used." The laughter was back in his voice.

"By the Goddess, after you made sure the whole damn palace knew about us, what is the point in hiding?"

"Does this mean I can finally take you out to dinner then?" A sinful smile on his face.

The small, hopeful part of me wanted nothing more than to be carried away in bliss at his invitation, at his relentless persistence to turn us into more than friends and lovers. Yet I didn't, and as painful as it was to admit it, Ivo had little to do with it.

Instead, deep in my heart, I knew this was more than a simple invitation, it was an unspoken proposition.

Truth was, I couldn't spend the rest of my life pretending to be the sweet, innocent woman he expected me to be. Not for the first time, I wished we were not heir and spy. Not for the first time, I wished I was just a normal girl with the chance to figure out if she could fall for a normal guy.

But I wasn't a normal girl, so I fixed a smile on my face. "Let's not get ahead of ourselves."

"Breakfast, then? I'll ask Karl to bring us something. Dream cakes included," he asked, already halfway to the door.

"Fine. I expect a *pile* of dream cakes. Alongside some pancakes and strawberries!"

Moments later, Aiden left to request what I could only assume would be enough food for the whole palace, and I took the time to drift through the room. Curiosity getting the better of me.

Somehow, he managed to have even more books than I scattered throughout the room and as I approached the pile on his desk, something else caught my attention: his signet ring. The dark gold glinting under the day light, Niram's fiery crown etched atop of it.

I couldn't break into the Royal Archives, but maybe I could still get the reports out of there, with the right letter, and the right seal.

Before I could think better of it, I reached for the ring and concealed it inside my dress bodice. Its round, rigid form a constant presence during my long breakfast with Aiden.

◆

It was hours before I found myself back in my own chambers. I took my shoes off in a swift movement and left them forgotten by the door as I sat in my favorite chair in silence.

It would be so easy to forge a letter, to request that the reports be delivered to Aiden and to lurk in his room long enough for me to read them. One night in his chambers would be all I needed.

I turned his ring in my hands, wondering if using it made me any better than Ivo. Maybe I'd been turned into a well of poisonous darkness, or maybe it was who I had been all along.

One way or another, this time, I refused to follow my master's orders.

Which meant I would have nothing to placate him with and, short of betraying my best friend some other way, I had only one choice: I had to get leverage on Ivo, leverage enough to keep myself, and Aiden, safe.

I was not naïve enough to think he would have any nostalgic mercy for me when I dared to cross him, to uncover his secrets. If Ivo caught me – and he would, sooner or later – the only thing left for me to do would be beg for a quick death.

As ruthless as Ivo was, he was never careless. He would not risk his own position, his rewards. He would stop at nothing to get what he wanted, which also meant he had a lot to lose. All I had to do was find something big enough to tip the scales in my favor.

Without a second for doubt to descend, I tossed the ring and the half-written request to the Royal Archives, into the secret drawer in my desk and peered around the room savoring every detail, committing to memory every piece of comfort and safety I was risking. In the dark, quiet room I wondered if loyalty to Aiden was worth it, if one friend that didn't even know the whole truth about me was worth risking so much. I contemplated the ugly part of me, the part of me that couldn't be so easily convinced to do what was right.

Then I started planning, because no matter how insane the idea of challenging Ivo was, it was the only choice I was willing to live with.

Chapter 9

I needed leverage.

Ivo was no different than any other human being. He had secrets, weaknesses. I just had to find them.

I visited old friends, stalked some of his other spies and visited every place in the city where he was a regular. Still, all I could find was what I already knew.

He was a self-made man, who appeared in Niram out of thin-air twenty years back with nothing but a relentless ambition and an endless grudge against his former Kingdom, Tlaloc. There was nothing to find but an enviously spotless record; a testament to the spy master's foresight. But ambitious, powerful men rarely had clean histories, no matter how spotless their records may look.

Through all the years I lived with him at the villa, he never shared much of his own past. Nothing beyond vague reminiscences of his childhood. Over the years, he and that henchman of his, *Billy*, had erased every mention of what brought them to Niram.

Coming myself from a past I'd rather forget, I never questioned his reluctance to talk about his.

My mind was rushing ceaselessly when I arrived at the dance studio. I knew I had followed every lead I had on Ivo, questioned everyone I dared. *Except for Dara,* I realized when I saw her organizing the weapons rack.

She wasn't Billy, but then no one was as close to Ivo as his bodyguard, yet he trusted her enough. More importantly, she didn't hate me, so all-in-all I probably had a better chance with her than I would ever have with that damned henchman.

I changed clothes and went through our normal routine as I tried to find an innocent way to steer the conversation towards Ivo.

Until she finally knocked me over and held me nailed to the floor with her right foot on my stomach. The air went straight out of my lungs and a shock of pain flew through my spine with the impact.

"Out with it," she said, exasperated.

I knew I was being sloppy, but her smugness was still as hard to take now as it was when I was ten years old. I took her foot off my belly and sat up.

"I'm distracted, that is all."

"What is it?" A woman of few words.

"Nothing, really. Ivo asked me to do something, but I'm not sure how yet."

"You have a few days, then."

"Do you know when he'll be back?"

She looked at me sideways. "If he wanted you to know, he would have told you, don't you think?"

"Please," I cried out with big eyes. My pleading had never worked on her before, but there was always a first for everything.

She glared at me, extending a hand to help me get up.

I sighed. "I'm just trying to get my shit together before he comes back, that is all. The Goddess knows I can do with some peace right about now."

"Trouble with the princeling?"

"Is there anything my dear uncle doesn't tell you?" I didn't hide the scorn in my voice.

"Plenty! And the whole town is talking about you, not exactly a topic for Ivo's spies." For a split second I thought I heard laughter in her voice.

"Are you mocking me, Dara? After twenty years, did I finally put a teensy-weensy smile on your ever so serious face?"

She let go of my hand and I dropped ass first back on the floor.

"Ouch!" I couldn't stop the surprised wince in my face. She laughed. A low bark of a laugh that I'd heard only a handful of times. Somehow, that lightened my tension as much as it softened her posture.

"He will be back in a week or so. You still have time to put your head in the right place," she finally said.

"I'll try." I got up and stretched as casually as I could, before continuing, "Where did he go anyway?"

"Not my business, girl."

I nodded, unconcerned. "He always had his mysteries, I guess. To this day, I never managed to get him to tell me how he got to Niram. Believe that?"

She frowned and switched weapons in the rack. For a moment I thought she knew what I was up to.

"You never will. There are things better left unsaid. And unheard," she dropped her voice and signaled for me to prepare my stance.

"You know his story then?" I stared, letting surprise show in my face and faking the mildly excited tone from the court gossipers.

I saw a flicker of attentive judgement. Before the expectant silence could become uncomfortable stillness, I blurted, "Please, Dara?"

"There is nothing for me to tell. I know nothing more than you do. He doesn't like his past, so he doesn't talk about it. You should know better than to question him. I told you that court would turn you into a frivolous empty-headed girl, if you didn't pay attention," she mumbled.

We finished our training in silence and, against all logic, I believed her.

"Be careful," she told me before I left the studio that morning. A rare demonstration of worry.

A reminder I needed, because now I was sure the only person who knew anything about Ivo's past was Billy and the world would be reborn before he would tell me anything, willingly or not. He often underestimated me, but he also hated me too much to let his guard down with me around.

There were only two ways I would have a chance of finding anything about Ivo's past without showing my hand. Since I didn't have the time to take a trip to Tlaloc, I was stuck with the next best thing: I had to break into his quarters and hope to find something there.

◆

The madness of infiltrating Ivo quarters caught up to me. If he ever found out, there would be no coming back from it, no denying it. But there was no going back to my comfortable existence either, no ignoring the threats to Aiden's life, no hiding behind fancy, sheltered walls.

Even if a part of me doubted Ivo would hurt me beyond repair, I knew I had a slim chance and a lot to lose. Yet I was deft and at the brink of despair and, the thing is, despair has a way of making people do the most unthinkable things.

So, for bravery or lunacy, I focused on what had to be done and reminded myself of my skills, of my cleverness, of everything I was capable of; because, if this worked, I wouldn't have to break Aiden's heart and walk away. That alone, was reason enough to try.

My spy training had not always been formal. It involved all sorts of training: weapons, poisons, torture; but some of the most important things I had learned came from Ivo himself, from observing and listening to his speeches.

One of those lessons was that the best way to remain invisible is to become undeniably and unmistakably predictable. A part of everyone's expectations. Being Aiden's latest conquest gave me the perfect way to become just that.

The royal dinner was served in the main dining room. A round salon topped by a vaulted ceiling with dozens of glass doors and several round tables scattered in between. The space was richly decorated in white and bright orange, dramatized by dozens of candles projecting dancing flames across the walls and central floor.

Between the warm light and the never-ending music, the whole place had an intimate and whimsical atmosphere, offering a nightly escape to the well-dressed courtiers gorging on the extravagant drinks and food.

I arrived minutes after the meal had started. Faces turned as my laced, emerald gown captured the light. My hair bounced behind me, falling in big waves down my back and I smiled and bowed my way across the room.

My stomach grumbled in acknowledgement of the rich smells of the food. I wandered past a few tables, exchanging meaningless pleasantries with as many people as I could before finding myself at a table in the center of the salon.

I always enjoyed spending the court functions I attended with the three girls who now faced me. They had always been pleasant, kind, the type of people who often got crushed in vicious places like this. And they'd just came back from a few months in Kait – the second largest city in the Kingdom.

I sat down, beaming and let the relief of dining with familiar faces wash over me. I was never a sheepish woman, but those forceful nights in court always had a way of making me wish for the quietness of my room.

"You're back." I offered in greeting before glancing at the food eagerly. Steamy rolls and baked cheese, a tall steak and buttery potato. "By the Goddess, this all smells delicious!"

They were all roughly the same age as me. Two were sisters with silky ebony skin and the most beautiful curly hair I'd ever seen. The younger, Lorrie, had big brown eyes so deep they reminded me of melting chocolate, while the older, Cassie, had full sensuous lips. The third, Rose, was delicate and blonde, piercing blue eyes and sandy skin with a gentle face.

They were typical ladies, but there was a tranquil elation to them that never ceased to amaze me.

"The cook was inspired today," said Rose while offering me a glass of wine.

"We missed you in Kait," added Lorrie with a silvery

voice. "Things were not as much fun without you around."

"I'm sure it was still more fun than these insufferable dinners," I responded in a conspiratorial low voice.

"Maybe you have a reason to endure a few more of these now," Cassie blinked while pointing her chin to the front of the salon.

I followed her gaze to see Aiden sitting at the royal table, to the right side of his father, King Elran - a middle aged man with perfectly-combed dark hair and a sharp jaw. Serious and gruelling. For two years, I had made a point to avoid crossing paths with the King and yet, I knew all too well about his cruelty and hunger for power. In many ways, I was the result of it.

Rose brought my attention back to her.

"Tell us everything we missed. Especially that," she said glancing at Aiden.

Of course, they'd already heard about it. And yet, there was no judgement. Not even an ounce of the forced interest and jealousy I had grown used to in the previous few days. Still, I would keep Aiden out of it.

"Well, my uncle kept me busy," I said dismissively, "I think I've missed home a bit, so haven't really been to many court functions lately. You'll need to ask someone else for the juicier gossip."

Lorrie reached for my hand and squeezed it warmly.

"Adjusting is hard; home sickness still seizes me often, and I've been here for five years! But you don't need to be lonely," she said softly so no one beside our table could hear.

Her gentleness surprised me, touched me. It always did.

They told me about their days in Kait, the latest plays

they'd seen, the music they were memorizing and their plans for the end of summer. No gossip or ill-words, it was soothing.

I enjoyed myself, as easily and openly as I should. No plans or schemes, just dinner.

It was not until dessert that reality found its way to me, and I crossed eyes with Aiden.

He grinned and lazily raised a glass in my direction. A greeting.

I knew it was time, even if a part of me regretted it, I knew it was time. So, I gave him a shallow, pleasant nod as I raised my own glass in return, ensuring that as many people as possible saw it.

"So, it *is* true!" Lorrie whispered.

I still felt Aiden's gaze on me when I turned to her and nodded. "It has been for a while." I winked.

They didn't ask for more, and I didn't offer. We continued talking, and drinking, and laughing. Aiden, and his whole court, following my every move.

When the food stopped and the music grew louder, he finally offered me a hand, leading me to the dance floor, the court's attention heavy behind us. As we passed the royal table, King Elran joined them. Cold and calculating as he watched his son.

"I don't know if I'm more surprised with you being here or with you not objecting to a dance," he said on a whisper, his breath warm against my ear. "A very, very public dance."

I smiled and let him guide me in a waltz across the room, conscious of the risky bet I was making.

"I figured you had already sent everything to hell, so I might as well enjoy it," I replied. And I did. For the few minutes we danced across the room, I delighted in the moonlight through the window and savored the arms of my best friend on my waist under the lovely music.

When the song ended, most of the people had lost interest in us. But not the king. Elran's attention followed us through the rest of the night, along with Ivo's other spies.

◆

We repeated the same for the rest of the week. Quickly settling into a comfortable routine that always finished with us leaving the room mere minutes apart. With every night that Aiden devoted entirely to me it became less of a shock, less of an event. More predictable.

The night before Ivo returned, I knew no one would question where I'd be after dinner or with whom. I'd created an alibi so strong that once I left the room no one would suspect me of being near Ivo's quarter at any hour of the night.

I had the whole court enthralled in our unrolling affair, including the king. Yet I was not naïve enough to think that was not a terrible risk on its own. *I may have been simply replacing one daemon with another.*

Nor was I oblivious enough not to see the small cruelty I'd been offering Aiden by feeding him feelings he shouldn't indulge. But it was done now and later that night, I would either have found a way to keep us both safe, or I would have doomed myself trying.

Still, it pained me to see his happiness. The thrilling joy of someone who believed those nights were more than borrowed time, the type of happiness people like us – rulers and spies – don't get to enjoy outside of wild dreams. For even in a world where Ivo was no longer a threat to him, we still didn't have the kind of future I saw lurking in his face.

I guided him to a corner of the room and served us both a glass of wine.

"One of these days you'll have to share your attention, dance with a few of the other ladies."

"Why would I do that?" he came one step closer to me. "It took me two years to get you here, I'm not about to leave you and go dance with anyone else."

I knew I needed one more night of perfect romance for my plan to hold. Then, I could ease him out of his misguided hope. Still, I could feel his father's attention following us night after night. Tense, calculating.

"I'm just saying your father has looked very interested in us these past few nights. Too interested. Maybe it is wise to ease his worries and give some scraps of attention to the other girls." I kept my voice light, my tone playful. "I'm not going anywhere."

He smiled sweetly at me.

"You don't need to worry; I'm dealing with my father. I promised I would keep you safe, didn't I? In fact, I have something to tell you." He tenderly removed a strand of hair from my face and continued in no more than a whisper. "I know you still don't like the idea of being so publicly in my arms, but I've found a way to ensure my father won't hurt you."

Except I had no doubt, he would. No matter that Aiden was the most powerful wielder of the Kingdom and, hence the rightful heir. No matter that he'd been raised for it.

The King himself would kill him and bring his weaker brother back to court, and to the throne, if it meant he could keep the Crown under control and away from the influence of a non-wielder such as myself.

Seeing his bright eyes and flushed cheeks, feeling the eagerness in his touch, I knew how important it was that he saw it, as much as I knew there was no way he would. Aiden wouldn't stay away from me after the sliver of hope I'd dangled in front of him.

Not unless I found a way to lead him back to the resigned distance we'd existed in for years.

Thoughtless reflex seized me, and I yanked my hand from his as I considered crushing his hopes, driving his away. But I couldn't risk it.

One more night.

I would get him to forgive me later and we'd be fine. As long as I didn't betray him.

I saw a flash of anguish at my unexpected reaction, and immediately reached out to him, but before I could grab his hand again, a smoky voice, took us both by surprise.

"It seems you two are having quite the momentous night." Flynn stared at us with a honeyed smile and continued. "My lady, Aiden," he didn't bother bowing.

My blood froze. I already had too much in my mind without having to worry about *him* or why he did any of the things he did.

"Prince," Aiden corrected coldly.

Flynn ignored him and turned to me, his sight a pool of melted gold hovering over my body, languidly. "Lovely, as always." He kissed me on the cheek, hand lazily falling on my waist and utterly ignoring Aiden's presence.

Aiden's cold glare was fixed on Flynn's hands on me. Shaky shoulders and gritted teeth as the torch closest to us flickered. His control starting to falter.

At a loss for words, I took a small step out of Flynn's reach, but it was a moment too late, and the smirk that flickered on his lips told me he knew it.

Aiden's self-control vanished at the apparent intimacy of his kiss, his touch. I felt the torches and candles around the room shine brighter, its warmth increasing in response to Aiden's wild temper. His bitterness pushed me back to my senses and I graciously moved to his side.

"What the fuck do you want, Flynn?" he grunted.

Flynn simply smiled, slipping his hands in his pockets, relishing the moment.

"No pleasantries, this time?" He paused, waiting for a response before continuing. "I thought I could do you a favor. For old time's sake, you know? I can take lovely Lady Aila off your hands so you can attend to your princely obligations. Lady Sarah has been throwing dreamy glances at you the whole night."

The words between them were full of contempt and old history. Flynn was arrogant and deceitful and maybe that was why a part of me was fascinated by him, mesmerized by his audacity and confidence. Deep inside I knew that, in some ways, we were equals. The more I tried to ignore him, the more allure I felt.

When Aiden didn't reply Flynn pierced me with a lewd stare. "Go ahead. We had so much fun the other night, I assure you, I won't let her miss you." His voice was sweet venom as he offered me a hand. "Shall we, love?"

I tried to look away from him, to walk away from this whole conversation. It had gone too far already. But I couldn't. I still didn't know what kept me silently in place, but I didn't move, didn't speak. A shameful part of me too lost in the burning memory of his body against mine. It didn't entirely surprise me when Aiden walked away from us.

Flynn's stare didn't balk, his extended hand never

wavered. Not a single part of him acknowledged Aiden's rage. Not a single part of him lost its focus on me.

"Happy now?" I finally snapped at him.

"Not even remotely." Somehow, I knew that to be true.

Chapter 10

After Aiden's departure, there was no point in me staying behind. I left Flynn before he could stop me and went quickly back to my room, hoping no one had noticed my heated conversation with the prince.

I thought about waiting until later that night when the servants would be resting and the palace asleep, but that was also the time in which Ivo's own guards would be patrolling his corridor more intensely. I had one window, and that was before the evening entertainment was completely over. I would act during the sweet time in which families slept and unexpected lovers started to find each other in a frenzy of music and alcohol.

My light dress was quickly replaced by black fighting clothes: a pair of tight pants with simple daggers in scabbards strapped on each of my legs, long boots that covered most of my shin and a long-sleeved shirt with a low neck, all in a light, breathable material only reinforced in the most essential areas. Lastly, a functional belt with tools to break in.

I arranged my hair in a single braid while debating if I should take a short sword with me. But I'd planned a silent break-in, I needed to be swift and agile, not ready for a rundown with the guards.

The position of my quarters meant a limited number of permanent residents with prying eyes and enough freedom to come and go as I pleased. I'd never been so grateful for it.

Until dinner was over, patrols would be few and far between, so I waited, leaning against the door, and when the guards' footsteps faded, I silently left the room.

There was no need for shadows in the quiet and deserted night. I quickly made my way to the closest entrance to the servants' passageways.

I reached Ivo's corridor in no more than a few minutes and observed the patrol movement, hidden in one of the closest servant's pathways until I was confident there had been no change to the usual schedule and that there was no reinforced security and no sign of Billy.

I took an L-shaped pin and a small hook from my belt and inserted them in Ivo's lock, working on the mechanism. Wasting time in a very visible spot was not the safest action I'd take that night, but using my power seemed even riskier. Ivo was not oblivious to my abilities and my best chance of surviving this was for him to never suspect anyone had entered his office, let alone me. At least, not until I was ready to show my hand.

Seconds stretched before I heard a click in the mechanism. I entered and closed the door behind me, sighing in relief.

The door gave way to a large antechamber. It was dark and empty, with no sign of any movement besides my own. I went directly to the room he used as his private office, steps echoing behind me.

My hands made quick work of finding and disabling the alarm on his door. *Never the trusting type.* It wasn't until I was inside that I took a long breath to steady myself and carefully observed the room.

I hadn't been in his quarters more than once or twice, and never alone. Ivo used to say he preferred meaningful conversations to happen in less official surroundings. I always wondered if, in fact, he wanted to keep this little haven of his true self hidden.

The rest of his chambers were elegant, yet cold and ordinary. But this little office was different – a small room that showed a completely different side of him, a comfortable and eccentric space that felt almost like a personal retreat, an unexpected coziness to it. I wondered if it bore any resemblance to whatever home he may have had in the past.

First, I closed the curtains and sent a veil of darkness over the windows before lighting the lamps. His room faced the ocean, but I was not taking chances.

Then, I walked around, under the warm yellow light, examining the shelves and paints through the walls, looking for hiding places. On the corner of the room, I recognized two figurines: one he used to keep in his room at the farm, a token from his old Kingdom, or so he told me when I asked about it. I took the piece in my hands; it was heavy and uneven, a nightmarish humanoid carved out of ancient wood. I always wondered what type of memory he was trying to keep alive by looking at it.

The other was a small rendition of the Goddess, a black candle between them. Ivo had always been devoted, always found solace and strength in the church. Somehow, he found refuge in his constant visits to the temple, but I never found anything other than a sense of entrapment and useless obligation.

I focused my attention on the shelves. They were home to hundreds of books and, even though there were volumes from all over the world, nothing compared with his Tlaloc collection: from legends to historical registers, many bearing the Tlaloc Royal family crest, a stone-like jaguar head, singed on the leather spine.

He had dozens of books with the crest, side-by-side, forming a mesmerizing pattern of continuity. I scanned the books trying to piece together the little I knew about his past, the contempt he seemed to dedicate to his former Kingdom and this interest in its history. I couldn't understand how he could have acquired so many official books, or why. The more I tried to connect those dots the more convinced I became that I didn't really know much about him at all.

I sat at his desk and started going through the documents scattered across the surface and drawers. There were reports from his spies, a few letters with instructions from the Premier and the documents I had stolen during the ball, the letters still not decoded.

Unable to find any hidden compartments, I reclined on his chair, feet atop the desk, and observed the entirety of the room for the first time: the way in which some of those documents were laid out seemed intentionally careless. Ivo was not a fool. If he was willing to be negligent about this information, it was only because there were much higher stakes at play.

The longer I studied walls and shelves, the more drawn I felt to his Tlaloc collection. With no other clues to follow I started examining each book more closely, mindlessly touching each of them. My fingers eventually traced a worn-out volume; its leather lighter and smoother, its crest faded and its marking nothing more than a good replica of the other ones. Yet, an undeniably more frequently manipulated volume.

My heart jumped as I took the heavy book off the shelf and turned it in my hands. There was nothing on the cover other than the big and elaborate crest of Tlaloc. Smiling, I opened it to find a hidden compartment with a few envelopes inside.

I dumped the contents on the floor, kneeling, and scanning through them. I found half a dozen wrinkled letters dated from over a decade before; a large iron key with a simple brown ribbon attached to it and a very thin journal with a black cover and pristine white pages.

I flipped through the journal: a diary, with dozens of pages filled with a language I didn't recognize and sketches of people I had never seen. Without even noticing it, I went from the automatic flipping of pages to a careful examination, fascinated by the delicate and elegant calligraphy covering almost every space.

Until I saw the familiar circled arrow with intertwined branches, the Alliance symbol. I traced it with my forefinger, surprise flickering through me. A long-lost melody prickling at my memory.

I was absently reaching for the maps and documents on the desk, when I heard the hollow noise of the office door shutting behind me.

◆

"What do we have here?" Billy growled behind me.

I slowly turned, putting distance between myself and

the desk. If this ended up in a fight, I was not going to be cornered.

Billy was blocking the door with his heavy body, he didn't have any big weapons, but I'd always had the feeling he didn't need them in order to be brutal and murderous. He glanced at the documents on the floor and a satisfied glow transformed his expression when he looked back at me.

"Always knew you were a little bitch," he said with a crooked smile.

I calculated my options and figured I had none. We had too much history and distrust between us for any of the obvious options – denial or seduction – to work. He had me; the trick now lay in not letting him know how badly.

I relaxed my body as much as possible and willed my face into a bored expression: "I think you should measure your words, Billy-boy. After all these years, you should know better." I winked in a subtle reminder of all the times Ivo took my side over his in the past decades.

His face went red with anger.

"You are not getting out of this one, you brat! I have proof – "

"Do you?" I interrupted him. "The way I see it, all you have is your word against mine. We both know how that usually ends, don't we?"

He laughed. "Yeah, but this time it isn't a hunch, is it? This time you are here, in his office. I just have to keep you here until he comes back. It's not even gonna take long." His teeth glinted through menacing, parted lips.

I had wondered if I could take Billy in a fight, but I never truly expected to find out. Not until tonight anyway, when I saw myself trapped in Ivo's office with direct combat being my only option.

The odds seemed stacked against me.

"Don't you ever get tired, Billy-boy? Being his faithful dog must be tiresome." Working him into a senseless rage was as much of an advantage as I could get.

His hands closed into fists, but he didn't move. Scorn twisted his features as he replied. "Being his whore can't be much better."

I smiled sweetly before replying.

"When I was a child," I started in a confiding voice, "I was so afraid of you. Big, strong Billy! I would hide from you and refuse to train or even eat by your side. You see, I knew you hated me, even if I didn't understand why, I still knew it. Then, there was this one night when Ivo came to my bedroom and told me I had nothing to be afraid of. He told me you would do as he commanded and that, if need be, he would make you kneel to me." I saw the rage begin to boil under his skin, cracking the mask of patient reason.

The first lesson I'd learned from Ivo was that a person can always be manipulated through their greatest desires and fears. The second was that the best kind of lies were a delicate combination of truth and fantasy.

I gave Billy a split second for my words to sink in, to cloud his judgment before continuing. "He told me you were no more than a stupid, loyal dog, and that if I was smart, I would make you love me as much as you loved him." I shrugged. "I guess I wasn't smart, but at least you and I had our fun."

My words hit the mark. Billy's love for Ivo was never a secret to anyone close to the two of them. Their friendship was probably the oldest relationship my master had ever known. After two decades of seeing him taking my side on every single one of our bickering matches, it wasn't hard to guess what the sore point between them was.

As soon as I finished speaking, he lunged for me. I dodged his attack with a swirl as I took my two daggers from the scabbards, a snide smile on my lips – he'd always underestimated me, and I intended to use it to my advantage this time.

Billy hit the desk, knocking over a lamp, and sending a few pens to the floor.

I took the chance to elbow his neck with my right arm while aiming my left dagger at his ribs, but I wasn't quick enough. He turned and punched my stomach with a strength that threw me into the wall shelves, breathless.

I heard a crack accompanied by a sharp pang on my left side, my rib probably broken. The sheer force of that man was beyond anything I had ever faced, and I had just worked him into an unstoppable rage. Before I could get to my feet, his kick fell on my face, knocking me over just before a brutal stomp descended on my stomach. Faint dizziness seized me as I tasted the coppery blood on my mouth before it dripped onto my chin.

I rolled over before a second kick hit the floor where I had been laid a moment before and, in a quick motion I managed to put my dagger through his calf.

As he howled, I found the balance and speed to stand and charge at him again. I swirled around him, evading his attacks, my ribs and stomach shouting in pain with every movement.

The injury to his calf had slowed him, and it wasn't hard to find an opening to slice his shoulder after he failed to punch me once again. A superficial cut, just enough to get him angrier.

Only then, he drew his own dagger and came at me

with renewed energy. I was faster, but he was stronger, and more seasoned in combat. We both knew it.

He opened his stance as he charged at me once more, luring me into attacking his exposed stomach just to feel his left elbow connect with my face and his dagger cut my lower back. I managed to step back and gain some distance from him.

My body was slowing down, my breath growing heavy.

Sensing the lure of victory, he charged again.

I stilled my mind and summoned the darkness around us, forming thick tentacles that twisted around his arms, holding him in place before I jumped towards him, dagger in hands prepared for a final attack.

Surprise and confusion tinted his face with the unexpected force on his arms. The shock quickly replaced by understanding as the ripple of dark power leaked from me to the tentacles holding him in place.

My dagger hit his neck in a swift movement. His blood splattered across me and, when I looked at him again, there was nothing but emptiness facing me.

With painful movements, I got the journal and wrinkled letters from the floor and left, leaving the only friend Ivo had ever known dead on his rug.

◆

I ran to the servant corridors, barely missing three guards rushing from the main hall. The pain shooting through my abdomen with every step was enough to keep me distracted. It took me several minutes to notice the shouting in the distance. The unusual noise filled my ears every time I crossed one of the bigger corridors.

There was no sign of movement through the servant's passageways, but the main areas of the palace were louder and more frantic with every passing minute. I took a deep breath, clearing my head and pushing the pain aside.

Slowly, the sounds became recognizable; boots on the floor, weapons against armor, and orders shouted at a distance. The guards were looking for someone.

Terror started to creep under my skin when I remembered the guards outside Ivo's room. Those were not the usual patrols; they were looking for whatever caused this commotion. It hadn't been enough time for them to have found Billy's body, yet the guards flooding the corridor would hardly help me to get to my own chambers.

I ran a hand over my face and torso assessing my injuries. Cut lip, eye starting to swell and, of course, Billy's blood was all over me, tinting my face and neck red. There was no explaining any of that in a rational way and, even if there was, Ivo would not be deceived by sweet words.

Billy was dead. No matter what leverage I could find, Ivo would never forgive me for that.

All my hopes started to crumble, and I had to will myself together before I took the first step towards the grove behind the palace. First, I had to get out of the guard's reach, then I would figure out my next move.

My progress was slow and laborious, and it wasn't long until movement leaked from the main corridors to the smaller passageways, leading me to a longer path to avoid the patrols.

I turned the last corner before the corridor that would lead me outside and almost stumbled into Aiden, sword in hand. Shocked disbelief pooled in my gut.

He recognized me immediately.

First, worry contorted his expression. He dropped his sword and promptly embraced me.

"Aila, what are you doing here?" he breathed against my head, our earlier misunderstanding momentarily forgotten.

I did not reply, surprise and fear running through me. I searched for the combination of words that would stop him from understanding how much I had lied to him over the past two years.

He held my arms and took a step back, surveying my swollen face. "What happened to you?" he asked as he looked for the source of the blood on my face and neck.

Then, his gaze darted to the rest of my body and I watched as understanding cleared the concern out of him, as he released my arms and took the smallest step back.

I whispered his name in a plea as he noticed my clothes, the blood on my hands and finally, the corridor from where I was coming. When he looked at me again, I saw nothing but hollowness and pain.

Words failed me. I tried to call for him, to mutter an explanation, but I knew there were no easy and quick words to be said. I needed to explain it fully, he needed to know everything. And even that might not be enough.

"Where were you? What did you do?" His voice was cold and sharp. No more a friend and a lover than I was a lady in distress. It pained me deeper than I expected.

"Let's find a place to talk, Aiden." My voice was surprisingly firm.

He took another step back at the sound of his name, shaking his head slightly as if trying to clear his thoughts.

"Were you with Valran, Aila? Was that you?"

Command leaked through his words. A Prince used to being obeyed.

Him asking about Valran was unexpected, but I had no time to think about it, or to even consider how all this commotion could be related to him.

"I have no idea what you are talking about." I mustered all the honesty I had. "I know seeing me like this must be troubling, but I promise you I can explain. If you let me."

"Why are you covered in blood? Carrying weapons?"

The sounds of patrolling guards echoed around us, closer with every breath. I was on borrowed time, now more than ever.

"Tell me!" The words were a plea.

"Please, Aiden." I offered him my hand. "I'll tell you everything, but we need to leave now. Just trust me a little longer."

He lowered his head and reached for his sword. For a moment, I believed I had convinced him. I believed he would listen to my story and maybe I'd be able to make it right.

Then he said under his breath: "Trust?" He scoffed and shouted bitterly "Guards!"

In a blink of an eye, my whole world crashed down around me.

The guards had been set into motion with his call, and I knew they were not far. Still, for the longest second of my life, neither of us breathed. Aiden didn't make a move to attack me, or to delay me.

I forced myself to run towards the grove, but my path was interrupted by two guards appearing on my right, from a side corridor.

I dodged the first guard's blow while running my

dagger through his leg. Solid wall on my back, guards at my front. My way out of the palace completely blocked.

The injured guard cried in pain as he stood and prepared to lunge for me again. I waited and they both attacked me in a coordinated motion. Despite myself, a small part of me relished the challenge and I ignored the pain on my ribs as I swirled between them finding an opening for a slice on the second guard's waist, shallow enough that he would recover.

I was conscious of Aiden observing my every move and I knew each blow only solidified the reality that I'd lied to him the whole time we'd known each other.

A glance beyond him showed me more guards approaching and I knew I could not take them all, not like this. I tried to pass between them, to find a way out of this corner, but they were relentless and well trained. I didn't want to kill anyone else; I didn't want to take that undeniable step under Aiden's watchful eyes. Yet, I couldn't see a way out that wouldn't further tarnish his image of me.

An uninvited, bitter smirk found its way to my lips as the harsh truth unrolled in my mind: the only way I could survive, the only way I would ever have a chance to explain myself to him was by revealing the very thing I'd spent my whole life hiding. The only way I would leave this palace on my own legs, was by showing him my ugliest part.

I summoned the darkness from every corner of the room and in a single movement formed two tentacles that broke the necks of the guards in front of me while a wave of intense darkness claimed the whole corridor.

I drew a deep breath as Aiden disappeared in the blackness, wondering if I would ever see his face again.

Chapter 11

The palace grounds were buzzing in a chaotic swarm of soldiers scouting for any sign of movement. Even if they didn't know who they were searching for, a quick look at my bloody figure would send them running for me.

I kept to the darkness, using my power and the night to hide on my way to the grove and, eventually, to the quieter streets beyond it. Luckily enough, whatever search party Aiden had organized, had not yet reached the city itself.

One look at the sky told me it would be dawn soon and it would be hard to go unnoticed, magic or not. I took a shuddering breath and glanced over at the distant palace. My stomach strained with the memory of Aiden's face disappearing under a sea of darkness and the painful comprehension I thought I'd seen in his face. I allowed myself a minute of silent goodbye before darting to the only place I could think of.

I reached the dance studio shortly before sunrise. The street was sleepy and quiet, utterly unaware of any of the events from the last few hours. I had only a short time before the sun surged over the street and rendered my shadow cover a pit of solid moving darkness. I looked at the pipes on the side wall of the building and knew that what was usually an easy climb would take several painful minutes, but I had no other choice.

Luckily, I'd dismissed Dara today, assuming I'd need all the time I could get before Ivo's return. No one would search for me here. Not even her.

I took a shuddering breath and started climbing before I could convince myself otherwise. I made slow, but sure progress, muffling a few yelps of pain through sheer willpower. But the pain of climbing a wall was nothing compared to the agony of jumping through the open hatch at the roof.

The air left my lungs as I dropped on the floor awkwardly and I hoped I didn't make my already broken rib much worse as I fell in the middle of the empty training room.

The bathroom at the corner of the room was small but large enough to clean myself and exchange my stained, torn clothes with one of the training garments hanging in the many wardrobes. I examined my injuries and although I would probably have a very hard time fighting, I didn't seem to be in any immediate danger.

I found the familiar loose floorboard under the weapons rack and retrieved the black leather bag I'd left there two years before, shortly after moving to the capital. At the time, I figured it wouldn't hurt to have some basic items stashed around the city. I just never imagined I would be using them to run away from everything I knew.

I sat and spilled the contents in front of me, side-by-side with what I'd retrieved from Ivo's office: a couple of poison vials, a few coins – *too few coins* – and an envelope with Ivo's sigil.

Slowly, I held the envelope in my hand: a presentation letter Ivo had written years ago in case I ever needed to use his spies' network around the city. I sighed at the thought of it now, his spies and the guards were the last people I should get anywhere near. Yet, the thought was too tempting when I had nothing that could take me to safety. Hell, I didn't even know if safety would ever exist for me again.

My life was crumbling, and I didn't really understand why. All I knew was that Aiden wasn't meant to be in those tunnels, the guards weren't supposed to be running around the castle.

Then something clicked into place. *"Were you with Valran?"* He had asked. *"Was that you?"* I remembered his shock as he noticed the blood on me, my clothes, the daggers at my thigh. Something had happened to Valran, and I'd been caught right in the middle of it.

For that many guards and the Prince himself to be after the person responsible … *Shit*, I thought.

If things were that bad, they wouldn't constrain their search to palace grounds. I needed to leave town. Now.

I went back to the bathroom and assessed my face in the half-broken mirror. There was no hiding the purple patches already blooming on my cheekbones, the cut on my bottom lip or my swollen left eye. There would be no walking through the streets in broad daylight without calling a fuck-ton of attention.

Royal fucking shit!

I had to wait. The sound of music and dancing started to fill the room, leaking from the floor below in a sign that the day had finally started. It felt like I hadn't slept in days, but I was restless, unleashed.

So, I sat down, spreading all the little clues I had taken from Ivo's office in a big puzzle in front of me. The reality of the last few hours sank into my mind. In one night, I'd lost my best friend, killed my master's right hand, and got the whole Royal guard hunting me.

I may not need to worry about being forced to use Aiden anymore but, after Billy, I'd need leverage for a whole different reason. Ivo wouldn't even listen to me otherwise. So I forced myself to remain practical, to ignore the thunderous feelings trying to take hold. Instead, I focused on the papers in front of me. Because, if I had a chance to fight Ivo back, the first step had to lay there.

I studied every page of the journal with a reverent touch. I didn't understand the language, but something about the delicate lines and drawings made me think it was telling a deeply intimate story.

This wasn't just fragments of memories written down to avoid getting lost. It was a rendition of someone's life, recorded for generations to come.

I left it aside and started reading the wrinkled letters. There were over ten, all addressed to Ivo. All dated from years back. All seemingly unanswered appeals from his mother for him to come back, to forgive her, to let go of his need for revenge.

Except for one, dated only three years before.

"Dear son,
I grow weaker and with the long and painful days, also goes my hope that I'll ever see you again.

Before I'm too tired and lost to put pen to paper, I beg of you once more ... come home! Come back to me!

Your father knows the position you've achieved in Niram and I know even if he can't concede, a part of him is proud. You've proved him wrong at last, and now you can come home to serve your brother and your Crown. As you should always have.

Come back, my darling son, before there is nothing for you to come back to.

*Forever yours,
Mother."*

I re-read the letter over and over again, and every single time I was drawn to the same line, my mind racing around the same idea *"to serve your brother and your Crown."* I remembered all the detailed stories he had told me about Tlaloc over the years: the traditions, the tales, the description of the palace. It always felt so dear to him, so personal.

I remembered the bookshelves at his office, the number of books on Tlaloc Royalty, their official appearance.

Until that moment, I'd always believed him obsessed with a country that failed him, a country he loved and hated. I had always thought Tlaloc was a place he longed for as much as he despised.

But now, now I wondered if it was more than that, if his obsession was with the Royal family, his family. It made me curious about what could have happened for him to want to erase his origin so thoroughly.

When I finished going through everything, it was already late afternoon. So, I packed a few clothes, the venom vials, letters, and the journal. Finally, I got a pair of daggers from the rack and stored them carefully inside the satchel.

When I was done, I sat down at the darkest corner, in complete silence. I held the handle of my favorite sai and contemplated the utter disaster my life had turned into as I let the distant music numb my senses.

In the quiet room, I let my thoughts fly and patiently waited for the day to give in.

◆

The water by the bathroom basin had been enough to keep thirst at bay but, by the time dusk descended, I was tired, hungry and deeply on edge. None of which helped when I heard the door unlocking. I went still, thickening the shadows around me and hoping that whoever was entering would be quick and inattentive.

Instead, I saw Dara.

Never-miss-a-thing Dara.

Loyal-to-Ivo Dara.

Knew-all-my-tricks Dara.

My heart tumbled to the floor as I saw her calmly entering the studio and locking the door behind her.

"You can come out now," she called out even before she turned on the lights.

In the background I could hear the street movement slowing and the whistling of faraway guards growing progressively louder and more frequent than usual with crepuscule approaching.

I knew there was no bullshitting her, so I went for the best alternative. I faced her head on.

I left the shadowed corner of the room and emerged into full view, doing my best to look unfazed and relaxed. My hands casually in reach of the throwing knives at my belt, my hair in a braided bun that gave easy access to the pair of sai sheathed on my back, as I stood silent and proud, holding her stare. Her stormy grey eyes revealed nothing.

"What did you do to cause all the fuss going on out there?" Her own hands seemingly relaxed by the side of her body.

I tensed further. There was nothing more dangerous than Dara appearing calm.

"I had an eventful night. It seems not everyone was happy about it," I said noncommittally.

"Ivo won't be happy you blew that sweet disguise of yours." Wary and cold.

I shrugged.

"He might well cut you loose for that," she continued.

Despite myself, I asked, "Is he back?" I needed all the information I could gather.

She didn't reply immediately, every fiber of her being solely focused on my stance, my words, my breathing. After a minute or more she finally shook her head.

I opened my mouth to ask for more, but she spoke before I could: "Very soon, though."

I nodded. An urgency to move, to leave, built in my core.

"Is it true?"

"You'll have to be more specific," I said coldly.

She laughed. A rasp and hollow sound.

"I know you did Billy, willingly or not," she said pointedly glaring at the many visible injuries, "but Valran seems too far-fetched, not your style."

"What the fuck happened to Valran?" I snapped.

She smiled. "Knife to the throat, no fight. Messy, but effective if you ask me. Too blatant for you."

There it was. The royal fuck-up of my night.

The smirking face of a certain captain found its way to my mind, unease churning my core. Flynn had access; he was lurking the palace grounds as often as I was. Yet, as usual with him, the big question was why? What did he have to gain by killing his own master?

"They think I did it."

It wasn't a question, but she nodded all the same.

Fucking Flynn!

"How long until Ivo comes through that door, really?" I challenged her again, my focus back on my immediate problem: Getting the hell out of this city.

Her brows furrowed: "How would I know, Aila?"

Disbelief coated my every sense. "Are you saying you won't give me up on a plate? I killed his best friend."

"Oh, he will be pissed alright. But I don't see why I need to get involved. Billy was an asshole and he had it coming."

She never had the same love Ivo had for Billy and I always liked to think it was because of how he treated me, that it was because of some sense of protectiveness.

But now was not the time for foolish trust, not with Ivo's employees anyway.

"You could gain his position, money. You know he'll give you anything."

"Are you trying to convince me now?" Exasperation cut the air between us.

"I'm trying to understand where we stand. I don't wanna fight you, but I do intend to leave this fucking city on my own two feet." My hand moving to the handle of a throwing knife.

"Easy girl," she said. "I'm not fighting you for this shit."

She scanned my body, and I wondered how much of the wariness, tension and alertness she could sense. She let out a deep breath before continuing.

"Look, Ivo and I have an understanding. A fruitful relationship, if you will. But I bear no love for him or any of his cronies. Fuck the Goddess, I *raised* you! So, don't be a brat and believe me when I say I have no intention of turning you over to him. He can hunt you at his own will. And take heed: nothing will stop him from finding you."

I said nothing. A part of me wanted to believe her, to trust she would listen and help, but I had already made that mistake earlier in the day and I was not about to do it again.

There were enough shadows through the city for me to hide now. From a distance, the end of the last class of the day filled my ears with hollow laughs and frivolous conversations in a horde of over-excited girls. It was time.

Silently and with my attention fixed on her, I got the satchel I'd prepared earlier and made my way to the door.

"Let me help you," she said in a rough gasp, more quietly than I had ever heard her. "Guards are already patrolling the whole city."

Sorrow and something else flashed through her face. Concern, maybe.

"I'm fine," was all I said. I didn't know if I dismissed her for lack of trust or for fear of what it would cost her.

"You are far from being fine, girl."

"I will be."

I could see the struggle in her face as she watched me crossing the room. The silence lingered between us. We both knew this would be the last time we saw each other. Her stare pinned me the whole time and the fifteen steps it took me to cross the room felt like a marathon.

When I reached the doorknob, she finally asked.

"Can you really summon darkness?"

I stopped, frozen. I had feared this question for so many years, feared this knowledge spread into the world. An eternal sword hanging over my head.

A mix of terror and relief filled me. My life would never be the same. Yet I never felt freer than in that moment, never more myself than when I started running away from everyone and everything I knew and cherished.

I sent a swarming of darkness behind me. Black tendrils of shadow trailing my steps like vanishing smoke. For the first time I could remember, I let my power ripple from me and fill the space of the room. Finally, I let it caress her in goodbye.

"There is something you need to know." Her voice was low and deep. Serious enough to make me stop.

"Ivo didn't find you by chance. He was searching for you, hunting you. I never knew why. Until now."

I turned to her, wary. "How can you be sure?"

"He hired me months before he found you. I swore to never tell a soul."

The words dropped on me like a boulder. Shattering the remaining honey-laced beliefs I still had in a single, heavy blow.

I was five-years-old when he found me in the middle of a town raided by bloody soldiers, when he rescued me from a painful and slow death.

That day flashed in my mind. I saw the certainty with which he made his way through the soldiers, the conviction with which he took me from there and settled me in his own life and, deep in my soul, I knew she was telling the truth.

Everything I knew, everything I'd ever believed was wrong. No more than crumbling lies.

A whistle sounded at a distance. I had no time and no voice to question her.

So instead, I nodded and crossed the threshold. Away from the only life I had ever known.

"Be careful," were the last words I heard before a talon of pure darkness closed the door behind me.

◆

The streets were full and buzzing despite the night that was descending over town, much of the activity due to the patrols sprawled through the main streets. I made my way through a set of small alleys, to the stall market by the harbor, hoping it would take the guards a few hours to get to the more undesirable areas of the city.

There were still a few stalls left. Most of the sellers left at sundown, but there were always a few desperate or brave enough to risk the darker hours.

Stale fish and oily water flooded my nose as I observed the products displayed on every surface: old barrels, broken chairs, ragged cloths on the floor. It was messy and oddly hypnotic.

I didn't visit this part of town often. The shabby surroundings of the harbor were usually attended either by the poor looking for cheap produce, or by local criminals searching for easy prey. Even though the true crime lords were based in much more prominent parts of the city, the stall markets, along with the slums were still the key source for shady business and illegal substances. Or, in my case, the only place where I could find a one-way ticket out of town.

I wondered how long until Ivo was back at the palace. I knew he would play the mess I left behind to his advantage. Valran's death gave him the opportunity to angle for his job. While my own move against Billy gave him the excuse to feign surprise about my abilities – magical and otherwise.

He would play my unexpected revelation flawlessly: the portrayal of the betrayed uncle, the search for retribution, the role of protector of the Kingdom. Hell, if he was smart enough, and I knew he was, he would even play my secretive relationship with Aiden as what he always tried to turn it into: a cold and calculating move on the throne itself.

I choked a bitter laugh. I had unwittingly given him all he needed to be appointed Niram Premier. Undoubtedly, his first action would be to find me before I could spoil any of it.

Behind the distinctive pang of fear clutching at my stomach, there was a different kind of pain. Even as I ran for my life, my heart broke a little further, a little deeper.

In my soul, I knew there was too much hurt and deceit between us, too many lies and vileness for ours to ever be a normal relationship. Still, beneath it all, he was the only father I had ever known. In our own messed up way, we had found respect, love, and some semblance of trust. Until now. Until I'd betrayed him.

Except that was also a lie, wasn't it? I'd betrayed him, yes. But he'd lied to me my whole life. Dara's words played on through my head over and over until I found myself fighting for control over my body and my magic. Until I found myself clutching my hands and grinding my teeth.

The voice within me was no longer quiet, no longer small. It howled.

He was hunting you.

Hunting me! What else had he cost me? What life had he robbed me of? What other lies had I happily accepted? What other price would he want me to pay now?

Because of his threats I'd lost the only friend I'd ever known, because of his games I'd been forced to lie and kill, forced to abandon everything I held dear, to flee the only life I'd ever known.

I stripped the satin silver chocker he'd given me nearly a decade before from my neck and let it drop to the floor. I had no more space for his presents.

My only choice was to leave town quickly, to buy a way out by foot or river, before he could find me. But I never really had a chance. The patrols had already reached the market and eight guards were covering every entrance to the harbor while two more were making their ways through the ships, turning everyone uneasy and edgy enough to refuse questionable passengers.

I turned back discretely, head down and weapons hidden. I made my way to the slums beyond the market and the harbor, trying to keep as far away from the guards' whistles on my back as I could. Still, every street I turned down presented me with the sight or sound of a new patrol. Whether the order was coming from Ivo or from the King himself, they were intent on not letting anyone leave that damn town.

It wasn't long until I was trapped between different patrols, with no hope of remaining invisible in the small empty street - darkness or not.

With no more than a second to spare I entered the big oak doors in front of me and was greeted by a crescent moon encased by a copper triangle. The symbol of the Goddess stood proud and glimmering in front of me.

Chapter 12

My first thought was how opulent the temple was; far more impressive than any room I'd seen before. White marble with delicate silver veins and several carvings of a crescent moon encircled the round central room. In the center, a proud statue of the Goddess herself stood – a hooded figure with a crescent moon encased by a copper triangle hanging above her head.

Under the shiny night light, I was greeted by the holy keeper who bounded the fate and crossroads of all humanity. At her feet piles of different herbs burned, sending a sweet and intoxicating smell through the whole room.

The high ceiling gave way to a round opening, guaranteeing constant light and a direct view to the sky that fostered spiritual access to the Goddess Herself - or so Her followers believed.

Among other things, Nuri was famous for being home to the biggest temple dedicated to Her cult in the whole of Niram, if not the world. Still, I'd never set foot inside of it.

I didn't believe any of Her teachings strongly enough to warrant a visit.

So, when I found myself in the big, clear room, I wasn't any way prepared for the complete, deep silence that greeted me. If I closed my eyes, it would be easy to believe myself alone, safe. Maybe it was the fact I was out of options, desperate. Or maybe it was that this was the first time I had entered a temple of my own free will, but in that fraction of a second, I finally understood the refuge Ivo sought on his weekly visits, the faith and belief he devoted himself to.

Through the years, I had grown used to the burgundy robes of the priestesses as they walked across the city and palace, but amid their sacred place, they were somehow more ethereal and magical. The light, shimmery fabric of the sleeveless robes flew around each of them gracefully with movement. Small, wooden buttons and delicate golden seams decorated the hems and collars in flowery patterns. Long hoods covered most of their faces, leaving only their mouths visible underneath the fabric. The only ornament against the rich robes was a large copper medallion on their chest - the crescent moon, their holy symbol. A token of the belief to which they dedicated their lives.

They were as graceful and shadowy as travelers that once crossed the veil between the worlds. Wholly part of this world and yet from somewhere else entirely. Truly daughters of the night, as they were called.

I kept walking through the room, pretending to examine the carvings and reverently take in the details. There were three discrete doors on the opposite side of the entrance. Only the last was unlocked.

A quick glance at the interior told me it was a servant's cabinet: brooms and dustpans leaned against the side of the room. Stashed by its side sat a couple of laundry baskets full of burgundy robes.

Without a second thought I entered the empty room and threw one of the fine robes over my clothes, concealing my weapons the best I could and pulling the long hood over my face. I contemplated hiding inside the building but, without any knowledge of what lay beyond ... I shook my head at the hopelessness of my situation and opened the door back to the salon, shortly before the first soldiers came into view, taking the temple by storm.

I breathed in. Slowly. The robes demanded blunt respect from most of the citizens in Nuri and its hood covered enough of my face to disguise anyone who didn't know me too well. With some luck, it could grant me enough anonymity to evade the guards.

Maybe it would work well enough for me to brave the city again, reach the sewers. If I could get to an entrance unseen, I could find my way below ground to the edge of the slums in the outskirts of the city. A gamble, yes. But one I was desperate enough to make.

There was no more time for uncertainty, so I let the view of the guards ground me, I let it dissolve the pure panic and give way to cold resolve. I descended into the calculating space I'd forged in my mind over the years and let all the instincts I'd honed under Ivo's tutelage take the reins as I stepped back into the salon.

◆

A slim female figure cloaked in black stepped in front of me before I could reach the center of the room. I had never seen one of the priestesses in black before, but the making of her robe was so similar to the burgundy fabric and style that there was no mistaking it.

The seams were as fine as the ones on the other priestess and yet different, stronger. No delicate golden flowers, her robe was covered with intricate silver patterns giving way to torches and animals, in a mesmerizing tale I couldn't quite decipher.

I gazed under the hood, trying to face the person in front of me, but either by my own tiredness, or by an effect of the faint herb smoke coating the room, what I saw was more mystical than I would like to acknowledge. Her face was no more than an amalgam of cloudy white shadows in constant movement: she was all and nothing. A person and a void.

I jumped at the sound of hounds howling in the distance and shook my head, trying to clear the fogginess in my mind. In silence, she beckoned me to follow her to an empty area near the central pillar. To my own surprise, I did. Momentarily forgetting what had led me inside of the temple in the first place.

It was not until we reached the central figure that she broke the silence:

"I've wondered when you'd come to find me."

Her voice was a soft whisper full of command.

"You must have me confused with someone else," I said as politely as I could, half remembering what I was doing there and scanning the room for the guards.

"And yet you are in need of refuge and council all the same," she motioned to the guards behind me, clear and assertive.

That gained my full attention and I tried, once again, to see any part of her. The herb smell, now stronger and more oppressive, fogged my senses.

She pressed. "What do you seek, my child?"

The question forced some clarity into me. Taking me away from that limbo between reality and delusion.

"Just some time for meditation, daughter." I used the common title hoping the different robe didn't indicate some sort of hierarchy I was oblivious to.

"You'll need more than that if you wish to succeed. You'll need me."

"Succeed at what?" I asked before I knew why. A part of me dismissed it as an attempt to stall, evading any suspicion that I was, indeed, running from the guards. Yet, there was a ring of truth in my question.

She studied me for a minute, and I wondered what answers – and questions – she was reading in me.

"We all have a higher purpose in life, princess. Whether we accept it or not."

"I'm not a princess, nor am I in need of a purpose."

"I must be mistaken, then," she mused in a voice too amused to mean she believed it. "Yet, it seems you've reached a crossroads. Haven't you? One that the First Woman could never have predicted."

I stared at her, confused, the part of my brain that had been keeping track of the movement of the guards inside the temple was now completely focused on the strange woman before me.

The First Woman was as much legend as she was religious canon. A woman born under a moonless sky, the first to bear any arcane power, chosen and blessed by the Goddess herself to control all of the arcane elements. With her death, each arcane element passed to one of her children and a millennia later resulted in the five Kingdoms we now know, each ruled by the most powerful wielder of each element. The wielders' magic ability had been diluted over the generations, but their greed for power never sedated.

Eventually, the head of each arcane house – our kings – formed the Elementalists. In theory, a council dedicated to ensuring the balance of power across the Kingdoms, in practice an order consumed with finding ways to restore the immeasurable magic the First Woman once held.

This legend explained the surge of arcane wielders and their control of fire, water, air, earth and light, but it did not explain my own power. It never mentioned darkness.

"Well, even if she existed, there is a lot she couldn't have predicted, isn't there? Else, she would have better educated her descendants." Sarcasm laced every word.

"Blame is rarely a one-way avenue. Do you know how magic truly came to be, child?"

A hundred legends crossed my mind. There were so many stories about the First Woman, about the blessing of magic. Regardless, I never got a chance to respond before she continued.

"It was before the Goddess fought her brothers and sisters for the control of this realm, before She used the veil to hold the other Gods on the other side. The humans needed help, for in a world full of frivolous Gods fighting for power, there was no one else to protect them. So, she chose one of her most devoted daughters to know the secrets of the veil, to manipulate the very energy beyond it, the magic ... The First Woman." A brief, heavy pause before she continued with a strained tone. "The Goddess made many errors when blessing her with the means to access arcane power. But one was bigger and more dire: Magic was never meant to go unchecked in a realm isolated from the veins of power. Yet, when the time came, the First Woman refused to leave the humans unprotected."

"She gave it away." Something in her tale kept me enthralled.

"The woman was wise. She knew the hearts of men. So, she broke her power down and passed bits of it down her lineage in a bid to grant protection, safety for generations to come. Yet, in doing so she ignited the very flame that destroyed the Gods themselves: greed."

Angry disbelief started churning in my stomach, but the guards were circling too close, so I held the leash of my temper as I said,

"Wise? Tell that to the people being kidnapped and experimented upon. To the ones who have no hope of fighting against magic, who have no one to protect them." My voice a pool of bitter sharpness.

The greed of the Elementalists was the very thing that started the Great War, sixty years before. Generations of mixing between wielders and non-wielders led the magic to weaken. With the desire for power came the Light Wielders' experiments. A desperate attempt to use the vital force of a non-wielder as an amplifier to their magic abilities, an attempt to bind the life of those who are powerless to tap into the very fabric – and power – between the realms: the veil.

After many deaths, the non-wielders rallied, rebelled. They formed the Alliance in a final attempt to protect themselves.

The Alliance ignited the war, but the experiments caused it. The Elementalists got involved, and with time, the war destroyed Kalindi – the Kingdom of Light – and decimated the Light wielders lineage. Yet, the experiments never truly stopped.

Even fifty years after the Great War ended, children

disappeared from their beds, old men disappeared from their fields. No Goddess or magic woman to protect those who needed it the most.

"As long as someone needs protection, there will always be someone to protect, child. Even if it takes time for all the pieces to fall into place."

"Well, tell your Goddess to hurry up."

"Do you know why she is called the Guardian of the veil?" she asked in a pensive voice as if I hadn't said anything.

I shook my head. Religious studies had never been an interest of mine.

"She wanders through the worlds, guarding humans and magic and preserving the veil that separates us from the Old Gods' domain. She listens. Long ago, She bent the rules by giving humans the power to wield the elements. But She never left them to fend for themselves; She gave her own power to her followers - Her daughters - to heal and to fight. Even if many have forgotten."

Her healers were famous, high members of the church, valued by the arcane houses, but fighters? Legend or canon I never heard about fighters.

"The church," I said, full of contempt.

"Her daughters and Her blessing have no need for robes and walls. That came much after."

The woman continued before I found the words to ask anything. "She underestimated the lure of magical power, but She never stopped looking out for humanity. Now, we are coming to a crossroads, and even through the veil She sees the hope for freedom and justice beginning to fade, as much as she hears the murmurs of an Heir of Light and Dark getting louder."

My mind reeled. She told me the legends of our

world, of magic and of wielders. Yet, she didn't. Every word felt more meaningful than empty fairy tales.

"The Heir? That is just a rumor spread through rebellious camps. A glimpse of hope to distract people from the hardships of their lives." The very reason why my own power needed to be a secret; anyone bearing the control of dark was a threat to the very existence of the Elementalists, a threat to our whole world.

The guards were almost done with their sweep, and I knew I should have left, but I felt tethered to her, held in that spot as if I needed to hear what she had to tell me.

"Even your scriptures say that no one has ever controlled two elements. Beyond that, Light was lost during the war, and no one has ever wielded Darkness." The practiced lie rolled off my tongue. "Your own church negates the heir."

"There are many truths that were never captured in books. Sacred or not. Even more truths that the church would prefer to remain hidden. Never forget the church doesn't know what the church doesn't know." I thought I felt a hint of amusement in her voice.

"Do you really want me to believe that the heir is not just a fool's tale?"

She considered it for a few seconds before replying in a gentle, old voice, "Not even the creatures beyond the veil know everything. That, my child, will remain to be seen."

"Unless your Goddess's fighters are an army hidden somewhere, a single wielder, heir or not, won't change what the Elementalists are capable of."

"It will be a long time before the world finds Her fighters again. Until then, there are other ways to tip the scales." There was ancient kindness and sorrow in her voice.

"The First Woman found a way to pass her gifts to her line and everything that can be given, can also be taken away."

"Take away magic?"

"Destroy, pause, distribute. It is all one and the same for the energy lines in the world. Magic exists beyond your kind, in spite of it. Not even the most powerful of wielders can change that. Even the first woman needed help to manipulate the lines and bind magic to her family. For that, she needed to use the Goddess's blessing one more time, she needed Her stone."

The guards' boots were closer now. Only respect for the priestess kept them from removing all hoods. Only my years of training kept me from fidgeting as I pulled my own hood lower.

My life hung in the balance, and I had to figure out an escape route, yet I couldn't bring myself to stop listening to the woman in front of me long enough to take the first step.

"Why are you telling me all this?" was all I could say.

"Because it is time for you to know."

Her words were too fantastical to believe and yet a sense of urgency emanated from her. Words kept evading me, and I couldn't stop the feeling she knew more about who I was than anyone should.

I grew up believing the idea of a promised wielder able to manipulate Light and Darkness to bring revenge upon the Elementalists was just that: an idea. An empty myth. A story designed to rally innocent folk behind desperate rebels.

But then, no one should be able to manipulate Darkness and here I was hiding an unprecedented magic for twenty-five years.

Besides, if Ivo had lied about how lucky we were to find each other among the bloodied streets of a destroyed town, then what else could he have lied about? Could this be the reason he had hunted me? If he had deceived me about the most fundamental of things, then how could I believe anything else I'd learned from him?

She was silent for a few moments and then the amused tone was back into her voice: "Your guards have left. It seems a good time for you to start your journey."

There was not a guard in sight. Still, I didn't move.

I didn't know what to believe anymore, I didn't know where to find the truth. I only knew that even though I didn't have a drop of Light in me, I *could* manipulate Darkness. There was more to my story than Ivo had led me to believe.

She took her medallion and extended it to me. "Take it. The road ahead of you will be long and dark, I trust this will help you find your way to Urian, and to the Moon Stone."

It was the second time she talked about a stone, but the image of the map I'd stole from the Premier popped into my head. To judge by the many red marks. the Alliance was all around the small town.

"Urian? Why would I go there? And what is a Moon Stone?"

"To find yourself." Her voice was no more than a caress. "And regarding the stone, that is one of the answers you'll have to find at the end of the road."

I was about to ask her what she meant when she handed me the medallion, cold fingers brushing my hand as I felt the warm, tingling wave spread through my body relieving the pain in my ribs, easing the swelling on my face. I inhaled sharply. *Healing magic!*

I'd never been healed before. Healing powers were different from arcane power. Not inherited, given. A direct gift from the Goddess, forbidden to anyone other than Herself.

"Who are you?" I finally whispered.

"That is a tale for when I see you again."

She turned away, adding before disappearing in the small crowd: "Remember even a moonless night only remains dark for so long, Princess."

I glanced at the medallion still in my hands, the metal warm against my skin, and pulled it over my head, still wondering what I could find in a small city in the middle of nowhere.

I needed the truth. I needed information. Annoyingly enough, Ivo might well be the only one capable of giving it to me. He'd deceived me my whole life, he'd entangled me in so many lies that I didn't even know where to begin to unravel the mess. How could I ever hope to best him?

I needed to settle myself if I wanted to escape. I squeezed the medallion in my hand and took a deep breath. *I will face Ivo, I will make him give me the answers I need. Even if I have to destroy myself doing it*, I vowed.

So, I had a choice: I could search for leverage that I knew I would only find in Tlaloc. Or I could search for the reasons Ivo didn't want me to investigate the Alliance.

An invisible pull rattled my core at the thought that, short of the palace, the only other place where I had a chance – even if slim – to find any leads, was at the premier's home estate, in tiny Urian.

The same city that was surrounded by the Alliance, the same city where the Premier was amassing an unnecessary number of soldiers. The very same city where, if the words of a strange woman where to be believed, I would find myself.

The woman was right about one thing. I was going to Urian.

Chapter 13

I threw myself back into Nuri's chaotic streets. Hood pulled over my head, weapons hid under the shimmery burgundy cloak, and the medallion against my chest, its weight strangely comforting.

The guards had cleared the block, but I could still hear them on the main streets, whistling and screaming as they progressed to more remote areas of the city. Their search was getting more intense, and my resolve to get to Urian more urgent.

When I approached the slums, there was no ignoring their presence anymore, the guards were everywhere. Slowly, the noisy alleys grew quiet and empty. No open doors or windows, no hard-working people, no degenerates. No one risked crossing the path of the units rushing by.

In this part of the city, there was no beautiful architecture, no luxurious houses and no well-tended streets. There, on the side of the hill that harbored the slums, away from the palace view, the streets were narrow, the houses old, and the sewer entrances uncovered, rather than disguised behind beautiful tiles and small drains.

In these forgotten alleys, the sewer entrances were as big as a grown man - doors to a maze of underground tunnels, secured by big iron grids and padlocks.

I only knew of the vastness of the underground tunnels from gossip yet, in the dead of night, with the royal guard on my back, the prospect of searching for a path in the dark was inviting.

I threw myself at the padlock the minute I saw it. It was an old mechanism that would take precious seconds to disarm without magic - seconds I didn't have, to protect a secret I no longer held.

Aware of the futility of hiding my power, I willed the darkness around me into a thin tendril that exploded the padlock from within and pulled at the bars.

But the grid was too heavy.

The footsteps and whistles of the guards grew closer.

I pulled again and not a speck of dust moved. It was stuck.

I took a step back and with a deep breath, mustered the shadows from every corner. A long and strong tentacle wrapped around the bars, easing the grid with a ferocious pull that opened half the entrance. It wasn't a large passage, but I could squeeze through it.

"Phew! Cool trick!" The sound of the young, excited voice startled me. Dark talons immediately formed at my back as I turned around.

"Ok, ok." She raised her hands facing me with laughter in her voice. "Awful trick, then!"

The slender girl was in her early twenties. A brilliant, playful smile was on her face as she peered at the entrance behind me. Cornrow braids adorned with thick golden threads flew behind her in a big ponytail, illuminating her ebony skin.

She leaned against the wall, satchel hanging across her shoulder as she took another bite of a half-eaten apple, relaxed and confident. A simple enough movement, but so careless that it made a part of me long for the same easy freedom.

"Want some?" she offered in earnest between one mouthful and another.

I shook my head as the dark tendrils behind me, slowly dissolved back into the shadows around us.

She took my silence as a sign to continue. "Quiet type, then? Fine. I take this is all for you?" She jerked her chin in the direction of the shouting guards.

I nodded.

"Damn, you really pissed someone off, girl!"

"That is an understatement," a smile bloomed on my lips despite myself. To my disbelief, her own smile got even brighter in response.

I don't know if what kept me frozen in place was the ease with which she stood in that alley biting her apple, or the lack of questioning and judgement at the sight of my magic.

"That tunnel closes off about a mile from here. You'll be stuck." She pointed to the half open grid behind me.

"Fuck." I spat, following her gaze.

She took the last bite and measured me for half a second while tossing the apple core to the side. "There is another entrance two blocks from here. I'll take you."

"I'm fine." I said, scanning my memory for any other entrance.

"Well, the twelve assholes closing on you say otherwise." Exasperation tinted her tone for the first time.

"Shouldn't you be hiding behind thick doors like everybody else?" I snapped at her, mirroring her own exasperation too easily.

"Maybe, if I had one." Not a waver on her silvery voice or stubborn face.

A vague memory from the few years before Ivo, surfaced. A part of me still remembered how it felt to have no home, no one to look after me, no one to care for me. In some ways, I still didn't.

She rolled her eyes before I could say anything else. "I get it, ok. You are just fine on your own and can do everything alone. Except when it comes to those tunnels. It is a fucking maze down there and no one in this freaking city knows it better than me. Also, I don't think the church will be interceding for you when the pricks get hold of you, robes or not." She looked pointedly at my clothes before continuing. "So, unless you want to finish the night in shackles, I suggest you swallow your pride and follow me."

Without another word, she walked away.

A moment later, I followed.

◆

We ran through alleys I had never braved before, narrow streets only familiar to those born and raised in the slums.

The night and my own Darkness kept us hidden, our skills kept us silent. All while the girl lead me with unshaken resolve, her focus solely on the noises behind us and the path ahead.

She never stopped to see if I was following, still I knew she kept track of my position as we raced together.

In the silent, tense minutes I feared I'd been wrong to

follow her, feared she would lead me back to Ivo. In spite of this, I let her guide me, embracing the only option I had with a fool's determination and a heart prepared for battle.

As we rushed through the murky streets, I wondered what path had given her the ability to hide in the night, what fate had forged the knowledge and skill to survive these dangerous streets. No matter how bright she seemed, how sincere, the world had not been kind to her, not if it led her to someone like me.

It wasn't long before the footsteps of the guards became heavy and constant behind us. Their march a beating reminder of my growing urgency. Louder and louder. Closer and closer.

The sewer entrance stood in front of us, similar in all ways to the first one, except for the missing padlock and the marks on the street where the grid was constantly dragged.

The girl flashed me a devilish grin and a wink before pulling the heavy, iron gate. I lost a shuddering breath as relief poured through my senses and hope slowly engulfed my thoughts.

Though relief and hope are not for people like me. Those are things laced with privilege and innocence, born in the happy and safe childhood I wish I had known.

Before I could join her at the gate, the first unit reached the end of the alley, weapons in hand. There was no running anymore, no hiding behind cloaks and tricks.

I threw my hood back and placed myself between the guards and the girl.

"You go through the gate the minute it is open."

I didn't wait for a reply before I delved into my power, summoning as many shadows as I could in the short time I had, hoping it would be enough to stop the guards running toward us.

The patches of shadow around us turned into long tentacles and sharp talons as I unsheathed the pair of sai strapped under the robe. I welcomed the weight and coldness of the hilt in my hand, testing my grip as the noise grew closer.

All guards wore the palace insignia, but the surprise on their faces at the sight of the shadowed talons made it clear they didn't know who or what they were chasing and they hesitated just long enough for me to launch my own attack.

An uncanny yet harmonious dance of shadows and strikes.

In mere seconds, the alley was overtaken by an uproar of pouncing and screams, pierced skin, and bloodshed. Yet, they were too many, too fast.

More guards kept coming from nearby streets and I couldn't do anything other than pounce and strike, pounce and strike. I was so used to hiding my power, that I didn't think about amassing my magic as we moved here and now, there was not enough time to summon sufficient darkness to swipe them away or to consider a different strategy. There was only pounce and strike.

The gore had started to pile around me when I heard the girl yelling: "Get in!"

"You first."

"I know how to close it off. They will only keep coming, if I don't." Not a prick of fear on her voice.

The guards were too close to argue now, so I focused my talons on the closest ones, hoping I could slow their attack enough for us to disappear into the sewers.

"Move your ass, now!" The girl shouted as I jumped through the hole, into the dark and fetid sewers of Nuri.

The first thing I noticed was the splattering sound of

my feet reaching the bottom. It was not a high fall, but it still unbalanced me enough to make me kneel. Sludge immediately started to seep into my boots as the stench clung to everything else.

The second thing I noticed was the lack of another pair of boots splattering besides mine. The girl had stayed behind.

I stood, intent on getting as far away from here as I could but, just as I took the first step towards the endless tunnel, I heard the girl scream. *Fuck.*

The gate above me was still open, shrieks flying through the empty tunnels in a reminder of the pain and death that would surely await me at the palace.

Maybe I should have counted my losses and risked the tunnels, maybe I should have ignored the lifeline she had thrown me just minutes before, maybe I should have deemed it too late to do anything for her. But I didn't.

I pushed one deep breath down and started to delve into my power, collecting a small cloud of shadow around me before I climbed the few rustic steps in the wall, back to street level.

I told myself I would not find my way through the tunnels without the girl, that I was merely repaying a debt. But the thing that kept coming back to mind was her utter lack of fear and judgment at the sight of my power. The thing that kept me moving was her offer to help me.

She had put on a fight. Not a fair, or easy one, but enough to distract the guards from immediately jumping after me. I sent a single tentacle of pure darkness from the tunnel, thrusting through the shoulder of the closest guard and giving the girl the distraction she needed to break free from the man holding her.

Without a second thought, she jumped into the tunnel and I used the last of my power to pull the gate back into place behind us.

I found her tumbled on the floor. As breathless as she was fearless. Unrelenting strength beamed through her. A fighter.

She grinned and pushed herself up. "I'm Ruby, by the way."

"Aila," was all I said, not quite believing the easiness with which she fell back into the carefree bright girl I'd seen before. Not a sign of distress.

"I know. Shall we?" She signaled the tunnel to our right. And I followed her as guards shouted and pulled at the bars above us.

◆

The tunnels spread beneath the whole city in a never-ending, dark maze and, in any other circumstances, it would have been easy to lose the guards tracking us.

Except these were not normal circumstances and those were no ordinary guards. Aiden had selected his best officers and they would not disappoint their prince.

We ran through the tunnels for what felt like hours, deeper into the city, in the hopes we'd lose them. Until the girl stopped on a darkened corner and whispered, "If we don't lose them down here, getting to the exit will do us no good."

"Any brilliant ideas?" I spat.

"Well, can't you darken their path or something?"

"Doesn't work like that. I can cover a tunnel in darkness, yes, but I need to know where to command the shadows. I hear them all around and, without knowing the tunnels, I'd need to throw a huge cloud and for that I'd need more time to summon than we have."

"Shit."

"Yeah ... shit."

"Well, we better figure out something soon, cause every day at sunrise this tunnel gets cleaned – so it will fill with water from the city."

I didn't know how long we'd spent inside, but sunrise couldn't be far away.

"How many do you figure are still following?" I asked.

"Hard to say. Four? Five? The rest may be making their way to the exits."

Her estimate wasn't too far from my own and the more I tried to find an alternative, the more convinced I was we would need to face them.

"Teach me the way out." I told her.

"Why?"

"I'll stop them before I continue."

"Ok." A simple knife found its way into her hands.

"What are you doing?"

"You don't expect me to face them with my beauty and sense of humor, do you?"

"I don't expect you to face them at all. I expect you to tell me the fucking way out and then to disappear."

"You can expect that all you want."

"I don't need your help."

"Good for you."

"I'm serious."

"Me too. You are not asking for my help, and you don't need it, but you'll have to take it anyway."

"Why? Why not run?"

"Now is hardly the time to discuss our world views, but if you must know, I'm tired of watching life go by."

"You have a death-wish is more like it."

"Maybe, but like it or not, I'd rather die doing something, feeling something."

I didn't know if she was the most reckless person I'd ever met or the wisest. Once again, I wondered if she was just finding a way to take me to Ivo, but if that was the case it would have been easier for her to lead me to the guards. One way or another, I needed her to get out of the damn tunnels.

"Fine," I said just as I cloaked us under darkness, and we made our way back to the nearest guards.

We approached them silently. I would take the blunt force of their attack and Ruby would reach them from behind, using a lateral tunnel to encircle the small party.

I stopped in the middle of the way, sai sheeted at my back, robes stored in my bag, head angled down. I listened as their rough steps stopped, as they went in formation carefully approaching me two at a time. All while I plummeted into my power.

"Don't move," one of them said.

I glared at them, a wicked smile on my lips.

"So bossy," I said. "You almost make this fun."

"Drop your weapons," he continued.

"And why would I do that?"

"We'll take you back to the palace. The Prince wants you alive."

"Sorry to disappoint, boys, but I have other plans. If Aiden wants a word, he can find me in person, can't he?"

They exchanged surprised glances at the familiarity attached to Aiden's name, but they didn't break formation, didn't slow their steps.

"Now, you have two choices. You can go back from where you came on your own feet, or not at all."

They continued to approach me, ignoring my words. I tsked. "I really wish you'd chosen differently."

With that, I threw myself at the first two guards, as talons of shadow thrust into the two behind them.

They were well trained and well armored, which made my tired advances hard. I aimed at the soft areas of their armor while I moved around them in a series of quick movements. I soon found an opening behind a knee and, eventually, a neck, the blood gushing over my hands. My talons did faster work than my arms and pierced through the stomachs of three of the guards.

It didn't matter that I'd been healed just hours before, I was tired and hadn't slept in over a day. And not long after, I found myself cornered between a wall and two very skilled guards. The last one running back through the tunnels in search of reinforcements.

"You can come with us the easy way, or the hard one," a guard said through gritted teeth.

"We had this conversation already." I needed to buy time. Power thrummed through me, but I was too tired, and too afraid I wouldn't hold to consciousness if I delved further into the Darkness.

Before I had to find out, a knife jolted through the temple of one of the guards and he toppled to the floor with a thud. The second was surprised enough not to offer much resistance as I buried my sai under his chin and through his skull.

In less than a second, Ruby was retrieving her knife, a bitter look on her face.

"I thought you'd left," I said.

She ignored me and I turned in the direction the final guard had run, listening for his steps, trying to figure out how long until he came back.

"He didn't get far," she said in a low voice.

"You got him?" I asked as I handed her one of the dead guard's short swords.

She didn't reply immediately, but eventually her voice found a way out. "I couldn't let him get out."

I recognized the sorrow of a new kill, the penance I once felt at the weight of my hands interrupting a life. So instead of questioning her further, I increased my pace and followed her through the remaining tunnels.

◆

We walked silently and more somberly than before on our way out of the sewage system on the outskirts of town. We left the tunnels beyond the hills that housed the slums and near a small river that went all the way to the ocean.

I climbed the path to the top of the hill to take one last look at the city. My eyes traced the edges of the distant orange cliffs and the seaside beyond it. The horizon slowly turning lighter as dawn approached.

The ocean had been my first sight of Nuri years before, its white sandy beaches, the terracotta cliffs, and the stunning view of the palace were a few of the things that made me fall in love with the city. It seemed fitting this would also be my last sight of the capital.

Ruby waited for me, seated on a large rock, facing the breaking dawn. Under the warm light of the early sun, I could see how beautiful she really was behind the rugged and worn-out clothes. How delicate behind the apparent fierceness.

"Thank you," I said in a small, sincere voice.

It was enough to break whatever thoughts or memories had seized her.

"My pleasure." She offered me a delicate head bow, a quiet smile cracking her gloomy surface and chasing away some of the sorrow I'd seen on the tunnels.

"Was it your first kill?" I asked.

A shadowed look flickered as she shook her head.

"Not the first, but I still hate it."

"Why did you do it?"

"They would have killed you."

"You owe me nothing," I said, surprised at the sincerity in her voice.

She faced the sky and took a deep breath and, for a second, I thought she was going to say something, but then she seemed to think better of it. In a blink, the pensive expression was gone.

"You didn't owe me anything either."

I'd gone back for her. I couldn't fully explain why.

"You know who I am." I remembered her words in the tunnel.

"I bet the whole city knows your name by now." She chuckled, never looking away from the sunrise. "But that doesn't mean I know who you are."

I nodded. Once again, an unexpected gratitude filled me at her lack of judgement.

She took a deep breath and got up, as if storing away the sadness before asking with a brighter voice, "Where to now?"

"North."

"Ok." She started walking towards the green field behind her. "This path should lead north, but that's as far as my knowledge of the area goes."

"Wait!" I said in surprise. "Thank you, but you can go back now. I'll be fine."

"I have nothing to go back to." She shrugged. "It is beyond time I accept that."

"Not every escape is good." I managed to push the words out of my mouth. More edged than I wanted it to sound.

"I'm not escaping, I'm moving on." The edge of a sweet smile. "I might as well keep you company as I do it."

"You don't even know me. You said so yourself."

"True. But I know you were the first one to come back for me in a very, very long time, and that is enough to make me wanna change that," she said in a thick voice.

I truly noticed her eyes for the first time, as brown and rich as warm caramel, as bright as beacons of hope and gentleness. Whatever demons she'd faced had not been enough to break her, or dull the light in her.

She'd saved my life. She'd been the first to do that in a very long time. The only one to do it without a hidden agenda.

In that second with only the green fields and the new sky as my witnesses, I thought of Ivo and all he'd done for me and to me. I thought of what he'd made me into.

I wished I could trust her. I wished I could one day fix the broken parts of me, if only to deserve that unexpected, blind kindness.

"Fine," I said quietly, as I joined her.

For the rest of the day, we walked away from the river, the city, without ever looking back.

Chapter 14

There was an unexpected beauty to the Golden Sea.

After a month of hard travel through half-hidden tracks, the famous green fields beyond Nuri slowly gave way to a mesmerizing, live savannah. A sea of yellow and green and white.

Tall paepalanthus flowers unrolled in an uninterrupted wave to the far horizon. Thick brown stems as high as my knees, each flower a bright green and yellow core giving way to dozens of wide and delicate florets tipped in pure white.

Under the golden sun on the mid-afternoon, life poured from all around us and beneath the cloudless, blue sky.

The savannah covered most of the northern Niram territory, stretching from the edge of the capital to the distant border at the base of the mountains. Uninterrupted miles of plain fields sometimes covered with flowery valleys and large ponds, sometimes with no more than tall grass and twisted trees. As I breathed the fresh air, watched the clean water, and listened to wild birds I couldn't help but feel in awe of the peaceful beauty, nature and the life that went on despite my own struggles.

This far from the capital, there were none of the leafy trees that required magic to thrive. Here, away from the hands of earth wielders, the trees were taller and more real, their leaves less prominent and yet more beautiful. The villages no more than a single street full of white-wood, plank houses. We'd crossed from the city, into nature's domain.

There was a quaint beauty to the landscape, inviting and enticing. In those last days of summer, it was almost too easy to get lost in the scenery, in the pleasantness of the days, in the silent invitation of every creek.

A part of me wished I could simply enjoy the crystal-clear water, lazy afternoon sunsets, and starry skies that accompanied us every day. Sometimes we did just that. Allowing ourselves that small indulgence.

For the first few days, fear and worry trailed our every step. No matter we didn't see any trace of soldiers, no matter we stayed away from any towns, all I could think about was getting North.

Until we reached a small lake. Until Ruby shoved me inside and jumped after me. The cold shock of the fresh water was enough to startle me out of my emotional turmoil and with every laugh I felt some of the fear loosen and give way to surprised easiness.

That was the first night I honed Ruby's knife and short sword, before falling into a deep dreamless sleep.

"Thank you," she murmured when she woke up to find the weapons resting by her side.

"Not used to taking care of them, are you?" I asked.

"Never really learned how."

"I could show you," I offered and after the silence stretched for a few seconds added, "could show you how to use them as well."

She nodded and thanked me, but it still took her a few more weeks to accept my offer.

Yet, despite the easy camaraderie building between us, we *were* fleeing. Running from the king's guard. A knowledge that danced in our minds and tinted every conversation we had.

We didn't dare stray too far from the occasional villages without a map and yet we never risked the larger cities and main roads. We dwelled on the quiet limb between the small towns and wild fields.

We walked for as long as the sunlight allowed and rested only in the dark hours of the night. We ate nimble animals and small, bitter fruits, and I missed the luxury of my bed and the scrumptious food from the palace. But we carried on, day after day.

Until, one night, I noticed the sky.

It was starry and bright. The Dragon Stars were almost invisible, disappearing over the horizon. Soon, the constellation would vanish from the sky and the preparations for New Year's celebration would keep the whole country busy. A month later, like magic, the Dragon would once again emerge, and with it a new year would begin.

That day, the first, was my favorite of the year. It was a small flower in bloom, a new dawn, an ellipsis sentence. It was a magical moment when history could be created, and even my wildest dreams were possible.

If only I could hold on to that feeling.

"Are we quieting, raging, or crying?" Ruby asked as she laid by my side.

"Quieting, I guess."

Not even a minute later she said, "What was it like? Living in a palace?"

"Weren't we supposed to be quiet?" warmth in my voice.

"Sure ... if that was what you wanted. But we both know it's not. So, how was it?"

I sighed before replying: "It was restrictive, but damn luxurious. Most of all it was lonely."

"Sounds wonderfully horrible."

"It was." I laughed. "But the food. Fuck, the food!"

"Well, you have my company now. Which I can only assume is much better."

I winced exaggeratedly.

"What?"

"Well ... it's just that the food ..."

She elbowed me playfully. "Was it as fancy as people say?"

I considered what type of gossip would reach the slums, how the palace excesses would look to people who had little more than a day's meal in their belly and the blue sky over their heads.

"More," I finally said. "But you know what I miss the most?"

She waited silently, studying the skies.

"The library," I said wondering if it was for the books or for Aiden's presence. "And dream cakes!"

"What a fuck is a dream cake?"

I looked at her, perplexed. "You never had one?"

"I never *heard* about one."

"Think a fluffy bun, stuffed with vanilla custard and sprinkled with sugar. It is like eating a sugary cloud."

"I'll take your word for it." Laughter lingered in her voice.

"Maybe I'll take you to a bakery one day."

"I'd like that."

We fell asleep talking about palace luxuries and food. The next day, we made our way towards one of the villages.

"If I'm not back in an hour you keep going north, ok?" I told Ruby, as we observed the little town from a distance, hidden by tall flowers.

She looked at me bluntly, pure defiance in the lines of her jaw.

"Like hell you are going there."

I sighed. "Thanks for the concern, but I'll be fine. No one is looking for a Priestess." I carefully unfolded the robes I'd cleaned in a creek days before.

"You couldn't pass for a Priestess in a million years." She fought to hold on to a chuckle.

Her disbelief was a bit disheartening, but I ignored it. "It served me well enough last time."

"Well, last time it wasn't the middle of the day and you were mostly hiding. So, I wouldn't count it as a win." She yanked the robes from my hand and started putting them over her own shoulders.

"No! They saw you with me, Ruby, and if they catch you …" I wasn't sure if I was more afraid of them catching her or breaking her. "It is better if I don't risk it." My voice was more tired than I'd expected. More sincere than I wanted.

She was a survivor, not a warrior. What kept her alive were her wits, not her training. If someone found her, there was no way she could fight her way back to me.

She smiled. Soft and oblivious.

"I doubt they even noticed me. But even if they did,

they are either looking for two people or for an entitled, white, fake priestess." She pointed at me. "I intend to give them a feverous, black devotee," pointing at herself. "It is ok, Aila. The Mother will keep me safe. She always has."

I knew she was truly a follower of the Goddess – not that She had guarded her before – and that even though she'd been on the streets for longer than she should have been, it never corrupted or broke her.

She had seen the same cruelty and felt the same pain as I had, and yet she turned out my opposite in every way that counted. She turned disappointment into decency, hardship into an innate virtue and sorrow into hope. In more ways than one, this half-reckless and impossibly wise girl made me believe in a better version of myself.

I'd grown used to her careless joy and genuine bravery and somewhere over the course of those days, I had truly started enjoying her company. I didn't know then how much she would change me; how much she would become a part of my life. All I knew was I didn't want to lose her. Not yet.

"Be careful, please," I said looking in her eyes as I placed the few coins I had in her hands and wished her Goddess would truly keep her safe this time.

◆

The last rays of sun were tinting the sky an intense orange when Ruby finally came back. I had been pacing the same spot for hours.

At first, I kept to the now familiar routine and set out a small camp. It was better to keep my mind busy than to allow it to wander back to Ruby or the palace. So, I found the clearing we'd scouted earlier, placed our few things behind a large rock and collected enough wood for a few hours of fire.

I summoned tendrils of darkness to clear the ground of our small camp area. I'd started using my magic at every opportunity and the irony of using my power even in the smallest of tasks was not lost on me. I had been so afraid of relying on it that I'd never allowed myself to discover how deep the well ran.

Ivo couldn't have procured anyone to teach me without revealing what I really was, but he found me every book he could on arcane theory and history. He encouraged me to learn my true power, said it was a part of who I was.

In spite of that, I was desperately afraid of being found. So intent on keeping my power a secret that I never truly explored it. Never learned how much I was capable of summoning.

A wielder's power was always limited, the core of their magic naturally finite, even if that limit could be stretched with training. Proper dedication could increase control of an element, reduce the energy required to summon and lessen the time to recovery. Proper training was the difference between commanding an element and being consumed by it.

Now that I had no secret to keep and the whole of the Royal Guard was hunting me, there was no point in hiding. So, I trained, pushed my limits, and learned how to stretch my energy.

I used the endless days in the fields to descend into the pit of Darkness in my soul and explore it, until I learned to truly wield it, until I came to cherish it like I never had before.

Turns out building my magic fortitude was

exhausting, tiring like nothing I'd done before. It was also liberating.

For the first time, I felt free. Free from the secrets, free from the need to hide, free from the fear of judgement.

Free to find out who I really wanted to be.

For better or worse, Ruby seemed fascinated by the dark, never afraid of it. And every time she didn't balk from it, I felt a little bit surer, a little bit more focused.

As I paced the clearing, and the hours passed by, I couldn't stop worrying that someone would recognize her, that staying close to me would harm her, until she finally stepped into the clearing, briskly as ever. She had a satchel of old bread and soft cheese, some apples, and a bottle of wine and was oblivious to my spiraling thoughts and dark temper.

"This should last us for about three or four days - I couldn't risk bringing more without raising suspicions."

"Where the hell were you?" I asked searching her for any signs of hurt.

"Getting information," she replied matter-of-factly. "Relax and drink." She tossed me the bottle of wine.

I drank enough to placate my thirst, but not nearly enough to quench my worries. She waited with squared shoulders and hard eyes, the most serious I'd seen her.

"Look." Her voice was kind but firm. "I'm new to this whole 'being cared for' thing, but I'm not a child, in case you didn't notice. I can take care of myself; I wouldn't have survived if I couldn't. So, you have to stop worrying and treating me like an innocent bystander."

She was filled with unwavering determination. She was also right. She had done fine without me hovering over her, better than I had on my own, at least.

"Ok. But you have to be careful! They won't be

kind."

She nodded in agreement. "That is *not* an understatement."

I sighed at her remark and reached for the food, offering her some pieces of cheese and bread.

"I ate at the tavern."

"So, what's the news?" I asked half-heartedly.

"They don't have a very good description yet, but you really do have half the Kingdom looking for you. At least they want you alive and they think you are traveling alone."

That *was* good news. If we were lucky, we would get to Urian before anyone recognized us.

"Do you know where they are searching?"

"Random sweeps. No one seemed to pinpoint a location."

Ivo knew me as well as I knew him. Better. Because infuriating as it was, even now I felt he was one step ahead.

He knew I had been in his office and, by now, he knew what I had taken from there. He would have found Aiden's ring and the half-written letter on my desk. He would have guessed what I was looking for even if he didn't know why.

I thought about Dara, serious and loyal Dara, about the truth she'd offered me before I left. *I hope I can thank her one day.*

"They will be monitoring the Tlaloc border," I spoke the thought out loud. I didn't believe Dara had told Ivo about her parting gift. So Ivo might as well think I was just searching for leverage. Presumably, he'd dismiss the letter for the Alliance reports as a desperate way out of his command. He would still use it to prove my guilt, but I didn't think he would pursue it. Not yet, not until he had to turn his eyes to

Urian and the Alliance, but by that time I expected to be long gone.

"Why?"

"They may have reason to believe I would look for …" I searched for the right word, but not even I knew what exactly that was. "Information there."

"Are you?"

"Not there, no. We need to get to Urian before they have reason to think otherwise. We need a big city; we need a map."

"We are two weeks away from Kait."

I considered. Kait was the second largest city in Niram. It would be swarming with guards, at best, and courtiers who might recognize me, at worst.

It was still my best chance.

"Ok. We leave at first light."

She nodded. "So, are you finally going to tell me how you got half the Kingdom after you?"

If she was going to cross half the world, she needed to know exactly what she was getting herself into. And with whom.

"I guess you just need to piss off the right man."

She smiled and I continued.

"There were two murders at the palace. The Prince thinks I'm behind both."

"Are you?"

"Does it matter?" I asked half hoping I could keep her from knowing *that* side of me a little while longer.

"It does," she said simply.

"Not both. I did kill someone that night. I killed more than once that night." She had seen some of those.

"Why?"

"Because I didn't think I had another choice? Because I was running, and they were in the way?" I took a deep shuddering breath. "Because I was trying to protect someone I cared very much about?"

"Killing is rarely the best way to protect someone, Aila." A gentle, wise reminder wrapped in an echo of sorrow.

I smiled a pained smile. Full of lost promises and broken memories.

"It is the only way I have ever learned." My voice was rough, and I didn't stop her as she closed the distance between us. "I was made for lying and killing, Ruby. Those are the only things you'll find by my side."

"I don't believe that."

"You don't really know me," I reminded her.

"You've cared for me. You came back for me."

"I killed for you, Ruby!" My fading smile felt bitter and rotten, tainted with the last words I'd exchanged with Aiden. Pained by the lies I knew Ivo would be feeding him, the lies I'd made so easy for him to believe.

It was time for her to see me for who I truly was. So, with a deep breath, I continued:

"You are strong and bright, Ruby. I'm not. I've never been … I trusted the wrong people, and I let them turn me into something dark. I relished it, savored how it kept the fear at bay. The world tried to destroy me, so I learned how to make it burn."

She stayed quiet for a long time, long enough for the stars and the moon to conquer the dark sky above us.

"I'm not strong and bright, Aila. I just choose hope over hate, life over death. I choose to make the world worth living for. Especially when it threatens to destroy me."

◆

I slipped into an unconscious world of pain and blood.

The streets around me were drenched in gore as I searched for refuge in the wreckage of the village. I barely registered the destruction of the houses and the bodies of the people who had cared for me in my few, short years.

Screams grew louder, and I knew the few men standing wouldn't be alive for much longer. There were no wielders, the King didn't think they would be needed against a handful of farmers and peasants. He was right.

There was no organized attack, no military precision. Just chaos and noise and stench. Too fast and too strong for me to do anything other than hide, breathless and trembling. I half-expected the noises of a massacre to be metallic, but what I heard the most was the swoosh of sword against flesh and the never-ending dripping of blood.

Until silence started to fill the air and I became unable to move. That was the first time I knew the paralyzing fear of death. Soldiers started to turn against the few women and children hiding. No light nor humanity in their faces. Just numbness disguised as a lingering desire for death and a rising thirst for pleasure.

It wasn't long until one of the soldiers marked me. Our gazes locked and over what felt like an eternity he peered at my bloodied arms, taking in the small body behind the ragged clothes, assessing how much he would enjoy it – me.

The wolfish smile that pulled at his lips spurred me into action. I didn't know how to use my power and there was no calming my mind to keep it hidden, so I willed myself to run, leaving a trail of uncontrolled shadows in my wake. He chased harder, the want on his face replaced by rage.

I crashed against broad shoulders and strong arms, darkness uncontrolled around me, enveloping both of us.

Except, this time, when I looked up, I didn't see the face I'd seen twenty years before; it wasn't Ivo's slick hair and triumphant smile facing me. For once, I didn't relive the moment in which he saved my life and gained control over my soul.

This time, I saw the face I'd come to admire. I saw shiny armor with Niram's fiery crown stained in blood. I saw Aiden, holding me tightly and ominously as he said, *"Guards,"* right before I jolted, suddenly awake.

◆

"It's ok! It's just me!" Ruby repeated crouching before me, holding my face. Her voice was certain and constant, not bothered by the dagger I had put to her throat in a reflex.

I don't know how many times she had repeated the same words before I understood that I was in the Golden Sea, safe. How long she kneeled before me until I could feel the cold air of the night on my face and force my lungs to take long and deep breaths. I put the dagger back under the bag I was using as a pillow and murmured, "Sorry."

She offered me a cup of her nightly tea. It was sweet and soothing with a crisp tang of peppermint.

Tension gnawed at me and my thoughts spun out of control.

For the past few weeks I'd tried to keep my focus on what I had to do, on what I needed to find. I'd kept thoughts of Aiden and Ivo at bay, but still they ate at me, day after day.

They were looking for me and because they were the only father and friend I had known for a long time, and I loved them, I didn't fully want to flee from them.

I couldn't rest until I faced them again. Until I got answers and spilled truths.

Anger and frustration seized me once again, that same voice roaring inside of me. What chance did I have to get answers when my master knew me so well? When Aiden had the whole guard hunting me? What chance did I truly have to escape the destiny in which Ivo had so carefully trapped me?

My life had never been a blessed safe haven, it was a luxurious prison bounded by secrets and fear. And even if Ivo built the cage, I had only myself to blame for believing in it.

As it always happened, Flynn found his way into my messy thoughts. It innerved me that I didn't understand him, as much as it enraged me that I felt so attached to him. He'd questioned and helped me. The more I thought about it, the less I understood why.

Then there was Valran. Flynn was the only person who could have got close enough to kill him, but why would he? A captain would never be able to claim his position as premier. Maybe he wanted to increase his influence? Make himself essential to whomever replaced Valran?

The tea's warmth and deep breaths slowly calmed my senses. When I finally spoke, my anger was safely leashed.

"I now understand why people drink this. Thank you."

"My mum used to say there was nothing a good cup of tea couldn't fix. She offered me one, every night before bed."

I smiled, silent.

"Are you ok?" she asked.

I nodded and added, "Just a silly nightmare."

"It didn't sound silly. Wanna talk about it?"

I considered her question, but even as I knew I would feel relieved to open up about my unspoken story, to rely on someone other than myself for once, I still couldn't force the words out, couldn't bring myself to trust anyone else with that deepest piece of me.

"I think some things are better left unsaid."

She finished her tea, eyes fully on the dark space where the remnants of our fire were still glowing.

"You know, I've been thinking a lot about my mum these past weeks. I think she would have liked you."

Ruby had never talked about her family before, and there was pure love and bitter sorrow in her voice.

"I doubt she would think I'm a good influence on you."

"I think she would find you loyal. Yeah, you have issues, clearly," she added gawking at me, "but you're all right."

I remained in silence, raw emotion stopping me from joining her little attempt at humor.

"My mum was beautiful, and so bright," she started in a small voice after a deep breath. A faint smile danced across her face. "She was the life of every party and even with no money she made our lives so magical. She wanted to show us the world someday. Me and my brother, I mean."

Her eyes dulled and her smile slowly vanished as she continued.

"Eight years ago, a customer, a fire wielder, followed her home. He thought he was entitled to more than the drinks and food she'd served him earlier. He looked like a warrior, or a mercenary, I still don't know how to tell them apart." She shrugged, pain coating her voice. "I just know he was much stronger than the both of us."

"My mum distracted him so me and my brother could flee, but I couldn't. I tried and I couldn't." Her voice broke and she continued in barely more than a whisper. "I shoved my brother through the window and told him to run, I promised I would find him later."

She seemed to have lost herself somewhere between remembering and reliving it, but eventually, she clenched her fists and forced the words out.

"He killed her and burned our house while I watched. I was too paralyzed to do anything, too afraid to kill him, and *she* paid for it," she finished in a haste, jumping through the words as if she couldn't bring herself to dwell too much on them.

I reached for her hand, holding it tight in mine.

"It's not your fault, Ruby. You couldn't have done anything."

She tried to smile at me, but it was hollow and sad.

"Your brother?" I asked.

She shook her head. "I've searched for him every day, but I never saw him again. I failed her twice that night and for the past eight years, I've been too afraid to accept it."

Her shoulders were tense and her hands cold and sweaty. I could see in her eyes she blamed herself; she had been holding on to guilt rather than grief. It pained me.

"You were just a child. I'm sure you were fierce, but you were still just a child." I tried to speak as softly as I knew how. Anguished by the cruel reality that I had never learnt how to offer kind words and friendly support. Never needed to.

"I know," she said.

The only choice we both had was to continue to

move, to continue to hope.

"I'll help you find him. Your brother," I said into the night. "One day, we'll find him."

We held hands and sat together until she broke the silence again.

"I told you about my mum because you gave me the courage to stop feeling paralyzed by her loss and start trying to live again. I told you because when I saw you fighting for our lives with all you had, for the first time in a long time, I wanted to do the same, no matter the price." She took a deep breath, head dropping, and continued in a small voice, "I know you have killed people, but I don't think it makes you a killer. A killer wouldn't have come back for me."

Chapter 15

Every step away from Nuri was laced with clarity and peace. In the midst of the never-ending savanna, with no one but a bright girl for company, I was, in many ways, free.

Free from spy missions, free to use my magic, free to laugh. The more I did, the more I stopped missing the false safety of my gilded cage and started letting go of my fear.

Until Kait emerged from the horizon.

If Nuri was the jewel of the Crown, all rich streets and buzzing commerce, Kait was its heart, a place of arts and delightful quietness. It was the destination of most nobles during the warm summer months, and one of the places I had always dreamt of visiting. It pained me that I would do it under dreadful circumstances.

"We keep our distance inside, ok? We don't let anyone know we are traveling together," I declared before we left the cover of the trees.

"Aren't you being just a tad over-dramatic? None of

the cities before us got more than a verbal description of you. Not even a good one, by the way. Half the guards I saw wouldn't recognize you if you kicked them in the balls."

"Yeah, yeah. But Kait is a big city, and many courtiers spend part of the summer here. Someone could recognize me. I'm not risking it."

I gave her the familiar robes and tucked her cloak around my shoulders. There was no need to hide the sheathed weapons as we travelled through the rough roads; in fact, I made a point of keeping most of them visible and easily accessible as I pulled the hood of Ruby's green cloak over my head and waited for her to gain some distance before following.

Nothing I'd heard about Kait prepared me for its beauty, nothing did it justice. The city was perfectly placed around a crystalline lake at the foot of a mountain plateau. A large marble arc, flanked by unending white walls, marked the entrance of the city, and gave way to a paved road that led straight to the lakeshore.

Countless houses sat orderly in perfectly neat streets, built not to intrude on the view, but to frame it, enhance it with pastel colors and expensive materials. Everything in the city was designed to enchant and delight.

Dusk had taken over the place when we arrived, and I couldn't stop myself from gasping at the view. The last of the sun was still nestling behind the flowery hills on the west edge of the city, the final luminosity giving way to thousands of small glass lamps hanging on tree branches and nearly invisible poles across the streets. Small orange flames, burst to life in a breath-taking wave of dimmed, magical light, no doubt powered by the fire magic that ran in so many of Niram's traditional families.

No one stopped me as I crossed the entry arc, too distracted to look for signs of the royal guard. I didn't halt until I was facing the lake, mesmerized by the movement and brightness of the hanging lights following the shoreline and encompassing the city profile in playful shadows.

In another life, I could have spent hours exploring the streets beyond and surrendering to the beauty and tranquility of the lake.

Ruby remained ahead of me, seemingly as awestruck as myself, but no one paid attention to either of us. For a few glorious moments we were lost in surprising anonymity, nothing more than two of the many travelers passing through the famous ethereal city.

But Kait was still a large city, with a likely well-informed guard. I forced myself to focus on what lay beneath the fairytale beauty and started observing the movement around me, searching for signs of the royal guard, listening for whispers of my name and sketches with my face stamped on it.

There was none. Yet.

Ruby moved firmly away from the main street, searching for a pub where we wouldn't draw too much attention – *"nice enough to draw a small crowd and cheap enough not to have many sober souls,"* she had said earlier.

It didn't take her very long to find a two-story corner pub that fit the description. She made her way swiftly among drunken farmers and through the doors. From a distance, the pink flowerpots hanging from the black windows made the building rather charming. It could pass as an expensive and stylish establishment, but a closer look showed the cracked paint and chipped window frames.

I followed her inside, finding a place at a half-hidden

table at the end of the saloon as she made her way upstairs, a barmaid in tow with bread and wine.

Loud laughter and conversation flew through the room, eased by the constant flow of alcohol. Most of the people there were either too drunk or too distracted to notice me. I studied the area, the people and soon bits of conversation reached my ears freely, bringing news of the city and the Kingdom beyond.

Inconsequential gossip gave way to news as three recruits sat behind me, teasing and chatting.

They were barely over their first round of ale when they caught my attention.

"Do you believe him?" said the one on the right.

"What? That she's behind the Alliance? Nah! Too young to be causing so much trouble." The one on the left offered. Adam, they'd called him.

"*I* heard they almost killed the king," the one in the middle said with surprising certainty.

The other two laughed openly and Adam eventually responded,

"You've lost it, Brian!" Another laugh erupted before he could finish, breathless. "A girl? No girl can pass the Royal guard."

"That's why she seduced him. Tried to kill him in his bed," Brian added even more seriously.

The other two fell into a roaring laugh and I wasn't sure if I was offended or amused. Either way, it was clear some sort of news – or misinformed gossip – had reached Kait.

"Why else would they be hunting her so fiercely? Killing so many?" Brian asked with a tint of resentment and defiance.

None of them replied immediately, the laughter snuffed out of them, replaced by solemn silence.

The third one broke the silence.:

"Maybe she *is* their leader and they just found her now … I mean, why else would the Premier be doing the raids now? The public trials?"

"Trials! That is a nice word for the carnage," said the quieter one, resentment leaking from his voice. "You've known half of those people your whole life. They have nothing to do with the rebels."

Another silence fell between them. This time grim and heavy.

No-one other than Ivo could have been appointed Premier so quickly, I knew he would try to discredit me, to ensure I couldn't reveal any of his secrets. But what was the point of connecting me with the Alliance?

Was he just using the easy narrative I had inadvertently built for him to consolidate his hold on the Premier position? Or was there something else behind his move?

It didn't matter that I wasn't sure what was driving him, I recognized his resolve. I knew he would not stop until I – and everything I knew about him – was destroyed. If waging war against every innocent city he could find helped him do that, he would not hesitate.

"Do you really think he is killing this many people just to get to her?" Brian asked in a whisper.

"I think some girl messed things up in the palace. Right under everyone's nose. Now he will kill whomever he needs to stop the whole Kingdom from finding out."

The boy had no idea how right he was, no idea of what was still to come.

I couldn't listen anymore.

Ivo's face crossed my mind, the sweet, silver-lined smile that I so rarely saw, mocking me, teasing me. The father I wished for, but no longer knew if I'd ever had. I knew he could be cruel; I knew how much he loved power, yet a silly part of me believed there would be a limit. I believed there was at least a few lines he would not dare cross.

But this was the man who had hunted a five-year-old for Goddess knows what reason.

I could feel the ravenous voice bellowing in my core again. The Alliance's cause was never mine, but Ivo was hunting them just so he could flush me out. *How many more lives will he destroy to keep me under control? How much more death will I be responsible for before the end?*

Because that was the truth of it, whether I was dealing the killing blow or not, all this blood was on my hands.

For better or worse, I had nothing else to lose. Nothing but rage and violence waiting to roam free. Nothing but the inevitable question of how much more hurt he would cause before I started hurting him back.

And this time, I would not hold back.

◆

When I snuck onto the second floor and found the sign Ruby had left on the door, she was already peacefully asleep in the narrow bed.

The room was rustic, but clean. It could have been a charming place once, but now the old furniture made it shabby and cheap. It had no more than a narrow bed, a small table with two chairs and a large trunk.

Across from the door, a round window gave view to

the thousands of hanging flames covering the city and casting a faint, yellow light on the room. It was at its foot that I sat down, spreading all the little clues I had from Ivo's office once again.

At first those letters reminded me even more of the pain and hatred in Aiden's eyes when he finally truly saw me.

Still, as much as losing the comfort of that relationship pained me, I couldn't change the last few months any more than I could change who I really was.

I learned to live with the pain and sorrow, and I told myself there was still time for me to find my way back to him. As long as I was still alive, there would always be time for him to hear the truth and, maybe, for us to find out what could have existed beneath the masks and lies.

"You look like shit." Ruby's voice startled me, taking my thoughts away from Ivo.

I looked through the window to find dawn lurking behind the small buildings and was suddenly aware of my tiredness and hunger.

"Good morning to you too," I said not getting a hold of my temper.

She ignored me and jerked her chin towards the pieces of paper in front of me.

"What's all this?"

I lost a long breath before putting it all away. "A puzzle ... one we can solve later."

"Did you hear something last night?" she asked helping me fold the letters.

"Well, they want me. Badly. But no surprises there." I shrugged. "At least I don't think they know I'm traveling with you."

"Who exactly are *they*?"

"The guard, the prince, the premier, maybe the King himself." I threw my hands in the air and looked at her. "At this point, does it even matter?"

"No," she said after barely a second. "So we stick together from now on. Throw them off."

I considered her suggestion, it would make it easier to blend in if they were specifically looking for a loner, but that was relying too much on the speed of communication between the cities. Relying on them having nothing other than a verbal description – a bad one.

I shook my head. "I don't know how good of a description they have of me, who we may cross paths with. It is still too risky, Ruby. They don't know about you for now, and I intend to keep it that way for as long as I can."

"Then what?"

We needed to leave as quickly as possible, with as much information as we can. I wouldn't risk another big city even if there was one between us and Urian.

"What do you know about the rebels?" I asked her as I finished storing everything safely in my over-used, dirty bag.

"The Alliance?" Surprise lifted in her voice.

I nodded, aware it would take too long to explain it fully.

"Not much, really. Why? What do they have to do with us?"

I took a moment, trying to figure out how to explain it simply and quickly. We didn't have time for the story of my life, and yet it felt like everything that was happening had started long before Ivo invited me to that ball. In a way it felt as if it all had started long before he even found me.

"Ivo is spreading rumors that I'm connected to them,

that what happened at the palace was an attempt on the king's life. It's his power play. He gets to destroy the biggest threat to the Elementalists and bury all the secrets I know with a single move." *Nothing short of brilliant.*

Her eyes narrowed at his name. Everyone in Nuri knew of him. People at the palace knew of his influence and money, but the ones living on the streets knew of his power. That is where he took his pick of his lower spies, where he used violence to command and to compel, and no matter how secretive he was, some whispers are just too important not to be shared in deep, dark holes.

"Ivo? As in Ivo Timal?" Uncertainty tainted her tone.

I nodded. "Newly appointed premier."

A flash of fear crossed her as she realized the amount of power he now controlled - second to none but the King himself. And a second later, a deep frown appeared between her eyebrows as she noted the intimacy in which I referred to him.

"You need to give me some serious answers, Aila." she finally let out in a burst.

I took a deep breath and nodded. She had never pushed me to reveal anything I wasn't ready for, but there was no dancing around it anymore, no sugar-coating it either.

"For years, Ivo was the spy master for the Kingdom. But that was never his biggest secret. He saved my life and raised me from a very young age. He is the closest thing I ever had to a father, the only family I truly knew. He protected me and cared for me, he kept me safe. More importantly, he trained me relentlessly, turned me into a weapon, a spy." I didn't dare look at her as I spoke. "Then, he took me to court a couple of years ago and infiltrated me into the highest circles, hidden from everyone, including the king."

I paused for a second, unable to talk about Aiden. Still not wanting to volunteer that piece of my story, that piece of my guilt.

"I've been loyal to him and to the safety he offered me. Until ... until I wasn't. I chose someone else's life over his ambitions. Which means he no longer trusts me to keep his secrets, and for that alone he will hunt me to the end of the world."

I let out a shuddered breath: "I also killed someone he cared for, so whenever he catches me, he will make sure I beg for death. And he'll do the same to anyone helping me. He'll do *worse*, to anyone who helps me."

To her credit, she didn't budge, didn't flinch. When I faced her, she had that fierce expression, again. The same resolve I'd seen when we left Nuri.

"He knows about your magic?" she asked.

"He knows everything there is to know about me. He knows more than I do," I scoffed.

She nodded. "What do you want with the Alliance?"

"I don't know yet. I need something to help me fight Ivo and during my last job he was very intent on keeping me far away from them. He never interfered before, but he did it this time and I can't stop thinking that there is a reason for that."

She nodded. "All I know is they have strongholds in all the Kingdoms. They whisper in the streets, calling for people who dream of change – wielders or not. I've heard their calling in Nuri a few times, but I never followed. I once heard they have a base somewhere in the north and they are preparing for something big."

"How would one find them? Join them?"

"People on the street spread their message: kids,

elders. And they watch, searching for those who ask questions, who believe their message. If they trust you, they approach. The thing I always heard is that one doesn't *join* the resistance, one gets chosen, recruited into it."

I reached for her hand and squeezed it in gratitude.

No matter how sound I believed my plan and what I told Ruby, there was another reason why I needed to find them. If anyone could help me make sense of all I'd heard at the Goddess's temple, it would be the people waiting for the impending appearance of the heir.

"Did you hear anything about them waiting for an heir of some kind?"

She shook her head, surprised. And I believed her. All I had seen about the heir was in Ivo's reports or through Aiden's knowledge as next in line to the throne. It was a story only passed among the rebels and snuffed out by the Elementalists since I was a child.

"We need information and supplies. And I want to get out of this city before sundown. The former Premier was monitoring Alliance movements in Urian, and I don't think it will take Ivo long to follow suit."

I was getting back into the calm easiness of planning, my mind welcoming the familiar rhythm. It was the first time in days that I felt like myself. We discussed what we needed to do, what we had seen of the city and the areas we should try to avoid. Ruby would search for directions and supplies; I would search for the Alliance.

"I'll meet you at the main gate in four hours," I told her, as I sheathed a dagger before leaving.

"Be careful," she responded giving me a hug. A strong and welcome hug.

"Ruby, you can still leave, forget you ever met me."

"I'm not hiding again," she said with unwavering determination.

"If I'm not at the gate you leave, ok? Promise me."

I held her softly by the shoulder and stared her in the eyes until she agreed. Then I nodded curtly, leaving the room before she had a chance changed her mind.

Chapter 16

The Goddess medallion felt cold and heavy against my chest. I'd been using it as a disguise for the past few weeks and even though I'd never been a religious person, something about the cold weight of the metal against my bare skin felt comforting as I walked through the city in search of signs of the Alliance.

I had no contacts in Kait and only four hours until I had to meet Ruby, but every big city functioned in a very similar way, if you knew where to look.

I made my way to one of the busy streets in the central area and waited for the pick pockets to appear. It would be easy to follow them into what would likely be a cheap pub in a poor neighbourhood. From there it would be a matter of approaching the right person and hoping they would lead me the right way.

Even though I felt the prickly tension in the air, the restlessness of the guards, I didn't allow myself to stop. It wasn't until I was inside said cheap, alcohol-smelling pub that

I heard whispers that the Royal procession was approaching town.

I jolted. If the Royal family was approaching town, I had to find Ruby. Not landing myself in a dungeon just became priority. I'd find the Alliance later.

The nearer to the central lake I got, the more crowded the streets became. It was a far cry from the peaceful beauty I had witnessed on the previous night. I pushed and shoved my way to the main gate as the conversation around me drifted towards a common topic: the Royal visit and the open trials.

The memory of the previous night's conversation flashed in my mind and I finally realized that whatever trials happened, they happened here. In Kait. It wasn't only the Royal guard that I'd have to worry about, but the Premier as well.

A mix of fear and excitement ran through the rushed conversations around me. No one knew much about the new premier, but they had all witnessed the trials, and they had all heard about the bloody trail he was leaving behind.

I was a few meters away from my meeting point with Ruby. That is, if I could cross the central square unnoticed. I pulled my hood low and peeped at the guards every few steps. Royal guards, clad in the yellow and red livery that I'd grown so accustomed to.

I grew more unsettled with every passing breath and forced step, my hands clammier and my breathing shallower. Before I could leave the crowd behind, I saw the horses approaching, the people's frenzy growing.

Even from a distance, I could see the city gates were flung open, the path from there lined with a throng of onlookers on each side of the street.

A hastily erected wooden dais stood in the center of the square – Niram's flag and Ivo's black banner on a pole by its side. A row of elder prisoners filled the plank, waiting with the sagged postures of those who were already defeated.

And in front of all, Ivo.

My world went impossibly still, impossibly quiet. It had been months since I'd last saw Ivo and, as I gazed at him, there was no familiarity left. I saw nothing of the man who had raised me, trained me, cared for me. Nothing of the man I'd learned to love and fear, whose approval I'd sought for so long. I couldn't help but wonder if I had imagined it all, if I had seen tenderness where there was only pain. For this was not a savior, this was a villain.

This was the man who had lied to me, the man who had destroyed any chance I had at the normalcy I craved. This was the man who owed me answers.

An ember of anger stirred in my core as I studied his tight jaw and cruel eyes under the roaring of the crowd. Maybe for the first time in my life I saw him for what he was: a wicked man with unchecked power. In that moment, I knew he would crush whoever got in his way. With a flinch I realized just how responsible I was for all the power he had and for all the pain he would bring into the world. A burning wrath ignited in my soul, my magic threatening to explode out of me. Even as I grasped for control, even when facing the ugliest lie of my childhood, a small, shameful part of me still had to stifle a sorrowful cry.

He glanced in my direction, and I lowered my gaze, my hands trailing to the daggers hidden under my cloak and my magic collecting around me.

For luck or destiny, something else caught his attention before he saw me.

Horses approached, and the atmosphere changed. The people went in uproar at the sight of the Royal banner and the strong Prince leading the soldiers. Horses, wagons, and foot soldiers marched behind Aiden.

It was disheartening looking at him now. All the pieces I knew so well were still there: the strong jaw line, the fiery hair, the large, strong shoulders. But there was an aloofness, a quiet vileness in his stance. A bitterness that didn't belong with the gentle and vivid memories I carried in my heart.

Ivo bowed deeply to him, and with a simple sign from the premier, the crowd fell silent. Tension filled the air as his voice traveled through the square.

"My Prince. People of Niram." He paused, giving time for his voice to carry. "The Alliance has become daring. They strive to spread dissent among us, to attack our Royal family. But they've failed. They will continue to fail as long as I breathe, for I'll lay down my life for my Kingdom if I have to.

"Today, I bring forth another group of prisoners found guilty in an open trial. They stand ready to submit to their sentence."

The crowd roared again and, with every shout, I flexed my fingers and deepened a bit lower in the well of my magic. Ready to lash out at every one of them.

Thankfully, before I could do anything stupid, a firm hand squeezed my arm in an urgent, trembling touch. Ruby.

"They have children chained in the courthouse. Children!"

Children. I half-listened to Ruby's words, but I was frozen in place.

Ivo was still speaking, Ruby still holding my arm with unusual urgency. Yet, I had stopped hearing them. My mind too consumed with Aiden, too focused on trying to reconcile the man in front of me with the man I cared for.

Ivo's speech was lost in the murkiness of my mind but when Aiden replied, his voice was clear and loud even for me:

"I won't tamper with our justice system. Nor will I offer mercy to those who attack our people."

No-one but me could have noticed the quiver of his voice or the small drop of his chin. No-one but me could notice the discomfort with which he held the pommel of his sword or understand how disgusted he felt at his own words. Despite all of it, he didn't hesitate to condemn the crying women and elders.

Moments later the ten prisoners on the dais were beheaded in a coordinated motion.

I'd grown up believing the Alliance was nothing more than a barbarian group inciting needless violence, yet it was the Kingdom –my master and my friend – spilling innocent blood.

"No," I whispered to no-one as the hope I'd felt of making peace with Aiden was crushed. It was like falling from the razor-edge of a tall cliff, like plummeting into nothingness.

I knew him with all my heart, I knew his quirks, his hopes, his dreams. I knew his heart better than I knew my own. And there was nothing of him in the shell of the man in front of me.

My control must have slipped, for Ruby was shaking me now. A touch of despair in her usually bright face.

"You have to pull yourself together, Aila." She was rushing through the words. "If anyone sees you, we are done for."

I followed her gaze to my hands and only then I noticed the darkness swirling between my fingers, spreading over my body.

The sight of it was enough to take me from my stupor. The feeling of Ruby's hands on my shoulders enough of an anchor for me to leash my magic.

Ruby didn't give me a chance to breathe, she yanked me away from the square, step-after-step until we crossed the city walls.

◆

We walked the whole day, as I battled the cold clutch of guilt and the burning fire of rage. It wasn't until the full moon was high enough in the sky that I remembered her agitation when she found me.

"You were trembling," I said in a throaty voice as we sat down to eat. "What happened?"

"It was nothing. You need to rest." Her own voice was low and sorrowful.

"You said they had children?"

"You heard that?"

"A part of me did. Sorry I was …" I trailed off, not knowing where to begin, how to explain. "Doesn't matter. I'm listening now."

It was a long time before she spoke, and when she did, she blurted the words as if she could no longer hold it in her heart.

"The children were locked away, chained. What will happen to them?" Hands white knuckled with the tension of her closed fists.

"They won't kill them," I said without knowing if it was a reprieve or a curse. "The King will want them for his experiments."

"They are *children*!" She could barely control her rage as she pushed through gritted teeth. "Will no one intercede for them?"

"Aiden would have, once. But ..." I let the words die, reluctant to face the truth of my thought.

"*But* what?"

"The man I knew would never stand by when faced with senseless violence, would never condone it, but it seems I left enough damage in my wake for it not to matter anymore."

And how can I judge him when I have my own sins to atone for?

Because I'd killed to protect my life. I'd murdered under Ivo's command. Even if I made sure every one of those cold-blooded murders were justifiable, every one of those people corrupt and violent criminals, I still had their blood in my hands. How much better did that make me?

"It should matter!" Her face was pure determination. "It *has* to matter! Because those kids were as young as my brother when I lost him, too young to become livestock for heartless wielders. And no matter what you have done, he is *choosing* to ignore this."

I watched her for a moment, seeing the anger seeping through her. A mirror of my own.

I couldn't deny I'd scattered the lies that allowed Ivo to gain Aiden's ear. I'd paved the way. In spite of all that, she was right. He was Niram's heir, and he always had a choice.

Ivo was making his play: he was using me and the Alliance to solidify his hold as Premier as much as he was using Aiden's trust to increase his influence.

He'd finally found a way to use my relationship with Aiden to his advantage. It made me even angrier.

It was time I made a play of my own. It was time he regretted every skill he forced into me. It was time I made him regret finding me, as much as I regretted letting myself love him.

I will make him stop! And I will make him pay, I promised myself.

"Come." I offered Ruby a hand and led her to the closest tree. The short sword I gave her in Nuri at my hand.

We soon found a trunk large enough to take the anger out of us. I lunged the sword against it. Once. Twice. As many times as it took until I could breathe more deeply and think more clearly. Until the rage and guilt faded, leaving nothing but dull pain behind.

Then I made Ruby do the same.

When we were both panting, she asked, "The Prince meant something to you, didn't he?"

"He did. He does."

"Should I hate him? I mean, for besides the obvious reasons?"

I couldn't suppress a tired smile.

"I don't know."

"Will you let me know?"

I nodded and after a few moments of silence, I let the thought I'd been trying to ignore, find its way to my lips.

"I wonder if I broke all that was good inside of him, Ruby."

"I don't think anyone but him has the power to do that, Aila."

I knew she was right, even if it didn't ease the pain in my heart. I knew she was right.

◆

We kept a rigorous pace during the following weeks, an unforgiving routine that kept us walking from dawn to dusk. New Year came and went without a hint of hope or celebration.

We complained about the hard floor and dry bread, exchanged few words and made quick and quiet progress, but I spent most of my days lost in thought.

I still missed the comfort and protection of the palace walls, the sense of belonging and purpose, as fake as it was, but most of all, I missed Aiden's presence. The lack of his vivid laugh and simple humor left a hole in my chest, a space I didn't even know he had occupied so thoroughly. A hole that was suddenly haunted by the image of the cold shell I'd seen in Kait.

I focused my remaining energy on getting to Urian. I had no other leads to follow on this side of the border.

On our last night, with the Urian walls lurking on the horizon, I didn't feel like being quiet anymore. I didn't know how many peaceful nights waited for me and I wasn't ready to part with the easy friendship that had built between myself and Ruby.

I knew she was aware of all the uncertainty ahead of us, that she was as worried as I was. Yet, she hummed a merry tune, absently throwing a small rock between her hands and observing the starry night. That gesture alone was so typically

Ruby that it instantly eased some of the tension in my heart.

I sat and looked at her.

"Have you ever heard about the Goddess having fighters or warriors?" She was the only Goddess follower I knew – apart from Ivo, of course. A bitter smile tugged the corner of my mouth at the thought of asking him to engage in a philosophical conversation.

"No. She gave magic to the world, she blessed healers. But that is it. Maybe one of the old Gods blessed fighters? I never heard anything about it, though," she offered casually.

"How about a thing called the *Moon Stone*?"

"Old scripture stuff, only … a few believe it is a metaphor for the gift of magic, but there are some that believe it to be a real stone used by the first woman to access the power beyond the veil. Sort of like a bridge between the two sides."

I vaguely remembered the religious books Ivo had made me read when I was little. He never forced his faith on me, but he ensured I knew about it and not once had I seen any reference to warriors, heirs or stones in those books.

"I'm surprised *you* heard about it."

"Why?"

She shrugged. "Even among Her followers there are very few people who talk about it. The church doesn't really encourage the common folk to read the scriptures, you know?"

Looked like Ruby was one of those few people. For years, I'd wondered what leads someone to blind obedience to a being that, even if real, doesn't care about anything happening in this world.

"Why do you follow her?" I asked, absently holding the medallion on my chest.

"The Goddess?"

I nodded. "You don't strike me as the brainless type."

She laughed and sat to face me. She reached out for my medallion, trailing her fingers over the intricate details. When she let go, she had a faint smile on her lips.

"Ah! I'm nothing like those idiot pricks at the Cult of the Keeper. They pray on people's belief for the money and power that comes with it." Her smile grew into a grin. "No, I see my Goddess in the world, not inside the walls of a Temple."

"What do you mean?" I couldn't see any difference between following a priest or a God. For me, it all felt useless, even if a part of me longed for the unwavering faith of the believers.

"Well, the church wants us to believe we need priestesses and buildings to connect with the Goddess, to find her blessing. But I believe that She is all around us. She is time and fate. Constantly guarding our paths and the veil between the worlds. She is right here, right now as much as in a temple. The lectures and churches and priests are just mankind's thirst for power."

"Shouldn't She have protected you, then? Your mother?" No judgement or irony, just plain curiosity.

"Who is to say She didn't?" Amusement flickering.

"I don't get it. You lost your whole family, your whole life! Where was She?"

"Well, the way I see it, I'm here with you. I survived, I found a friend, a good one." She winked at me. "She made sure I got exactly where I needed to be, to learn what I have to know, even if I don't understand it."

A part of me was jealous of her certainty and unwavering faith, envious of the belief, of never being alone and helpless.

She continued. "There are old legends that say She is always at the crossroads, guiding us. They say She never truly left our world, just learned how to disguise Her true self. They also say we can recognize Her if we know where to look. And that is the thing: I feel Her, I've felt Her in all the big moments of my life. I know deep in my bones that She is always guarding my path."

Peaceful silence grew between us.

Once again, I remembered the priestess I'd met in the temple, the sound of her voice, the look of her skin and a shiver shook me.

"What would Her true self look like?" I asked in a small voice, gaze dropping to the locket on my hand.

Ruby looked puzzled but replied nonetheless: "I don't know for sure, but if all the legends are to be believed She would be all and nothing, look like part of this world and yet, not. She wanders through the veil and I don't think this is the type of power that can be hidden under flesh. I guess it would be scary and mesmerizing, all at once."

I remembered the feeling of peeking inside the cloak of the hooded priestess in the temple, the cloudy shadows replacing her skin, the glimpses of a face that looked like many and none. A being that looked like nothing I had ever seen. Old and sacred.

All the same, there was no faith or devotion in me, so, even if all those old legends were true, why would a Goddess bother to come to me to talk about heirs and stones and the legend of creation? More importantly, why would she send me to a small town on the edge of the Kingdom?

I guess a part of me knew the woman in the temple was something different, but it was not until Ruby's quiet words echoed through the silent night that I could admit it.

"Ruby, I think I saw her." A small gasp slipped my lungs. "The night I met you. I think she is the one who sent me to Urian. The one who told me about the Moon Stone."

Chapter 17

I don't know what I expected of Urian, but it wasn't that. Not the number of beggars and vendors mixed on the street. Not the high fort in the central square, still bearing Valran's livery. Not the constant flux of guards trailing every street.

There was nothing special about Urian: no relevant roads nearby, no booming merchant market, no trade route.

It was nothing more than a small town lost in the middle of nowhere, its living fully centered on the fort and its military. With a few stalls and pubs around the fort, soldiers and residents mingling and a paralyzed quietness in the air.

Yet, everything about it was special.

The central fort – Valran's former estate – was large and well maintained, a stark contrast to the simple market and the small town.

The proximity to the Alizeh border was strategic but the lack of conflict with that Kingdom and the natural protection the bordering mountain range offered, made the excessive manpower out of place. Unless, this was, indeed an Alliance outpost.

I remembered the maps I'd seen at Valran's office. The sheer number of red crosses in the whole region. It was the only explanation for a couple as ambitious as Lidya and Valran to choose it as their official residence. The only excuse for the Crown to reinforce its military presence to such levels.

The only thing that still didn't make sense was why in hell a Goddess would be so intent on me getting there.

Ruby and I explored the city for the better part of the afternoon, but we could find nothing. No whisper of the Alliance and none of the silent humming of a city with a conflict brewing. Civilians and military coexisted peacefully, or would until Ivo's bloody campaign reached this far north.

We used the last of our coin to secure a cheap room at the edge of the city where we could rest and plan. Ruby had spent the past few years living out on the street and the information it could offer, so tomorrow, she would pry for rumors and knowledge.

Tonight though, I would do my own thing.

I waited until the night was set and the streets quiet before I left the old inn through the back window. I found my way to the fort, cloaking myself in darkness.

It wasn't easy to find a safe and dark path around the building, but eventually I saw an alley from where I could observe one of the side gates. The less well-guarded one.

The guards were more organized than those I'd seen at Valran's capital home: better trained, more alert. Still, there was no high-ranking official in sight at this late hour. I remembered Valran's captain and his overconfident demeanor, the swagger in every movement. If this is where Flynn had spent the two years I'd been in court, I had a feeling these men would be well-trained and well-disciplined.

I let my mind drift to him, and wondered how he'd played my role in Valran's death. He'd helped me escape scrutiny once, but this time I wondered if he was among those hunting me. *Well, I do make a very convenient, and desirable, scapegoat.*

As always, unease grew in me at the thought of him. I hated that I couldn't read his motives as much as I hated that I couldn't predict his actions. It was like walking on uneven ground, like chasing a ghost.

I forced my thoughts back to the reality in front of me: trained guards, a fortified building, no conveniently distracting ball, and no idea what lay beyond the walls. I sure as hell hoped Ruby would find enough information for me to avoid having to brave a break-in.

A break-in started it all, maybe a break-in will end it, the irony was not lost on me. If my own life didn't depend on the dire bet I was about to make, I may have laughed.

The bitter truth was that I was completely adrift in what felt like fate's cruel game. Nothing short of a miracle could save me from doing a very reckless thing.

When I woke up the next day, a warm light gleamed through the empty inn room, a reflection of the orange, painted sky beyond the window.

No sign of Ruby in the room, beyond the discarded clothes on a chair and some food atop the dresser. I sighed, remembering the banquets at court, longing for the dream cakes and chocolates Aiden used to bring to my room. I was sick of the rancid cheese and hard bread we'd been eating for months.

Ruby entered the room minutes after I woke up. A perky walk and bright smile, but I could still see the deeper dark circles under her eyes and the slightly dropped shoulder. She had made a habit of keeping positive and happy, but she was as tired as me.

"Aren't we looking rested today?" she threw in way of greeting.

"Hum ..." was all I offered.

"Not in a good mood, I take it?"

My silence was answer enough as she sat by my side and threw a small paper bag at my lap. A sweet coconut bun inside of it,

"No dream cakes around here, apparently. How was last night?"

I smiled at the small cake. It was dry and flavorless, and we could not afford it, but it was still the sweetest thing I'd tasted in a very long time.

"Where did you get this?"

"I have my ways."

There was no forcing answers out of her, so instead, I said in between one bite and another: "Quiet and gloomy."

The darkness in the room was growing, the afternoon quietly giving way to the night. I twirled long ribbons of shadow around with a flicker of my wrist, drawing them to me, willing them to envelop my hand. Just a small release of the power in me, much like flexing a muscle.

"I wouldn't go as far as to say the soldiers are unbeatable, but they are alert. There is no entering that place without at least knowing the layout first. You?"

She shook her head, letting a deep, breath loose.

"Street kids are usually wary, that is how they survive. What they are not is quiet and shy. Except here. There is not a whisper of anything, it is as if this is the quietest, safest city in the whole world." She dropped herself onto the bed, staring at the ceiling.

"You should rest," I said after a few minutes of silence. "I know you're tired."

"I'll rest when I make those kids talk." The tight sound of exasperation brewed in her voice.

"If somehow an Alliance stronghold survived right under the nose of the former premier, I doubt someone will talk."

"Then what?"

"We'll make do."

"How?"

"Watching, biding our time … learning as much as we can before I need to do something crazy." I shrugged. "We'll need money, though."

"Good thing I found a job, then."

"What?" I turned to her, surprised for the first time since she came back.

"The bakery across the street needed a waitress." She jerked her chin to the empty bag in my hand "I know you don't like it, but we need the money, and we both know you can't risk walking around in broad daylight. Besides, it will give me a chance to get to know people, to hear them."

She didn't have to work too hard to convince me this time. We didn't have another option other than staying alert, waiting and planning. Preferably with a roof over our heads.

She spent most of her following days either at the bakery or working out in the streets in the hope that we would eventually catch the eye of the Alliance.

If the chatter on the streets was to be believed, the movement was growing, fueled by rage at Ivo's campaign and the scattered word about the appearance of a Darkness wielder. Rumors were everywhere, but other than gossip, disguised as news, we heard nothing.

As for me, I spent my nights in the shadows, rotating the alleys around the fort, and when I wasn't counting security patrols, I was tracking guards and officials; I hid in busy taverns as they drank and bitched about their days until I was fairly sure they didn't have a good description of the *"wanted girl from the capital"*. Only then, did I approach them.

We drank, we talked, and I learned as much about the fort layout as sweet smiles and flirty glances allowed me.

Yet, lethargy is a short-lived thing, and we were soon forced out of ours. The Premier was on his way.

◆

Barely a fortnight after we settled in Urian, Ruby raced through the room in the middle of the morning.

"He is marching," she said as the door slammed behind her, jolting me from a shallow sleep.

For the first time since I knew her, there was no measure of calm in her face.

"Ivo?"

She nodded. "He departed Kait a few days back, the men in the bakery were saying he'll be here in less than a fortnight."

"Did they say if he is alone? Or how many men he is bringing?"

I didn't dare asking about Aiden, but if what we saw on Kait was any indication, the Prince wouldn't be too far behind.

"I don't know, I couldn't overhear much more."

I dropped myself back in the bed. "If Ivo is marching again, we can't afford to wait anymore, we have been here for days and there is no sign of the Alliance. I need to be done with this and out of this forsaken city before he gets here."

"What choice do we have?"

"I'll enter the fort. Tonight."

"I thought you didn't know enough."

"I don't," I said as I silently went through every piece of information I'd pieced together. It amounted to very little, but that wouldn't change in a matter of a few days. "I'll find a way."

"Are you planning to try your luck against the contingent of the whole damn fort?"

I sighed: "One of the boys I've been tailing seems rather inexperienced. He'll invite me in."

"He may not."

"Appreciate the confidence," I forced a hurt look, trying to look more humorous than I felt. "Believe me, he will."

"And when you are inside?"

"I'll figure it out, Ruby. I promise you I'll be fine." *I don't have another choice.*

"Is it really worth it?" I heard the streak of fear and uncertainty in her voice.

I considered her question for a long time. I had been asking myself the same thing. Asking myself if I was doing this to find out what Ivo wanted to keep from me, or if deep down I still had hopes I would find something to help me find a way back to Aiden.

"I don't know," I answered, "but right now, Ivo has all the power, and he is using it to kill a lot of innocent people. I need to find something that will make him hesitate, something to help me fight. I have nowhere else to look."

Hopelessness had a way of making people do stupid,

desperate things.

She nodded, something like stubborn resolve flickering in her.

"Then let me help you get in."

"No."

"You'll need someone to watch your back."

"I work alone, I can't get distracted worrying about you, Ruby!" With a sigh, I held her hand and studied her face. "I need you to get out of this city tonight and not look back. I'll find you if I get out of there."

It sounded a lot like a good-bye, even to my own ears. But I wouldn't make the same mistake again. I thought I could protect Aiden, I thought I could keep him close and safe, and all I did was spoil the little we had, break it.

"I can't force you to let me help you, but I won't leave you either. Like it or not, you are not alone!"

Her jaw was tense, a small vein throbbing on her neck, not a drop of doubt in her posture.

I heard the decision in her voice, the terrible dangerous decision, and remembered how it felt every time Ivo forced my hand, snuffed my resolve out of me. I couldn't control her the same way I'd been controlled my whole life. I also couldn't live with myself if something, anything happened to her.

I sighed, hands running through my hair.

"This is not about you, Ruby! I made the terrible mistake of thinking I could protect someone from Ivo once." My voice cracked and failed, but I continued in a rasp. "I was wrong, and I can't bear to be wrong again. If he finds you, there is nothing I can do to keep you safe."

"That is not your decision to make. I've let doubt and fear own me for far too long and I've lost too much because of that."

"He'll kill you, Ruby! He'll kill you out of spite. He'll kill you just to get back at me."

"You are my *friend*, Aila. The only one I've had in a very long time. If my death gives you a tiny bit of a chance to stop all he is doing, if it helps to do for those kids what I couldn't do for my brother, then it will be a good death."

I felt the tightness around my chest, the blur in my vision and the sting behind my eyelids. There were no words left in me, no rational thought. There was just an endless pounding in my ears.

My heart filled with tenderness for the brave woman in the same measure my body filled with fear - for her and for myself. I wondered if that hopelessly sweet feeling was what made people do reckless things, if that impossibly inebriating, secure bond was what made life worth living.

She took my hands in hers, carefully, tenderly. "You don't have to be alone anymore, Aila."

"I don't know how to do the whole 'friends' thing, Ruby."

"For someone who doesn't know how to be a friend, you sure as hell have been a loyal one to me."

I squeezed her hand, silently hoping we would get out of this city together and alive.

Chapter 18

Night had barely settled when I made my way to the pub nearest the fort. A few hours was all that I needed and then I could meet Ruby in the woods near the city and never think about Urian again.

I missed the weight of my sai, but there was no way to hide it in the simple dress Ruby had found me to wear. The two daggers hidden in my boots would have to be enough.

People never suspected simple, innocent girls. Which was all they could see beneath the shabby dress, the headband, and the dirty nails. I'd been giving them what they expected out of any girl who'd just lost her only family in a far away farm. For the past week, I'd been having dinner at the bar, asking mildly interested questions about life in Urian and spilling dreams of seeing the capital.

Soldiers after a long shift were as needy for attention and fun as some of the more bored ladies in court. So, it didn't take long for some of them to engage, even less for them to make their intentions very clear.

I smiled, I blushed, and I flirted as any gullible girl would. I coaxed them into telling me stories about their jobs and about what the insides of a big fort looked like. Carefully assessing the ones ready to spill as many truths as sugared words and suggestive glances could buy.

By the time I had to act, I knew exactly who my target would be. Dan was young and innocent. Easily manipulated, overly trusting and with enough access to the fort to get me in, but not so much that his every movement – and company – was noticed.

That night I arrived earlier but, instead of eating my usual dinner I ordered a pitcher of wine and let the sweet smell of it intertwine with my own before Dan found me.

"Hello, beautiful," he said from behind me.

I took a moment more than I needed to turn to him and offer a lazy smile.

His pale blond hair was disheveled, and his ashen face carried heavy dark circles. He wasn't a beauty, and he wasn't particularly kind. Just another numb soldier, too tired to consider anyone's pain but his own.

"Dan," I exclaimed pulling him to the seat by my side, "join me. I'm celebrating."

"I can see that. What happened?"

"I got a job today! I'm the newest maid at the Mountain Inn." Ruby had heard about their opening that morning.

"I'll drink to that." He poured himself a glass of the watery wine at my sign.

"Oh Dan." I touched his arm mimicking the shameless intimacy only alcohol can elicit. "If I save enough, I can go to the capital! Can you imagine?"

"I'm sure you'll fit right in." he hovered from my

hand on his arm to my lips, to my cleavage. No more than fleeting glances, but enough to tell me he was hooked.

"Perhaps you could come along?" I lowered my head slightly in sign of embarrassment.

He didn't answer. Frowning with a shadow of doubt. *Come on, Dan!*

At his silence, I started to pull my trembling hands away, letting my lips drop and my eyes float around.

At the last moment, he held me in place and said under his breath: "Perhaps I could."

After that, it was easy to keep him enthralled, busy with the suggestive touches and flirty smiles. I kept pouring glass after glass and as my voice slurred and my touches advanced, he stopped taking notice of whether I was draining my own cup or not. By the time the moon was high and the pub empty, he finally asked,

"Shall we get out of here? It is a beautiful night." It was a terse, embarrassed question, but I beamed and nodded all the same.

I made a show of stumbling on my feet, letting him half-carry me through the empty street around the fort. As we left the pub lights behind and his grip on my waist tightened, I dropped my weight slightly on him, forcing us to half-collapse against the wall.

He straightened me up with bold hands and an unmissable hunger. I didn't hesitate before kissing him. Awkwardly and hastily.

To his benefit, he didn't waste time on pressing me against the wall and moving his focus from my lips to my neck.

"Can we go to a quieter place? More private?" I whispered against his ear.

"My house is a few blocks away," he pushed in between too-wet kisses on my shoulder.

"I don't think I can get that far," I pretended to repress a moan and stuck my nails on his back, pulling him to me clumsily.

I didn't want to spell it out, I didn't want to shove him through the door of the fort. *Think, Dan! Think!*

I noticed his hesitation. He glanced towards the top of the wall – no sentry in view – and then to the door mere feet from us.

Before he could rationalize any of it, I bit his earlobe – just slightly – and shifted my body against his.

He grunted and I knew I had him.

He pulled me by the hand whispering: "You have to be real quiet, ok?"

I nodded, the image of innocence.

In no more than a couple of minutes, I was crossing the courtyard through the hidden side of the wall, stumbling and suppressing small giggles.

The main building beyond was old but well-tended. Made of sandstone walls with over a dozen high windows. Colorful plant pots hung beneath each of them.

With every step, I summoned my power, gathering it in a small reserve in the deep part of my soul, in the small place where I always felt the tug of magic, the comforting silk-like texture of it.

This was a foolish, reckless plan and my stomach contorted in a knot with how little control I had over the many variables. Not for the first time that night, I felt my hands clammy and my heart thumping.

All the while, Dan kept pulling me through small stone corridors. The deeper I went, the more I noticed the lack of resemblance to the fine and luxurious estate Valran held in Nuri. This was a war estate, not a home. A building meant to withstand an attack, a building managed by warriors, no matter how many plant pots Lidya had hung throughout the grounds.

Dan shoved me inside one of the sleeping quarters on the first floor. The split second in which he let go of me to lock the door was all I needed to twist under his grip. I landed an elbow on his stomach and a punch to his face and when he straightened up, one of my daggers was already at his throat:

"Easy now, Dan!" I said leaving the drunk disguise behind and building a darkness shield around the room.

The gleam of lust was quickly replaced by anger.

"Who the fuck are you?"

"Now, where would be the fun in telling you that?" a side smile tugged at my lips. "You don't have to get hurt; you just need to tell me where Valran's office was."

"Fuck you! There will be a battalion here any minute!" He spat.

"That is not very polite, Dan."

I retrieved my other dagger without ever losing sight of him or relaxing the blade on his neck. I angled the second dagger into his groin and pressed enough to elicit a guttural sound from his voice.

"Now, are we going to make this conversation fast and easy or long and painful?"

He closed his mouth, intent on not saying a word. Until the dagger on his groin drew a small drop of blood: "Second floor, third room to the left."

"Thank you." I retorted before the hilt of my dagger clashed against his skull and he collapsed at my feet.

He could have lied, but I didn't believe he had enough

spirit to do so, not with a knife at his balls. Still, I had to be quick and careful. Wandering through an unknown fort with nothing more than two daggers and a hidden journal was far from a sane plan.

I checked that the journal was still safely tucked against my back. I told myself I couldn't risk losing it if I was separated from Ruby, but the reality was I couldn't afford to leave it behind anymore. Its delicate lines and realistic drawings were now painfully familiar and comforting. A gleam of hope in a very long and dark tunnel.

I ripped pieces of the sheaths to bind Dan in case he woke up before I was out of there. Then I cloaked myself in darkness and followed the main corridor to a flight of stairs: a large, open stairway with no hiding place in sight. As I reached the middle portion, I saw four soldiers coming down, side-by-side.

The shadows curled around me, hiding my face and most of my body. But they'd seen enough to move into formation. The swishing sound of swords being unsheathed filled my ears as they moved in synchrony. *They are well trained, after all.*

I scattered the darkness, willing it into a silky shield around the stairs, stifling any sound. Four long, silky talons sprang to life in a snap, darting towards the ears of the soldiers, crumbling their brains and leaving nothing more than limp, lifeless bodies behind.

There was no time to hide them, no time to hesitate. I ran to the second floor, making quick work of finding the third room to the left.

Luckily, it was empty and unlocked. Protected from outside threats by the fort itself.

The room was more a study than a real office. Walls

were lined with maps, there was a small coffee table and chair in the corner, and a large mahogany desk in front of the closed window and its velvety burgundy curtains. No rich decoration or personal items, just a comfortable, practical study.

A sweet smell enveloped my senses, flowery and rich. *Lilies? Maybe Jasmine?* I searched for the source of the scent: a vase, a flowerpot. Nothing.

The desk was clean, organized. Not a piece of paper scattered around. Atop of it, laid a big map of Urian's surroundings, small pins marked what looked like scattered forces. Red pins laid on the fort itself, the king's forces, and tens of black pins – for the Alliance, I assumed – were scattered close to nearby cities, stretching around the base of the northern hills and continuing toward Isra Mountains, the shared border with Alizeh.

There were many of them. I couldn't tell if they were intended to represent settlements, soldiers or battalions. But this was certainly much more than a handful of people causing trouble, it was a vast movement, far more organized than the news let on.

My step faltered and my vision blurred, heat burning on my ears. Dizziness struck me. *Get ahold of yourself.* I shook my head.

I moved my fingers across the desk as I circled it, using the feeling of the firm wood to steady myself. My heart started to pound, strongly and uncontrollably as I scanned through the desk drawers: guards shifts, bills, tax trackers, and beneath it all a few letters from Valran to Flynn with update requests on the estate and the rebels. Mostly on the rebels.

I dismissed the rest of the documents and pocketed the letters, hoping I'd find a clue later.

I yanked one of the maps from the wall and used a

pen to mark down the locations set up on the desk, fighting to control my quick breathing and fast-beating heart. If there was nothing in the letters, at least this would lead me to the Alliance.

When I finally reached for the door, my steps turned leaden, my vision mostly a blur of shapes. My head was foggy, dizzy and I didn't know if my racing heart was from whatever was taking over my body or from the sheer panic seeping through me.

As I stepped into the corridor, three heavily-armed men waited on each side. *I'm too late*.

I willed the darkness into long talons. Nothing.

With a jolt of panic, I reached for that place inside me where the comforting presence of my magic stood, the place I'd been fueling. Nothing. Empty.

No one moved, all the guards calmly frozen into place. No weapons drawn. One of them, an official I'd followed a few times, took a step towards me, a relaxed and almost bored step.

Something was wrong.

"Funny thing those silent traps, ain't they?" he said in a raspy, humorous voice.

I remembered the sweet smell coating the office, the jasmine-like smell. The dizziness, the racing heart ...

"This time it got us a big prize, eh?"

Venom.

The word echoed through my mind as my blurred vision turned black and unbound darkness engulfed me whole.

Chapter 19

I woke to a clanging sound in my ears and a cold, damp floor against my back. My head throbbed as I slowly, so very slowly, sat up. Drowsiness weighed on my head and muddled my thoughts.

Stone walls and heavy iron bars locked me in a small rotting cell with sturdy and humid floors, covered with mold in between irregular grey stones. No windows, only a few small holes to the seemingly empty cell to my right. Beyond that, nothing but a long, poorly-lit corridor.

I tried to stretch, carefully feeling for damage on my body. The journal and maps were gone, along with my weapons, but at least I wasn't hurt. Yet.

From where I was, I couldn't see any of the other cells, but from the constant clanging, I could assume another prisoner was bored enough – or desperate enough – to try to get the guards' attention.

A metallic taste lingered in my mouth, and I realized it was probably the after-effects of whatever poison I'd triggered before. *Stupid, utterly stupid.*

The memory of the seconds before I blacked out came back to me and, with a flash of terror, I reached out to the shadows around me, inside of me, willing them to move, to encase me, to do anything. But there was nothing beyond numbness. The piece of my soul that held my power seemed empty, probably hindered by the magic stifling venom. *Hydrangea? Smart*, I conceded.

Whatever was hidden in that office was bigger than a few maps. It had to be if Valran invested in silent traps in the middle of a damned fort! Keeping an intruder in was certainly more expensive than keeping someone out, but it was also more effective.

I waited. If for hours or days, I couldn't tell. It was impossible to follow the passage of time without natural light and with an erratic food offer at best. If I could even call the greyish porridge, food.

I ate the little they gave me, and I drank the foul-smelling water they offered. I tried to sleep, I tried to wield and when it all failed, I waited again.

I waited with nothing other than my awful thoughts to keep me company. I waited as worry, guilt, and unease ate at me. I waited even when I wanted to scream and to cry and to thrash against the unmoving bars.

At first, I could do nothing but think about Ruby. I would spend hours searching for a glimpse of other prisoners, listening to the guards, trying to be sure she wasn't rotting in another cell, mere meters from me. Time passed and I saw nothing of her, so I began to hope she'd left to travel the world and find her brother, that she would stay far away from Ivo's reach, far away from me.

My mind wandered to the past. To the life I had left,

to the hurt I had caused; to Aiden. In the dark solitude of that cell, I allowed myself to think about him, about the unwavering faith he'd had in me and the lies I'd offered him in return.

There'd been so much fear in me, so much blind trust and love for Ivo, that I'd drowned. Unable to even recognize the lifeline he'd offered me, afraid to trust him with the truth of who I was.

I was blind to everything other than the false safety of Ivo's protection.

"I never thought you would prefer to be a pawn for your uncle ..." the words Aiden uttered months before still echoed in my mind, in my very soul. I'd been so worried with not depending on anyone, so worried with not being vulnerable again that I didn't even realize how much I'd relied on Ivo, how much I'd craved that weird sense of familiarity he'd built in me. *"A pawn ..."* Aiden was more right than he could ever dream.

As misguided as my loyalty to Ivo was, it had been enough to make me kill, to make me cause pain. In the dark, lonely cell, I couldn't help but wonder what kind of monster it made me.

My eyes started to burn with the weight of tears that promised to undo all that I was, that threatened to rip open every little wound I had ever concealed. And a part of me knew I couldn't do it, not yet. That if I opened that door in my heart, it would turn into a crack I couldn't possibly fix.

So, I fought against it. Too afraid to let myself get lost in all that pain, too afraid to face so many old demons.

Instead, I let the silence wash over me, and I grieved the loss of everything I could not fix, hoping the darkness would claim me, embrace me like so many times before. I waited and waited, until the shadows around me became hollow, foreign and I realized this time there would be no comfort in them.

◆

No one came for me. For hours – or possibly days – I remained alone and in silence.

Maybe that was part of whatever game they wanted to play, maybe they had no clue who they had caught. Maybe both. Maybe neither.

I felt numb, with no hope of reprieve and no will to fight. I was, once again, alone and defenseless. No matter how much I tried to wield my power, it was always lacking, leashed. As if my connection with that fundamental part of me had been shattered, interrupted by the venom running in my system, and with it, any chance to shatter that damn cell to crumbs.

I slept poorly and inconsistently, unable to quiet my mind into a dreamless sleep. Quickly, the long silent hours turned into a painful contemplation of every mistake I'd made, every lie I'd told, every secret I held.

When my hopes of escaping vanished, I turned my mind to other paths. I looked for an advantage I could press, a secret I could trade, a favor I could call, but there was nothing I could use without revealing more about who I was, without putting Aiden at risk. Ivo might have his ear, but I doubted he would hesitate to hurt him if it held my hand. If it held my tongue.

Time bled over and I simply waited. Eventually I surrendered to the nightmares, and a quiet resignation fell into place.

Only then, as if my hopelessness had summoned them, three guards made their way inside my cell with a loud clank of the door. They didn't offer a word before pushing me up and chaining my hands and feet.

We moved left through the long corridor, my body tensing under the weight of the shackles.

As they dragged me through corridor after corridor, a distant sense of reflex took root and my trained mind half-memorized every cell and small passage we walked by, making note of the ones from which I could hear distant shouting and faint wood swords banging against each other.

I half-expected my brain to be rushing through potential paths, forming a plan. But that part of my mind felt distant now, dormant. Almost content to conform with whatever destiny waited for me.

I took every step deliberately slowly, peering inside the cells in cold curiosity, studying the faces of the few prisoners who looked back.

We moved through a short flight of stairs and finally arrived at a silent, cold room covered with the same old, irregular stones as the cell walls. A window, a blessed window gave way to fresh, limpid air. It was located near the ceiling, across from me, revealing a wistful blue-grey sky.

The rest of the room was nearly empty. Only the chair where I was chained, a large table with weird-looking small tools and a rack. And a bald, middle-aged man leaning against the table, facing me.

A crooked, yellow-toothed smile danced on the face of the short man, somehow highlighting the hollowness of his cheeks. An unnerving and odious sight. I let my gaze wander to his face ever so slowly and rested my attention solely on him, waiting. Let him deal his hand.

I watched as the silence stretched, and with each heartbeat his face grew more attentive, hungrier. Anxiety peeking through his expression.

One side of my mouth tugged up, barely. Challenging.

He nodded to one of the guards by my side and a second later a heavy hand connected with my jaw and sharp pain shot through my brain. Blood dripped from my lip, either cut by my own teeth or by a ring on the soldier's hand. I couldn't tell. It didn't matter.

I looked back at the officer in front of me, licking the blood from my lip, smirking. He would need to do more than that to break me.

And he did.

A set of punches shot through my body: face, stomach, ribs. One shot of pain after another.

Yet, never a single word. Nothing but a sickly smirk on his face.

◆

I woke up on a makeshift hay mattress in my cell, barely able to open my bulging eyes. Pain pulsated ceaselessly across my whole body. Quick, light fingers told me my whole face was swollen and tender, but nothing was broken.

I had no idea how long they'd beaten me or how long I'd been unconscious. Even so I knew it could only get worse, *would* only get worse. Either by their hands or by Ivo's, I would die, and it wouldn't be pretty or serene.

The thought was enough to break me from my stupor, the pain propelling me forward. I tried to summon my power over and over again, tried to find something, anything, to pick at the lock, to use as a weapon.

Too soon, they came back. Too soon, I was chained in the same chair, facing the same odious face.

"Enjoying your stay?" I recognized the raspy voice from the night I'd been captured. "Shall we introduce ourselves this time? I'm Tyler."

I let my gaze wander to the small window and the orange sky beyond. His sweaty fingers held my chin, forcing my face back to his.

"It is only polite to offer your name in an introduction. Did your mother not teach you that?" Unchecked anger showed in his tone. "We don't take lightly to thieves, but maybe we can get to an arrangement? You can tell me what you were doing here, and I can preserve this beautiful face of yours." He ran a finger along my cheek. "Moving forwards, that is."

His face was inches from mine, demanding. A self-entitled man, believing himself righteous and powerful. A fool with no idea who I was.

I spat.

He smiled, the same venom-laced smile from before, and nodded once to the guard by my side as he retreated to lean on the desk again.

Sharp pain cursed through my abdomen as the soldier punched my ribs.

"What did you want?"

I kept silent, focused on the window, imagining the warm sensation of the sun on my skin.

Another punch, and a steady pattern.

"Who sent you?"

Punch. Silence.

His voice grew angrier and more frustrated with

every second.

"Where is the Alliance?"

Punch. Silence. Question.

Punch.

Silence.

So, we went, until I could barely raise my head or think through the constant pain. Until he gave up.

"Take the night to think on whether your loyalty is worth it. We will continue later," he said motioning the guards to take me back.

The rich Jasmine-like smell of Hydrangea took over my senses as the guards shoved a damp cloth over my mouth and empty blackness claimed me again.

◆

I woke up back at my cell, as destroyed and dizzy as the first day. The same metallic taste on my mouth. The same emptiness when I reached for my magic.

They came back sooner this time, more eager. Anxious.

A starry sky was the first thing I saw as I entered the room. I had always found comfort in the dark night, and even through a tiny, barred window the stars made me feel more like myself.

Up until that moment, I didn't know what was driving me, what was making me resist but, as I held onto the stars, there was no denying the power of the rage burning at my core; there was no ignoring the hope that I could still make Ivo stop, make him pay. I was holding on for me, as much as I was holding on for every innocent suffering at his hands.

With startling clarity I knew that, over the previous

months, I'd shattered Ivo's silky shackles and found a part of myself I didn't even know existed. I'd set my own soul free from the crippling fear and control, from the need for his approval and love. I'd learned to accept myself. Scars and all.

They could beat me to death, but no one would own me again.

"How do you fare today?" The rasp was nothing more than a nuisance in the back of the room that I didn't bother to acknowledge. I kept admiring the sky, taking slow breaths, holding on to that flicker of clarity and purpose I had just found.

He turned my face with forceful fingers, his mouth close to mine as he whispered, "I'm growing tired of your stubbornness. I won't be polite much longer."

He motioned for a young woman to approach from the back of the room. Not a woman, a priestess of the Goddess.

My stomach twisted at the sight of the robes, identical to the ones Ruby and I had shared in the past few months.

Her clothes were immaculate, but the silver pendant on her chest was somehow flimsier than mine.

The priestess's hood was cast down, showing her light hair and blue eyes – fickle and unattainable as a traitorous ocean. Her delicate, plain face was arranged in a mask of indifference as she moved through the room, haughty and entitled.

Her cold hands slid over my skin as her healing power swarmed through me. A similar touch to the woman at the temple in Nuri, and yet less intimate, less certain.

A subtle yellow glow slowly spread between us as a warm tingling unrolled through my body, reaching my bones and beyond. Then the throbbing pain eased, and my muscles relaxed. For a glorious moment I forgot where I was and why I was being healed in the first place.

The light grew warmer and brighter as peace and bliss dominated my brain. Until, to my surprise, it washed away the grief, sadness, and regret I'd been losing myself into.

A faint voice echoed through my mind, the same voice that had told me tales about stones and heirs: *"Hold to your strength, Princess. Find your Light."*

Something akin to surprise flicked over the priestess's face as a gentle calmness took root in my soul. I felt surer than I had in days, less alone.

"Much better now." Tyler's rough fingers caressed my cheek as he tilted my head to face him. "I can see what poor Dan saw in you now … maybe I'll find out what he missed out on."

I tried to muster regret for the boy I'd played, or disgust for the implication in his words, the intent touch of his clammy hands, but I felt nothing. I averted my eyes, measuring the space around me. It was the same room I'd been brought to before, the same guards, the same conceited middle-aged man in front of me. Yet, with the panic and grief no longer boiling in me, I saw it all a bit more clearly.

The rusty torture rack took half of the room, and I wondered if that was why he had a priestess this time. Torture and heal. I wouldn't have thought the church would deign to participate in something like this, but even I had to admit the effectiveness of the plan.

"We don't need to resort to that. We could end this much more amicably … you just need to ask nicely," he offered following my gaze.

Despite myself, I laughed.

"Did I say something funny?"

"Oh, you are in so far over your head," I said in a whisper, a touch of insanity coming through my voice. He had no idea how much praise or trouble I could bring him. Even caged. Especially caged.

Delivering me to Ivo could be his way out of this hell hole of a city but breaking me before it … I was a threat to Ivo, a problem to be eliminated … yet he loved me enough to kill anyone who lay a hand on me without his blessing.

"Is that so? Why don't you enlighten me?"

"Where would be the fun in that?" My lips curled as a glimpse of doubt flickered in him.

Playing on his vanity and sense of self-importance would be my only hope for escape. If I had enough time.

He held his stance and signaled to the guards as he left the room, priestess in tow.

The guards didn't bother to ask questions in between the punches that time and the clarity in my mind didn't resist the sweet venom they brushed into my face before dumping me back in my cell.

◆

I didn't know how long I spent like that. The venom blurred my sense of time, and I couldn't tell how many times a day they took me, nor for how many days.

Thoughts of the Goddess and Heirs and Stones flickered in and out of my mind. *Some good it did me to believe in Gods and their lunacies. Some good it did me to believe there was more to me than I'd thought.*

Because, legends aside, I had no Light power. Even if I did have it, what good would it do if I couldn't purge the hydrangea from my body?

The priestess became part of Tyler's little routine: heal me, question me, beat me. But I didn't feel the same surge of clarity and peace again. Whatever had happened that first time, the girl made sure it stopped.

Sometimes, I would stay in the room for mere minutes, annoying him so quickly he wouldn't bother with questions; sometimes, they would keep me for hours, taunting me, questioning me. He would give great speeches about how he had found a new rebel camp and destroyed it, always trying to coax a reaction from me. And every time, they would make me smell the same hydrangea-laced poison before they threw me back in my cell, unconscious.

I played my own game, waiting for an opportunity, but every time I woke up to a throbbing pain, hopelessness was an inch closer, panic stretching its claws towards my heart once again. Panic that I would be sent back to Nuri, that I would have no chance to explain it all to Aiden. More than anything, panic that Ivo would find a way to own me once again.

◆

Tyler paced around the room as the priestess worked. Slowly, taunting. There was a different sort of tension in the air, silent, anxious looks on their faces.

He finally stopped in front of the torture rack, picking up some tools, examining them. He had been hinting at their use for a few sessions now. But the way he handled the tools told me he wasn't as experienced as he tried to let on.

"Tomorrow you won't have a chance to be nice anymore," he said with his back to me. "You know, I don't really like to use these fancy tools ..." he raised a particularly thin scissor to me before dropping it back at the rack with a loud thud. "I'd rather feel the work with my own hands, but I suppose there is a sort of elegance in it."

He approached me until his face was inches from mine.

"I still think you are way too pretty for that …" he looked at the rack, "but tomorrow my opinion won't matter anymore."

I willed myself to remain motionless, keeping the questions from my mind. He would not bait me.

"You see, *tomorrow* you'll be in the hands of more powerful and blood-thirsty men than I."

Pure panic struck through me. I knew Ivo would arrive sooner or later, but I'd foolishly convinced myself that I would find a way out before he got here, that I could play this arrogant small-town guard before Ivo ever set foot in Urian.

"He even sent us a colleague beforehand …" he continued, gesturing to the priestess who nodded once in acknowledgement, confirmation. "And you have seen yourself how effective she is at keeping you alive. I imagine what wonders she'll do with nastier wounds."

There were no smart retorts, no taunting remarks, just raw panic. It took all my lingering self-control not to tremble, not to betray the boredom I showed on my face. I could only hope I'd been successful.

"Nothing?" he finally said after a few silent seconds. "I guess you'll have enough to say tomorrow." He shrugged as one of the guards approached me.

When Hydrangea-laced oblivion started to take me this time, I gladly let it.

"We'll keep you presentable tonight. Consider it a kindness, the last one you'll have in a long time." The muddy words reached me from a very long distance, and I knew they were the truest words I'd heard since I first woke in that cell.

Chapter 20

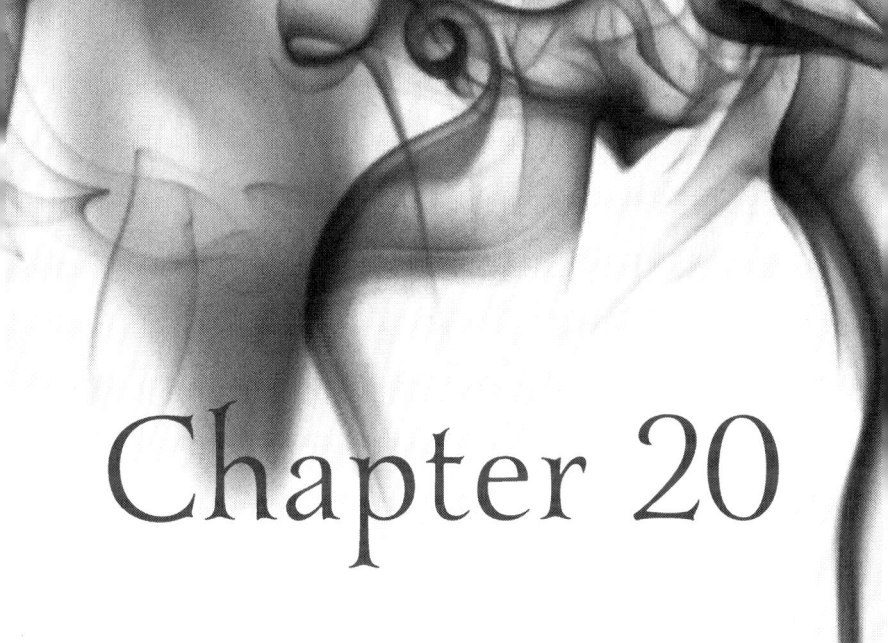

The sweet embrace of oblivion did nothing to keep the panic at bay, if anything I woke up more restless, unbound.

Tyler had taunted me about the pain, the torture, but Ivo would be more creative, crueler. *"Play the long game,"* he always told me. So, I wondered how long he would play with me for my disobedience, for Billy – daughter or not.

I could almost see his face, the anticipation of having me under his control again, even if rotting in a forgotten dungeon. One look at me and he would know I'd tasted hope and warmth. He would delight in breaking it out of me, in breaking *me*.

Sorrow took root in my heart. So unending and strong that I could drown.

For the first time in long years, I wept.

An unending flow of tears for the cold man I'd accepted and worshipped as a loving father, for the lies he'd fed me my entire life, for the role I'd played in what Aiden had become. But mostly for the love and caring and trusting that I had only begun to find.

"Don't." said a steady male voice through the wall. "Swallow it, bury it, revolt against it! Just don't give in to the despair, to the sorrow. Never to the sorrow."

The walls were familiar to me by now, and although I had seen the small hole on the right wall days before, I didn't make much of it. It was too small for me to see the other cell properly and I had just assumed it empty. Until now. Until I heard the firm voice and saw the piercing almond eye and wrinkled eyelids peering through it.

There was such intent and warmth in that glimpse of his face, such certainty in that voice. I could only ask, "Why?"

"Because the moment you break, they win!"

A bitter laugh escaped me.

"They already did. There is nothing left, nothing other than this ..." My voice was barely more than a broken rasp. I couldn't find the words to explain that maybe I could have built something for me, maybe in a different life I would be worthy of something more than pain, but not in this one.

I leaned against the wall, feeling the distant presence on the other side, letting the tears dry. It was not until my breathing became lower, calmer, that he continued.

"There is always something left, child. His voice was low, but still firm. "As long as we breathe and love and hope, there is always something worth fighting for."

I let his words fill me, find their way into my heart, and shift something deep, invisible. A hidden part of me recognizing the truth in it.

"Why do you care?" I asked him. No bite, no swagger, just plain curiosity.

A calm and contemplative silence filled the space between us. I thought he would not reply, but then his voice became gentler, laced with something warm – *a smile, maybe*.

"Because no one else does, not for us."

I knew that all too well, I'd lived it and survived it. The indifference and loneliness pushed me towards Ivo and slowly turned me into a cold shell, too afraid to open up.

But now, a brave, bright girl had offered me a scrap of friendship and, with it, a sliver of hope found a place in my heart.

Hope that I could be better, more. That I would be free.

With a jolt of clarity, I finally saw it: hope was a fuse waiting to ignite. It was what kept the rebels fighting. It was not despair; it was hope that defied the Kingdoms.

One thought rang louder than sorrow in my mind as the tears dried on my face: that was the ember Ivo needed to destroy, the fire he was trying to stifle, and it was that blazing, hot fire that was going to bring him down!

I would face Ivo again; I would bide my time and let him break my body if he had to. Until it was *my* turn. Then, I'd burn his world to the ground.

◆

I carried that resolve with me as I walked to the torture room the next day. I knew there was nothing I could do to escape what awaited me, so I would face it knowing the small taste of freedom had been worth it.

There were no more words floating between cells the previous night, whoever sat at the other side remained quiet. All the same, the sense of his warm companionship cradled me to sleep, and his words lingered in my heart giving me courage.

It was with a peaceful mind I resisted the urge to wonder about Ivo's absence and held the gaze of the thin, blond man in front of me as Tyler, with a wicked smile, described some of our *conversations*. Nothing but bored distaste in the new guy's gaze.

His brows crinkled and mouth tightened at each description of Tyler's brutish methods and loathing filled his features with every word.

He looked at me coldly, no acknowledgement sparking in his face before he reached for the tools in the side rack and selected what he needed. He either didn't know me, or he simply didn't care.

Unexpected softness laced his touch as he knelt before me, hand on my knee. His gaze locked onto mine, deep intent and devotion burning behind piercing silver eyes. He would be beautiful, if not for the cold viciousness on his features, if not for the shiver that his touch sent through my spine.

"Hello, I'm Kiran and I'm delighted that I shall be the one to hear your story. I'm sure we'll be good friends before the end." A limpid and light sound, completely at odds with what lurked beneath the polite surface. "I apologize for the barbaric treatment you've received so far, I'm going to introduce you to some friends of mine and then we'll hear what you have to say. Sound good?" He stood up before I had a chance to reply and motioned the guards to move me to the sprawling table near the rack as he added, "we may need to ruin your clothes. I'll make sure you have something more ... convenient for tomorrow."

Cold sweat ran down my spine as I did my best to

hold onto the courage and strength lingering in my heart. I searched for the window, concentrating on the blue sky and the smell of buttery corn coming from the street beyond. The room went utterly quiet and even Tyler seemed suddenly uncomfortable near the wall. The only noise, the clinking of the iron shackles holding me to the table.

Until the door opened in a sudden jolt and a very familiar face came through it.

Flynn's golden eyes flared in unexpected recognition the second they landed on me. There and gone so fast I wondered if I had imagined it.

Not Ivo. Not the premier, or the captain of the fort. *Flynn fucking Wheelan!*

He dismissed the guards' salute and slipped his hands into his pockets, walking lazily through the room and barely acknowledging a surprisingly meek Tyler. Every inch the arrogant captain I'd met in Nuri.

Last time I'd seen him, my life had been utterly different, *I* had been utterly different. I could still hear the sweet venom in his voice, see the streak of suspicion in his gaze. I turned to the ceiling and drew a deep breath, bracing myself for the sarcastic words, for the revelation of who exactly they had in their hands, for Ivo to burst into the room.

Nothing.

Flynn leaned against the wall underneath the window, one leg up and arms loosely crossed in front of him, laced in somber silence. He had a clenched jaw and something like revulsion shone on his features.

For a moment the world froze around me as I waited for triumph to appear on his face. He had to be the one responsible for Valran's death. The mess I had created had given him a free pass. Why look for another killer when they had *me* to blame? Finding me here of all places was his golden ticket. A very satisfying scapegoat delivered to his doorstep. Or shackled to it, in this case.

Yet, even as I silently questioned him and his motives, the memory of a dark night against a wall crossed my mind – and his own, if the way he tensed against the wall was any indication.

I was so tangled in my own thoughts that I barely noticed Kiran until he cut the upper part of my dress open, exposing my naked body. His fingers traced my skin with the gentleness of a caress and the precision of a healer. Prodding, choosing. Until he settled for the sensitive area under my collarbone.

I felt every inch of the blade slowly flaying my skin, piercing and agonizing pain stretching for seconds, minutes. Only sheer willpower kept the screams buried in my lungs, but no amount of control stopped my body from trashing against the tight shackles and my eyes from filling with painful, unwanted tears.

He mimicked his movements across both sides of my body, slowly moving towards my breasts.

"The face is a messy business, too much blood, too fast. I think we are both happier not touching it for now," he offered as means of explanation between one cut and another. Never breaking his concentration from the task at hand.

As he started working on my left breast, a hoarse scream escaped me. Guttural and raw, as foreign to me as the unrelenting pain thrashing through my limbs. The edges of the world darkened, and an unreadable golden gaze was the last thing I saw before I fainted.

◆

Tingling warmth spread through my torso as I opened my heavy eyelids. The priestess's face furrowed in concentration, Kiran patiently at her side.

She healed me enough to stop the bleeding and clot the wounds, but not enough for the pain to vanish. Not even enough for the pain to lessen.

Kiran came into full focus with a polite smile. "There you are. We don't want to miss you so soon." A reassuring squeeze on my shoulder, or so he intended.

I did my best not to flinch away from his touch. I couldn't tell if my body obeyed.

"Maybe now you can tell me what you were doing here the other night?"

His hand remained casually on my shoulder, his unflinching attention on me.

Despite my best resolutions, I considered what I could give him, what secrets could buy me a reprieve from the pain. I remembered all the rebellion locations I'd seen on Valran's maps, the few lines I memorized from the coded letters.

Then I remembered the quiet words of the stranger in the cell beside mine and the seed of courage I'd found at last.

Flynn was still under the window and despite the casual posture and bored face, I could see the tension in his shoulders, an ember in the gleam of his eyes. If his silence told me one thing it was that no-one else in that room knew who I really was. And, if Ivo was willing to put so much effort, so much energy into questioning a random girl for some scraps of information about the Alliance, he was more afraid of them than I thought.

Hope! That was the thing that would bring him down.

If only I could hold on to mine long enough to find a way out of this place.

I didn't answer, didn't offer them anything.

Kiran was patient but he eventually tired of my silence and probed me again: "Nothing?"

Still looking at Flynn, I mustered all the contempt in me, all the rage I ever felt and by the time I faced Kiran again, a defiant silent smile tugged at the corner of my mouth.

He smiled back, as if acknowledging a challenge.

"Oh, I knew we were going to have fun." Kiran placed a stranded lock of my hair behind my ear and started again.

We stayed there for hours. The dimming sun on the window, was my only way of telling the passing time. A darker sky, every time I came back from the healing.

He asked little, flayed a lot.

I offered nothing but silence and muffled screams. Expected nothing but swift death. Yet, I never let the defiant smile and contemptuous look leave my face.

Between one scream and another, I searched for Flynn, wondering if he would help me again, if he could read that wretched question in the lines of my face. Eventually, I stopped searching for answers and let his stare hold me. His deep golden eyes glimmering with a hint of defiance of his own.

After a few hours that was my only thread out of the mind-shattering pain.

A thread out of my own body.

Until there was no thought left. Just molten gold keeping me sane before empty darkness claimed me.

◆

Consciousness and oblivion battled. Swift and foggy. My mind reaching for the edges of awareness and my body collapsing before I could open my eyelids. For a while, I couldn't tell dreams from reality.

I thought I heard hurried whispers and muffled conversation. I thought I saw movement. But when my eyes fluttered open, as tired as the rest of my pain struck body, there was nothing but silence and the hard cold floor at my back. These were the dungeons, nothing but desperate moans would find me here.

Every muscle ached, a silent reminder of the shackles and ... I couldn't let myself think about it.

I dragged myself up, slowly and carefully, sight fixed on the irregular edges of a large stone near the hay pile I used as a mattress. It was not until I managed to sit that I noticed my new clothes: large pants and a buttoned old shirt, stained and patched. A rugged cloth was scraped against the tender skin on my breast and even though no blood peaked through it I still didn't have enough courage to examine what lay beneath.

I hissed and cursed my way to the nearest wall, and, only when I rested my back against it, did I notice Flynn leaning by the bars, loose shoulders, unfussed face and piercing golden eyes on me. Contemplative, careful.

"Not a lady after all," he finally said in a quiet voice I hadn't heard before.

He barely knew me, had barely exchanged a word with me that wasn't laced in sarcasm and edged with mind games yet, there I was, at a loss for words for the memory of him tethering me to sanity.

Whatever he saw in my face was enough to force him

out of his contemplation. He straightened himself never taking his sight off me and slowly slipped his hands into his pockets.

"I thought you'd be happy to see me," he enticed in a more familiar tone. A poor evocation of the double-edged banter that was our only way of communication.

Somehow, his stoic silence in the torture room made me forget the smugness and confidence that roiled through his every word, his every movement. It annoyed me … no it enraged me! For even if I didn't know what he wanted or why he acted the way he did, I knew he was free and I was running, I was suffering.

And yet … those golden eyes.

That single memory unnerved me.

Suddenly, I found myself too tired to question him, too tired to try to understand him.

"Go away," I countered in a small voice. Turning my attention back to the dirty shirt, but not missing the slight frown between his brows.

He shook his head deliberately. "What would dear old Prince think if he saw you now? His beloved …" he paused, searching for the right word "friend?"

Renewed anger flashed through me as I shot my face to him. My voice more certain, demanding. "Out!"

A quick, small gleam passed through his face.

"I suppose he would want to save you. Or was that before he realized it wasn't a sweet damsel that had been warming his bed?"

The anger melted into something else, into vicious guilt and regret. The memory of what I'd seen in Kait still too tender in my mind.

"Why are you here, Wheelan? Why am *I* still here?"

I hated the pleading note in my voice, the deep tiredness lacing every word.

"Hoping for a trip?"

"Just wondering why I haven't been shipped to Nuri yet, I'm sure you have more advanced methods there."

Something I couldn't place shifted in his face, lips twitching, shoulders sagging. Something I wouldn't even notice if not for the hours I'd just spent lost in him. If I didn't know better, I could have convinced myself it was regret.

"Oh … Kiran is good." A flat, clear voice.

"Where is Ivo?" I finally asked. Unable to stop the dread anymore.

"Dear old uncle? Busy, I suppose."

"He is not here?"

His gaze turned more intense, deeper as he silently shook his head, studying me. A shudder escaped me at the small, useless relief it brought me. It was just a matter of time, anyway.

"Why *are* you here?" He cocked his head to the side and asked in a quieter voice than before.

I sneered; *Just another way to get an answer then? Was that why he was here? Why he didn't say a word? Was this just another brand of torture?*

I mustered all the disdain I could summon, turning the rage filling me into something sharp. "Is that the big plan? Offer a hand, charm the girl, get the information?"

"Is it working?" He gave me a simple smile.

"Does it ever?"

He shrugged. The portrait of arrogance. "More times than I bother to count." Seductive charm in every word.

"Someone thinks mighty highly of himself." Never mind that he had the looks to back that up.

He held my gaze, silently. A small streak of defiance peeking at his face as he stared at me. Deeply and intensely enough that I remembered how he never looked away, how his eyes never left me, not even through the worst of it.

I thought he wouldn't speak again, but he did. Just as he turned away from me, leaving.

"I made her heal the worst ones completely. You'll be sore, but no risk of infection."

Some sort of offering, even though I couldn't understand why.

"Why didn't you tell them?" I blasted before he disappeared. He knew what I meant, could probably see the question there for that entire conversation. "Hand-delivering me keeps them from looking into you, and Ivo would give you anything … I suppose a lot of people would give you anything at this point." It was the truth. Between the power in my veins and the lies I'd told Aiden, I doubted I could find a single ally back at the capital.

He halted just enough to throw me a conceited smile as he said: "I have all I need, love."

◆

Echoes of anger and annoyance lingered for a long time after Flynn left. His perfect grace and arrogance were able to incite my temper in that dungeon as easily as in any of the palace rooms where I'd met him before.

Except this time there was a hint of gratitude tangled with it. Doubt and gratitude.

I muffled a scream, momentarily forgetting not to pity myself, not to worry about what the next hours would bring.

I sat beside the little hole to the side cell and before I

could stop myself, I said to the empty space beyond, angling my head to the high ceiling, "how long have you been here?"

The dragging sounds reached me before his voice, as if he was moving through the cell.

"Couple of weeks, I think."

The prospect of spending weeks in this hell sent shivers through my skin, doing nothing to muffle the pit at the bottom of my stomach.

I held onto the anger, remembering Flynn's smirk, his relentlessly self-satisfied voice. Anger was better than pity, better than fear.

"How have you not clawed through your own heart by now?"

He chuckled. "You're angry."

I simply grunted, doing my best not to let the fading feeling dissipate, not allowing myself to contemplate my real alternatives, or lack thereof.

"Good," he continued. "Anger is good! It suits you better than desperation. It'll serve you better as well."

"Yeah, yeah. Still pointless and empty. But hey, we can't be picky now, can we?"

His silence was enough for me to imagine him nodding behind the wall, contemplating my words.

"Maybe. But in a place like this, pointless anger can keep you whole."

"What difference does it make?" When I really wanted to ask why should I try to survive, try to do better, try to keep innocent people safe? What good did it do me?

"Only you can decide that, child," he said quietly.

Tiredness seeped into me. All the silly rage at last dissipating into the gloom.

I took a long, deep breath.

"It is not like I have any choice over what happens to me next." I quietly opened the shirt to examine my pained body.

Flynn hadn't lied; most of the nasty patches were healed completely, but still tender. The smaller areas along my collarbone and high chest though, had been barely touched, and were still painfully raw.

"They can break your body, yes. But only you can give them your soul."

I heard the kindness in him, the quiet embrace he offered me. I was grateful, deeply grateful.

"Tell me about yourself?" It was tentative, quiet. For a moment, I was afraid he wouldn't deign to respond, he wouldn't want to relive whatever horror he must have gone through in those dungeons.

But he did.

He told me about his home, about how much he loved working crops and tending to the earth. About how he had been arrested weeks back on the road and accused of conspiracy with the Alliance, how they had questioned him in the first few days, but grew tired of him when I arrived, a week earlier. Then, he talked about his loved ones, and how they meant everything to him, how they were the reason why he held on to his sanity in any way he could.

I drank his words intently, silently, and felt my heart tighten as he talked about the first time he saw each of his grandchildren and how his biggest fear was not seeing them again.

I leaned on that stranger's companionship to travel through those dark hours, to escape the thunderous fear that threatened to swallow me again. I asked and listened. Until finally, his voice rocked me to a rare dreamless sleep.

Chapter 21

My eyes rested on the skin underneath the iron shackles as one of the soldiers strapped me back onto the table. What used to be untouched fair skin, was now marred and raw. I followed the irregular edges of the sore bloodied patches the priestess never bothered to heal, wondering if it would eventually scar.

Flynn was already in the room. Under the window, holding my stare whenever I bothered to find him. And even as a part of me was angry and bitter with his freedom after killing Valran, with his apparent easy demeanor, I couldn't help but be grateful for his silence.

He didn't mention my connection with Ivo nor visit my cell again, and after a while, I stopped wondering why. I guessed he'd either use me or not; either way there was nothing I could do about it. For now, his unflinching stare made me feel less alone.

Kiran lowered his head over mine, gently taking a lock of hair away from my neck as I averted my gaze, focusing my thoughts on the clear blue sky beyond the window.

He flayed my arm. In tiny, precise motions until darkness claimed me. When the healing magic brought me back, he pulled my face toward his with a small smile and intent look on his face. As if searching for an answer.

I turned away in denial, mindlessly searching for the comfort of Flynn's golden eyes, for the balm of not being utterly alone.

And then he started again.

And again.

And again.

It became our ritual, the structure of our time together. Only rarely broken by a gentle comment or probing question.

In between the flashes of agony, I started thinking about Ivo with surprising yearning. A shameful part of me started believing him my most merciful option, wishing for the family he'd once been. For no matter how cruel or dangerous he was, beneath all the lies, I knew he loved me enough to offer me a less painful death.

But then, Kiran stopped. For a few minutes he simply looked at me. Intent.

I mustered all my draining strength to spit in his face before pursing my mouth in a half wild smirk.

Unfazed, he took his time touching the loose, dry skin on my chapped lips. The water had gone scarce since his arrival, and this morning it had finally ceased completely. Maybe that was why my thoughts felt slower and my head heavier, or maybe it was just the maddening pain.

His hands on my lips and skin were tender, horrifyingly caring and expectant. It sent my whole body into a frenzied tremble I had no hope to stop. Each stroke of his finger was a memory of the pain he'd inflicted, each touch reverberated through me in a terrifying jolt.

No amount of willpower stopped me from thrashing against the chains in the empty hope that I could get away from his soft hands. I whimpered even as I refused to cry. I scrambled desperately for the darkness, praying it would answer, I fought the grip of every single guard that tried to hold me, until I had no fight in me.

I found Flynn's face with a hopeless plea. A fire burned in his eyes at my desperation. If the guards hadn't been so busy holding me in place, they would have noticed his clenched fists and raging face. If I wasn't so panic stricken, I would have mused at that little crack in his always careful pose.

Instead, I braced myself for Kiran's next horror, closed lips, and deep breaths. Then calming air was replaced by burbling water in my mouth and nose, demanding, suffocating. Consciousness slipped through my fingers and I drowned in the invisible, magical water filling my lungs.

Kiran studied me, a satisfied and eager face as he commanded more water through my nose. I coughed on it, the pressure on my chest and throat increasing, my body convulsing.

Only when blurred darkness threatened to take me away, did the water vanish, giving way to limpid fresh air. A pleased smile peeked on Kiran's face at the utter control he had over me.

Without pause, he caressed my face and shoulder until setting on my exposed forearm, tracing the scar of a burning mark he had placed there … a day ago? An hour? Before?

He turned back to his table and the metallic sounds of his tools interrupted the chirping birds beyond the window as he searched for the small blade that pierced through my skin only seconds after.

Deep and unrelenting as I held my lips closed together, containing the coarse scream threatening to erupt as my body thrashed against the irons holding me in place.

Warm blood leaked from my arms as Kiran examined the inside of me, opening and stretching the skin until he touched bone. My body went limp with every precise movement and the ensuing pain.

Still, no words, no questions.

The little strength I had leaked out of me with every drop of blood and soon enough the pain was all that existed. I searched for Flynn's gloomy eyes and held to his gaze with all I had. Maybe it was just my desperate imagination, but I thought I could read a silent command in there: *Look at me, stay with me!*

His solid, unflinching stare felt like relief and understanding. And that was enough to send silent tears rolling down my face.

I passed out when Kiran broke the bone inside my arm.

◆

When I woke up in my cell, my arm was healed. Tender, but completely healed.

"Are you okay?" The familiar whisper got me moving to the small hole in my wall. I lay beneath it as fatigue washed over me.

"I think I'll live." My voice felt hoarse, my throat

painful.

We never talked about the dungeons and the torture, never talked about anything other than beautiful things, so I was surprised when he asked, "Why don't you give them what they want?"

I didn't answer at first, I didn't know how to explain I couldn't surrender my soul again, that I couldn't give up the freedom I'd only recently found.

That my only chance was to hope … hope that I could get away from that dungeon, that I could live to defy Ivo and stop his senseless bloodshed.

I didn't know how to explain that I finally understood the rebels and that it didn't matter if there was any truth to the heir legend anymore because it wouldn't help me out of there.

My consciousness drifted away as I tried to piece together an answer, and I don't know how long it took me to make sense of my feelings and words.

My eyelids were heavy when I finally managed to speak. "Someone once told me I should dream, that I was *allowed* to dream. But dreams … dreams are a dangerous living thing. And I may have believed them too much."

◆

I was barely awake when they came for me again.

They half dragged me from my cell, hauling me through the corridors as I tried to muster enough strength to stand on my own feet.

Halfway down the corridors a bundle of golden threaded braids caught my attention.

I missed the next step and the floor fell out from under me when Ruby's full face came into view. The guard's chatter went muffled and the walls seemed to grow closer and heavier with each frantic heartbeat. Once again, I desperately tried to call out for the shadows around me, just to be met with the deep void that was now my constant companion.

She seemed unharmed and lucid; her expression lined with recognition and concern. Emptiness and despair washed over me at the sight of her inside one of the cells. I realized how much I missed her bright, easy way. How much the memory of her had kept a kernel of hope buried deep inside of me.

I went limp and slipped into a pure stupor. I let the guards pull me and tie me, without even registering whose hands were touching me or what words I was hearing. There was nothing left to give, nothing left to hold on to.

This time, I didn't fight, I didn't seek the sky beyond the window. And when the pain started, I didn't bother to search for Flynn's stare because this time I deserved to be alone.

Instead, I screamed and I didn't hold back.

◆

Flynn entered my cell at what could only be a very silent night. I'd woken up hours before with fresh thin scars along my lower neck, but the memories of how I got them were hazier than usual. Tinted by the desolation numbing my senses.

After a while I had learned to dissociate my senses from whatever horror Kiran had chosen, to distance myself so that pain became just pain, sharp pain, throbbing pain, never-ending pain. I had learned to track his vicious imagination through the pattern of thin scars and half healed wounds left behind.

Yet this time, I couldn't even say if he had cut, flayed or broken. This time, there was only pointless pain and a new lump in my throat that no amount of tears could ease.

I had sat as far from the small hole to the next cell as I could, unwilling to let anyone drag me out of my agony. For the past few hours I'd stayed there, unmoving even long after my tears had gone dry, and my legs were frozen in place.

Flynn tossed me a small vial. "Drink it."

I frowned at the small bottle fallen on my lap. Flynn may not have told them who I was, but I didn't trust him. Not enough to risk him connecting me and Ruby.

"One more time," I thought and collected myself. I pushed all the spiraling thoughts away from my mind, shoved down all the numbing despair. I silenced the part of me that wished Kiran would cut a bit too deep, that the priestess would get sloppy enough to allow for the little blood and life still in me to bleed out.

I held the vial between my fingers; a red clear liquid whirled around inside of it. Whatever it was worked in very small doses. I let a smile reach my lips and slowly faced him.

"Tired of watching, already?" voice full of wicked contempt "I didn't take you for a weak stomach, Wheelan."

"Need I remind you that you are as good as shackled to a wall and barely able to stand, love? There are easier ways to end your misery than poison." No humor or arrogance laced his words. Just pure, logical reason. And, maybe, a note of shame, but that could have been only my imagination.

"Still underestimating me? I can do more in this cell than you could ever imagine." A cheap bluff.

He approached me, one graceful step at a time, and hunched over to face me. Warm, strong fingers caressed my skin as he gently moved a strand of hair from my face and whispered into my ear.

"Can you, though?"

His rain and green-grass scent enveloped me as fresh and sweet breath brushed my neck. For a brief moment we were back at a long-ago night in Nuri. Then I reacted. I knocked my head against his nose and tried to raise myself up, just to fall on my knees when dizziness and pain shot through me. My head throbbed with lashing pain.

"Good. You still have some fight in you. You're gonna need it." No amusement or mockery in his tone.

He looked down at me, hand on his bleeding nose, and offered me a small flask. "Water," he said when I didn't immediately pick it up. "Pace yourself, you've gone too long without it."

I stashed away the doubt and drank the crisp, fresh water in small sips. Neither of us spoke again until I drank it all.

His attention never shifted from me, never swayed from the serious, contemplative look I always failed to place. As if there was a whole part of him that I couldn't begin to understand.

When I finally handed him the flask back, he pointed to the small vial laying by my side. "Now that one. It will counter-act the Hydrangea. You'll have to leave tonight. Can you manage the pain?"

I reached for the vial, examining it: "Why would I?"

His shoulders sagged and he faced the ceiling, letting out a deep breath.

"What, love? Why would you what?" His voice was tired.

"Drink this? Listen to you? Trust you in any way?"

Continue to stare into those damning eyes?

He ran his hands through his hair and for the first time since I first saw him, he seemed unsure. Open. Utterly human. His gaze burned and sparkled with a fierce intensity that prickled at my skin; his voice tinted with a pain I've never heard before. "For fucks sake, Aila! By all means, don't trust me! The Goddess knows I don't. Ignore every word out of my mouth, but drink the damn potion all the same." His smoldering gaze locked on mine. "I may be the only one who recognizes you for who you are in this hell hole, but this changes tomorrow. Ivo is on his way, and I'm sure you don't need me to remind you of what he will bestow on his ... niece."

Maybe it was the unwilling intimacy of my name on his lips, or maybe it was the shivering that coursed through me at Ivo's memory or maybe it was just my imagination. But I could swear something softened his expression before he reached for the door offering me nothing but a side glance.

"Just drink it. And turn right at the main corridor."

"Left," I said. "I have to go left." Ruby was to the left.

"You'll find nothing but death in that direction," he said in a quiet, small voice before disappearing from view.

There was only lonely emptiness left when his footsteps finally faded.

◆

I could wait for death, or I could knock back the red liquid and take hell to Ivo's doorstep.

I didn't trust Flynn, but whatever his reasons were, he'd had about a million chances to reveal who I was, to look away when I searched for him, but he did neither. Instead, he tethered me firmly to sanity and life.

Now there I was, holding another lifeline he'd thrown my way.

It didn't matter if I trusted him. He was keeping me alive. I swallowed the bitter red liquid in a single gulp.

Warmth spread to my temples and neck, slowly tracing its way through my skin and merging with the steel resolve that firmed inside of me. I'd given up enough, offered all the decent parts of me and held on to the shame I felt I deserved. I'd happily recoiled from the suffering I witnessed in the world, content to step into the vile role Ivo outlined for me as I let him prey on my worst fears. Year after year, I let him convince me the path he offered was righteous, convince me I wasn't worth affection and love.

But no more!

I wouldn't go down sheepishly, I might be going to my grave, but I would do it as grandly and loudly as I could. I would fight for myself in all the ways I knew how. If I were to die, I would die making it count.

I ripped a piece off my shirt and swiftly tied it over my mouth and nose. I wouldn't risk Hydrangea getting in my way again.

The cord around my power snapped, ripping a deep breath from my core with the strength of the Darkness building inside of me. Every tendril of shadow around me flickered in response.

I called it to me, letting it engulf me, welcoming the comforting feeling of its presence after so long. A deep breath escaped me as I felt it in place, filling me, lending me strength. For the first time since I landed in that cell, I was whole.

Only when I had enough, when it was coursing through my body and trailing my movements as long-lost companions, did I form a large talon to yank the door of my cell from its stone hinges.

The sound reverberated through the corridors and less than a second later I heard shouts. They may not know what was coming for them, but Flynn had trained them well, that much was certain.

I snapped the door of the cell beside mine free with the flicker of a hand. The man inside was old and short, his brown skin seemed frail with age, but his build was strong and his appearance serene as he took me in with a satisfied look in his warm and tired face.

"Aila," I said, "It is a pleasure to finally meet you."

Anger and power burned in my veins, in my whole body. Shadows trembled around me, but he didn't falter. The lines of his face brightened with something akin to awe and surprise.

"I'm Ezer," he said in the deep voice I'd grown so accustomed to.

He followed me without question, more surely and swiftly than I thought him capable. The ache in my body was a constant throbbing, but not enough to stop me, to slow me.

I opened every door I passed. Freeing every prisoner I could, offering a hand to every lost soul in my path.

The shouting and clanging grew closer, and it wasn't long before the first two guards reached us in the corridor. Blood drained from their faces as I smiled and two spikes of pure darkness impaled them in a single, swift movement.

When I reached the main passage, a small battalion had started moving, taking the left corridor by storm, in perfect formation.

I started moving towards them as I sensed the other prisoners moving to the right, running for the open sky. I threw talon after talon at the soldiers, ripping through flesh and breaking necks.

But my power began to flicker, and my body began to falter, too frail after the torture and the days with no water and food. My legs buckled without warning and I felt a strong hand under my arm, urging me to stand, to move to the open skies. Ezer.

"I need to get to her," I screamed through the chaos, in between slowing and weakening blows.

"You won't pass through them."

"I won't leave her behind."

"They will kill you!"

"They'll kill *her* because of *me*," my voice broke off.

"If they knew of her, they would already have used her. She would already be dead."

I knew he was right. If they had any idea of what she represented to me, she would have been right by my side in that torture room.

Ezer sensed my hesitation and pressed.

"Live to fight another day, Aila! Live and you can come back for her."

I finally nodded, doubt still clouding my every thought. He didn't give me a chance to reconsider before yanking me from the ground and taking me outside under the cover of the dark shield I threw around us.

Chapter 22

I could barely stand as we moved through the fields beyond Urian. The surge of power that allowed me to cover half the fortress in a black cloud was far from anything I'd done before and left me fully drained, half-fallen on the street. Still, it was a priceless distraction that bought us enough time to disappear into the night.

For the second time, Ezer dragged me toward safety. And either by trust or by tiredness, I let him guide me through hidden pathways in the fields without so much as a question.

Between the exhaustion and the throbbing pain of the unhealed wounds, there was not enough of myself to dwell on rational thoughts. There was only the immediate need for survival, and yet every couple of hours Ruby's face would spring to life in my mind and I would fight against my sluggish instincts and reach for the power inside me, too afraid that it would somehow be bound again, taken from me. But even if stripped bare, that deep place inside of me wasn't vacant anymore. An essence of Darkness remained live and flickering.

We walked quietly and surely.

Ezer wasn't the fragile, half-forgotten prisoner I first expected. He walked nimbly along paths I couldn't see. Certain and agile, old and attentive. His short hair was mostly grey and even though his body was weakened by the weeks in captivity, there was nothing frail or helpless about him.

He stopped as frequently as he could and let me rest for as long as two runaways would dare, but he didn't question nor push me out of my silence. Soon enough I came to appreciate the quiet, steady company.

I kept a step behind, focusing on nothing but the irregular terrain and the bright and silvery rays the large full moon cast on our path. We made slow progress and, with every breath, the sounds of the woods became louder and clearer: cicadas, crickets, the crisp running of a river. With every breath we left more of the city behind. Ruby with it.

We stopped at a riverbank, no bridges in view, only the relentless flow of a river too large to cross by foot and the grey sky, lightening up with the approaching sunrise. Ezer kneeled by the side of the river, half washing his face, half gulping as much water as he could.

"You've gone too long without water." I remembered Flynn's words and forced myself to crouch and drink, even if I wasn't thirsty. I took small sips near Ezer and felt the crispy water descend to my gut in a wave of iced relief, quietly easing some of the throbbing pain that had spread through my body.

"I'm afraid we can't stop for sleep," Ezer's voice was low and tentative "can you keep going?"

I nodded, never looking away from the river.

"Ok. We can spare some time, though."

There was no rock slowing the water flow. Just a steady strong stream that we couldn't risk crossing. So much uncontrollable water. I felt my lungs constricting, my eyes burning to the memory of drowning under Kiran's watchful stare and satisfied smile.

I looked away before the memory took hold of me. Dragging my attention back to Ezer. "How long does she have?" The words slipped through my mouth before I could stop them, as if to chase my memories away.

Either from my haunted face or my trembling hands, he knew who I meant.

"Most of the people there are left alone."

"How long?" I needed an answer as much as I feared it.

He took a long breath before saying: "Days. Weeks if they don't suspect a connection with you."

"And if they do?"

"They will use her in whatever way hurts you the most."

Days. I had days to take her out of there, and I would make them count.

"I need to find the Alliance," I said half to myself. I didn't know if I could trust them, but I needed allies, and we had at least one thing in common: we needed to stop Ivo.

He regarded me for a long moment before offering a curt nod. The certainty in him so palpable that I knew he understood.

So, I ignored the tiredness and the pain, and we walked through the rest of the day, never speaking another word.

◆

We arrived at the farm shortly before dusk. From a distance it looked like a vacant building in the middle of an overgrown wheat field. It was only when we got closer that signs of movement became apparent.

The wheat field around us stretched as far as I could see and worked as natural cover, high enough to disguise the curtains on the windows, the small vegetable garden on the edge of the terrain and the clean steps to the preserved front door.

Even when there was no mistaking this for an abandoned house anymore, there was no obvious movement, no people walking around the front of the house. Whoever the inhabitants were, they kept to the back of the property, where the barn and small orchard worked as an added barrier to unwanted scouts.

I didn't know what awaited me inside, but I knew I needed somewhere to re-group, a place to consider how I could get to Ruby.

There were no more than twenty people in the main room, a mix of men and women younger than Ezer. In spite of the cheers and hugs they offered him, none seemed surprised with our arrival, even if some still seemed a bit wary of my presence.

Ezer led me outside, to a wooden stool placed near a large and inviting hearth. He offered me a bowl of hot soup so fragrant it sent a rumble of hunger to my core, and when he sat across from me, I was conscious of the many eyes on us, and yet, I was too tired to care.

"I'll get a bed ready for you and a healer is coming in a few hours. Until then, you are safe here."

"Thank you." My voice was no louder than a whisper, my attention fixed on the untouched soup in front of me.

"I know you want to go back for your friend, but you need to find your strength first." He pointed to the bowl in front of me.

"I may not have the time."

"You'll be no good to her if you can't fight your way through." I couldn't argue with that. "You'll find your way back to her, I'm certain of it."

I examined him further. This was not a helpless man, not frail. He wasn't in that cell by mistake and this was not a common farm.

"How do you know?"

"You didn't break," he said simply. "You found something worthy to protect and you let yourself be dragged to hell for it. Not many choose that path, even less come back from it."

"Maybe I didn't come back from it. Not entirely, anyway."

He hesitated, as if searching for something in the lines of my face. I wasn't sure there was anything to find.

"You want to go back for your friend. I say the part that matters found a way back."

"What is this place?" I asked finally.

He looked around and I could see he was pondering how to answer my question.

"It is a safe-house. I'll explain everything. Just eat first, rest. You'll need a functioning brain when we talk."

A tall woman signaled to him before going back inside, never sparing me more than a glance. He nodded, rising to his feet, but settled his attention on me once again before leaving.

"Why free me?" he asked. The first real question he asked, the only one that truly mattered.

I faced the fire, its untamed rage matched the roar in my soul.

"I'm done sitting by as people suffer; I'm done being a docile pawn in someone else's game."

◆

Sunlight brought me back from sleep and, for the briefest moment, I had forgotten everything. As I blinked myself awake, there was nothing but the soft, simple mattress on my back and the birds singing by the window.

Then, the memories flooded me. Almost unconsciously, I commanded the shadows around me to rise, reassuring myself that my power was still within my grasp.

The room was simple with a jar of fresh, clean water, two other unused beds, a corner table and a chest sharing the space. I half-remembered someone bringing me here after the healer's visit and, even if I was too sleepy to remember more than that, a part of my brain had still registered surprise at the healing magic that flowed from the hands of a girl who looked nothing like a priestess.

A part of me felt exposed by how deeply sleep had claimed me, how utterly vulnerable I'd been. Yet, I was grateful for the dreamless night the healer's potion granted me.

I marveled at the painless movements as I dressed myself in the clean light trousers and slightly too-big shirt that'd been left on top of the chest. The bruises and wounds were all gone, not a trace of ache. Still, thin scars marked the several places where Kiran had worked harder, deeper. Not even healing magic could completely undo his creations.

I traced my finger over the faint marks on my wrists, remembering not the pain, but the reasons I had endured it. It was worth it, and I would never allow myself to forget it. None of it.

I washed my face carefully, letting the fresh water on my skin chase away the memories from the last few days.

Wary, tired, green eyes looked back at me from the basin's reflection as I tried to get a sense of my new reality: No luxury and high walls around me anymore. I was stranded on a farm in the middle of nowhere, circled by people who were conspicuous at best, dangerous at worst, with no weapons or maps, and the only ones who had ever offered me any type of love or friendship were either hunting me or stuck in a dungeon because of me.

In those silent minutes I ran through the few memories I had from my life before Ivo, the short years where I barely scraped by, where I'd seen more death and loss and violence than a child should ever have been allowed to. I remembered the attack when he found me and how happy I'd been to fall into his open arms.

"You are safe here, little one," he told me when we first arrived at our Villa. *His* Villa. "I won't let anyone find you here."

I was barely five then, but I'd already felt so much loss: parents that I didn't remember, a whole city dead around me.

"They will come for me, someone always does when they see the shadows," I whispered back.

"Then we'll hide it from those who can hurt you. I'll always keep you safe."

"I can't control it." My voice was so low, so embarrassed that I didn't quite understand how he heard me, but in no more than a second, he was kneeling in front of me, taking my hands in his.

"You'll learn to if you wish. And you should. Practice! Use your quarters, I won't let anyone follow you there." He tilted my face, so I looked at him "Make sure you are its master, little one. Not the other way around."

Ivo taught me not to fear my power as much as he taught me to need his protection.

Kiran and that dungeon changed me. For the first time I thought of my power as more than a sentence to death. Of Ivo as anything but my rescuer.

For years, I followed his every whim. I'd given all the blood and life I had in search of safety, but no more. From now on, I would honor love, not fear.

So, I finished cleaning myself, mustered all the frail confidence I felt in my heart and left the room, ready to find a way back to Ruby.

◆

No one paid me any attention as I followed the chatter to the outside camp. In the late afternoon light and after a long, deep sleep, I could finally see that the back garden had been transformed into a camp of sorts. Small tents were set around the big hearth to the edge of the field and the orchard seemed to buzz with excitement as a few younglings harvested its plump fruits.

The barn doors were open, indistinct shouting coming from it, Ezer stood in the entrance with the same young woman from the previous day. He interrupted whatever conversation they were having and made his way to me, hands on his back and a warm smile on his face.

"You seem better. Rested," he offered as way of greeting.

I nodded. "How long was I out?"

"Almost a full day. You must be famished."

I let him guide me to the hearth and offer me a bowl of broth, a piece of warm bread and cheese. I devoured it, not realizing how hungry I was until I tasted the rich, delicious flavor of the broth.

When I had made my way through half of the food he spoke again.

"Your wounds?"

"Healed." I looked at him, needing to acknowledge the words bubbling inside of me since I first heard his voice. "Thank you. You saved me in more ways than one."

He smiled faintly. "I just gave you a direction, you walked the path on your own."

I offered him a curt nod. Once again grateful for the direct simplicity of him.

"The healer," I asked. "She didn't seem like a priestess."

"That is because she isn't one." A bright smile spread through his whole face.

I must have seemed as confused as I felt because he continued. "The Goddess blesses the believers, not the ordained. Healing is not bounded by the church, even if they benefit from the belief that it is."

There was a simple logic to his words and yet I'd never heard of a healer who was not a priestess, never seen healing magic used without strings to the rich and powerful.

"They simply hide?"

"Ah!" His expression softened. "You, more than anyone, must know what it is to be hunted, what an incentive it is to stay hidden when your very existence is what puts you in danger."

I found no signs of fear or surprise in him at the mention of my power. No doubt or wonder, just the certainty of someone that had seen more of the world than I could guess.

Then, of course, he was right. I knew what it was to hide your power for fear that it would get you killed.

Comfortable silence stretched between us once again and I only spoke when I'd finished the rest of my food.

"I need to go back."

"I know," he nodded, "but your friend is fine for now, and she will remain fine for a few days."

"How can you be so certain? You've seen what they did to me, they could be doing the same to her."

He looked back at the fire before replying, considering.

When he finally continued, his voice was tired, pained. "Why did you break in, Aila? What were you doing there?"

It was an earnest question. Even if it felt laced with more than curiosity and fueled by knowledge he shouldn't have.

I took a deep breath before replying.

"I think I was led there. At first, I thought …" I didn't know where to start, but there was something in him that compelled trust, maybe it was the way he'd saved me when it mattered, or his kindness, or the simple fact that he had none of the things I saw when I looked at Ivo's eyes. Either way, I found myself pouring out truths.

I shook my head and continued. "Look, I've made many mistakes in my life; I've entangled myself with very dangerous people and forced my mind to believe it was fine, that I had nothing to lose. Until that changed and I cared enough about someone to risk everything else, even if it destroyed me in the process. In a way, that was the very choice that led me to that dungeon."

I knew there was no way he could understand it, and yet he didn't push me.

"What did they want from you?" he continued.

"I don't know, really. Something about the Alliance, but they didn't know who I really am, so they didn't know the right questions to ask." I dropped my head on my hands. I was so tired and so lost.

"But you still had answers." And even if it wasn't a question, I nodded. "Why not give it to them? It could have bought you time, maybe a reprieve?"

"No point on hiding behind the illusion of safety anymore."

He seemed to lose himself in thought, but I broke the silence before he could.

"So, is this the Alliance?"

A small and warm smile flickered. "What makes you say that?"

"Well, for one, you were not supposed to know how I was caught or what they wanted."

"You didn't miss that, did you?" Laughter laced his words.

I waited.

"Well, I told you this was a safe house. Not one that you would have seen in the maps you found, though."

"You know about the maps? You knew about me?" I asked with a shock of surprise.

"Not at first, no. It took me a while to piece things together. We knew the Premier was circling us, but it wasn't until you left Nuri that we suspected you were more than Ivo's niece. And I didn't suspect it was *you* in the cell beside mine until a couple days back."

"Who are you really, Ezer?"

"I'm one of the many people who keep the Alliance alive. I have been doing it for fifty years now."

I took a deep breath, connecting the pieces of everything he'd told me, of all the things he knew about me.

"You have people inside. Maids?"

He observed me for a long time, as if pondering what to share, how much to share. Until, he finally said, "Your friend was arrested for a disturbance; they don't have any idea of her connection to you. Not yet."

I lost a deep breath at that, a heavy weight immediately lifting from my shoulders. And yet, it was all too much. I had been chasing ghosts for months. Now I had landed right in the middle of an Alliance camp.

"Aila?" His voice was expectant enough that it brought my mind back to our conversation, my attention back at him. "We have a council meeting tonight and I would truly appreciate if you would agree to join me."

◆

Three people gathered around the big table in the main room of the house. Small plates of fresh bread, cheese and cured meat were spread between them and, as I crossed the door, they turned to me in a single movement.

The walls were unadorned and slightly cracked in a few places, with orange brick showing beneath the white paint. Heavy, worn curtains protected the window from view and candles and lamps spread across the table and floor offering enough luminosity for it to become a bright and vivid room. It was like anything else in the place: humble, old, and clean.

Ezer sat beside a woman - the same young woman I'd seen a couple times now - a man across from them, both about my age, if I had to guess. No one occupied the head of the table. An easy familiarity was apparent in their relaxed, informal demeanors, even behind the earnest, grave faces. Ezer smiled encouragingly and bade me to come closer.

I gave him the faintest nod and sat down close to them, facing the red-headed woman, unsure of what I should do next. A thin, pale white scar ran from her right ear to her chin, fiery, short hair moved a bit wildly with her precise movements. And under the gaze of her piercing stare, I wondered what had turned her into such a fierce, lethal force.

"It seems we owe you a debt of gratitude." She jerked her chin towards Ezer. Her voice was clear and full of authority.

"He saved me well before I could save him."

She nodded once. "So, your Darkness power or your role as the Fox's pet? Where do we start?" She leaned back in her chair, focus solely on me. It took me a second to realize she meant Ivo, and another to hold my amusement as I thought of how much he would hate the nickname.

"Easy, Bren!" Ezer said before I could reply.

"What? She is here, she saw all of this, and her fucking uncle has made it his life's mission to kill every last one of us. Is succeeding at it, by the way. We need to know where she stands! Dancing around it won't change anything."

I knew I wouldn't find easy trust among them, which was fine since I wasn't prepared to offer it either.

Besides, the fact remained that Ivo would do exactly that. It was his way-in with the king, a way to secure the job he'd worked his whole life for. But it was something else, also. I wondered if they knew exactly how afraid he was of them, or why.

Still, hearing her words and knowing I helped him get to such a powerful position, it stung.

"I didn't know this was an interrogation," I replied defensively.

"Think of it as an exchange of information, if it sits better with you." She was brash. A part of me couldn't help but like it.

The room remained silent, and even Ezer seemed to recoil from her words. I could see the unspoken truth in his gaze: he'd trusted me because I'd saved him, and as a result I knew more than anyone with ties to the Crown should. But I was yet to prove I deserved it.

"Ivo isn't my uncle, but he did raise me, which you already know. He is also dead-set on destroying everything I ever cared about. You'll find no sympathy towards him in me. Quite the opposite."

"You've lied for him before, many times I'd wager."

"I've been a happy pawn for most of my life, if that's what you're asking."

"And now?"

"Now he pushed me too far and I'm no longer inclined to let him threaten what I care about."

"Would that be our dashing young prince?" A snide smile slowly curled her lips.

For a brief moment everyone's attention shifted to her, the air in the room tense to the point of breakage.

Cold calm stilled my senses and my voice dropped to a dangerous, low rasp.

"*That* is none of your business. And I'm not your enemy, Ezer wouldn't be standing if I was. You should remember that."

I could see the thoughts running through her mind, the considerations, the choices she was making. Ezer could be the older person in the room, probably the wiser, but she was the strategist.

"Darkness?" she finally said, tension leaving her face.

It was my turn to smile. I summoned the shadows to me, letting them trail around me, dancing.

"Interesting," she said, "how did you stay hidden?"

"Ivo is a piece of shit, but he is damn good with secrets." A sarcastic smile tugged at my lips and she replied in kind.

I definitely liked her.

"I'll need more than that."

I took a ragged breath and let the words flow without thinking.

"I was young, he … *found* me, took me to a secluded villa and told me to learn my power and then hide it, taught me how to kill and spy. You know, fatherly stuff."

"Of course. And now, you are here."

I leaned back in my chair. "Now, I'm here."

"And what do you want, Aila?"

"What do *you* want? After all these years, what do you fight for, really?"

She considered me, and I could see the thoughts ravening through her mind. Then, a defying look took hold of her. "We fight for the impossible. We fight for a chance!"

It was my time to consider her. I had so much to ask, but it all came down to whether I could place my trust on them. And that was assuming they had the people and focus I needed to stop Ivo. There must be a reason why he feared them, why he wanted me away from them, but even if the Alliance knew why that was, I doubted they would spill it out so easily.

"For now, I need to get a friend out of that forsaken dungeon, and …" I studied every one of them, "I won't think twice before I kill anyone who gets in my way."

That seemed to break the spell that was keeping Ezer and the other man fixated on my conversation with Bren. They both moved, but Ezer was the first one to speak.

"No one will stand in your way, Aila. You are welcome here, but we won't hold you."

"I think I could like you, girl." The woman said with a bigger smile now. "I'm Bren. This is Leon."

Leon winked at me, barely dipping his chin. Mischief dancing on his deep eyes.

"What comes after we get your girl out?" he asked biting a piece of bread.

"I'm sorry … we?" I sounded more confused than I'd liked to admit.

"Smooth," said Bren under her breath.

"We'll help you get your friend, of course," Ezer explained "It is the least we can do."

For a moment, I didn't know what to think. I didn't know why they would even offer such a thing. Because it was true, I wasn't their enemy, but I wasn't their ally either. I wasn't sure about how I felt owing them anything, not so soon.

I shook my head slowly, never looking away from him. "I'm in your debt, Ezer. I wouldn't have a shot at saving her if not for you … I wouldn't be here if not for you. And I appreciate any information your contacts can give me, but I don't need any more than that."

"You'll need more than our contacts, Aila. And we don't leave people behind when we can help it."

"Besides, hun, where would the fun be in a long, safe life?" Leon added.

"Shut up!" Bren said with what seemed like a kick under the table.

I ignored them both.

"Why would you do that? We aren't one of you. You don't need to rescue us," I told Ezer.

"You could be," Bren interrupted.

"You were just grilling me. Now you want me to join you?" I snapped at her.

"I was getting to know you." she corrected with a hint of a smile.

Maybe driven by the disbelief in my face, she sat up straighter, leaned her elbows on the table and glared at me.

"Look, you stood up to those shitty guards and you gave them nothing. I know you kept secrets that weren't yours to keep. You brought Ezer back, and you gave hope to many of us. We all have a past, but as far as I'm concerned, yours is only relevant if you want it to be."

"How do you know what secrets I kept?"

"Let's say we have good contacts. Besides, there is no way you had the access you had, with the company you kept without seeing one thing or another." She was right.

"Why should I trust you?"

"You don't have to, but we are willing to help anyway. Think of it as a token of gratitude. No strings," she offered simply.

"Thank you," was all I had to offer, "all of you."

She nodded once.

"None of it matters now." Ezer drew my attention back to him. "You'll need a few days to recover, and we will need to prepare for our trip back to Urian. We'll have time to talk later."

We had a normal meal after that. As much as a former spy to the Crown could have with the leaders of the Alliance, anyway. They told me about the camp and how Ezer had been arrested. They talked about the worry when he was gone and the relief when we appeared at the camp.

They were like a family and something in me ached with the familiarity and care I could see in their shared jokes and silly arguments.

We never talked about the Alliance itself, nor about what bonded them to the movement. But I had the distinct feeling Ezer meant it when he said we would have time for those things. They were giving *me* time.

After what felt like a long and unexpectedly satisfying dinner, I bade them all goodnight and started to make my way back to my room. But before I made it to the door, Bren called out to me:

"Aila! For what it's worth, I don't think your business will be your own for much longer ... your princeling has been traveling with Ivo for weeks now. He is passing judgment on the rebels they've captured."

I remembered the execution in Kait, and the floor threatened to slip from under my feet again. He had once believed the rebellion had merit, he had believed we could all live in peace together. Before me, he had believed in a lot of things.

"He is not my …" She shrugged and I continued. "He … he wasn't always like that." It sounded like a poor excuse even to my own ears.

"Well, he is now."

Chapter 23

I didn't see Bren again but, at some point during the night, someone slipped a small pile of documents under my locked door with a blank note that had nothing but her name on it. It was a concise and complete report with accounts of Aiden's and Ivo's travels from Nuri and the judgement they'd passed on every single person accused of ties with the Alliance. All had been found guilty and executed in what could only be described as a mockery of a trial.

A few were active members or mid-level leaders, but most were only distant sympathizers. Some didn't even have ties with the movement. The more I read, the less I recognized the man I'd known and the farther Aiden seemed from the dreams he had defended so fervently.

I thought about the things Ivo would have found in my room, about how easy it would have been to convince Aiden I was working with the Alliance all along. I'd made it almost too easy for Ivo. Still, I didn't want to believe it had been enough to erase all that he knew of me, to convince him there was no truth in our time together.

I spent so many nights hearing him criticizing his father for similar empty violence, and now ... this was murder and he wasn't only condoning it, he was ordering it.

Hot rage burned in me, and I no longer knew if it was only for Ivo's manipulations. He wasn't acting alone, and he certainly didn't get there without my help.

I considered what my actions had set in motion and what my own responsibility in all of this was, until, unable to think about any of it anymore, I pushed the files aside and settled for fresh air instead.

It wasn't long before I found myself standing by the entrance of the barn I'd seen the previous day.

It had been converted into a training ring: archery targets to the right and two big rustic rings to the left. A large weapons rack rested by the side of the door with mostly wooden swords and spears.

The whole barn was empty, probably too late for the morning training, so I took my time tracing my fingers over the weapons. I'd never gone so long without training, never felt my body so weak and frail.

I didn't notice Leon until he spoke from behind me.

"Are you planning on dragging your ass to that ring anytime soon?"

Without the coat he'd worn the previous night, I could see the line of muscles on his arms and chest. He was slim built, but fit and strong, nimble if his silent approach was any proof.

He had the same mischievous glint in his amber eyes from before as he offered me a daring, playful smile. His hair was so light that it looked almost grey. Beautiful, not in an arresting way, but somehow enticing all the same.

"Maybe later, it's been a while."

"The longer you wait, the harder it'll get."

The barn door shut closed with a metallic clang, and I jumped. In the blink of an eye, my breath turned shallow, and my hands darted to the scars at my chest. The metallic sound so similar to the clang of shackles against a table iron frame that it sent my mind right back to Kiran's clutches.

In a split moment that felt like an eternity, the memories seized me: the pain, the feel of Kiran's fingers coldly tracing my body, the chain ripping through my wrist, Flynn's unwavering presence holding me together. It would swallow me whole. I breathed and breathed.

Leon took a step closer, angling his face to capture my attention. Careful enough not to touch me unexpectedly, but attentive, as his simple presence embraced me. His voice gentle as he offered, "it'll get easier ... eventually."

Instead of dwelling on his words, I asked the first thing that came to my mind, in desperate need of distraction. "I expected more of you. More people, I mean."

Mercifully, he heeded my silent plea and started to speak as he stretched his arms and shoulders, somehow never losing his jesting, relaxed posture.

"We are well spread, and always moving. There are never too many of us in the same place, not this close to Urian, at least."

He stretched his legs before continuing. "This is safe enough, but too close to the King's grasp. It is probably our emptiest outpost."

"Are there more people on the council?"

He nodded. "Nahla. She stayed at ... well, home."

I didn't miss the mild hesitation, and I had to remind myself I never accepted their invitation or committed to their cause. Even though I wished them no harm, I was still the fake niece of the man hunting them down.

I couldn't expect them to trust me any more than I trusted them.

"Is she your leader?"

"We don't really enforce rank. Let's just say she looks after the people."

"And you?"

"I keep our forces in line, train young recruits. Bren is our intelligence master; she keeps our safe houses and ensures we communicate. Ezer is our older advisor, the voice of reason if you will."

"So, half of your movement leadership just happened to be in your riskiest safe house at the same time?" I smiled, trying to inject a bit of light humor in my voice. "You may need a better strategist."

"Want the job, smarty?" he laughed it out, but for a moment I thought I'd seen a flash of hope. He finished stretching and continued more seriously. "We came for Ezer. You saved us a lot of trouble hand-delivering him. He is like a father to many of us, I'll be forever in your debt."

I met his gaze and mustered all the sincerity I could. "There is no debt to be paid."

He nodded once and I had no trouble reading the gratitude shining in his face.

"Sure you don't want to join me?" he said as he walked to the ring. "Show me what all those years of fancy classes you took can really do?"

I smiled faintly, but honestly, to my surprise. I searched the weapons rack again and Leon, sensing the shift in me, pushed. "If nothing else, it'll keep your mind busy."

Before I could change my mind, I reached for a pair

of short swords and joined him in the ring.

◆

"Ready to get your ass handed to you?" he asked after I stretched.

And then, he handed my ass to me.

My breathing was all wrong, the weight of the two swords in my hands too heavy and my balance off. It seemed like a few months of travel, followed by a few days of crippling torture and little food was all it took for someone to fall completely out of form.

For the first time, I understood what their offer to help me rescue Ruby truly meant. I had no hope of pulling it off on my own, magic or not. I was too tired, too weak, and too out of form. I barely escaped the first time and that was without Ivo and his guards in the city. Their offer gave me a real chance of freeing Ruby.

"You are not bad, Timal! For a skinny girl trained by fancy tutors, I mean."

I was laying on my back, panting, but my mind was gloriously empty. No uninvited memories.

"Not Timal." I corrected. "That is Ivo's name, not mine."

He nodded once and stretched out a hand to help me stand. There was an ease between us now, a level of familiarity: "Seven tomorrow?"

"Don't you have anything better to do?" I teased.

"Than kicking the ass of the most wanted face in the Kingdom? Nah, I'll clear my day entirely for you."

I scowled as I nodded in agreement.

"A couple days of training, food, and some running

will get you back on your feet. You'll be fine by the time we go get your friend."

"Ruby," I offered "Her name is Ruby. And thank you."

A gentle breeze passed by me as if in response. I looked around, surprised. There were no windows, and the door remained firmly shut, and then I saw the tricksy smile on Leon's face.

"You are a wielder," I whispered in disbelief.

In response, he made the wind run a bit wilder, scuffling the loose strands of my hair and yanking a small laugh out of my chest. The Royal library came to life in my mind with a perfect image of Aiden sitting across from me: *"They have wielder sympathizers now,"* he'd said.

"Why? How?"

Leon shrugged and replied in a serious voice, "My magic doesn't give me the right to cruelty. It is not a free pass to hurt people."

"But it gives you a lot of privilege. It gives you freedom and safety and a dignified life," I said pensively after a few moments.

"It does. And for a long time, I used it to hide from what is happening out there, but our silence is as damaging as their actions, and that is not good enough."

His face was intense, trained on my reaction. No more sign of the playful mischief in his face. Only hope and passion and wild resolve.

"We are beyond silence, Aila. We don't have a choice but to be part of the solution."

"And then what? Peaceful coexistence?"

"No, a thriving, loving world! One that we build to be equal and fair to everyone," he smiled. Gently and sweetly, as if remembering something, "You could see it for yourself. *Our* home, I mean. The world we've started to build."

The longing and hope in his face were so raw, so real, that I surprised myself. "One day."

His grin grew a fraction wider before his voice became loud and humored again. "One day! Now go feed your skinny ass so you stand a chance tomorrow."

◆

Ezer was waiting for me when I walked out of the barn. The fresh air – and his people, I assumed – had done him good. He was a far cry from the old man I'd freed from the dungeon.

"I see Leon got you into the ring."

"It felt good to be out of my head for a while," I admitted.

His attention lingered on the space behind me, Leon still organizing the weapons rack.

"He is a good kid, they all are." He turned to me before adding, "Walk with me?"

"Is Bren around?" I asked once we started moving.

"She left this morning."

My face must have shown some sort of surprise, because he added, "I'm afraid she won't be back at this camp for a while. May I help you instead?"

"It's ok. She left me a few documents I wanted to return."

"Ah, that."

Maybe I should have been surprised he knew about them, but I wasn't.

"Yeah ..."

"I'll make sure they find their way back to her," he

assured me.

The day was pleasant, but the chilly wind of mid-winter had most people indoors, so we walked silently and unobserved by anything other than the yellow wheat strands and the extinguished hearth. The faint fragrance of food and seasoning filled the air around us.

Maybe it was the lack of witnesses, or perhaps the reassuring peace his presence commanded, but I found myself speaking without restraint.

"What does your symbol mean?"

He took a deep breath and faced the sky, taking a few moments before replying: "That is the Heir Crest."

"I didn't know there was a crest."

He shot me a side glance. "How much do you know about the heir?"

"Not much," I admitted. "But I think you are about to educate me."

He laughed and eventually continued in a pensive, lower voice.

"The crest was created to represent the unexpected love that was born out of the hate between two sides of a war. A love that gave life to the Heir of Light and Darkness," he paused, and I sensed he was collecting himself so I waited. "Tell me, do you believe in the heir?"

"I was taught it is nothing more than a rumor spread through rebellious camps."

But since then, I'd accepted the world was not as simple as Ivo had taught me, I embraced my own power, and I met a Goddess who'd told me I would find myself in Urian.

"Now, I don't know anymore," I continued. "Do you?"

"Depends. There are many stories." He faced the fire

before continuing,

The most famous one was the most tragic. It suggests that the disappearance of the young Kalindi Prince – the last known Light wielder – was a betrayal. A ploy by his followers to preserve the royal heir. They tricked the Prince into leaving the island in search of rescue while the Elementalists obliterated every woman, elder, and child of his Kingdom in a bloody end to the great war.

The uncertainty of what happened to the Prince became a myth and fueled the idea of a lost heir, the last bearer of Light, cursed with Darkness and bound to bring reckoning to the Elementalists who doomed his Kingdom. A legend murmured across some of the rebel camps. A promise, not of liberation, but of revenge.

I'd been obsessed with the myth for a while. I hoped I would find an explanation as to where my darkness came from.

Eventually, Ivo convinced me the story was just that, a story. The last scrape of hope for people who'd known death too closely. For as imaginative as they were, none of the stories ever explained where the heir's darkness came from, and I'd never shown any light power. So, whatever happened to the young prince, it had nothing to do with me.

"Many believe the young Prince was deceived and lost to the war, but he didn't leave Kalindi in search of conflict. He left it in search of peace, he left to strike a treaty with the Isra warriors. Instead, he found love. Consuming and passionate love that resulted in a child and a new magic lineage, one that has been lost, hidden. Until now."

"I don't get it. How would that create a new magic lineage? How does Darkness play into this?"

He nodded pensively before replying, as if guessing

what those words would mean to me.

"The Isra warriors were able to control the shadows once. But this is a story for another time. A long one."

"You can't throw half a story at me, Ezer. Not about this. You've seen my power; I've searched my whole life for an answer to it."

"I know. Yet if you are to believe my tale, you'll need to trust me and right now you don't. Not yet."

My head was in uproar, my heart thundering. I wanted to pull the story out of him, to beg, to threat.

"And who gets to decide when I trust you enough?"

"You, Aila. Always you. I promise you the next time you ask me, I will tell you everything I know. I swear it." He took a deep shuddering breath before continuing in a softer voice. "But I have to warn you, once you hear it, there will be no going back, there will be no forgetting any of it. You must be sure."

"Will it explain where I come from?"

"I believe so. As much as it will show you your legacy." There was an ancient sadness in his face.

"Does the story also speak of the Moon Stone?"

A line appeared in between his brows, a sign of confusion.

"I'm afraid all I know about the Moon Stone is what is mentioned in scripture, my dear." Once he saw the disappointment in my face, he added "But I know someone who may have heard more. I can ask her if you wish."

I nodded.

A part of me wanted to push for more answers. But something in his tone, in the intensity of his stare made me hold my questions. Unsure of what I'd do with the answers.

"I've spent most of my life believing you were

lunatics waiting for a promised heir to bring revenge upon the Elementalists."

"Our fight is not about revenge; it is about hope. The prince's story and ours is one and the same, Aila. For the love that young Prince found, was the beginning of this rebellion, the first seed. They were the first ones to dare to fight for people like me. *That* is why we use the crest."

"Hope," I whispered.

"Symbols have power, Aila. I won't deny that the legend of the heir rallies people."

"There is not a drop of Light in my whole being," I answered his unspoken question.

"So, it seems."

"But I can't be the only one able to hide my abilities, can I? Maybe your heir is out there, somewhere."

"Maybe."

I looked at him in time to see the smile he was trying to repress.

"You don't believe me, do you?" I said in an incredulous voice. Amusement flickering in me at the sheer naturality of him.

"I don't believe in coincidence. That is all."

"Just in crazy legends?" I raised my eyebrow at him in fake disbelief.

He laughed. "Something like that."

Silence settled between us again and I knew he was right. Symbols did have power, symbols inspired people to hope and to fight. And ultimately, that was what both of us wanted.

I took a deep breath. "I'm no heir. Just a regular girl who has made a whole lot of mistakes. But I want to stop Ivo as much as you do, I've seen too much death and I'm sick of it."

He studied me for a long time, there was no one near us, nothing but the sound of the wind rushing by.

"You are not a regular girl, Aila. You slipped through the fingers of the King and his premier, you faced their torture chambers, and you didn't break. And you *are* the only Darkness wielder. So, light or no light, *you* are a living symbol now. And symbols have power." When I didn't answer, he continued. "Have you asked yourself why the executions *now*? Why is Ivo promoting a death procession now of all times?"

"He is freshly appointed, I messed up his credibility when I left Nuri. He needs to control the narrative again."

"No, child. He knows you can ignite the movement. Already there are whispers about your magic in the streets. You can ignite the whole rebellion. You can tip the scales!"

I was stunned, lost for words. A turmoil began in my stomach. Memories of what I'd seen in Kait blending with the reports I'd read a few hours before. *Was that why Ivo tried to keep me away from them from the beginning? But why would I aid them before all of this? Why would he think I'd betray him?*

Ezer held my arm, gently but firmly, and waited for my eyes to go back to his before pushing his next words out.

"The Crown decided to stifle hope with violence, but war is still coming. Soon enough you'll have to decide what role you will play in it."

Ivo was making his move, and a part of me knew he'd been making it for a long time.

Dara's parting words burned through my soul as the same words kept ringing in my mind: *pawn or rebel?*

"Make me your symbol, Ezer," I finally said back.

♦

I had dinner outside, along with some of the people staying in the farmhouse. Mostly some new recruits and a couple of soldiers.

We sat around the hearth, and I took the time to know them, to hear their stories, talk about their families. I didn't ask them about the movement, that was not why I was there. I wanted to know who they were fighting for.

Ezer and Leon came and went. They had dinner with their people, they laughed and chatted with them. Although they saw me, they let me be. Later that night, I found them in the room where I'd first dined with them. Papers and maps scattered over the table.

"Missing me already?" Leon said with a side smirk as soon as I crossed the door.

He had his legs on the table and a glass of wine in his hand. The portrait of easy amusement.

"I'll let you know tomorrow morning," I threw him a wicked smile.

Ezer hid his laughter, but I could see the hint of a pleased look on his face.

I went straight to the reason why I was there. "I know you have no reason to trust me, but I don't think you are safe here."

"No one is ever really safe, kiddo," Leon offered. His playfulness never fading.

I scowled. "Isn't my name good enough for you?"

"Nah ... we need something more personal," he winked. A natural and easy movement.

"We know the risks, Aila. This place is as safe as it

can be." Ezer declared, bringing my mind back to why I was there.

"Ivo is not a mere courtier; he has been the spy master for years and he has been collecting intelligence on your movement for a while now. He has a list of locations and names connected to you. I know him, it is just a matter of time until he finds this one."

I didn't miss the glances between them. Leon's amusement suddenly fading. He straightened himself in the chair and opened a map on the desk. It was like seeing him for the first time: not the warm boy, the general.

"What do you remember?"

I stepped closer to him and started pointing at the areas I remembered from Valran's maps. I never managed to decode what the locations meant, but it didn't matter now.

"He... *I* stole a lot of information from Valran for him and I don't know what else he may have collected on his own. There were things in his office I didn't have time to examine properly." Not for the first time I wished I still had the journal.

He gave Ezer a quick nod before holding my hand and facing me fully.

"Now I understand why we never got close to Ivo. Even so, we fed every single location to Valran, Aila. These are all inactive or flat out false," jerking his chin towards the locations I'd pointed. "We've been playing a dangerous game, but we've been playing it for a long time."

"He has more, Leon. I don't know where he got it from, but he had documents and a journal with your crest stashed in his coffer. I just never ..." my voice broke as I felt the control slip from me. I'd had my hand on all of this, I was also to blame for their losses.

Ezer was the one to fill the silence. "We'll ask Bren to

look into it. Maybe now that we know what to look for, she can dig something out. Until then we will double the scouts, stay alert."

"I'm sorry," I offered in a small voice and felt Leon gently squeeze my hands.

"You have nothing to apologize for," Ezer interrupted before I could say anything else.

"We all have a past, it is the future that counts," Leon followed.

I nodded, thankful for his words and reassuring touch.

"Now, what is this I hear about you being ready to change the world with us?"

I threw a glance at Ezer just to find some emotion I couldn't recognize on his face. A dimmed, unexpected emotion.

"Let's make it crumble … maybe we can build a better one," I confirmed with no short amount of fierceness.

Leon dropped my hand just to stand and throw his arm around my shoulder as he said with a grin, "Welcome to the Alliance, smart-ass!"

"You'll never stop with the damn nicknames, will you?"

"Not until I find the right one."

I rolled my eyes and asked unsure, to none of them in particular, "Now what?"

"Now, we train your skinny ass, and we rescue Ruby. The rest can come later."

◆

I trained with Leon every morning for the next four days, and we grew closer with every jab and joke. His constant jesting helped me to put distance between the present and the horrors etched in my memories. It was in that makeshift ring that I calmed my mind and reclaimed my control. It was also when we started crossing the line from allies to friends.

I told him about the little I recalled from my childhood and about Ivo. Soon I realized this was not about sharing Ivo's weaknesses, it was about sharing mine. Leon was the first person to whom I opened up. about how it felt growing up with him, being protected by him and about how sometimes, beneath the fear and anger, he still felt like the closest thing I had to family.

He told me about when he joined the Alliance and how it had been to be one of the few wielders in their forces. He talked about the resentment some of the rebels had towards him and how he'd been trying to recruit more wielders to their cause. *"There are more of us out there, I know it,"* he would say.

Yet, I never talked about Aiden, and he never talked about his life before the Alliance. That new thread of friendship still too young and fragile for the whole truth.

My afternoons were spent somewhat alone, diving in my own mind and power. I had never wielded my power so openly and it felt deliciously satisfying, so I made a big show out of it, covering the barn in clouds of darkness and countless shadow talons. I relished the feeling of the Darkness spreading through me, diving lower and lower in my own well of power with every day. Soon enough I had an audience of recruits as I did it.

At night I would join Ezer, and sometimes Leon, trying to predict Ivo's next moves, guess his defenses. And together we would prepare for Ruby's rescue.

He'd been in Urian for days now and there was no

indication that he knew I was ever in that dungeon. Even so, during that time, he'd changed recruits on the fort, maximized defenses and taken complete control over the city. The whole Alliance network in Urian was suddenly quiet, too afraid of catching the premier's attention.

Still, they assured me their contact inside the fort remained secure.

I tried to convince Leon to face Ivo now. Swift and unexpected. But there was no arguing with the fact that we were utterly unprepared to take on the number of soldiers he had on the fort.

Then, news arrived.

I found Ezer and Leon by the hearth. Grave faces watching a piece of paper burn on the bright flames.

"Is everything ok?" I asked without preamble.

"Bren sent news," Leon said without facing me "Ivo is preparing to sweep these fields. There are a few camps he could hit depending on the route he chooses."

"Our contact doesn't have his exact plan; we don't know how much of our location he has. You were right," Ezer joined.

"Ruby is still ok, though. Silver linings, right?" Leon's face marred with an unusual bitter smile.

I sat down by their side, watching the remnants of Bren's note disappear.

"When will he start?" I asked.

"Tomorrow," Leon answered.

"Then we evacuate people tonight, set a trap he can follow, and hit him when the fort is vulnerable."

Go on," Leon said turning to me.

Ezer's eyes remained focused on the fire as he followed my words.

"He won't go with the soldiers, not at first. He will want to be sure they have found something before making an appearance. Which he will ... to claim the win.

"So, we lay the groundwork, we leave him crumbs, make it look like they found us, show enough to entice them, to force them to send word to him. It will give us some extra time for evacuation. It will also leave the fort more vulnerable than it has been since he arrived. We won't have a better chance to get to Ruby."

Ezer was looking at me now as well. I remembered the spectacle Ivo organized in Kait.

"I don't believe he will travel hidden in the night. He'll want to make a show out of it. But we should still start evacuating now. We take no risks."

Ezer turned to Leon. "One night isn't much time for an evacuation but, if we focus their attention in one spot as the other camps draw back, and then attack the fort ..."

"We may just slip through the cracks," Leon finished. He faced me, all the general, and continued "Will you be okay back there?"

He'd seen me jump in panic at ordinary sounds more than once.

"I know what to expect this time. I have my magic and my power is stronger under the night sky. If I time my entrance ... I'll be fine."

"We keep it small and swift, and you are never alone in there, understand? We go in and out under my command." Every bit the damn general.

I nodded and, as if in response, Ezer started giving orders. "We focus their forces here. This is the closest camp to the city and the easiest in which to fake movement. Send Rorin to update Bren, she can organize the other camps and set up the fake leads to bring them here. Who are you taking with you?"

"David and Yan ... we'll brief them tonight," he added looking at me.

"Fine. I want everyone else out of here before sunrise. We move to the mountains," Ezer finished.

I watched the precise exchange of words, the orders that followed, and it hit me; they were a force to be reckoned with. Lethal. They might actually stand a chance in a war.

"Where in the mountains?" I asked before Leon left to put the orders in motion.

He smiled. "Home, Ace. We are going home."

◆

The next few hours were a haze. Leon, David, Yan and I memorized the dungeon maps and all the routes in and out. We hadn't intended to move so quickly, but we had put a basic plan in place for rescuing Ruby and we would have to use it.

"Our guy can't open the door for us without compromising himself, but he will leave this section free for eight minutes at the eleventh bell," Leon said pointing to the southern wall. "After that, we are on our own."

"Climbing?" I asked.

He nodded, never looking away from the map. "It'll be close, but we can make it. Can you keep us hidden from the sentinels on the other side?"

"Yes," I said.

We kept at it for hours. We discussed the role each of us would play over and over again, until we could recite every step in our sleep.

There were only a few hours and no space for errors.

We would all enter the fort, but only Leon and I would go to the Dungeon. Yan and David were our backup at the entrance, giving us enough time isolated with the internal personnel before any of the external guards could get to us.

With some luck, we would get Ruby out before an alarm rang. But, if an alarm did ring, we only had short minutes before the whole contingent was on the patio.

"They strengthened the protocols after you escaped," Leon said when it was only the two of us in the big room; David and Yan long gone to get a few hours of sleep before we had to leave. "If that alarm rings, we won't get out as easily as you did last time. We may not get out at all."

"You call that easy? Maybe I kicked your head a bit too hard this morning."

He sneered. "It was a fucking miracle that you escaped that dungeon in the condition you were in, but you had surprise on your side. The protocols they have now … what you did last time will look like a walk in the park."

I knew what he meant. I'd seen how Flynn kept those guards trained, and with the extra forces from Ivo. … By the time I spoke again, Leon's attention was back on the maps.

"I had help," I finally said. "The fort captain. I'm usually very good at reading people, but …"

He gave me a look I couldn't ignore.

"Ok. Maybe not Ivo or …" Aiden's name died on my lips before I could force myself to say it. "Anyway, I don't know where this guy stands. He always does the opposite of what I expect. It's like he is toying with me."

He didn't look at me when he said, "He won't be a problem."

He tossed me a small red vial. Shockingly similar to the one I'd gotten from Flynn days before.

"Drink it before we go in," he said. "Call it extra-safety."

I examined and pocketed it before forcing myself to find some troubled sleep.

Chapter 24

By the time I found Leon the next morning, there was no one else at the farm. The hearth had been filled with enough wood to burn for the whole day and into the night, the curtains had been opened wide and a few lanterns were burning on top of desks and chests, the barn doors wide open.

What seemed like a vacant building at first, now beamed with staged life. Hopefully enough for the house to pass as an occupied place from the wheat field beyond. At least for a few hours.

I had only a short time to rest, but sleep is a fickle thing for troubled hearts. So, with the first signs of light, I braided my hair tightly, put on the clothes Leon gave me and arranged the belts and straps in place. I let every movement center me, steel my mind, chase away the doubt and worry.

The short boots and sleeveless, black jumpsuit were a perfect fit, adjusted through small straps that could hold small tools or vials and reinforced with extra pads and precious cushions over the more vital areas of my body.

I stashed a dagger in one of the hidden pockets and left the straps of the large belt empty. I'd get some weapons from the training rack before leaving.

Finally, I arranged the long black cloak around my neck and held what looked like a neckerchief in my hands. It was a type of thick black scarf with a golden clamp on top of it to hold it on my face. I tested it out, adjusting the elaborate golden clamp on the bridge of my nose, and studied my reflection on the window glass. Between the fabric and the hood of the cloak only my eyes were visible and, despite the thick mask filtering the air, I could still breathe surprisingly well. *Very clever.*

Leon was wearing an identical set of clothing as he honed a long sword by the hearth. It made him look more serious and lethal than the man I'd grown used to.

His gaze followed me from the moment I left the house.

"Any trouble with the straps?" he eyed the belt on my waist.

"No. Fits like it was made for me."

"It was. I mean, I had to guess some of the measurements, but I had it made for you. Bren took the request with her when she left."

"That is … thank you!" I truly meant it. "How did you know I was going to join you?"

"I didn't. But it didn't matter. You'd need it either way."

Gratitude filled me and I nodded once. There were no words, but I knew he could read the emotion on my face all the same.

"It is clever. I've never seen a suit like this."

"I designed it over the years. I haven't tested the mask in the field yet, but we'll know soon enough."

He signaled to a box on the bench and said, "I honed them for you this morning."

A beautiful pair of short swords lay inside. Intricate mother of pearl handles and slightly curved blades with delicate etchings. I raced my fingers across the blades in awe of their beauty.

When I said nothing, he added, "I know you'd prefer a sai, but I couldn't find a pair."

"No," I said quickly, "these are perfect, beautiful! Thank you."

"I thought if you were going to go down to the fox's lair, you might as well do it in style." He winked.

Warmth found its way to my heart and a smile broke free.

I strapped the swords to my side as I asked, "How did you know about the sai, anyway?"

"Told you we have good intel, ace!"

I wanted to ask more, but Yan and David joined us and the easiness between us was suddenly replaced by focus and an edge of adrenaline.

We left the farm an hour later, not daring to stay longer and risk meeting the guards on the field. We moved silently, taking the time to cover our tracks and making careful progress towards the city. Even with our slow pace, it was still much faster than the rhythm I'd been able to set with Ezer days before.

It was early night by the time we approached the city and found a place to rest and wait for the eleventh bell.

♦

When the bell rang, we were in position, hiding in dark shadows by the Southern wall. Only Leon and I took the red potion and used the neckerchiefs, but we all had arm bracers in place and hoods drawn as low as possible over our faces. Yan climbed first, with a rope in tow. He was incredibly fast, an agile spider running up the wall, brick after brick.

We only had eight minutes before the next patrol, and we used every second well. By the time the patrol reached this side of the wall, we were safely hidden on the patio beneath. We kept close to the walls and made quick progress to the dungeon, my shadows hiding us under a cloak of darkness.

With the map in my mind, I moved precisely and intently, yet I kept searching for hidden doors and threats, part of me waiting for the one that would get me locked up again.

I slowed my breathing, consciously letting the measured rhythm calm my senses. Leon touched my arm in a silent, and welcome, reminder that I wasn't alone.

When we reached the entrance to the dungeons, I commanded a soft tendril of shadows around my fingers, needing the reassurance that my power was still dancing inside of me. I was in control, and it was time.

David and Yan remained at the main corridor entrance, ready to warn us if any extra guards approached. Leon's contact would keep our route understaffed, but there was no room for error.

We went straight to Ruby's cell and soon chatter found its way to us. Two voices rose and recognition ignited immediately. The two guards who had fetched me and held me, standing by as I was beaten and tortured. The two young men who given the choice, had decided to do nothing.

I felt the air shifting, Leon had started to draw the air

to him; a quick, silent kill was smart, I knew it. Still, I found myself reaching for his arm, halting him in a wordless command.

I unsheathed the short swords in a precise movement and understanding shone through his face. I needed to feel their blood on my hands, I needed this small revenge.

And he let me have it.

The breeze started to move in a different direction, forming a shield behind us, muffling the sounds. I stepped into the corridor, moving shadows engulfing me as I ran towards the two stunned guards. By the time I let the darkness reveal me there was no time for them to draw their own weapons.

I thrust my right blade through the neck of the guard on the left, releasing it as I swirled behind him and pierced the second guard on the back with my left blade, holding him in place as I sliced a clean cut on his throat.

It was quick and brutal, and I welcomed the iron smell of their blood as I watched their bodies splay at my feet.

Leon touched my shoulder, breaking the influx of memories trying to flood me from the depths of my nightmares. His clear, non-judgmental features brought me back to the present and I ran to Ruby's cell, a mere ten paces from where we stood.

She was curled up in the far corner of the small, dirty space. Hugging her legs, forehead touching her knees. Her luminous hair was dull, hay stuck between the braids. The image alone sent a shiver through my spine and I moved before I had a chance to picture myself in the same position.

The dark tendril I sent through it easily dismantled the lock on the door and, in less than a breath, I was kneeling in front of her, holding her shoulders as gently as I could.

"Ruby?" I whispered.

She raised her head slowly, focusing her big eyes on me before noticing the open door at my back.

"You're alive." She held my face, tears starting to roll.

"I'm fine! *We* are fine! Are you hurt?"

Her face was still frozen in disbelief, but she shook her head and my heart cracked with relief.

"Are you strong enough to walk?"

"Yes, yes. He always brought me food and water," she murmured.

"Ok, we have to go now. We'll need to be quick."

"You came back for me."

I squeezed her shoulders and whispered, "I didn't leave you behind before, I'm sure as hell not leaving you now."

Leon was dragging the second body to the cell when I ushered Ruby up. I motioned for her to follow us, and we traced our steps back to the entrance of the dungeon. No alarm, silent, and swift.

Moments later, David and Yan joined us, remaining behind Ruby, covering our flanks. The promise of safety built between us, stronger with each step closer to the door.

Then the smell of hydrangea made Leon and I stop dead. We glanced at each other, knowing too well that our fragile plan was starting to crumble.

Leon directed a small breeze to take away as much of the venom as possible while I motioned to the others to stay behind.

The two of us crept furtively to the door, observing, assessing. Outside, the full contingent of the fort waited. Ivo at the center, Flynn a step behind him.

Leon swore under his breath, his face strained as he

searched for exit points. But there were none. Not a single route was unprotected.

Ivo outplayed me. He knew I was there, and he wouldn't let me out without a fight.

I held Leon's arm, turning him to face me. There was not a trace of warm humor left in him. Only cold, calculating fury.

"I'll buy you time." I said, high enough for him to hear me clearly.

"Not a chance."

"I'm the only one who can distract him long enough, Leon. You know that."

"You can't fight all of them."

There was no arguing with it, they were too many.

"I don't plan on engaging in single-handed combat."

"I know you are powerful, but they may have wielders too … and I don't know how much the mask and the potion will hold against more hydrangea."

"I don't intend on winning …" I didn't hide the sadness in my voice. I wished I had more time to know him and the others. To help them.

"I'm not leaving you behind," he said in his general's voice. But not even his will could change the odds stacked against us.

"You just met me, Leon. You'll survive." I knew it wasn't the time to banter, but I needed the ease between us to come back, and there was nothing else to say.

"I won't leave you, Aila."

I lost a breath: "You are not *leaving me*; you are getting *them* out! No matter the cost."

Maybe it was the certainty in my tone, but he nodded slowly. A small crease between his eyes as he shifted back to planning, so I continued. "If I don't follow, you make my death count, you make me a fucking martyr if you have to." There was no time to offer them anything but my death.

He nodded once.

"I'll make it count." his voice was thick as he kissed my bloody hands.

"Tell Ruby …" My voice broke but I pushed the words through anyway, "Tell her, thank you. Tell her it was all worth it."

"I will," he whispered.

I wiped the tears threatening to fall on my cheeks as I faced the door, head high. Before I crossed the threshold, I pointed at the side entrance I'd used with Dan not so long ago. "There. I'll keep you hidden for as long as I can."

I walked into the open patio without waiting for a reply.

◆

The guards were in tight formation, line after line in front of Ivo, shielding him. Flynn was a step behind, but I didn't see any other familiar faces, not Kiran, not Tyler.

I summoned all the arrogance and malice I'd learned from Ivo to my veins, stepping back into the role I'd played for so many years, and walked deliberately slowly, letting shadows trail behind me, dancing and swirling. I willed them towards my hands, veiling my fingers slightly, letting the image of talons confuse their senses, heighten their fears.

Only when I heard the soldier's gasps, their attention fully on me, did I make a show of measuring the whole space, slowly glancing from man-to-man, except for Flynn, afraid of what the sight of him might unravel in my mind.

I used the moment to make sure Leon and the others were in position and gathered some cover for them through the forgotten Northern wall, willing the shadows there thick enough to offer hiding.

Then, I lowered my cloak, eyes fixed on Ivo, a poisonous smile on my face.

We stared at each other for a few moments before he advanced a few steps and broke the silence with a cold voice.

"You really thought I wouldn't see you? It is one thing to break into a prison with a second-class staff, but it is quite another to come this close to me unnoticed. Tsk, tsk. I taught you better than that."

Unease stirred the nearby soldiers.

"You look well, uncle." Pure boredom leaking from me.

The soldiers shifted again, uncomfortable. Still, no one broke formation.

Ivo ignored my reference to our familiarity.

"You've made quite a mess of things, Aila dear."

"I thought it was time to see what power really tastes like."

"Is that what you are after then?"

I shrugged. A perfect portrait of entitlement.

"Let's just say it was time to leave the nest."

I thought I saw a flash of pain and regret on his face, but I knew I was just seeing what I wanted because his voice was as cold and amused as ever.

"That could have been arranged, of course. Still can." He paused slightly before continuing. "Maybe we can even ease your punishment, provided we improve your current company."

He glanced at the door behind me. But I knew the

others had started moving the moment I got Ivo's attention, I just had to keep him talking a bit longer for them to reach the small gate.

I laughed ironically. "I don't think that will work for me." I paused slightly, twisting my face into a purely vicious expression. "You see, I've become quite used to being the one giving the orders, and after the little talk Billy and I had, I'm pretty sure you and I would have irreconcilable views on what being leashed to you really means."

Anger flashed through his face at Billy's mention. Barely perceptible for anyone other than me. There and gone, instantly.

Yet, part of his amusement faded away. He steeled his features and said lower than before, "You'll do well to remember that you need me, dear. Now, more than ever."

"Ah, yeah. Premier. Congratulations are in order, I guess. Good for you, you've sulked on that one for long enough."

He laughed, dangerous and wild. "Oh, Aila, you've never learned, have you? You could have had the world."

For a moment I recognized his passion, I remembered the emerald necklace I'd left in Nuri. And it was enough to remind me that his power over me never came from the secrets he held. Not really.

I clenched my hand in a tight fist even as I tried to keep the emotion out of my face. Leon and the others would be close now, I just had to distract Ivo a little longer.

"With you behind me." Not a question, an acknowledgment. One he understood.

"With a King by your side. If you'd just had the patience, you could have had all the love you ever wished for."

I felt my blood burning at this mention of Aiden, at the idea of the poison he must have spilled in his ears to make him go along with so much death and violence.

Ivo was the source of every pain I'd ever felt, and yet a thousand warm memories flashed in my mind at the sight of him.

I locked away every image of Sunday lunch with him, every time he rocked me to sleep with a story, every proud look he gave me when I learned a new sword maneuver. I shot down a whole life with him as I lay the bitter question burning my soul at his feet.

"The love you robbed me of? Was it you, Ivo? Did *you* burn that town to the ground when you hunted me? Did you kill my parents when you searched for me?"

A flash of surprise crossed his face and, before he could recover, I continued, rage spilling through every word as the angry voice inside of me roared. "Why did you want me so badly? Was I worth so many lives? So much pain?" Despite myself my voice broke at that word, at the weight of it, at all I had lived and learned in the past few months.

It was enough for Ivo to regain his control.

"There it is ... you got emotional, attached. You've become a pathetic, weak thing."

I wanted to scream, I wanted to beg him to stop it. I wanted to kill him, but I didn't. It was still too soon for a fight to break out.

"That is why you are here, isn't it? To find your prince, to demand I stop hurting people for you?" he pressed in a sharp cold voice. "You care too much, Aila. It'll be your doom; I'll make sure of it."

He knew just how much all of it hurt me, just how much guilt I'd be taking from his actions. And he knew exactly how to exploit it.

Then I felt a familiar breeze touch my face, soft and certain. A sign and a good-bye. They were in position.

I closed my eyes and breathed it in, holding to its feeling against my skin long enough to wish them good luck and then I unleashed a dark hell on the earth.

◆

Chaos erupted as I raised a translucent shadow dome around me before sending two talons of shadow through the closest soldiers' lines. Men began screaming and advancing in a rehearsed motion and not a second later I heard the small side gate jerking from its hinges with the force of Leon's howling wind.

Hydrangea bottles smashed against my shield, and I prayed silently that the potion I'd taken would hold long enough to buy Leon and the others the time they needed.

My first attack decimated the two front rows, but it scattered the other soldiers so much I couldn't get the same effect again. I willed the darkness into large spikes instead, taking out two or three soldiers at a time as the others hammered at and shot long arrows against the shield between us.

Ivo and Flynn remained unmoving, watching from the back as I wielded every scrap of darkness in the patio into an unwavering killing shape. When the terror of the first attacks faded, the soldiers recovered their grasp on logic and started facing my shadows with shields and swords.

Soon enough, they learned the talons were nothing but shadows made solid and, even though deadly they could still dodge, deflect and defend from them in a similar way that they could from any sword. Suddenly I was fighting on eight different fronts and maintaining a full domed shield. My power drained, the well inside of me emptying with every breath.

Still, I kept fighting beyond any limit, beyond any fear, for I knew every second I lasted would make a difference to the others.

My grasp on the shadows flickered and the soldiers gained ground. I wouldn't last much longer. At my command, a cloud of darkness spread across the patio in an attempt to unleash panic once more. A draining divisive tactic, but the only one I had.

The shouting increased as the blows on my shield grew stronger. My balance was off, my head and limbs heavy and uncontrollable. Still, I unsheathed the beautiful blades sitting on my waist and waited for my power to vanish. I was ready and I would go down fighting.

Then, I felt it. Waves of scorching fire laced sure, strong steps. Barely a second later he advanced through the walls, from the tall building beyond the patio. "Enough of this!" A strong and certain command.

The blows stopped at the same time my grasp on the darkness slipped and my knees collapsed me to the floor.

The clouds, the talons, the shield, they all vanished into thin air as I gaped at the sound of Aiden's voice. At the sight of him walking through the high walls, trailed by flames. A stronger demonstration of his place as Heir of Niram than I'd ever seen him make.

He walked to the middle of the patio as I rose to my feet, studying his face. Seeing him in Kait had been disheartening. But seeing the hollowness in him? It was devastating. Heart-breaking.

"You're here," was all I managed to say. Never losing the grip on the swords that were my only means of defense now.

"Did you expect me to wait behind the walls of the palace as you plotted to destroy my Kingdom? Everything my family worked for?" His voice travelled over the whole patio, full of a hatred I didn't know he could muster.

"I expected you to protect your people, not slaughter them." My own rage flared up in response to his.

"I do what you forced me to do, I *am* what you made me," coldness laced his every word.

I examined him as if his whole face was new, and in a way it was. The silence around us was paralyzing, the soldiers seemed confused with the tale unfolding in front of them. Yet, they remained in position, waiting for their prince's command, oblivious to all the history between us.

Ivo and Flynn tersely followed every word, every breath and glance between us.

I wondered if he'd heard anything that Ivo had said, if I still had a chance to show him the truth. So I looked past the audience we had amassed, ignored Ivo's vile smirk and extended Aiden the trust I never had the courage to give him in Nuri. I offered him the truth.

"The thought of you kept me moving, it brought me here. The hope that I could explain everything, that I could—"

He cut me off. "Could what? Claw your way back to my bed and my favor?"

I scoffed. "No, it was never about power with you, and it is not about that now, either."

"Then what is it about, Aila? What is it that you want to explain so badly? Why shouldn't I order you executed right now?"

"I was afraid, Aiden! Afraid I would lose you, afraid I would scare you away. But now I can't stop thinking that if I had shown you the real me…"

"I've seen the real you! You fled into the night *because* I saw the real you." The sarcasm in his voice was painful and I felt the loneliness behind the lies I'd told him. Once again, I remembered how many times I wished he could see beyond the image of the docile lady I projected. How deeply I hoped he'd look at me as much as I looked at him.

Bitterness made its way into my heart and my voice. "You've seen what you needed to see: a perky defenseless girl, someone you could be a hero for." I smirked. "I've never been that innocent girl, but you should know that. You, of all people, have seen things I never dared show anyone else."

I took a deep breath and looked around. I measured the soldiers in position, Ivo's satisfied face, Flynn's unreadable expression, before settling my gaze on the fiery crown atop Aiden's head, taking in the symbolism of it.

Then I remembered his face as he passed judgement in Kait and I steeled myself as I continued.

"I thought I could show you the truth, *my* truth. I thought we could find a way to figure out what we could be without the lies, but now that I see you standing against everything you ever wished for, I know it is not about what I can show you, it is about the choices you are willing to make." I spread my arms. "This is all *your* choice. Go ahead and make me the villain of your story if you must, Aiden! But remember, I'm not the one sentencing good people to death. I'm not the one standing against my own people." My voice was raw with pain and anger, for whatever my hopes, we'd never be more than spy and prince.

"I loved you." he screamed. The words he'd never

had the courage to say out loud, that I'd never had the courage to consider. "And you lied and betrayed me for *them*? I was ready to face the world for you, Aila, and you chose a fucking rebellion."

I saw the pain flickering in him, the ache in the way he said my name, soaked in suffering and regret. My grip on my sword loosened a fraction in response. A sliver of hope flashed in my heart at the thought that he wasn't all resentment and maybe there was a way to mend some of the damage I created.

I softened my voice this time, letting some of my own pain show. "I never betrayed you. I tried to protect you, and I did lie, but not for them. I lied for …"

I never managed to say Ivo's name as two life-altering things happened.

The first was a throwing knife flying through the throat of a guard who had used my distraction to approach my open flank. A guard that would have struck me from behind a moment later.

The second was Flynn fighting his way through his own defenses. Flynn, landing by my side, back against mine, a sickle blade in each hand and a missing throwing knife on his belt.

Aiden froze at the sight of the two of us back-to-back, the pain I'd seen on his face completely replaced by cold, empty hatred. Before anyone could react, Ivo was back in full command, issuing orders and reforming the lines.

I was no longer alone, but I was still surrounded and depleted.

"Northeast," Flynn said under his breath, voice sharp and urgent. "If we leave this patio alive, we go northeast. It is our only chance to break the city blockade. Do you understand?'

"Our guy can't open the door for us without compromising himself," I remembered Leon's words as all the other clues clicked into place. I didn't allow myself time to second guess it.

"Stay close to me, Wheelan," I said as I delved deeper into whatever power I had left. I'd never reached such limits before, but I had no time to worry about consequences.

I sent a wave of crushing darkness through the archers on the top of the walls, freeing us from the long-distance threat, and immediately felt the lines between my own consciousness and the Darkness bend, my view of the world blur.

Some primal part of me felt a connection with all the untapped power around us. I *saw* with astonishing clarity when Aiden's Fire started collecting, pure flame building around him in preparation for an attack. I was beyond thought, beyond controlling the power flowing through me. All I could feel was Darkness. All I could see were the lines of power flowing through the veil of the world.

Images of the years with Ivo surged in my mind and I watched, once again, the death of the child I could have been, the death of the love I could have met. Loneliness ceased and all I could feel was the familiar comfort of the shadows beckoning to get closer and closer.

My body felt heavier than ever, completely out of my grasp. I was at the end of the well, lost deep into my own soul and there was nothing but eternal loneliness and death in it.

But then a new set of images flashed through my mind. I saw Ruby smiling under the starry sky, Leon's mischievous smile in the fight ring, I heard Ezer's voice flowing through a small hole in a dark cell, I saw nameless faces around a bright hearth, and I realized that somewhere along the line, the world had become less lonely and less scary.

I felt a tiny slit on the dark place where my power had always been. There, among shadows, a luminous dot waited, too fragile to touch but undeniably bright.

As bright as the golden eyes tethering me to life when I was about to give into despair, unwavering through the pain and horror.

Then the luminous dot exploded out of me in searing, blazing sunlight. Free from its hold, shining bright through my skin and spreading scorching heat into the world beyond.

Chapter 25

I remember Flynn shaking me, the buzzing in my ears, the scorched bodies and destroyed walls around us. I remember destruction and charred marks.

Even if there was not an ember anywhere, there was heat and there were ashes all around us. There was the feverish feeling of my own skin and the searing white light I kept seeing in my mind.

Flynn half-carried me out of the wreckage and into the woods as I tried to hold myself up, to take one step after the other. Yet awareness was quickly slipping away, my body failing me.

"Don't you die on me." was the last thing I heard before my world went utterly dark.

I dipped in and out of consciousness as Flynn carried me through the streets and wood tracks, never faltering.

When I finally woke, we were in a small, silent clearing. The sky was the pink-grey shade of a quiet early morning, and a hot fire kept the biting autumn cold at bay.

My first thought was for the ache in my body. A throbbing, exhausting pain in my limbs, core and head. I felt empty and yet, full. I couldn't begin to understand what had happened on that patio, or how we had survived, but a part of me was too afraid of reaching to that hidden corner of my soul where my power lay, too afraid of the sliver of light I would find there if I did. Of what it proved.

I turned my face to the fire instead, relishing its warmth, breathing in its smoky scent.

Flynn sat across it, throwing what looked like small twigs into the flames. He was lost in his own thoughts, seemingly oblivious to me waking up.

For the first time, I observed him. Not measuring an opponent or searching for the response to a puzzle, just studying him. It was three times now that he had saved my life, three times he had held my destiny in his hands and *chose* to not let go.

The thought I'd buried in my mind during the fight found its way to the surface. He had been the one sending false intelligence to Valran all those years, keeping the Alliance safe. And he had risked his cover by protecting my secret and helping me escape.

I mustered the little energy I had left and sat up, attracting his attention.

"You're up. Good," he gave me a quick glance before turning his attention back to the fire.

"How long have I been out?" I winced. My voice was hoarse, and each word felt like a painful scratch in my throat.

"Couple of hours."

The scent of herbs hit me. He wasn't feeding the fire, he was cooking.

I got up and walked to his side, sitting between him

and the small pile he'd made with our weapons. My swords and dagger had been cleaned and laid atop of it.

A small fish was roasting on a makeshift spit and my stomach grumbled at the sight of it.

"It's almost done," he said as if in response.

I nodded and silently observed the flames roaring.

After a few minutes I blurted. "You saved my life."

"Not bad for a jerk, I guess," he said not bothering to look at me.

"You're Leon's contact. You were there for Ezer." I finally put in words the suspicion I'd refused to acknowledge since I arrived at the farmhouse.

He nodded.

"Is that why you killed Valran?"

He didn't offer me an answer as he started to cut small pieces of the fish for us. And I didn't need one.

We ate in silence, the only noises the crack of the wood in the fire.

It wasn't until we were both done that I dared speaking again: "Why did you do it, Flynn?" his first name felt surprisingly familiar on my tongue.

He went taut for a moment. Maybe it was a foolish question, but I needed an answer anyway. He'd taunted me at every opportunity, he had all the reasons to let me rot in that dungeon, but he didn't. Even now, he was choosing *my* life over his whole movement.

"Because the world needs changing and he was too close," he offered simply. Valran clearly still on his mind.

"No. I didn't ..." I shook my head and started again "I meant why did you bother saving me so many times, you had no reason to."

He turned to me, and we faced each other fully for the

first time since he had freed me from that dungeon. His eyes twinkled with something raw and deep, and I thought he would say something revealing and cathartic, instead he offered simple words in a husky voice. "I had to."

I raised my eyebrows. Maybe I didn't understand him completely, but he didn't strike me like the type that does anything because he *had* to.

"Fine," he said, a flicker of irritation flaring before he faced the fire once again: "Whether I like it or not, your very existence gives people hope, it gave *me* hope."

"The heir thing," I mused.

He was silent for a long time and when he spoke again, his voice was lower, hoarse: "That is what I keep telling myself, but seeing you on that patio ... I just couldn't let you die thinking you were alone." There was no banter or audacity in him. Maybe for the first time since we met.

"You blew your cover so I wouldn't die alone?"

He looked at me once more, this time holding my stare as he said in a wobbly voice. "Don't make me regret it, Aila."

I didn't know if it was the raw look in his face or the sound of my name in his voice, but I didn't look away. For the first time there were no masks or games between us, no banter or irony.

For whatever it was worth, in that silent clearing there was nothing but the rawest parts of us and I refused to shy away from any of it.

So, we sat there, holding each other's eyes in the same way we'd done many times before. Except now, there was no doubt clouding my mind, no fear or concern. This time I knew he had as much to lose as I did. And he'd still risked all of it for me.

After what felt like an eternity he said, "You should rest, we still have a few hours before we need to move again."

He was right so, without a word, I crossed our little camp and went back to the improvised bed he'd laid out for me, covered myself with my cloak and let the crackling of the fire cradle me into a deep and dreamless sleep, without ever considering retrieving a weapon.

◆

We avoided the roads and, instead, walked silently and painfully slowly as grassy fields gave way to tall, green mountains with plateau like tops.

I'd never dreamt of being in these mountains, never imagined there would be anything for me here. Strangely enough, that was also comforting: the lack of salty air, the unexpected height, the lack of visible cities and people … it all seemed new and unexpected. It all seemed to fit with the changes I'd lived over the past few months.

As I watched the untouched mountains with their never-ending green blend among hard rocks, I realized that I could finally breathe easily, a part of me at last allowing myself to feel free.

There was no clear path ahead of us, but Flynn seemed familiar enough with the way to keep us in a steady, due direction through the quiet and crispy days.

It was mostly empty that far deep in the north, and the closer we got to the mountain itself the farther it seemed to stretch, the larger the plateau at its top seemed to be. Real highlands, a new world on top of this one.

It was still late autumn, but the altitude alone was enough to make the unrelenting, chilly wind keep me cold and tired. Still, Flynn was surprisingly attuned to my exhaustion, and we made several stops a day to prevent me from collapsing.

After five excruciatingly long days of tracking we reached the base of the mountains. The invisible path Flynn had been following gave way to a narrow passage in between two massive mountains and, eventually, to precarious steps carved between roots, green bushes and rock.

"There is a cave a few meters above us," Flynn announced glancing towards the top. "We would be more protected from the wind, there. Can you make it?"

I nodded and followed. Step after step after step for the better part of the afternoon. We had fallen into a quiet understanding, not back to our masks, but not comfortably at ease either.

Yet, I was more aware of him and his tells than I'd ever been and from the moment we started climbing the stone stairs I noticed the worry weighing on him.

We reached the cave at dusk, barely in time to settle before darkness fell over the whole world. It was a crack on the mountainside, midway to the top. Shallow but mercifully protected from the wind, large enough to fit two people squeezed against each other. Besides, it offered cover and a clear view of the fields we'd left hours before. We would see any threat long before it reached us.

Flynn went straight to the end of the cave and started turning rock after rock. "We use this cave as an outpost sometimes," he offered as way of explanation. He uncovered two blankets and a water skin. "I knew this would be handy one day."

After a few minutes, we sat under the blankets, shoulder-to-shoulder, and listened to the howling wind ravage the mountain side as he uncorked the water skin.

He took a big sip and offered it to me. "Surprisingly good, considering how long it's been sitting here."

Acidic wine burned my throat. It was terrible, but the only thing available to drink. I looked at the bottle and took another sip before giving it back: "So this is how we are supposed to spend the night, Wheelan?"

He looked at me sideways, a smug smile on the corner of his lips: "Have a better idea, love?"

I made a show of rolling my eyes, but something in my core eased at the teasing. The bare intensity was too new, but the teasing? That I could deal with.

"I'd rather try my luck back there." I jerked my chin to the valley below us and he gave a small silent laugh.

"I'm afraid we won't be able to light a fire tonight, but we are close now. We should arrive tomorrow morning."

I nodded. Maybe it was the growing darkness and the wine, but I found myself enjoying the warmth leaking from his body. The scent of green grass and rain engulfed me.

"That night ..." he started tentatively, his voice so low that I wouldn't have listened if we were not so close together. "When I killed him, I never imagined you ... I had no way of knowing."

He took a deep breath, and I didn't dare to break the short silence. "You got caught up in what I set into motion, and I can't shake the feeling that I had a hand in putting you in that dungeon, with *him*."

His revulsion at Kiran's memory was a mirror of my own. I felt the raw emotion taking root inside of me, the yelp building on my throat and the burning tears collecting on my face.

"I was caught up in all of this long before you came

into the picture, Wheelan. Whether I knew it or not."

The wind was howling around us, not a word audible beyond the small space of our bodies.

When he spoke again his voice was grave. "I won't apologize for what I did, for what I had to do, but I wish I didn't have to silently witness what they did to you. I wish I could have secured the antidote faster, given you a fighting chance earlier. I want you to know that I tried."

There was no regret in his voice, but there was pain. Searing pain and maybe a touch of guilt. A small part of me couldn't help but blame him, but I knew what he was fighting for, I'd seen it. I couldn't deny I would have done the same. Protected the hope and dream of his people.

"Why did Ivo think I had broken in before?" I asked remembering Ivo's words when he first saw me.

"Well, I couldn't let him know we had you, so I made it look like a break in. Like you and some of the others had breached the defenses to rescue the anonymous girl Kiran had been ... working on."

"So that is why he reinforced the defenses."

"Yes."

It was clever and well thought. I wondered how long he'd been treading that horrible line.

"I didn't see Kiran or Tyler," I whispered after a few moments.

"Ivo dispatched Kiran somewhere a few days ago. I don't know where. Tyler is ... dealt with." He looked sideways and added "I'm sorry, I know you also had a score to settle."

I wondered what *his* score was, but I simply nodded. Surprisingly relieved.

"I'll help you find Kiran if you want. I'll hold him for

you myself if I have to."

"I won't need anyone to hold him."

I sensed the hint of a smile on his voice when he said, "I don't doubt that for a second, love."

No judgement, just plain fact. And what sounded a lot like a note of pride.

"We evacuated the safe-houses. All of them. They all left hours before we did. I'm sure they are fine," I offered. I couldn't ease his guilt and pain, but I still wanted to relieve some of his worry.

His muscles trembled, his breath caught, and I wondered how much doubt and fear he was carrying, how many loved ones he had among the lines of the Alliance. He might have guessed it was Leon leaving the patio, but until now, he had no way of knowing what passed on the farm, what we had planned. He had no way of knowing how many friends he had lost.

"Thank you," he said under his breath after long silent minutes.

◆

We took turns sleeping until there was enough light to guide our steps. By the time the sun rose, we were reaching the main terrain.

The highlands were unending. Plateau after plateau, deep green cliffs and so many untouched green trees that a part of me felt the world was born anew.

It made me feel close to the sky and free from the violence and cruelty.

There were paths to the valleys beneath, Flynn explained, but none of them were as low as the valleys we'd come from. Not even in Alizeh territory, as most of that Kingdom sat atop high lands, so large that you'd forget yourself atop a mountain in the first place.

After a few hours of intense tracking, we started to descend. We crossed a large archway, sides encrusted on the rock in beautifully designed patterns and continued down a rustic path that followed the slope.

Beneath us, an ancient valley nested in the middle of the large mountains. There, protected by brown and grey rocks, meters above the base of the range, sat a perfect plain terrain and what could only be described as a small town.

I gaped at the combination of wooden houses and doors carved on the rocks, at the few grey-stoned buildings in the center of the delicate town. Completely integrated to the roaring nature around it.

Birds and waterfall noises reached me from a distance at the same time as children's laughter travelled through the wind.

I noticed Flynn observing me and turned to him. "Where are we?"

"Isra Mountains."

The name of what I had always believed to be a small range of uninteresting mountains, did nothing to placate my confusion, my wonder: "How ... I thought this place was nothing but an uninhabited mountain range?" The natural border with Alizeh.

"I guess not everything is what it seems, is it?" His lips curled in a side, suggestive smile.

Suddenly, Ezer popped into my mind. Ezer and the promise of a story about Isra warriors and their control over shadows. I wondered what answers I would find in this place.

"What is this place?" I asked Flynn.

His eyes wandered through the valley before turning back to me, and there was longing on his face when he replied. "Home."

The valley was called Shanti, and no one seemed to know how it had come to be, but it was believed to have always been a refuge to those in need of rescue and during the Great war it had become the heart and soul of the Rebellion.

The closer we got, the more easily I could identify houses, stores, restaurants. The sides of the mountains were covered with level after level of stone houses. The central valley was a tribute to life in community: a training ring, a vegetable garden, small benches and a hearth.

I remembered the other city I'd seen laying under the mountains. It was impossible not to compare them, not with the mountains tracing its edges. But while Kait was beautiful and charming and grand, Shanti was cozy and comforting. It was a home.

Flynn walked a few meters ahead, leading me to the valley below. I was beyond words for how fiercely they must have protected this place if it remained hidden after so many rebels had been caught and tortured since the war.

I saw Leon and Bren instructing a group of armed men and women just a second before they saw us, and pure relief engulfed me at the sight of Leon's smirk.

Before I could say anything, Bren was throwing herself against Flynn, holding his neck tightly, and I could swear I heard a long-shuddered breath coming out of him as he hugged her waist and squeezed her tight.

Leon was hugging me barely a moment later, alternating between bringing me close and pushing me away to inspect me. "What the fuck happened?"

"I'm fine." My voice was smaller than I intended.

"Tired, but fine. Alive."

He looked between myself and Flynn, a silent question dancing between them, but I had no words to describe the emotions inside of me, no words to explain how *they* made me do the impossible. I'd spent the last days shoving the memories of what happened in Urian aside, ignoring the power pulsating under my skin, but now … it all came back in an unrelenting surge: the fear, the loneliness and the hope.

"Are you compromised?" Bren asked Flynn, bringing me back to reality.

"I would have been anyway after another escape." He shrugged.

"How?" Leon finally found his voice, his gaze still jumping between Flynn and me. "What was that fucking blast?" he pressed.

I still didn't have the courage to ask Flynn about what he had seen, what it looked like. Yet, if the destruction I'd glimpsed was any indication, the blast would have been seen from the edge of the town. Maybe beyond it.

Flynn sensed my hesitation and said, "We got lucky, let's leave it there for now." I didn't miss the pointed look he gave Leon.

He was offering me a way out, a reprieve from the truth. Still, there was no denying what had happened anymore, no silencing what I knew had changed inside of me.

So, I spoke, instead. "It was me. The blast of light was me." I needed to say the words. "I don't know how."

Bren and Leon were silent, and I watched their faces go from confusion to understanding to awe.

And that was too much to bear. The little control I had over my own feelings threatened to dissolve.

"Leon," I whispered facing him fully. "That night …"

But I didn't know what to say. The part of me that had heard Ivo's words for so many years expected to find judgement and scorn. Instead, all I found on his face was tender acceptance.

He must have sensed the turmoil in me as he offered with a gentle voice. "What I saw that night was a brave woman willing to give her life for the people I love. Nothing else."

I felt the burden of the last days – months – crushing down on me, clawing its way out of the tight space where I'd locked it all down; my knees buckled, and my eyes burned with relief.

"She needs to rest. We barely made it here." Flynn's voice was quiet but definitive. I didn't know if he was reacting to my imminent break down, but I was grateful all the same.

Leon hugged me, tight and unwavering one last time: "Welcome back, Ace!" He breathed in my ear before going back to talk to the people assembled behind us.

Bren prompted me to move with a small nudge on my arm that got me out of my stupor. "Ruby?"

"She is fine. Resting. I'll take you to her."

I nodded and let her guide me, ignoring the easy intimacy between her and Flynn as she explained that her scouts had left the day before, and that Leon was about to lead a unit back to Urian. After us, after me.

She led me to one of the doors on the mountain side. A bright yellow door with small potted plants to the side. Her house. Flynn stayed behind as she took me to one of the two bedrooms. "We thought she would be more comfortable with me. You can share the room if you want," she offered with an earnest voice.

There was something in her open, sincere face that told me she would always offer me the truth, no matter how hard. There was nothing I needed more.

"Did everyone make it out of the safe houses?" I asked.

"Yes. They all made it." Then she added, "*We* all made it"

"Thank you," I whispered and meant it.

She nodded. "A healer will come by shortly."

I waited for her to leave before I motioned to the door, but she lingered, studying me. Finally, she said, with a glimpse of defiance, "You keep bringing my people back to me alive, and I'll most definitely like you."

♦

Ruby was fast asleep. In the room around her, two beds, simple yet comfortable, separated by a large chest of drawers. Delicate lanterns hung in four spots on the wall, colorful pictures in between them. A cozy throw placed on the bottom of each bed, handmade.

It was a home.

When Ruby started to shift in her sleep, I left my weapons belt on the empty bed and knelt by the side of her bed, suddenly conscious of my dirty clothes.

"Hey," I whispered when she blinked at me.

She looked around, adjusting her vision and recognition reached her. She smiled lazily, sitting up.

"For someone who doesn't know how to do the whole friends thing, you seem to have a bunch of them lying around."

I laughed. "Good to see your insufferable spirit is

untouched," and then added, "Why did I have to rescue you from a fucking dungeon?"

"I couldn't leave all the fun for you." A raised eyebrow.

The tension in me eased with every word I heard her say and every breath I saw her take. *She is alive,* was all I could think.

"How did you end up there, Ruby?"

She shrugged and her eyes dulled slightly as she spoke in a small voice: "I couldn't just leave you. I waited the whole night, and then the next day. And when enough time had passed and I could no longer convince myself you'd come back on your own, I remembered what *you* did and started to follow some of the guards, learn their rounds, find their families." She took a deep breath before continuing: "I did it for days but the more I learned, the less I knew what to do with it. I was desperate. And one day a drunk guard caught me. He thought I was going to rob him."

I shook my head, letting it rest on my open hands. "You should have left."

Resolve flashed through her features as she grinded her teeth. "We had this conversation, Aila."

We did. So instead of arguing, I hugged her.

"Did they hurt you?" I asked when we let go of each other.

"Not really. They taunted me, but mostly they let me be." She went quiet, sorting through the memories. "At the beginning they forgot to give me food and water, but after you escaped …"

I stopped her before she had a chance to continue talking: "I wanted to go back for you that night."

She nodded deliberately slowly before replying in an

almost unbearable whisper: "You did. Eventually."

She took my hands in hers, tracing the scars on my wrists: "What happened to you?" She rested her head against mine.

"Don't." I said in a rough whisper. Maybe I would find the strength to talk about it, but not now, not today.

We held each other, silently, for a long time. And when we let go, some of her perkiness had come back. She leaned on the back of the bed and said, "I heard some of the people here talking, you know?" amusement and curiosity made their way onto her face. "Remember when you asked me if I'd ever heard anything about their heir? Well, I have now … anything to share?"

I took a deep breath: "Do I really have a choice?"

"You know the answer to that." Surprisingly enough there was nothing but amusement in her face. None of the fear, concern or expectation that I thought I would see.

"Well, it seems I may fit the description. But I don't really know what it means."

"Do you want to figure it out?"

"I don't know," I said honestly.

"Well, I've got your back, girl, but I don't think you'll have too long to decide."

"I know," I whispered.

Then I remembered she never finished explained what happened to her: "Ruby? What were you going to say happened after I fled?"

She seemed confused at the random question for a moment, but responded nonetheless.

"The food and water, it never faltered again." She propelled her arms behind her head, lazily facing the roof as her usual grin found a way back to her lips, "A guy started to hand-deliver it actually."

"I figured." And I wondered what else I had to thank Flynn for.

◆

Two days later I found myself in the middle of a small library with the whole council and Flynn.

Until then, I'd spent most of my time in and out of consciousness. My body trying to recover after the effort of diving so much into my power.

Ruby had spent almost every waking moment by my side, and I couldn't deny that her overbearing protectiveness, although annoying, worked as a very convenient way to avoid thinking about whatever power dwelled in my veins, or to face a very present tall, golden-eyed figure.

But I still managed to catch Bren alone that morning: "I need your help with something," I'd told her.

"Spill," she said in between bites of a pear.

"I need to find someone. Ruby's brother … I know little about him, but he disappeared in Nuri a few years ago, after their mother was murdered by a fire wielder. I thought he may have wanted to join you, to fight."

Her face truly softened for the first time since I'd met her. "We lost many of our contacts in Nuri since Flynn was outposted in Urian, but if he is among our ranks, I'll find him," she promised. There was such a fierce certainty in her gaze I was sure she would.

"I don't want to give her hope yet."

"I won't say a thing."

Now, hours later, I knew there would be no Ruby to help me ignore my newfound power.

This room wasn't anything like the large, fancy libraries I'd seen before. None of the dominance of expensive, glowing furniture. Whoever had decorated the room cherished comfort and practicality over sophistication.

Bookshelves adorned every wall, comfortable couches and chairs were placed at its center. To the left, a big desk filled with maps, paper and an occasional dagger or two.

Ezer was alone when I arrived. The first moment we'd had without an audience since the farm, and I knew I only had moments.

"Is this place part of the tale you promised me?" He knew what I was referring to, I could see it in his face.

"In a manner of speaking, it is. Are you ready for it?"

That was the question, wasn't it? *Am I ready to face my story along with everything else it brings?*

"Not yet," I said.

The raw words were all I could say before the room filled with the rest of the council.

Each member found their place on the sofas with familiarity, and I could imagine the many nights they'd passed there. Planning, discussing, or simply enjoying each other's company.

Bren lounged on the biggest sofa, legs on Leon's lap. Ezer sat on the far end wingback chair, a tall brown woman by his side that could only be Nahla. Flynn leaned against the large desk, hands at its edge.

Laughter filled the room, and I found a place on the couch across from Leon and Bren, somehow comforted by the sight of them.

"Welcome to our little refuge, Ace," Leon said when quiet fell.

But it was Nahla who shifted the conversation. "So,

you found your way to Shanti!" Her voice was as sweet and gentle as her face. But there was no mistaking the respect she commanded with every movement.

She was tall and slender, short hair and infinite, limpid grey eyes.

I glanced at Flynn. Unreadable. If I was being honest with myself, it enervated me that even now I couldn't read him completely.

"I was lucky enough to find Ezer and to end up here."

"This place has a way of attracting strays, to guide them in unexpected ways, but luck has rarely anything to do with it."

She gestured to the others and continued: "You already met our band of renegades. I'm Nahla." She lowered her head in deference. "Now that you found your way to us, why don't you tell me what you want to do next."

"I don't know." I admitted faster than I expected. My whole world seemed to have shifted and yet, all remained the same. "Does it matter? What I want?"

"What you want will always matter."

Such a simple thing to say and yet so different from what I had heard my entire life. From what Ivo always had me believe.

"You said you wanted to help?" Ezer prompted before silence stretched.

I'd thought a great deal about this since I arrived there and at least that I was certain of.

"I never learned what a home really is, but that is what you have here, what I've seen in every corner of this place." I looked at each one of them. "I'd like to help protect it if I can."

"What really happened in Urian, Aila?" Bren asked.

Always cut-the-bullshit Bren.

"I don't know. I delved into my power further than I ever had and I lost control, I lost myself. I was collapsing, and then I wasn't."

"You shielded us, and then you blew up half the fort with the brightest light I've ever seen. Pure light," Flynn chimed in.

"Yeah, that," I said before facing Ezer. "Turns out I have a drop of light in me after all."

Leon snorted, eliciting a swift punch in the arm from Bren and a smile from me.

Bren said, "Our scouts came back today. Only a handful of people survived your ... blast."

"Did ..."

She understood my question before I formulated it: "Ivo and the Prince included, yes." She lowered her feet and leaned over her knees, "they found marks, two round areas unaffected by the explosion."

"It was all so fast. I didn't know if the dome would hold, but I figured it was better than nothing."

"Glad you did," Flynn muttered.

I remembered the feeling of Aiden's power, the sense of his Fire moving through the veil. He was preparing to attack, mustering his power.

"I felt Aiden commanding his power, collecting it. He must have shielded himself."

"Felt? As in literally feeling *his* power?" Leon asked. I nodded.

"That is ..." Leon searched for the right word. "Unheard of."

"I guess I like being remembered for doing impossible things." The attempt at humor eased some of the tension at my core.

I turned back to Ezer: "What is the goal here? Why have you been waiting for ... this?"

"I think you know what we want, Aila. I believe you want the same. We have been murdered and experimented upon for far too long, we want the right to live in peace. And I told you before, my dear, symbols have power."

"To rally people, give them hope," I said.

"To lead them," Nahla corrected.

"How do we do that?" I ignored the clutching in my stomach at the echoes of her words.

"We mobilize our forces, we face the Elementalists, we make them stop." It was Bren who replied.

"They are too powerful; they will decimate anyone who opposes them," I offered.

"Then we plan. We hit them where it hurts. We destroy the labs."

"Do you even know where those are?"

"On Kalindi," she said simply.

On a fucking island! A supposedly destroyed one, at that. Brilliant.

I dropped my head into my hands. It was all too much, all too fast. I couldn't *lead* people. We couldn't simply sail to the former light Kingdom. *My Kingdom*, I thought gingerly.

I took a deep breath and looked at each of them, at the expectation in their faces.

"It doesn't change anything," I said. "I don't know what this magic means, I can't control it. I don't know how to be your heir."

"You may have to figure it out, Ace. You tipped the scales, and they will hunt you with everything they've got.

Whether you want the role or not." Leon's words were as kind as they were truthful.

"I meant what I said before. If making me your symbol gives us a chance of fighting back, then do it." I smiled a bit wildly, eyes trained on Leon's. "And if they catch me, you make it count."

He smiled back. And I knew he was right. I would need to be more than a symbol, and very soon I'd need to find out what exactly that meant.

"We don't have to solve everything now," Flynn said, leading us back to practical, safe territory. "We had connections all over that court, but we never got close enough to Ivo and Aiden, not as close as you." He hesitated for a moment, and I didn't miss the brief look Leon and Bren exchanged. "You know them better than any of us could dream of. What should we expect?" Flynn came closer now, sitting on the arm of Nahla's chair. I couldn't help but think he was intentionally keeping some distance between us, avoiding me as much as I'd been avoiding him.

"Ivo will want to retaliate, to change the narrative. He'll use my story with Aiden to picture me, us, as cold and calculating. He may go to the Elementalists and try to coordinate forces to massacre every city that ever dared to whisper about the Alliance. But I don't know what the King will do. Aiden has swayed his father more than once, he is a …" I corrected myself, "he *was* a sympathizer towards non-wielders, a dreamer stuck in a vicious court. But now? I don't think I recognize him anymore. I don't know what he is capable of."

Flynn nodded, sorrow lining his face. "Things changed in the past months, I don't think Aiden will stop anything. Especially if it brings you pain."

"There's one more thing you need to know."

They all looked at me, waiting: "I told you Ivo is the king's spy master, right? There is something else. I think he is part of the Tlaloc Royal family and I don't know why he hid it or how I can use it, but I know it matters. And I will find out."

"This is personal to you." Nahla's voice was quiet.

"Isn't everything?" was my only reply.

◆

It could have been hours since I first sat on the log by the hearth in the center of Shanti valley. They kept it burning hot through day and night, building a flow of warmth that attracted small groups of people at all hours. I'd been sitting there since I left Nahla's library, quietly observing.

I saw Bren and Ruby talking by the central square, laughing, and a few people walking the streets. I watched as the valley emptied.

When there was no one else to draw my attention and keep me company under the starry sky, I faced the flames, tracing the movement of the dancing fire as I emptied my mind, not wanting to think about the details of the conversation I just had.

I told the council all I knew about Ivo's defenses and secret houses, about the letters from his mother and the Tlaloc ledgers, but I knew there was more. I knew that I would have to face the demons of my childhood and come to terms with the misguided trust I'd placed in him, that I would have to talk about Aiden eventually.

Flynn claimed the log beside me, two wine glasses in his hands, and a small, hidden part of me welcomed his presence as he offered me one of them.

There was nothing different in him and still, there was. As I studied his face, I saw all the same traits, the same intense look that puzzled me, the same arrogant smirk that enraged me. Beneath that, however, was the man who had saved my life over and over again.

For a brief second, I allowed myself to search his eyes, to look for the invisible tether that had grounded me under that dungeon. And he let me.

Until that inexplicable connection clicked into place.

He looked away, staring into the fire before breaking the silence. "Did you know?"

"That I can glow like the sun?"

He nodded.

I had avoided every question about my newfound power, resisted every topic even remotely connected with the heir. Yet I saw myself opening up to him.

"I had no idea." I stared at the flames again. "The Darkness always came easy to me. It was all around, embracing me for as long as I can remember. All I had to do was reach out and bend it to my will! Simple. But Light? I never knew warmth and ... hope. That is what I think it is: hope. I had never believed in it."

"Do you believe in it now?"

I considered his question. The question I had begun to ask myself in that dungeon. "For the longest time I watched the world from a distance, I let myself be used as a helpless pawn. Until I didn't. For the past few months, the world has shredded my heart apart as I learned how to piece it back together. And somewhere along the way I've also learned what hope feels like." My head fell into my hands as I found the words to continue. "I lost myself in the Darkness. I felt all the pain and loneliness that surrounded me my whole life and the wave of shadow almost engulfed me. I was free-falling and I thought it was the end. Until I remembered I wasn't alone anymore, that somehow, I had people now, people who mattered." I looked back at him then. "When I did, I found a kernel of light."

He seemed lost in his own thoughts, silently considering my words.

"Flynn?" It was still strange to hear his name come out of my mouth without mockery. "In that torture room" I swallowed hard before continuing. "You *saw* me. Really saw me. It's what kept me alive."

There was a question between us, one that I didn't know how to place. But he seemed to understand it, to feel it. He took a deep breath before saying, "I have spies across that palace and even from a distance I've learned everyone's secrets and dreams. Except for yours. You intrigued me and I knew I should keep my distance, but I couldn't. Because you looked every bit as much of an outsider as I felt." He paused for a few seconds. Eyes on mine, not hiding from whatever connected us now. "When I saw you in that dungeon, it felt wrong. Fundamentally wrong. But when you smiled at Kiran, defying him in the midst of the pain …" he trailed off and silence stretched a moment more. Deep and familiar.

"I couldn't risk all of this," he gestured around us "but I couldn't leave you alone either. I hoped, really hoped, it would be enough."

"It was."

We let the silence stretch between us and a few minutes later he offered me a small book – a journal – and a comforting medallion.

"How?" I asked, flipping through the pages of the

journal with a fondness I couldn't quite explain.

"The guards found it on you. Tyler saw the arrows and assumed you were one of us, one of our leaders. That is why he sent for Kiran to break you." It all made sense then. "It is also why I went with him."

"Because none of you would need to break in," I finished for him before adding, "You knew I would take Ezer."

"No, I didn't. But I hoped."

He jerked his chin back to the journal:

"I don't know where you got this, but I don't recognize the language. It is not ours, that I know of, at least."

"It was in Ivo's coffer," I said in a whisper, tracing my finger over the cover.

"Ezer knows many languages. He may be able to read it, if you wish."

"Have you shown it to him?"

He shook his head. "It didn't feel right."

"Thank you," I whispered.

We watched the flames together for a while. Then he got up and raised his glass to me. "To daring to be bigger than ourselves." A salute, an offering.

We drank to it and a while later I watched his figure bleed into the night, peace and belonging filling my heart. When I finally left the small bench, I knew that no matter what would come next, I would not face it alone.

Thank You

Dear readers, THANK YOU for taking the time to discover this world with me. Did you love Aila's journey?

Her story continues on Blazing Sunlight, the heart wrenching sequel to Among Shadows. Coming January 2023.

A bond forged through secrets.
A devastating, simmering attraction.
And beneath it all, the truth that will save or doom me.

When Aila dared to put the safety of Niram's prince – her closest friend and lover – above the spy master's command, she didn't expect to end up running from everything she'd ever known. As her deepest secrets were exposed and the prince became nothing more than a bitter enemy, she found herself thrust into the midst of a rebellion, with a bright orphan and a deceitful captain as her only lifelines.

Now, as the Elementalists prepare for battle and the whispers of the Heir of Light and Dark rise, Aila will be forced to deal with the consequences of her lies. And when her ties to the Rebel Alliance deepen and the inevitable pull towards the former captain becomes too strong to ignore, she will have no choice but to confront the truth behind her mysterious power.

With the stakes higher than ever, Aila will need to accept who she was born to become or watch as the world she embraced goes up in flames.

Acknowlegments

It was a long journey! A raw and very emotional journey! The past few years were filled with joy and excitement as much as with anxiety and insecurity. And as I sit in front of the screen trying to remember every turning point. I can't stop but feel in awe of the amazing people that had a hand in getting me here.

I'm deeply and irrevocably thankful to:

Andre, husband, friend and love of my life. Thank you for believing in my dreams even when I couldn't, for never let me doubt myself and for always make me laugh. My world would be less full of magic and light without you in it.

My little one: Victor. You changed me, you made me crave for a more meaningful life. And I wouldn't have gotten this far if not for the desire of showing you that it is never too late to find your true calling.

Mum, I wouldn't be the person that I am today without you. I owe you everything. Thank you for getting me through the hard times.

Marcos and Aline, you've been my family for over a decade, and I can't imagine my life without you! Thank you for giving me a second home and a space in your hearts.

Julianne, sister and friend. I'm so very thankful for the bus ride that brought you into my life. Thank you for being this ever-present figure through the good and the bad!

Luciana, my person! Thank you for never - ever - doubting me. For the hours on audio messages. And for always inspiring me.

Aline, Gabriela, Henrique and Thiago you are my family of choice and despite the ocean between us, I've never once felt alone or isolated!

Cassia, Denis and Marcio you were the best beta readers a girl could ask for! Thank you for the support, the chats and all the shared love for this story. You made me want to never give up!

Emily, thank you for the guidance and encouragement. This book would not be the same without you.

You, my readers! I'm humbled and honoured with your choice of trusting me with your time and mind as you go through these pages. I hope they help you to find what you need, may it be solace, companionship, or entertainment.

I would not have made it without each and every one of you. You have my heart!

About the Author

Aline Preto Mora is a passionate writer of the same strong and witty female leads that keep her hitched to a new book.

Growing up, she found some of her best friends and lived some of her best adventures inside the pages of a book. And, in time, she found solace in her own written word.

Now, after a decade of getting to know the most diverse type of people through her career in Marketing, Aline decided to follow her soul's desire and dedicate herself to writing, wishing she can provide the same hope and joy that she found within her favourite books to all those that are brave enough to search for it.

   Her debut novel Among Shadows is the first instalment of a new, exciting Adult Fantasy series.

Printed in Great Britain
by Amazon